OMEGA CRISIS

BOOK 1 OF THE *GEMINI GATE* SERIES

STEVEN E. WILDE

Omega Crisis (The Gemini Gate series, Book 1)
Steven E. Wilde
Paperback edition
978-1-77342-077-6

Produced by IndieBookLauncher.com
www.IndieBookLauncher.com
Editing: Nassau Hedron
Cover Design: Saul Bottcher
Interior Design and Typesetting: Saul Bottcher

The body text of this book is set in Adobe Caslon.

Also Available
Hardcover edition, ISBN 978-1-77342-078-3
EPUB edition, ISBN 978-1-77342-075-2
Kindle edition, ISBN 978-1-77342-076-9

Dedicated to Marilyn.
You are the inspiration and motivation for everything I do.
I love you with all my heart and soul.

"And ye shall hear of wars and rumours of wars: see that ye be not troubled: for all these things must come to pass, but the end is not yet.

"For nation shall rise against nation, and kingdom against kingdom . . .

"All these are the beginning of sorrows."

—King James Bible, Matthew 24:6-8

Prologue

On the TV screen, a smartly dressed man and woman sat behind a conference table in what looked like a schoolroom.

"Good afternoon. I'm Dennis Spaulding and this is Melanie Kearns, with Channel Eleven News. We're reporting from the Chantilly Elementary School in Chantilly, Virginia, about twenty-five miles from the capital, and our studio in Washington D.C. We have a crew in the Channel Eleven Skycam helicopter as well, currently getting in position for a firsthand report."

"If there's a nuclear explosion," Melanie said, taking over the narrative, "and we're told it's still *if* and not *when,* the mushroom cloud would spread downwind, with radioactive particles dropping out of the cloud as 'fallout.' With today's weather, we would expect the cloud to spread to the northeast."

"That's right, Melanie," Dennis said, taking over again. "Now we're told that our Skycam team is in position, so we'll hand off our coverage to Mr. Justin Chase, our reporter in the sky. Hello, Justin, what's going on up there?"

The picture on the TV split so that Dennis was on the left side of the screen. The right side now showed a young man with short, unruly hair and a pair of wraparound sunglasses propped on top of his head. The creases from his smile stretched nearly to his ears, and his tanned skin looked wrinkled where his headset touched his cheeks just below his ears. He was holding a microphone and there was a banner under his picture that read: Justin Chase, Channel Eleven Reporter in the Sky.

"Hi Melanie and Dennis," Justin said seriously. "It's beautiful up here. Clear sky. Gentle breeze from the southwest. It's hard to believe we're actually contemplating a nuclear explosion that could totally destroy the Washington, D.C. area. Wow."

"I agree Justin," Dennis said. "Hard to believe."

"Okay," Justin continued, "we're in the Channel Eleven News Skycam helicopter, ten miles west of Washington, D.C., at five thousand feet." He looked briefly at his watch. "It's 2:52 p.m. We're told the military still has teams in the area, checking for a bomb and watching for terrorists who might try to use the confusion of the evacuation to carry a bomb into the area.

"Our pilot says he can see a military helicopter now," Justin continued.

The camera panned away from his face to look out a side window, where a military helicopter flew rapidly from right to left below the news helicopter.

"Wow," Justin said. "He's really hauling. It must be show time."

The camera panned back to Justin's face, which was turned to the military helicopter. He wore an easy grin, a dimple in his cheek. It was obvious that he liked flying and speed, maybe picturing himself at the controls of the military helicopter.

"Can you tell if anyone's still in the city?" Melanie asked.

That brought Justin back to the present. As he turned toward the camera, he dropped the smile and the dimple disappeared, but his eyes still sparkled.

"It's hard to tell, Melanie. It's been eleven days since the president mentioned voluntary evacuation, and nine days since he confirmed that the terrorists have a bomb and plan to set it off in Washington, D.C. We've been watching people stream out of the capital and surrounding cities for days now, but we're told that there are likely thousands of people still in the city for one reason or another."

"That's amazing!" Melanie said. "Are the police and military helping with the evacuation?"

"We've seen them helping with traffic control, but whether or not they're going door-to-door telling people to get out is hard to say. Remember, they're also trying to find a bomb."

"Thanks Justin. It's 2:57. Do you want to take over and show us what's going on?"

"Thanks Melanie."

The view of Melanie in the schoolroom disappeared, leaving Justin and the helicopter to fill the entire screen. The camera panned right for a view out the side window and zoomed in on the National Mall.

"If you look closely at the spot where our camera is aimed, you can see the National Mall, with the Capitol building and reflecting pool on the left, the Washington Monument on the right, and the Smithsonian buildings running down both sides of the Mall in between."

What the camera couldn't detect from this distance were the people walking on the Mall and working in offices around the city. There were those who didn't believe the threat was real. There were young families on vacation who didn't want to lose their vacation time and the money their trip had cost, who were betting their lives that the bomb wasn't real. There were business men and women who didn't think they could afford to miss a day's work. And there were those who didn't hear the warnings, didn't understand, or didn't care, like many in the homeless population.

"I'll give you a second-by-second rundown of what's happening from our perspective," Justin continued. "We're putting on special dark glasses that we're told can withstand extreme changes in light, just in case we see a fireball. Whoa, it's like I'm in a cave. I can't see anything now." There was muffled laughter in the background. "We're waiting for the 3:00 p.m. deadline, which is coming up right . . . now."

1

"You are going to Chiapas, Mexico"

Damascus, Syria, 6 January (Six Months Earlier)

As he entered the airport luggage area, Saleh spotted his good friend and mentor, Ahmed, across the room. With a subtle nod, Ahmed left the terminal, walking slowly so as not to attract attention. A few minutes later, bag in hand, Saleh followed. He found Ahmed in a drab 1980s sedan at the curb, its engine running. He dropped his bag into the back and climbed into the passenger seat.

Ahmed set a _London Times_ newspaper in Saleh's lap, with the front page showing.

"Good to see you," he said in Arabic, as he pulled the car into traffic. "Another successful mission, my friend."

Saleh looked at the headline: **TERRORIST BOMB IN CROWDED NEW YEAR'S EVE CELEBRATION.**

Only slightly smaller was the subtitle: Suicide Bomber Kills 38, Wounds 147, at Victoria Embankment in Westminster.

Saleh would read the story, but for now he was satisfied with his good friend's compliment. He smiled at Ahmed.

"Khalid was one of the faithful, Allah be praised," he said.

"He will be rewarded in heaven," Ahmed replied. After a

pause he added, "We have another assignment for you."

"Whatever the Brothers require," Saleh said with a slight nod, still basking in his mentor's approval. He was surprised that another mission would follow so soon. He'd spent the previous three weeks in London preparing Khalid and his support team for the last mission, and three weeks before that planning and selecting his team. Still, he was hesitant to ask.

"What's this one?" he asked anyway.

Ahmed looked briefly at Saleh before returning his eyes to the traffic ahead, his expression unreadable. Then he smiled broadly through his heavy beard. Unlike Ahmed, Saleh had been required to shave his beard for his overseas missions, so he was pleased that the latest style favored a little facial hair—it allowed him to have a few days' growth. With his light skin and Queen's English, he was able to move freely around Europe. And his assumed name, Samuel, led many people to assume he was Jewish, which always made him laugh—when it didn't make him angry.

"You've performed flawlessly on your assignments, Saleh," Ahmed said. "How many students did you recruit for the camps? Twenty-seven? And you supported Rashid's team on quite a few successful missions. You've demonstrated that you know how to plan a mission and lead a team."

Saleh had been raised in Saudi Arabia, in one of the Wahhabi training camps, along with children from around the Arab world. That he had pleased his instructors was evident when, at age seventeen, he was sent to England to study at Cambridge and to observe for himself Western decadence. With nearly unlimited funding from the Brothers, he immersed himself in the culture—fast cars, alcohol, and women. But despite appearances, he'd never doubted the teachings of his youth for a moment, and only once questioned his own actions. Even then, he'd rationalized away his concerns without much effort. After all, he'd been sent to England to understand why the United States was referred to as the Great Satan, and why she and her Western allies were called godless. After experiencing the temptations of decadence for himself, he understood all the better why Westerners needed to be destroyed.

Called back from England after three years, Saleh had been given small assignments, and then gradually larger ones, taking messages and packages to Brothers in Islamic centers around the world. Eventually, he'd been assigned to Rashid's team in England, which recruited local Arab youths for the Wahhabi training camps. Then he was assigned to set up communications networks for young people returning to England from the camps—what they called sleepers. Having proven himself to be a resourceful and dedicated organizer, Saleh had found himself back in Cambridge, recruiting sleepers for suicide missions. His assignments had increased in size and complexity so that now, at age twenty-nine, he had completed two successful missions of his own.

Ahmed had stopped talking. Saleh was disappointed that he wasn't going to say anything about the next assignment, but then Ahmed surprised him.

"This one will be special, the most audacious mission the Brothers have ever planned. They have a lot of faith in you. It's not safe to talk out in the open. You will get the details from them." Then, as he stopped at a light, he turned to face Saleh, grinning broadly at his protégé. "This one will be solo. You are going to Chiapas, Mexico."

Matamoros, Mexico, 21 January

The sounds of gunfire pierced the otherwise silent air in Matamoros, Mexico. The guards standing against the walls around the room raised their rifles and moved toward the door. The battle between the Gulf Cartel and the Los Zetas Cartel had become the bloodiest war Mexico had seen in more than a century—almost two. Los Zetas was led by former elite members of the Mexican military who were notorious for their unmatched brutality. The Gulf Cartel had been the target of Los Zetas aggression for years, but never within the city—the battle for control of Tamaulipas and the production of cocaine had escalated.

One guard opened the door, while four others cautiously stepped through, crouching and fanning out. All of them were quickly gunned down by automatic weapons fire, dead before they hit the ground. The remaining guards closed the door, then ran to the windows to return fire. The drug lord and his captains, sitting around a long table deeper within the room, drew their guns, tipped the table over, and crouched behind it, preparing to defend themselves.

The Gulf drug lord was a veteran of the Mexican drug wars. Shrewd and careful, he'd risen to power by systematically eliminating all competition for leadership of the cartel. Then he'd expanded his franchise, learning how to grow coca plants in Tamaulipas and exporting the cocaine into the United States.

He'd stayed in power by mistrusting everyone, even his captains. He let each of them think that he, alone, was trusted, asking each one, in feigned confidence, to watch the others.

The Los Zetas were aggressive, but the Gulf drug lord and his men had bested them time and again. This latest escalation was different, though. *The Los Zetas must be getting outside help,* the drug lord thought, *but from where?* He'd never been afraid of anything in his life, but this was starting to make him nervous.

Suddenly, dozens of Los Zetas soldiers swarmed the front of the house. The first few fell to the guns of the Gulf, writhing in silence, but the room was soon overrun by Los Zetas gunmen. Within minutes, the Gulf Cartel's stronghold in Tamaulipas had been obliterated.

White House Situation Room
National Security Council meeting, 5 March

The president of the United States, Gregory McCormick, was a tall, dignified-looking fifty-year-old, his hair beginning to turn gray at the fringes. He sat in his usual place at the head of the table, leading a meeting he'd called of the full National Security Council—the NSC—to review recent world events and consider their potential impact on national security. Seated in the plush armchairs on either side of the long conference table were the statutory members of the council and some key advisers. Straight-backed wooden chairs around the wall, and folding chairs in the few remaining open spaces, held other regular attendees and staff. On the table, in front of the president, were a push-button phone with multiple lines and a small control panel that operated the large monitor on the wall to his right. Speakers lined the middle of the conference table.

As the last few invitees settled into their seats, the president thought about how large this group had become since the attacks of September 11, 2001. The participants represented virtually every government agency in the country, as well as those that dealt with U.S. interactions with the rest of the world. He was grateful that he was surrounded by so many good men and women, the best in their various fields. With such a diversity of priorities and opinions represented, he could count on this group to give him the best advice possible for him to make a decision for the country . . . under normal circumstances.

But the president had a nagging concern. He knew that the characteristics that normally made the council great could also make it slow and deliberate, and therefore ineffective in an emergency. Quick action would be nigh impossible—if they were facing a real crisis, he'd have to whittle this group down to a manageable size, keeping only those whose opinions he trusted the most. Ultimately, the real decision-making fell to him anyway.

McCormick looked to his right and left, confirming that his most trusted advisers were in place and ready. Then he turned to the Director of National Intelligence (DNI) Thomas Mitchell, seated on his left. A slender, fiftyish man, with thinning hair and a long face, DNI Mitchell didn't have an intelligence background—he was a political appointee—and he didn't manage the day-to-day operations of the various intelligence agencies. But Tom was a brilliant strategist. As DNI, he was the head of the sixteen-member United States Intelligence Community, and in that capacity he directed and oversaw the National Intelligence Program and served as an adviser to the president on intelligence matters. He was also a longtime friend of the president, and had managed his last two political campaigns—both successful—for the Senate and the presidency. Tom was one of the president's key advisers.

"Okay, Tom, what do you have for us?" the president asked.

Tom had some notes in front of him, but he didn't refer to them. McCormick knew they contained details such as names and dates, in case the president wanted them. He also knew that Tom had extensive knowledge of the history of the drug cartels in Mexico, including the latest developments, from months of working closely with intelligence experts.

"The battle between the cartels has escalated since the Gulf Cartel started growing coca plants in Tamaulipas," Tom began. "Up until three years ago, virtually all of the cocaine coming into the U.S. was grown and processed in Colombia. When the Colombian cartels shifted their attention to South America and Europe, the Los Zetas started growing coca in Chiapas with the idea of cutting Colombia out of the U.S. market completely. The Gulf Cartel was sidelined until about a year ago, when they brought in Peruvian farmers to teach them how to adapt coca plants to their soil and weather conditions. That's when the fighting escalated again."

Tom summarized the battle in Matamoros six weeks earlier and the takeover of the Tamaulipas territory by the Los Zetas. There were whispers around the room, including a few gasps as he described the intensity of the violence and carnage.

"There are indications of ongoing, isolated fighting on the plantations and in the streets. A few Gulf Cartel captains are holding out against Los Zetas, probably in hopes of setting up their own operations. Satellite images show fires at several sites, including the estates of two of the Gulf captains."

"That sounds like a good thing, doesn't it?" the president asked. "Let them kill each other off and destroy the crops?"

"You'd think," Tom replied. "But the last communication we received from one of our sources was that a player from the Arab world has approached the Los Zetas drug lord, Jose Mendoza, and may be supplying him with weapons."

The noise level in the room became distracting. The president held up a hand to stop Tom and looked to his right, where most of the noise was coming from. His vice president, Art Klemp, appeared to be holding a conference with several people around him. The president frowned, making a mental note of who was talking to Art.

"Quiet, people," he said, then looked back at Tom. "Be straight with me Tom. Is it Al-Qaeda?" When Tom nodded, he asked, "What do your other sources say?"

"We had three sources, sir. They've all gone silent in the last month, the last one yesterday. We don't know if they were exposed and eliminated, were lost in the battle, or are just lying low until things settle. With the fighting this fierce, we're not optimistic about their safety. And yes, we think it's Al-Qaeda."

"What types of weapons?" Secretary of Defense General James Seymour asked Tom. General Seymour, a barrel-chested man with a rugged face and a full head of gray hair, sat just to the president's right. As secretary of defense, commonly known as the SecDef, Jim was the leader and chief executive officer of the Department of Defense, and his authority over the United States military was second only to the president's. The SecDef was a statutory member of the NSC and an adviser to the president on all matters relating to the Department of Defense. Jim and the president had served together in the Gulf War. Afterward, Jim stayed in the military, eventually rising to the rank of general, while Greg chose government service. When Greg had become president, he'd seen to it that Jim became SecDef, and he'd been one of the president's key advisers ever since.

"Automatic weapons?" Tom shrugged. "We don't have any details. I assume it's stuff they can't easily get themselves."

"What does Al-Qaeda want in return?" Jim asked.

"We can only guess at this point," Tom said. "But my fear is that they're looking for access to the U.S. through the cartel's drug routes."

Texas–Mexico border, 5 March

The first man stuck his head out of a hole at the base of a small hill, looked around in the dim, early morning light, and listened for any sounds that would indicate people were nearby. His dark skin and rough clothing helped him blend in with his surroundings. Seeing no one, and hearing only the normal sounds of the desert, he enlarged the hole, quietly drawing the dirt toward him into the hollow where he was hidden. Then he carefully climbed out of hiding, immediately turning back and waving the next person out. In rapid succession, a string of thirteen men and women between the ages of thirteen and thirty-five climbed out of the hole and ran stealthily to a clump of tall bushes a few yards away. They were a few miles northwest of Laredo, Texas, in the middle of nowhere. They were a quarter of a mile from the border on the U.S. side, with that far again before they'd reach a dirt road where, they were led to believe, a truck would be waiting to take them north.

"Vámanos," *Let's go,* the leader whispered, waving the others to follow. As they started to move away from the bushes, eight U.S. Border Patrol agents moved out from concealed locations around them, carrying rifles and shining bright lights on the group.

"Alto ahí!" *Stop right there!* one of the agents yelled. "Levanta sus manos ahora mismo!" *Raise your hands right now!* The thirteen looked frantically around, only to see that they were nearly surrounded. All raised their arms into the air. Then one young man dropped his arms and started to run toward a gap in the circle of agents.

"Paras o dispararemos!" *Stop or we'll shoot!* The agent called. He fired a shot into the air. When the man stumbled forward without stopping, intent on escape, the agent closest to him took a step to the side, where he had a clear shot, and fired his rifle, hitting the young man in the back. The fugitive collapsed forward into the dirt, not moving. Several people in the group started to cry. One young woman took a few steps toward the fallen man before their leader grabbed her arm to stop her. He whispered something to her, and she stopped struggling, put her face in her hands, and wept in deep, wracking sobs.

One of the agents spoke into a radio, while two others went to collect the young man who had just been shot. The rest converged on the group, holding their weapons at the ready. Within minutes, two light-colored vans roared into sight and stopped abruptly near the group. The dead man was lifted into the back of one, and then the remaining twelve people were herded into the two vehicles. Two agents climbed into each van, weapons clearly visible, and the vehicles drove off. The leader of the agents turned to the three who'd stayed behind with him.

"Follow the tunnel back to its source," he said. "See what you can find, but be careful. We don't want it to collapse with you inside. If there's any reason we should keep it open, come back and tell me. Otherwise, destroy it on your way back out. You know the routine."

As he was speaking, another van pulled up.

"Yes, sir," one of the men said, as the other two went to the van, returning with explosives. The three agents went to the tunnel and crawled in, feet first. A short time later they returned, nodded to the leader, and turned toward the river. With the push of a button, the middle of the Rio Grande exploded, sending water and mud a hundred feet into the air.

White House Situation Room
National Security Council meeting

"We've been working with Homeland Security to locate and shut down drug routes," DNI Tom Mitchell said. "The problem is that the drug lords are very ambitious, the Los Zetas even more than the Gulf Cartel is . . . was. As soon as we eliminate one route, they open another one. I swear, they're more effective at identifying new ways to enter the country than Wal-Mart is at locating new store locations."

There were a few chuckles around the room. The president would have been amused as well, if not for the fact that the border with Mexico was as full of holes as Swiss cheese, which made the idea of stopping Al-Qaeda from bringing a bomb across the border a daunting proposition.

"An apt analogy, Tom," he said, looking around at the room full of people. "I assume you'll be watching for anything that looks like Al-Qaeda is involved, moving people or bomb-making materials?"

"Of course, sir."

"Anything else?"

"Yes, sir," Tom said, frowning. "As we discussed in our last meeting, our contacts in Israel have been watching activity around the Black and Caspian Seas. They've now confirmed that Al-Qaeda is meeting with representatives from Russia *and* North Korea."

The noise level in the room increased again, coming from the vice president's direction. The president tried to ignore it.

"Israeli intelligence believes it has to do with exchanging

weapons of mass destruction for delivery systems," Tom said.

The room erupted in noise and motion as people turned to talk to their neighbors. Several people stood and began motioning to get the attention of others in the room, while some others were frantically scribbling notes on notepads—the only option available since the president didn't allow electronic devices in the situation room.

The president held up his hand for Tom to stop. He knew the people in the room were seasoned warriors and professionals, not prone to panic, but considering his own growing anxiety, he let the group vent for a few minutes while he considered possible courses of action. When the noise finally died down, he motioned for Tom to continue. Tom took a deep breath before going on.

"As you know, Al-Qaeda has been shopping for nuclear weapons for some time. The most likely source would be the Russian black market. We have sightings of Arab suspects in Russia and in the Russian-controlled republics north of Iran. Connecting the dots, we have the possibility of Al-Qaeda buying weapons from Russian Siloviki—the former KGB and military officers who now control most Russian industry and banking—and sending them to North Korea, to be delivered on their missiles. Supreme Leader Kim Jung Un claims to have ICBM's that can reach the U.S. mainland . . . "

"He also claims to have nuclear warheads," the president interrupted.

"That he does," Tom agreed, "but either the warheads don't fit the missiles, or he's bluffing. Russian involvement could change that quickly. Our fear is that North Korea may have found a link with Russia through Al-Qaeda. We know that North Korea test-fired an ICBM that they claim can reach any one of several states—Washington, Oregon, or Hawaii. The test missile's trajectory was mostly vertical, so it landed in the Sea of Japan, but if they leveled it out, it's possible that they could reach the mainland." Tom shrugged.

"How would Al-Qaeda get a bomb to North Korea without us noticing it?" the president asked.

SecDef Jim Seymour answered, drawing the president's attention.

"The Navy monitors physical and electronic shipping manifests routinely, looking at contents, origins, and destinations. They haven't reported anything suspicious, but we haven't been looking for anything specific. If Al-Qaeda convinced someone to ship bomb components, we might never notice."

"We know Iran and North Korea have trade agreements," Tom said, "and most of the shipping stops somewhere in China going both ways. But China's made it very clear that any interference with their imports and exports, in their territorial waters, will be considered an act of war."

"Have we tried stopping and searching ships, Jim?"

"When we have valid reasons. But we have to be careful to stop only those ships that look suspicious. To do anything more than that could incite the Chinese *and* some friendlies."

The president thought about that for a minute before continuing.

"What about land routes?"

"It could take weeks, even months, to move weapons overland through Pakistan and China," Tom said, drawing the president's attention back to him. "And there's the issue of secure passage. Al-Qaeda would have to pay big for protection if they wanted a bomb to arrive safely."

"They *have* the resources, Tom," the president said. "Saudi Arabia has given them plenty of money over the years."

"Understood," Tom said. "Our sources say the meetings with North Korea are recent. Maybe we still have time to stop them before they ship anything."

"Get on it, and keep me informed. Anything else?"

The president looked around the table again. He could tell from the expression on Jim's face that the man was wrestling mentally with something. The president's stomach started to churn, anticipating more bad news.

"What is it Jim?" he asked, keeping the anxiety he felt out of his voice.

Everyone turned to SecDef Seymour as he began to speak.

"*If* Al-Qaeda obtains a nuclear weapon, and *if* they succeed in delivering it to the U.S. through Mexico or North Korea, what do we do about it? Are we prepared for a nuclear detonation on U.S. soil?"

The room went silent, each man and woman likely contemplating the possible consequences. Some of them were old enough to remember the Three Mile Island nuclear reactor meltdown in 1979 and the Chernobyl reactor disaster in 1986. And everyone in the room remembered the Fukushima Dai-ichi reactor failure in Japan in 2011—it had been a hot topic.

The thought of a nuclear bomb of any size going off in a major U.S. city was unthinkable—and yet they had no choice but to think about it.

The president rested his elbow on the table and closed his eyes behind his hand. After a moment he thought: *I need to pull myself together—they're expecting me to be strong.* He looked around the room. Everyone was watching him. *What do I tell them?* he wondered. *Any leak to our enemies, or the media, could damage our ability to counter whatever Al-Qaeda or North Korea are trying to do.*

"There are options," President McCormick finally said, "and we'll weigh those options if and when we face that situation. Tom and Jim, let's get the word out to start looking specifically for movement of nuclear weapons components." He pointed to his Chief of Staff, Eric Epstein. "Coordinate through Eric if you need me. Thank you."

The president rose, the others rising out of protocol—and respect. When the president didn't move, but stood looking down at the table, deep in thought, they all looked around, wondering what to do, then filed out silently.

2

"Rumors of a nuclear weapon"

The president's private office, the White House, 14 March
"Hello?"

"Amos? Greg McCormick," the president said. "How's the brain?"

"Mr. President," Amos said, laughing good-naturedly. "Good to hear from you."

"Cut the *Mr. President, Doctor* Blund," the president said with mock seriousness. "You know it'll always be Greg to you." Then he laughed, too.

"What's up, Greg? Haven't heard from you since that nightmare in the Senate. Another crisis?"

Greg paused. He was sitting in his comfortable swivel rocker in his White House residence office. The room was mostly dark—only the desk lamp was on. This was where he did most of his creative thinking, but he was far from comfortable at the moment. His old friend, Amos Blund, didn't have security clearance. The Intelligence Community would frown on the president making a call like this, crisis or no crisis. When he spoke again, he was deadly serious.

"You still have the secure phone I gave you?"

"Of course, Greg," Amos said, equally seriously. "I'll get it. Give me five minutes."

The president hung up.

"Hello, Greg," Amos said through the encrypted sat phone. There was little distortion with the encryption. The only problem they ever had on one of these calls was not having line of sight with a satellite. Greg had given Amos the phone when Greg was a senator and wanted Amos's advice on sensitive topics—he'd spent thousands of dollars on phones that he believed couldn't be intercepted and deciphered.

Greg had known Amos for more than thirty years. They'd met at a National Science Foundation Summer Math and Science Program in Flagstaff, Arizona, during high school. Amos had been the Sterling Scholar science candidate from his Utah high school, and Greg had been the candidate from his high school in Ohio. Both had been brilliant in math and science, and they'd hit it off immediately, spending all their spare time together during the ten-week course. They'd especially enjoyed the weekend outings with the twenty-two other students from around the country, camping and hiking in the area.

It didn't matter that Greg and Amos came from vastly different backgrounds. Greg's family was wealthy, with money from the oil industry, and his dad was a former linebacker for Ohio State who'd gone on to graduate from Harvard Law School. Amos was the son of a cattle rancher, and he'd paid his own way through engineering school, and then medical school, at the University of Utah. They'd stayed in touch over the years, often reminiscing about their exploits in Arizona. Greg respected Amos's analytical mind and systematic approach to problem-solving, and knew that Amos admired his charisma, organizational skills, and no-holds-barred approach to getting things done. Greg organized people to do what he wanted—Amos did his own thing.

When Greg had won a seat in the Ohio House of Representatives, and served on the House Committee on Science, Space, and Technology, he'd regularly asked Amos for advice on scientific issues. And when he'd moved on to the Senate and served on the Senate Committee on Commerce, Science, and Transportation, he continued to take Amos's counsel. When Greg had eventually become president, he'd asked Amos to be his Secretary of Energy. When Amos turned down the offer, Greg hadn't given up, asking him to be the Director of the Office of Science and Technology Policy, but Amos had turned that down, too. With every new offer, Amos had reminded Greg that he valued his time too much to squander it dealing with bureaucracy. Greg knew that Amos put a priority on his personal interests, family, and medical practice, but always offered advice when Greg asked about a specific problem. Greg was frustrated by the compromise, but they remained close friends.

Whenever Greg called, he was careful not to discuss details that required government security clearance, but he knew that Amos was well read and brilliant, which meant he was capable of reading between the lines. He valued Amos's perspective too much not to keep calling, though.

"Amos, I really need your brilliant mind on this one."

Despite the vast resources at their disposal, DNI Mitchell and SecDef Seymour hadn't made any progress on determining whether or not a bomb existed.

"Quit flattering me, Greg," Amos said seriously. "Tell me what you want."

"We've heard rumors of a nuclear weapon being obtained by an unfriendly nation and smuggled into the United States. What's the likelihood of that happening and what should the U.S. response be?"

"You know I don't have the intelligence-gathering resources you do. And I don't have the background for this type of analysis—"

"Yes, yes," Greg interrupted, "but you have better instincts than most of the people I have available."

"Come on, Greg. Tom has the best intelligence resources in the world at his fingertips."

"Amos, just indulge me for a moment. What do you think?"

"I only know what I've heard on the news and what I've read on the Internet, so keep that in mind." After a short pause, while Amos organized his thoughts, he continued. "Unfriendly nation, nuclear weapon, and smuggling," He was thinking out loud, repeating the key points like a mantra. "Al-Qaeda hasn't been successful in penetrating our borders since 9/11. But the Mexican border leaks like a sieve. The Los Zetas cartel took over Tamaulipas, just over the border, in January—they're aggressive, and they're looking for ways to expand their influence in the U.S. So, introduce Al-Qaeda to the Los Zetas and you have the potential for a bomb to be smuggled across the Mexican border using an undiscovered drug route." Amos paused again.

Without confirming or denying Amos's thoughts, or the direction they were taking, Greg asked, "Why would the Los Zetas help Al-Qaeda?"

"Well, there'd have to be something in it for the Los Zetas. With their drug sales, they've already got money, but maybe Al-Qaeda could provide weapons the Los Zetas haven't been able to get their hands on up to now, that would expand their influence in Mexico. I read that the Los Zetas takeover of the Tamaulipas was swift and bloody."

The president remained silent, waiting to see where Amos's thoughts would take him. After a moment, Amos continued.

"Russia might be a player. We believe they've been selling weapons in the Middle East. Al-Qaeda has unlimited money, they just need a willing Russian industrialist who's sympathetic to their cause or greedy enough to take their money. So, if Al-Qaeda could convince Russia to sell them nuclear components, then supply them to the Los Zetas, I'd also say the Los Zetas could smuggle a bomb, perhaps even a nuclear bomb, into the United States. How am I doing?"

Without answering, Greg asked, "Why would Vladimir Putin allow his industrialists to sell a nuclear weapon to Al-Qaeda? He knows the terrorists would use it—they place no value on life, not even their own."

"We're embarrassing Russia on the world stage right now, perhaps thwarting Russia's plans for expansion. Providing nuclear technology to Al-Qaeda would be a way for Russia to get back at the U.S.—bloody our noses, so to speak. Russia probably believes the U.S. wouldn't retaliate because we're more sensible than the terrorists. We know that could lead to another world war. We'd probably settle for massive air strikes against Al-Qaeda strongholds using conventional weapons."

"But we don't know where Al-Qaeda's strongholds are," Greg exclaimed. "Putin knows that."

"Does he? Maybe he thinks we're holding back. War spending keeps the economy strong and the public beholden to the government. That's what Russia would do," Amos added. Sarcasm dripped from his words. While the president thought about the Russia problem, Amos continued.

"I wouldn't be surprised if North Korea wanted in, too. They've been saber rattling for years. If they caught wind of a plot against the U.S., they'd probably volunteer to send a nuclear weapon our way. They'd love to prove their ICBMs can reach the U.S."

The president was quiet for a few moments while he thought. Amos had just taken what little Greg could tell him and made the leap to a conclusion that made perfect sense.

"If all of that were true, hypothetically speaking, what would I do about it?" Greg asked.

Amos laughed, but there was no humor in it.

"Greg, your advisers will tell you to find the bomb and stop it before it gets to the U.S. What more can I tell you?"

"You could tell me where to look," Greg said hopefully.

"I wish I could," Amos said seriously, then added, "The Los Zetas are aggressive. If they're also creative, they would be looking for ways to increase the frequency and volume of shipping. How could they transport more volume, more often?" He paused, thinking, then added, "North Korea borders Eastern Russia. How would Russia send bomb components to North Korea?"

"Good question," Greg said, wondering how he could use the insights Amos had shared. "Anything else?"

"Don't let me set U.S. foreign policy, Greg," Amos said seriously. "And good luck. I mean it."

"Amos, you never disappoint me. Thanks. Say hi to Lillie for me."

"I will. She'll be sorry to have missed your call. You give our best to Liz, too."

The president hung up. He sat, thinking, well into the early morning hours. Finally, he crept up to bed and lay down, careful not to awaken his wife. He knew Elizabeth worried when he didn't come to bed at a decent hour.

Situation Room, special meeting of 'The Panel', 11 April

When President McCormick entered the room, his key advisers were already there. When he sat, the others took seats on either side of him.

"What is it Tom?" Greg asked, skipping any pleasantries.

DNI Thomas Mitchell had asked for this unscheduled meeting, but it was the president who'd limited attendance to his most trusted advisers—what he referred to as 'The Panel.' Besides the president and the DNI, there was only Defense Secretary General James Seymour. The three of them were alone in the room with the ghosts of past presidents, whose faces gazed down on them from the walls. With the room almost empty, it was easy to imagine other crises, when other presidents had struggled with life-and-death decisions. President McCormick had selected which presidents' portraits would hang in the situation room—the ones he most respected and those who inspired him—Washington, Adams, Madison, Lincoln.

"As I mentioned last month," Tom said, "we haven't heard from any of our sources in Mexico. We believe there was an initial decrease in the movement of drugs while the cartels licked their wounds and replanted burned fields. When we were able to get assets in place in nearby locations, we noted a significant increase in communications into the area from the Middle East and Russia. Based on those comms, we believe Al-Qaeda has worked out some sort of deal with the Los Zetas, who have taken over Tamaulipas and the drug routes into Texas." Then he paused.

"Is there more?" the president asked.

"Only speculation at this point, Greg." The president had developed a close relationship with these men and had asked them to use his first name when they were alone. "I'd really rather wait until we can confirm the information."

"And when will that be?"

Greg thought about how quickly Amos Blund had analyzed the available information and drawn his conclusions. What would it take to get Tom and Jim to do the same? Tom looked frustrated, as if Greg had just chastised him.

"Well," he said apologetically, "our new assets are being careful right now—they don't want to give themselves away by being too aggressive. But, when you put Al-Qaeda, and possibly the Russians, in Mexico, it makes us think that they may be building a nuclear weapon that could be smuggled into the U.S. through a drug route."

He paused, looking at the president expectantly, as if he were afraid of being criticized for his leap to this conclusion, without evidence. As much as Greg didn't like the conclusion, he was pleased at his willingness to express his opinion. He smiled at Tom, thinking that he seemed to be confirming what Amos had said. *If Jim agrees,* Greg thought, *I'll act on this.* He was about to question his SecDef when Tom hurried on.

"Homeland Security has increased their surveillance of drug traffic from Mexico, but can't get ahead of it. They're barely keeping up, even with their increased budget. Our FBI agents are working all of their sources in the drug trade in major cities along the coast and the border with Mexico. We haven't heard anything that makes us believe things have changed."

Greg nodded, then turned to his SecDef.

"Jim," Greg said, his frustration increasing at the lack of information, "what's your take on this? Do you have anything from the Coast Guard?"

"Nothing unusual, so far. We've even turned a blind eye to some drug traffic in exchange for information. Nothing."

"Jim, does Al-Qaeda have a bomb?"

"I think it's a real possibility. But the military is not seeing anything unusual."

That's not the confirmation I wanted, Greg thought.

"*Anything* else on Mexico?"

Greg's question was answered with the shaking of heads. *Amos was right,* he thought, *we need to take action in Mexico, with or without confirmation.* Without mentioning it's source, Greg proposed Amos's idea: that the Los Zetas would be looking for ways to increase volume. He could see that Tom and Jim were turning the idea over in their minds. Tom was gazing in the direction of a portrait of Abraham Lincoln on the wall opposite, while Jim stared at the wooden table in front of him, lost in thought. Greg decided to move on—maybe there would be more information on the next topic.

"Fine. Tom, what about North Korea?"

"There's definitely something going on between North Korea and Al-Qaeda," Tom said. "There's been a lot of comms traffic between the two, all encrypted, and mostly in coded phrases. Even when we break their encryption, we generally can't tell what they're talking about. In addition, there's been an increase in activity at North Korea's ICBM missile site. Looks like they're gearing up for more missile tests."

"Jim, anything on your end?"

"We've been watching shipping between the Middle East, China, and North Korea, but haven't seen anything unusual."

"Can you do more than you're doing? Can you intercept and search?" Greg asked, shaking his head in frustration.

"Most of the ships stop somewhere in China going both ways. China doesn't want us anywhere near their shipping lanes—we've been over this. Any interference with their imports and exports, in their territorial waters, will be considered an act of war. And I don't think they're bluffing. So, we've limited our intercepts to the Arabian Sea and the Sea of Japan. I'd like to do more, but we can only justify stopping shipments that look suspicious, and the State Department is already receiving complaints through the UN."

"Then they can ship anything they want and our hands are tied." Greg realized there was a sharp pain in the pit of his stomach that had been building all day—it told him his stress level was too high. *I need to get out of the office and get some physical exercise,* he thought. *I'll have to get Eric to change my schedule so I can get to the gym.*

In Greg's silence, Jim said, "If you're willing to take more heat from China, we'll increase the intercepts and see how they respond."

Greg knew his old friend had no fear of upsetting their enemies—Jim had made it clear that he preferred action over diplomacy, and he accepted the consequences. But Greg also knew he would follow orders and do only what his president authorized. Greg didn't want to create more tension with China, but he needed Jim to do more than was currently being done.

"Thank you, Jim. Let me know if that creates a problem."

"Yes, sir. If it does, the secretary of state will probably hear about it before I will."

"Then let Secretary Hutchison know what you're planning so he's not surprised."

Jim nodded.

"Anything else?" Greg looked from Jim to Tom.

"Sir," Tom said, "we activated CIA assets in Russia to see if we could pick up anything directly between Russia and North Korea. Happy to report that, so far, they don't see anything."

"Good! Thanks." Greg repeated Amos's question about how Russia could send bomb components to North Korea on their eastern border. "Be creative. Think like your enemies," Greg admonished, though he knew it wasn't really necessary. "Thanks gentlemen."

The president stood and left the room, followed by the others.

3

We have confirmation

East China Sea, 17 April

The navy cruiser, nearly two football fields in length and bristling with guns, pulled to within a thousand yards of the rusted cargo vessel, which flew an Iranian flag. The cruiser had no trouble intercepting and running parallel with the vessel, chugging away at only ten knots. It had recently left the Chinese port of Taizhou and turned north toward the Yellow Sea. The navy had selected this particular location to intercept the vessel because it had yet to get up to full speed for its final run to North Korea and the shipping dock in the mouth of the Taedong River.

The radioman on the cruiser, an ensign, hailed the cargo vessel, first in Persian, the official language of Iran, then in Mandarin, then in Korean, all of which he spoke fluently, though with a slight Texas accent. He ordered the captain of the vessel to reverse engines and prepare to be boarded for an inspection. Initially, the vessel increased speed, as though the captain didn't understand or was going to ignore the order. But then the ensign heard a voice on his radio speak in broken English, at the same time the vessel began to slow.

"What reason do you . . . require for this . . . inspection?"

"We will ensure that you do not carry prohibited materials on your vessel," the ensign replied in English as the cruiser cut the distance between them in half. The deck guns on the cruiser were manned and pointed in the direction of the cargo vessel in case there was any trouble. The reply was in fluent Mandarin.

"Our ship manifest has been posted on the internet. We are hiding nothing."

"We will see for ourselves," the ensign replied in the same language. "Prepare to be boarded."

As the cruiser pulled alongside the cargo vessel, seamen threw anchor lines across the span separating the two ships. Deckhands on the cargo vessel tied them off to bollards on the deck. Seamen from both ships set out fenders to prevent damage to their respective vessels as the anchor lines drew taught and began to close the distance between the ships. Eight armed sailors climbed down to the cargo vessel, followed by a lieutenant carrying a shipping manifest.

The armed sailors dropped onto the deck of the cargo vessel and spread out to both sides, making way for those who followed and scanning the deck for hostiles with weapons.

"We will file a complaint with the United Nations in protest of this armed assault, lieutenant," the captain of the cargo vessel said in fair English, obviously recognizing the lieutenant's insignia, as they met on the deck. The captain was a gruff old sailor with a stout build, weathered features, and the rugged dress of a true seaman.

"That's your privilege," the lieutenant replied, touching his fingers to the brim of his cap in a respectful salute. The captain returned the salute angrily. The lieutenant was not intimidated by the captain's threat. "Now, please have your crew assemble on deck where they are visible to my men. We intend no harm to you or your crew, but we want no surprises. We will defend ourselves."

"We carry no weapons," the captain replied defensively. "They are locked up below. Complete your . . . illegal inspection and get off my boat."

The lieutenant nodded slightly to the captain, who turned and shouted orders to his crew. They straggled out of passageways and gathered on the aft deck.

"They are all here," the captain finally said. "All except my engineer and radioman."

The lieutenant nodded and waved to his men, who headed off in pairs to inspect the cargo holds. The lieutenant stayed on deck, surreptitiously watching the captain and his crew, as they openly glared at him and the guns pointed at them from the cruiser. After an hour, all the lieutenant's men had returned to the deck, informing the lieutenant that, as far as they could tell, the cargo holds contained exactly what the manifest said they held.

"Thank you for your cooperation, captain," the lieutenant said, as he saluted the captain once again and turned to leave.

"We have noted your registry identification number and you will be hearing from our government," the captain replied in broken English.

The lieutenant and sailors left the way they had come.

The president's private office, the White House, 24 May

"Hi, Greg," Amos's voice came clearly across the encrypted sat phone. Amos had promised to keep it close at hand now, in case the president called. "I've worried about you since our last conversation. How's the investigation going?"

"We're looking Amos—everywhere. If there's a bomb, we can't find it."

"What do Tom and Jim have to say?"

Greg had introduced Amos to his DNI and SecDef, along with other government officials and staff, two years ago at Greg's youngest son's wedding. The three men had hit it off immediately. Greg's respect for them had a lot to do with their impressions of each other.

"Tom is turning over rocks inside the country and across the globe. Every intelligence resource available has been activated. We're getting a few leads, but nothing solid." Greg sighed.

"Any of your leads solid enough for Tom or Jim to act on?"

Greg could tell where Amos was going with his question. They were out of options and out of time.

"I think we're to the point where we have to act on what little intelligence we have, while we still have time."

Amos was quiet for some time, but finally asked, "Is there a reason you called, Greg?"

His brooding interrupted, Greg said, "Just wanted to hear your deep, gravelly voice, Amos."

Amos's voice *was* deep—a very mellow baritone. Lillie had

told Greg more than once that she loved to hear Amos sing, on the rare occasions that he did. Greg had been teasing Amos about having a gravelly voice ever since Amos had suffered through a case of laryngitis several years earlier. They both laughed amiably, despite the seriousness of the situation.

"Nothing specific," Greg said more seriously. "Just wondered if you had any more ideas."

"Sorry. Fresh out. But I'll keep thinking."

"I know you will. Thanks, Amos."

Greg hung up, disappointed.

Cafe Helena, Washington D.C., 26 May

Vice President Art Klemp sat with his back to the wall in a dark corner of a dimly lit restaurant, periodically taking a sip of his beer. The restaurant was on a quiet side street in the nation's capital and difficult to find. When Art had told Senator Robert Stenger, the senior senator from Florida, that he needed someplace to talk without the president knowing about it, the senator had assured Art that they wouldn't be seen by anyone they knew.

"Everyone there is trying to not be noticed," the senator had said.

The senator arrived fourteen minutes late, a young man whom Art didn't recognize following closely behind. They crossed the room without attracting the attention of the few other customers and sat across the table from Art. The vice president nodded his head at the young man without speaking.

"This is Billy, one of my aides," the senator said. "We can

trust him." Art looked skeptically at Billy. "A meeting went late, we couldn't get away. We came directly here."

The senator waved at a passing waiter and asked for two beers. Art wasn't happy about the extra set of ears, but he pressed on.

"Bob, what do you know about these secret meetings between Greg—the president—Tom Mitchell, and Jim Seymour?"

"Nobody's talking," Bob said. "Either they really are secret or everyone except the three of us are in collusion with them."

"I think they really are secret," Billy said. "I can usually eavesdrop on conversations, because no one pays attention to me, and I haven't heard a word."

Art was surprised by Billy's comment. It seemed that the senator had been keeping Billy apprised of their ongoing conversations. He wondered suddenly if, by talking with the senator, he was repeating a mistake he'd made before. The president had threatened to ruin his career a few months earlier when he'd leaked information to the media. Party politics wouldn't save him if he had another run-in with the president. *Should I even be talking to the senator?* he wondered.

"Well," Art finally said, "keep your eyes and ears open. I want to know as soon as you hear anything. Greg can't keep cutting me out and get away with it."

The two men nodded, finished their beers, and left.

Perry, the vice president's head of security, sat quietly off to the side, listening to the three men talk. As usual, he was still, silent, expressionless, and watchful. Art didn't always know where Perry was, but he knew the security head would be close. As a trained secret service agent, Perry had pledged to protect Art with his life. In reality, they had developed such a close relationship in the year and a half that they'd been together, that Perry would have no reservation killing anyone to protect the vice president—even the president.

"What do you think, Perry?"

Art spoke quietly, guessing that Perry would be close enough to hear him. He couldn't see Perry's shrug.

"What do you want me to do?" Perry asked. He was a man of few words.

Art sighed.

"I don't know," he said, frustration in his voice. "I know the president only selected me as his running mate to win the California vote," he whined. "But I expected to have a role in running the country, like other vice presidents before me. When we were first elected, Greg included me in key strategy sessions with his advisers. He even let me pick my favorite projects to manage. Then he accused me of leaking classified information to the media and it all changed—he cut me out of everything and would hardly talk to me."

The accusation had been true, but Art had denied it. His new friend at the Post had assured him that it was how things were done on the Hill. You traded favors and information so everyone could get ahead. The information he'd given to the reporter had bought him insider trading information that had netted him over two million dollars, now in offshore accounts.

Greg's accusation had caught Art off guard and confused

him at first. When a military operation in Iran was compromised and six soldiers died, Greg had blamed Art personally. Over time, Art had become paranoid—he'd come to think that Greg would have him killed for his mistake. Art had told Perry all of this before and knew that Perry was amused by his obsession. But Art also knew that, by confiding in Perry, he had solidified Perry's commitment to protect him from danger, no matter the source.

"I'm going to confront Greg at the next opportunity," Art said firmly. "Maybe at the emergency NSC meeting he just scheduled. Maybe if I bring up the secret meetings in front of the NSC, I can catch Greg off guard and embarrass him into at least talking about them."

Situation Room, Emergency NSC meeting, 28 May

The room was once again full of NSC members, advisers, and staff. It was unusual for the president to call an NSC meeting for the middle of the week, so expectations were high.

"Go ahead and start us out, Tom," the president said to DNI Mitchell.

The vice president spoke up from the far-right side of the table before Tom could begin.

"Greg, I heard that you're meeting with some members of the NSC in secret, leaving the rest of us out."

"If the meetings are secret, Art," the president replied, smoothly and with a straight face, "how do you know about them?"

There were smiles around the room and a couple of snickers.

The president looked around, frowning, and the smiles quickly disappeared. Art's mouth opened, but nothing came out. Greg continued, unapologetically.

"The reason I have advisers, Art, is so they can advise me. When I need your advice," he tried a friendly smile. "Then I'll meet with you, too."

Art had already proven himself untrustworthy. Several things Greg had confided to his vice president, early in their term of office, had been reported on the evening news, and the fiasco in Iran that had resulted in the death of six soldiers had sealed the deal. Of course, Art had denied speaking to the press, or anyone else, but Greg didn't believe it. He could no longer trust the security of the country to Art's lack of integrity.

"I'm going to ask for Art's resignation," Greg had told the party's national committee chairman in a closed-door meeting with party leaders.

"You can't, Mr. President," the Chairman had said. "The party can't afford the embarrassment. We put everything we had into winning this election and only won the electoral vote by the narrowest of margins. You know we were behind in the popular vote. We have to tolerate Art until the next election, then convince him to decline the nomination for personal reasons."

"Fine," Greg had reluctantly agreed, "but Art will die of boredom before I allow him to touch sensitive information again."

"That works for me," the Chairman had replied.

Greg glanced over at Art, sitting in his cushioned chair, seething and glaring back at him. He turned back to DNI Mitchell.

"Tom?"

"We turned an asset in Mexico, a man who lost part of his family to the Los Zetas cartel. You don't want to know the details. He contacted the U.S. Consulate in Nuevo Laredo and offered information in exchange for protection for what remains of his family. He confirmed that at least one Arab is in Mexico building a bomb of some sort with the cartel's help. He doesn't know any more than that, except that they plan to use a drug route to bring it into the U.S."

From the set of Tom's jaws, Greg could tell there was more.

"What else?"

"An asset in Moscow is convinced that Russia is helping Al-Qaeda deliver a bomb to North Korea."

Exactly what they'd suspected. *Bingo!* Greg thought. *We have confirmation.* It was so quiet in the room that the clock ticking on the wall was audible. Greg thought again about Amos's assessment and wished he could bring his friend inside this circle. He would have to think more about it later. Finally, he broke the silence.

"Anything else?"

Tom shook his head, but he stared at Greg, his eyes saying,

we need to talk.

"Thoughts . . . anyone?" the president asked, looking away from the DNI so no one else would pick up on Tom's private message. It was quiet for a few moments, and then the president's chief of staff, Eric Epstein, who was sitting against the wall a few feet from the president, leaned forward in his seat and opened his mouth, uttering a quiet noise, a kind of choking sound. Greg, along with a few others, turned toward him.

The president considered Eric for a moment while Eric tried to find his voice. Greg had chosen him as chief of staff because he'd proven himself to be intelligent, educated, and sensitive when he worked on Greg's Senate and presidential campaigns. The man had a good sense of what needed to be said and of how the public would react. Greg believed Eric was among the main reasons he'd won his last two elections—but he also knew Eric could feel overwhelmed amongst the powerful people that surround a president. He waited patiently for Eric to speak.

"Is there a way to stop either of these from occurring?" the chief of staff asked apprehensively.

Once, when Greg had encouraged Eric to participate in discussions, he'd said that he didn't think such powerful men and women would take him seriously. SecDef Jim Seymour had been part of that conversation between Eric and the president. Now he stepped in.

"That's what each of us is considering, Eric," Jim said. "Keep in mind that there are international laws and treaties that set strict guidelines for military engagements on foreign soil. It wouldn't be unprecedented, but we need to tread carefully."

Jim's comment displayed a patience the general didn't normally have for non-military personnel. The president knew that what Jim *wouldn't* say in front of this group was that Congress had authorized the use of military force against militants in the wake of the attacks of September 11, 2001. Military action was also permitted under international law if a country was defending itself. Apart from those in the secret NSC Panel—DNI Thomas Mitchell and SecDef General James Seymour—nobody in the room knew that the president had organized the Panel. It had been set up to consider and, if necessary, to pursue the killing of individuals, including American citizens, who had been identified as suspected terrorists. No public records of their deliberations or decisions, or of any of their covert operations, were kept, so there was no reason for anyone outside the Panel to know about them. Under the circumstances, a covert operation was just what the president believed he needed in both Mexico and North Korea. Unaware of the president's thoughts, and encouraged by the lack of criticism, Eric continued.

"But laws don't stop the terrorists from operating on foreign soil. In fact, our unwillingness to engage seems to embolden them. Why should we hold back?"

He was getting worked up.

"Thanks for raising the concern, Eric," Greg said politely. "I'm going to adjourn this meeting to let everyone consider our options." As Greg stood, he looked around the table. Others started to stand. "Sit down, everyone," he said. They sat.

"I'd like Tom and Jim to join me in the Oval Office for a few minutes. The rest of you are welcome to stay and talk. Eric, will you stay and take notes on any ideas that come up?"

"Yes, sir!" Eric said enthusiastically.

Greg smiled—he'd known Eric would like that. It was rare for the president to invite him to be an active participant. As Greg walked out, he passed Art, who was less happy, his jaw clenched in anger.

Let him stew in his own juices, Greg thought.

4

Time to take action

Oval Office, special meeting of 'The Panel', 28 May

The president's secretary opened the door to the Oval Office as Greg and his NSC Panel approached, then closed it again behind them. To the left was the famous presidential desk, where past presidents had made world-altering decisions. Bulletproof, floor-to-ceiling bay windows behind the desk looked out on the lawn and rose garden. To the right was a comfortable sitting area. Antiques, some belonging to Greg and some carryovers from past administrations, decorated the room. Photos chosen by the president graced the walls.

The men moved to the sitting area, where the president sat in a comfortable swivel-recliner and motioned for the others to take seats on couches that faced each other on either side of him, across a glass-topped antique coffee table. Soft music emanated from speakers in the walls behind them. They all settled in comfortably, their stress lessening now that they were alone with others they trusted completely.

"Okay, Tom. Let's hear it."

The president was sure that his DNI had more information on Russia's involvement.

"Based on your suggestion that we consider how Russia could deliver bomb components to North Korea . . . " Tom started.

You mean, Amos's suggestion, Greg thought.

" . . . our source in Moscow began checking all east-west shipping options. He learned that an armored carrier unloaded two packages into a baggage car of the Trans-Siberian Railway. It left on Monday, two days ago, and will arrive next Monday in Vladivostok, on the coast, a few miles north of North Korea."

"Do you have a plan to intercept it?" Greg asked, looking between Tom and Jim. He was still thinking about Amos and his suggestion that it was time to take action.

Tom took a deep breath before he spoke.

"Yes, we have, but you probably don't want to know the details. This should be handled by the Panel."

"Okay. Tell me what you can."

"We don't have much intel on what's going on in Siberia—or Mexico, for that matter. You've heard everything we have. We believe we only get one shot at this in either location, so it would be nice if we had more information. Regardless, if Al-Qaeda is active in both locations, we probably have to hit both at the same time. Otherwise, one group will notify the other and something will change. We'll miss our chance altogether."

"What's the likelihood that we can stop North Korea and Mexico from receiving those bomb components?" the president asked, his brow furrowed in concern.

The SecDef took over. It would be his elite Special Forces that would be inserted into Mexico and Russia.

"It may already be too late in Mexico," Jim said. "With limited intel and a lack of planning time, all we can do is go in and try to upset their plans. There's serious risk to our assets in both locations, and a low probability of success. Nevertheless, we're prepared to proceed."

The president nearly told them about his discussion with Amos, but decided against it. So far, his team was heading in the right direction.

"So, you have a plan for the Russia–North Korea interface *and* for Mexico?" the president asked.

"Yes," Jim replied.

"When will these plans be executed?"

"We'll be able to report by next week."

"Fine. This meeting never happened. Do me a favor, will you?" Both men nodded. "Rejoin the meeting in the situation room and offer some input without giving anything away. Maybe something will come up that will actually help."

They nodded again and left. The president walked slowly to his desk, deep in thought. He sat and began looking through a stack of reports, but his mind was far away.

Vladivostok Sea Passenger Terminal, 4 June

At ten p.m. local time, two men dressed in black neoprene dry suits surfaced under the prow of an ocean liner docked at the Sea Passenger Terminal in Zolotoy Rog Bay. The older of the two was a Navy Seal commander, eight years the senior of the other, who had been in this situation many times before. The younger man, a Navy Seal lieutenant, while experienced in black ops missions and capable of leading missions himself, nevertheless deferred to the commander to run this operation. They had trained and worked together before. They were assassins, in a way, expertly trained to deliver highly specialized, intensely challenging warfare capabilities beyond the training of standard military forces. They had been chosen for this mission because neither had ever failed to complete a mission successfully.

After surfacing, the two men quietly climbed up the dock understructure until they could look across the wharf. There was nobody in sight, so they continued. Finding the shadows along a high railing near the edge of the dock, they removed their scuba tanks, masks, and fins, and lowered them into the water, tethered by lines secured to the understructure. Staying in the shadows, they made their way to the side of the terminal, where they knelt and opened their dry packs. The commander placed his night vision goggles over his head, attached his miniature microphone and receiver, and began initial surveillance. The lieutenant removed his handgun and attached a noise suppressor. Then they switched roles. They confirmed that their mics and receivers were functioning properly, then took turns removing their dry suits. Underneath, they wore wool pants, dark shirts, and socks. They removed lightweight hooded coats and boots from their dry packs and put them on. When each of them had removed a small bundle containing C-4 explosives, fuse, timer, and igniter, from their dry packs, and placed them in their deep coat pockets, they were finally ready to proceed. They dumped everything they weren't taking with them into a nearby trash barrel.

Resembling locals now, they moved casually through the Sea Terminal yard and jumped a turnstile. Staying in the shadows as much as possible, they moved toward the train station across the tracks. Parked by a back gate that led away from the station, near the end of the platform, was the military truck they had expected to find. As anticipated, it was guarded by armed men, eight in all. The two assassins watched the truck for a few minutes while the guards moved around, smoked, and talked quietly to one another. Discipline was lax. They were clearly not expecting any trouble, especially on Russian soil and at this time of night.

The commander motioned for the lieutenant to sneak around behind the truck and hide in the shadows, where he would have a line of sight past the truck to the tracks. The commander stayed on the platform side of the tracks, where he would be able to see the last few cars of the train when it arrived. The armored truck was positioned at the end of the station platform, and their assumption was that this was where the last train car—the baggage car—would stop, with the passenger cars being forward. The train was due in fifteen minutes, so the two men crouched uncomfortably, silently observing each other and watching the guards.

When the train arrived, just under a minute late, the armed guards were still leaning against the truck or sitting on the platform. Those who were smoking dropped their unfinished cigarettes and ground them out. Had they bothered to look around, they might have noticed the two men hiding in the shadows, but they didn't look. Two of the guards on the platform walked to the baggage car, while two of those leaning against the truck pushed off and moved into position, presumably to off-load whatever was being transported on the train. None of the guards had their rifles in firing position.

At a signal from the commander, both assassins opened fire from the shadows with their silenced weapons, dropping the four guards by the train before the remaining guards realized what was happening. When the remaining guards finally moved, it was only to push off the truck and run, or drop for cover. Two guards ran around the truck, only to get picked off by the lieutenant, who was in the shadows behind them. The two guards on the ground hadn't found cover, but it was difficult for the commander, still hidden near the platform, to get an angle on them.

"Can you get to the two on the ground?" The commander asked quietly, speaking into his microphone.

"Not without exposing myself. Can you see anyone in the baggage car?"

"No. I'll cover you while you get to the truck."

The lieutenant bent over and ran to the side of the truck. No shots, but so far he hadn't made any noise. He lay down and looked under the truck. The guards must have heard him this time— one was turning his way, while the other turned his head to look. He shot the guard who was turning, but before he could get off another round, the remaining guard twisted and quickly fired three shots, one of them striking the lieutenant in the right shoulder. His gun dropped from his right hand

and he had to scramble to pick it up with his left. As the guard twisted, attempting to aim again, his movement gave the commander the line of sight he needed, and a double tap finished off the guard.

"Status?" The commander asked.

"I'm hit in the shoulder. It's bad." The lieutenant moaned involuntarily as he moved to the back of the truck. "Let's set the explosives and get out of here."

"We need to confirm that the bomb is on the train. Where are you now?"

"I'm at the back of the truck. Still no movement on the train. I'll cover you while you check it out."

They expected there to be one or more soldiers in the baggage car, but they had to act quickly, before others noticed what was happening.

"Moving now," the commander said, leaving the shadows and approaching the platform at an angle that mostly hid him until he reached it, where he stopped to assess. He knew the lieutenant would watch the baggage car windows for any movement. They were still dark. He wished he'd allowed the guards to turn on the lights before signaling the attack, but they needed to be gone before the porters arrived to unload luggage.

"Here goes."

The commander pushed himself up onto the platform, keeping his eyes on the baggage car windows. No movement. He took a step, then another. Then he ran the rest of the way to the door, jumping over one of the downed men and stopping beside the door, which was slightly ajar. As he stood to one side of the door, ready to go in, he heard the lieutenant whisper,

"Movement in the window."

At that moment, a stream of bullets penetrated the wall of the baggage car, nearly cutting the commander in two. He fell to the platform without uttering a sound.

The lieutenant was on his own to complete the mission. He had no idea how many soldiers were in the baggage car, but he'd seen the shadows of two, at least. He decided to take the offensive and ran toward the baggage car at an angle, his right arm hanging limply. As he ran, he fired with his left, first through the windows and then, when he got return fire, through the wall to the side of the window on the right. At that point, the shooting stopped as suddenly as it had started, giving the lieutenant an opportunity to reload and reassess.

Moments later, he climbed awkwardly up onto the platform and continued to the door of the car. As he moved, he saw more guards, presumably alerted by the gunshots and breaking glass, running down the platform, guns in hand. He had the fleeting thought that he should use the explosives in his pocket, but there was no time now. He pushed open the door to the baggage compartment, firing to the right, then panning left. There was a dead guard on the floor of the car when he entered, and one still alive, reloading—a double tap put him down.

The lieutenant knew he had only seconds to find and destroy

the bomb, if there was one. There were two packages sitting on a crate in front of him, but nothing else resembling what he was looking for. He didn't have time to open them—he could hear running footfalls and voices calling in Russian just outside the car. No time to set his explosives. He emptied his gun into the two packages. The second one erupted in flames and caught some of the luggage on fire. He'd been told that destroying nuclear material would not necessarily result in an explosion, but he was still surprised.

Noise behind him caused him to turn back to the platform, where guards had arrived to deal with the situation. Seeing the lieutenant's gun, they didn't hesitate to shoot him, at the same time that he opened fire on them, dropping two of them before he died.

Evidence recovered later showed that the fire had been caused by a partially assembled bomb. A fully functional bomb would have destroyed most of the city.

Chiapas, Mexico, 4 June

At the same time that the two Navy Seals were engaging the guards on the train in Vladivostok, four Delta Force operatives wearing camouflage clothing were sneaking through a wooded area in Chiapas, Mexico. They were among the most elite, professionally trained assassins—approaching the status of mercenaries—that the U.S. military had produced. Neither the

United States government nor the military officially acknowledged their existence.

The four operatives crept silently through the trees in a jagged line about thirty yards apart, catching glimpses of each other periodically through the trees. They wore miniature microphones and receivers, carried suppressed handguns, and wore backpacks containing other specialized equipment. They had been inserted by helicopter fifteen miles away and had been walking for nearly five hours, through dense jungle, to get into position. Color was just beginning to tint the night sky to the east when they finally approached their destination.

The leader, "Alpha One," was on the far left. The other three, "Alpha Two," "Alpha Three," and "Alpha Four," were spread out in a line.

"One Tango ahead and left of Alpha One at twenty yards," Alpha One spoke quietly into his mic when he saw movement up ahead and spotted a sentry. Tango was the phonetic word for the letter "T." In this case, his team knew he meant that he had a target. His team members stopped and cautiously looked around.

"One Tango ahead and right of Alpha Four, thirty yards," Alpha Four said.

Alpha Two and Alpha Three replied in rapid succession with a double click of their mics as a silent acknowledgement.

The two sentries weren't alert, leaning in a relaxed way against trees close to a dirt road. One held his rifle limply in one hand, while the other had left his rifle leaning against a tree while he rolled a homemade cigarette.

Alpha One gave the signal for Alpha Four to approach and the other two to hang back. Alpha One and Alpha Four lowered themselves to a prostrate position on the damp ground, then crept slowly toward the sentries and, simultaneously, took them out at twenty feet with a single, silent shot each. They carefully approached the downed sentries, confirming that they were dead and that they hadn't activated radios or alarms.

The sentries had been positioned along the edge of a dirt road that curved off in both directions. *Some sort of perimeter access road,* Alpha One thought. The operatives dragged the dead men into the undergrowth and obscured their tracks. Then, from a crouched position, they looked around and spotted two more sentries, each about a hundred and fifty yards farther along the access road in each direction. After a brief, hushed conversation, they agreed to eliminate these two as well before moving across the road. Alpha One and Alpha Four backed into the woods and approached the next two sentries, repeating the process, before spotting two more, even farther along the road.

The sun wasn't up, but it was getting light. Alpha One and Alpha Four crept carefully back into the woods to ensure that they were out of sight, and then all four operatives crept to a central point. They crossed the road singly, carefully watching the roadway and woods in both directions, then continued on together toward their destination.

Fifteen minutes later, they reached a clearing they'd been shown in aerial photographs. As depicted in the photos, a small, single-story building, probably an office, sat about twenty yards to the left of a larger one, two stories tall. Both buildings were made of thick metal sheeting, with the same sheeting on their roofs. The buildings were draped with camouflage netting, and bamboo fronds had fallen onto the netting, adding to the effect. Alpha One knew the camouflage was intended to hide the buildings from airborne reconnaissance, but U.S. spy satellites had no trouble seeing through it.

While nobody was exactly sure, intelligence suggested that the larger building was likely a combination processing plant and warehouse. There were two old, rusting Ford pickup trucks parked outside the warehouse, and a pair of indolent guards lounged by the office door. A field of coca plants lay adjacent to the building, with a field of poppy off to the right in the distance. There were numerous peasants working among the poppies and a few armed guards overseeing the workers from atop wobbly platforms around the perimeter of the field.

The operatives stayed in the trees and crept toward the buildings, but quickly stopped and ducked when the door to the larger one opened. Three men came out, the two in front looking around as the one behind pulled a small dolly loaded with a closed crate. The man on the left looked Arabic, while the one on the right must have been the leader of the group, possibly the Los Zetas drug lord himself, Jose Mendoza, since the guards came to attention when the three appeared. Alpha One debated attacking immediately, which would have given them the best chance of success, but he hesitated too long and the three men made it to the office before he could act.

Intelligence suggested that this plant contained the bomb,

or at least the components needed to make it. The crate on the dolly certainly could be their target. Carefully, the operatives resumed their approach toward the buildings.

In his briefing in Syria before leaving for Mexico, Saleh had been told that the Los Zetas cartel drug lord, Jose Mendoza, liked to be called *El Jefe*—Spanish for *The Boss*. He had apparently earned the right to the title, and his fearsome control over the cartel ensured that his men complied with his every wish, including this one. He led the cartel with an iron fist and did not accept failure—at least, that's what Saleh had been told.

The Arab had cautioned El Jefe that the closer they got to completing their delivery of the bomb, the more vigilant the Americans would become—they might even send assassins.

"I will not be caught . . . surprised," El Jefe had said in heavily accented, broken English. "It is unlikely they could succeed . . . such an attempt."

They spoke in English, their only language in common. The Arab was fluent, the Mexican less so. Although the humidity and heat of the jungle were stifling, El Jefe had ordered his sentries on the perimeter of the compound to be vigilant. That comforted Saleh, but he still found it difficult to be nice to the bandit. After all, Mexico *was* part of the *evil west*. But during his pre-op briefing, Saleh had been told to treat El Jefe as a valued partner until he'd fulfilled his end of the bargain. After that, the Brothers didn't care what happened to the Mexican.

Saleh had found El Jefe ready to believe that the bomb they were building was no more powerful than those used in France, England, and elsewhere, to harass and frustrate a few of the United States' allies. "It's no more dangerous that the drugs we . . . and you . . . supply to the weak ones," Saleh had said with a conspiratorial grin. If El Jefe had had any reservations, the automatic weapons and body armor the Arabs had given him as part of their agreement had sealed the deal. Saleh would have to tread carefully for a few more days, but then he could be rid of El Jefe and his ego. The Mexican was almost as arrogant as the Americans and British.

Inside the warehouse, El Jefe motioned to his bodyguard to take the dolly and follow, and Saleh fell into step with El Jefe as they headed for the building's exit.

When our business is concluded, Saleh thought, *if I have an opportunity, I will personally eliminate you. But no matter. Once you help us secrete the bomb into the United States, with all of the national economies so closely tied together, the fall of the United States will mean the breakdown of most of the western hemisphere.*

"You have done well, my friend," Saleh said. He considered putting his hand on El Jefe's shoulder in an added show of friendliness, but remembered that while such a gesture showed friendship in England, and even in the United States, here it would be seen as a violation of the Mexican leader's personal space. It might be hazardous to his health, so he smiled instead.

"We are almost ready to proceed to the next phase of the operation," he said.

As they left the large building and started across the tarmac toward the office, El Jefe wondered—for at least the hundredth time—if the agreement he'd made weeks ago with these Arabs was worth it, given the insult it would present to the Americans. This Arab, Saleh, had told him it was a small bomb, but he didn't believe it. And the more damage the bomb caused in America, the more attention the American government would pay to his operations. But the automatic weapons and body armor he'd received in exchange had seemed to justify the risk. He'd used the automatic weapons in the takeover of Tamaulipas. The titanium bulletproof vests had yet to be tested, but he was sure they would prove their worth eventually. With these factors in mind, he settled his doubts.

"I am pleased with our agreement. The weapons you supplied have helped extend our control of the Gulf."

He smiled at the double meaning of the word "gulf," which to him denoted both the Gulf of Mexico and the Gulf Cartel, which he had virtually eliminated. The two men reached the office and entered, leaving the lone bodyguard to struggle with the dolly at the door. The two guards outside the door, who were not supposed to know about the bomb, pretended not to notice.

Once inside, El Jefe motioned for the bodyguard to place the crate on the conference table—which he did with some difficulty—while they reviewed the plan for getting the bomb to its final destination.

The American operatives watched the activity around the buildings for a few more minutes, careful to remain hidden within the deep tangle of undergrowth. Once the Mexican guards outside the buildings relaxed again, the operatives crept along the edge of the jungle canopy toward the back of the office building. Thinking they would have to work their way around and attack from the front of the office, Alpha One was surprised to find two small windows in the back wall of the building. After a hurried conversation, Alpha One and Alpha Two each approached a window and, standing to the side, simultaneously peeked in. Alpha Three and Alpha Four remained in the undergrowth at either end of the building, keeping a lookout. Through the window on the right, Alpha One could see the Mexican leader and the Arab sitting at a table in the middle of the room. A bodyguard stood to the side of the front door, opposite the windows. He faced the windows but was, thankfully, looking down at a box sitting on the table. He was clearly more concerned with what was going on in the room than with keeping watch.

Using hand signals, Alpha One told Alpha Two to prepare for their attack. Each man lifted his gun toward the window, but just as Alpha One pulled his gun back a little, preparing to thrust it through the glass of the window, he heard shouting and honking coming from in front of the building. Both operatives pulled back to a position to the side of the windows, crouching low.

It sounded as though a vehicle were approaching the buildings from the front. Alpha One carefully raised his head back to the window to peer inside just as El Jefe and Saleh rose from the table and the bodyguard raised his rifle, moving to open the front door.

If our luck holds out, Alpha One thought, *all three men will leave the room and let us get to the crate.* Unfortunately, El Jefe directed his guard to leave the room, while he and the Arab drew their own guns.

A quiet sound from behind him alerted El Jefe. His situational awareness was keen, as it had to be given his position. Over the past few days, he'd been wary of every noise, every movement in his peripheral vision. He acted as though the Arab's rumors were nothing to be concerned about—his men expected nothing less from him—but inwardly, he knew his life was at risk. He didn't trust the Arab, and he didn't trust most of his own men.

At the sound, El Jefe turned quickly and saw movement outside the window—what it was, he couldn't tell, but it didn't matter. He would shoot first and ask questions later. He raised his gun.

Alpha One, confident in his stealth, motioned Alpha Two to take out the men while he focused on the crate. They raised their heads and guns at the same moment that El Jefe began firing through the window. Alpha One got off a couple of shots just before El Jefe's first bullet hit him in the forehead. If he'd come from the side of the window, instead of from beneath it, the bullet might have hit his bulletproof vest and merely knocked the wind out of him. Alpha Two managed to fire a few rounds before he, too, was hit in the head.

Alpha Three and Alpha Four turned toward the building at the sound of gunshots from inside. Since their team members had silenced weapons, it was clear that the Op had been compromised. They watched Alpha One and Alpha Two fall and saw the blood and gore from their head wounds. They quickly retreated into the trees to regroup and consider their next move. As Mexicans with rifles surrounded the building, dragging the two dead operatives roughly to the front of the building, Alpha Three and Alpha Four fell back deeper into the jungle. Their pre-op planning said that in this situation they should wait it out in the jungle and try again at their earliest opportunity.

The cartel's men, armed with rifles, began to move noisily into the trees. They couldn't know if there were more operatives nearby, and it seemed they wanted to warn anyone away who *might* be there. It didn't work, but it did force the operatives to retreat even further. When the Mexicans finally returned to the clearing, Alpha Three called in their situation, asking for confirmation of the backup plan. Then he and Alpha Four found a good place to hunker down and wait.

El Jefe had been hit in the chest. His titanium vest stopped the bullet, but it knocked him down, taking his breath with it and leaving him in agony. As he fell, he saw, to his horror, bullets penetrating the crate, but there was nothing he could do. He also saw the Arab go down before he lost consciousness.

When El Jefe woke, he was on a couch with his medic kneeling next to him, looking closely at him and holding a cool damp cloth on his forehead. His vest had been removed and his chest hurt where the bullet had hit, but he was careful not to show any pain. His men expected him to be strong.

The Arab was on the floor with a pillow under his head, unattended. The bodyguard was standing at the door with his rifle hanging loosely in his right hand. He had a bloody bandage around his left bicep.

"What happened?" El Jefe asked his bodyguard in Spanish.

"We got them both," the bodyguard said, "but not before they damaged the package. You were both saved by the vests."

El Jefe looked quickly at the damaged package. *It wasn't destroyed*, he thought, *or we wouldn't be here.* "A good investment, it turns out. No?" Nervous perspiration broke out on El Jefe's forehead.

"Yes. We should get more."

"Agreed," El Jefe said, trying to rise and motioning to the Arab. "How is he?" he asked, quickly lying back down but disguising the agony in his chest.

The bodyguard pretended not to notice El Jefe wince. He knew it was important to his leader that his soldiers see him as being above pain, the hardest of hard men.

"Same as you," he said. *In pain,* he thought to himself.

"And the intruders? Can you tell who they were?"

"Caucasian. No ID. American-made weapons."

"Only two?"

"We couldn't find any others, but they killed four of our sentries."

El Jefe didn't bother to mourn for the sentries—they were just hired hands.

"No problem. We'll check out the package when the Arab wakes up."

He closed his eyes to rest. His pain was slowly being blotted out by a large dose of medication. He had a fleeting thought that they should leave the office in case the bomb exploded, but his tongue wouldn't cooperate and his body didn't want to move. He let his muscles relax, but his thoughts turned again to the rumors of assassination. The attempt hadn't come from his men or the Arabs. *Have the Americans figured out what we're doing?* he wondered as he drifted into a narcotic sleep.

The bodyguard sighed and stood over his boss to ensure his safety, his eyes on the medic. *No one can be trusted, not even the medic,* he thought, wincing at his own pain.

5

With each new twist of the knife

Situation Room, NSC meeting, 4 June
The president held the Daily tightly in his hand, hoping the shaking caused by his frayed nerves wasn't visible. The Daily, a report prepared for him each morning by his chief of staff, consolidated the reports of each day from individual NSC members and summarized important activity and intelligence from around the world. He had already read it, plus three major newspapers, cover to cover. It was his habit to rise early and read in preparation for the day—he wanted all the latest information about what others thought was happening in the world.

He wanted to ask if their people were responsible for the explosion in Vladivostok, but he couldn't do that in a room full of uninitiated witnesses. Instead, mustering some composure, he held the Daily up with one hand and smacked it with the other.

"What do we know about this explosion in Vladivostok?"

By previous agreement with the president, his advisers intentionally withheld sensitive information from him.

"It was in the baggage car of a Trans-Siberian Railway passenger train," DNI Mitchell said. "It appears to have damaged the last three cars,"

"Casualties?"

"Probably."

"Any Americans on board?"

"There were, but none were injured."

"Anything we need to do?"

"I've offered medical assistance, as per protocol," Secretary of State Cyril Hutchison said. "The Red Cross and other relief agencies are also aware of the situation."

The president looked at his secretary of state thoughtfully. Cy had served with Greg in the Senate for twelve years and had represented his home state of Illinois well. They hadn't always agreed on the issues that came before the Senate, but he'd always respected Cy's personal integrity, logic, and diplomacy. He'd been a natural choice for secretary of state and had come highly recommended, and Greg was grateful to have him.

"Russia's response?" the president asked.

"A thanks-but-no-thanks reply, as expected," Cy said.

"Okay, thanks Cy."

The president looked around the packed room. *We're not getting anything done,* he thought. *And I don't know who I can trust. This is a waste of time.*

"Let's move along," he said aloud, trying to change the subject.

"Wait a minute," Vice President Art Klemp said. "A week ago, Tom said Russia was going to help Al-Qaeda get a bomb to North Korea. Vladivostok is close to North Korea. Maybe the explosion *was* the bomb." As soon as he'd said it, he realized his mistake—a nuclear explosion would have caused far more damage—but he didn't get a chance to correct himself before DNI Tom Mitchell spoke up.

"I think a *nuclear* explosion would have done more damage, Art, but we've taken into account that it might have been bomb components." Tom turned to the president. "We're trying to get more information."

There was whispering around the room. The president nodded, looking at his Daily again. He was looking for something that wouldn't draw a connection between the incident in North Korea and the one in Mexico.

"Let us know if anything turns up," he said distractedly, then asked about a couple of relatively benign issues mentioned in the Daily. Finally, he felt it was safe to ask about Chiapas. "Tom, what do we know about this gunfight in Mexico?"

"Not a lot of details," Tom said. "Looks like a continuation of the drug cartel infighting."

"I thought the Los Zetas had wiped out the Gulf cartel," Art Klemp said suspiciously. There was murmuring around the room, whether in support of Art or not was hard to tell.

"We thought so too, Art," Tom said, keeping his voice neutral. "Unfortunately, we still don't have assets in place to get all the details, so we're guessing here. Maybe a third group has entered the mix, trying to take advantage of the situation." Tom raised his shoulders in a shrug, his eyebrows going up along with them. "We're trying to find out."

"Enough," the president said, agitated. His irritation was

supposed to be for show, but Art's inquisitiveness was actually making him angry. *This is the last time this group meets until we have something to share with them,* he thought. He decided to end this meeting. He needed to get the non-sanitized version from the Panel.

"This is unacceptable," the president grumbled in an unusual show of emotion—which he actually felt. "Tom, Jim, I want a discussion in the Oval Office, now. This meeting is over."

The president stood up to leave.

"Wait!" Art shouted, "What about Al-Qaeda and North Korea?"

The president glared at him.

"Weren't you listening, Art? We have nothing. I'll call another meeting when we have something to discuss."

Then he stormed out, followed quickly by Jim and Tom, who looked cowed by the president's anger, as if they were worried they might get reamed—or sacked.

The president noticed looks of disbelief around the room.

Good, he thought, *they're probably too grateful that they've been spared to wonder if the scene is being staged.*

As the meeting broke up, Art motioned for the senator to follow him.

Oval Office, meeting of 'The Panel', 4 June
Once they were seated, President McCormick began.

"There won't be any more meetings of the full NSC until the bomb issue is resolved one way or another."

He was angry—not at these men, but at the situation in which they found themselves. His advisers were surprised and relieved at the same time.

"You think that's a good idea, Greg?" Tom asked. "We can keep giving them a sanitized version of the facts."

"We don't have time to play games, Tom," Greg said. "I need you out there finding that bomb."

"I agree wholeheartedly," Jim said, "but Art won't be satisfied with that. He's already suspicious."

"Art's crazy," Greg snarled. "I'll have him locked up if necessary."

"No doubt," Jim said, "but keeping Art quiet is going to be a problem."

Greg glared at his SecDef without responding for a moment before answering.

"Besides, it's too easy to get tripped up by your own lies. So, was Vladivostok our doing?"

"Yes, Greg," Jim said. "The explosion at the rail station was our men destroying what was, presumably, a bomb. Lots of damage and injuries. The explosion wasn't big enough to be a nuclear warhead—probably bomb components. We don't know what we got."

"How many dead?"

"Two Navy Seals went in and they're MIA. Russia isn't saying how much damage the explosion caused, but from our satellite images and the passenger manifest for the train, we're estimating the collateral damage at about seventy dead or injured, including our two soldiers. Plus, the rail station is unusable."

Greg winced.

"Missing in action? I hate that. What about Mexico?"

"We sent four Delta Force operatives." Jim replied. "The Op was put on hold when two were shot and killed. The other two are waiting in the jungle to try again. We think they found the bomb, but we won't know until they get back to us."

"Anything from the Mexican government?"

"We don't expect to hear anything from them. Their president may not even know it happened."

"Well, I know," Greg said, quietly, "so she probably does, too."

"Don't lose faith yet, Greg," Jim said. "We'll make discreet inquiries, say that we saw something on satellite imagery, and then let them investigate.

"When do you expect to hear from the two remaining operatives?"

"We don't know when they'll have another shot at it."

"So, we blew up bomb components in Russia, and we don't know, for sure, if we've located the bomb in Mexico. Is that the crux of it?"

Greg looked from Jim to Tom, who both nodded their heads. It was time to let them in on his secret.

"I need to tell you," he said as he looked at each of them in turn, "I've spoken with Amos Blund."

"What did Amos say?" Tom asked, a surprised look on his

face. Jim just looked agitated, probably because it was a national security issue they were talking about.

"He reached the conclusion about a nuclear bomb coming through Mexico weeks before you felt comfortable telling me. He also gave me the idea to act in Mexico and Eastern Russia days before you suggested it. It was his idea to look for shipping routes between Russia and North Korea."

"Why don't you bring Amos in to help?" Jim asked gruffly.

Greg could tell from their reactions that they resented him consulting an outsider, even one as competent as Amos.

"He wouldn't come, even if I ordered him as his president. That's why I gave him a secure sat phone."

"A what?" Tom shouted, incredulous, and Greg frowned at him. "Sorry, sir."

"I bought encrypted satellite phones when I was in the Senate and gave one to Amos. I've had the software updated regularly to ensure constant encryption, and I've consulted with him many times over the years. I've never met anyone else who can put things together the way he does—he's always close to the mark. I'm addicted to him, I'm afraid."

Tom stared at the portrait of Lincoln, while Jim looked at the floor through the glass tabletop in front of him. Greg suspected that they were considering the difference between their approach and Amos's. Amos was free to speculate, whereas they had to have evidence to support their suspicions.

"Look," he said, "I realize that Amos isn't restricted by the need to obtain evidence. And I think it's time that we take the same approach—I mean, say what we really think. I need the benefit of your individual and collective thinking, or we'll never find a solution."

"Okay, Greg," Tom said, bitterness still evident in his voice, "what else did Amos say that we haven't said or done."

"He said to look for some way Los Zetas can ship more product, faster—that may be the key to how they're planning to get the bomb across the border—something we haven't thought of or looked for." After waiting a few moments to let them think about what he'd said, Greg asked, "Anything else gentlemen?"

Neither answered. From the sour expression on Tom's face and the lack of expression on Jim's, Greg wondered if mentioning Amos had been such a good idea—he might have just driven a wedge into his relationship with his best people.

"Any thoughts?" he asked again, but still neither man answered. "Okay, I see I've insulted both of you. I'm sorry."

They started to object, but Greg held up his hand to stop them.

"It's okay. I trust you two more than that whole room full of people down the hall combined, and that's saying something. I need you at your best, so please get over this and let's go stop the bomb in Mexico. I want to know immediately when the situation changes."

"Yes sir," Tom said. Jim just stared at the president.

"What is it, Jim?" He could tell Jim had more to say but was struggling with it. "Tell me what you're thinking."

Jim started to speak, then hesitated, as if sharing a mere opinion was difficult. He gritted his teeth, took a deep breath, then started.

"I . . . I didn't need to hear that Amos Blund is outthinking us."

The president opened his mouth to respond, but Jim held up his hand to stop him.

"No, just let me finish. This is hard enough as it is."

The president waited patiently for his SecDef to compose himself. He genuinely wanted to hear what he would say. Jim took another breath, then continued.

"I'm . . . so tired of the political wrangling. I was pleased when you decided to give us some rein and let us take action in Russia and Mexico. I'm sorry both missions failed to achieve their objectives. But I firmly believe the only way we're going to stop Al-Qaeda—stop the terrorists and their conspirators— is to take the battle to them."

The president tried to interrupt again, but once more Jim stopped him with a raised hand. Sitting forward, he went on.

"The military will keep looking for the bomb—you know we'll do our best—while you and the other politicians talk. But when you're through talking and find that it did no more good than all the other times, I hope you'll let me go after them and stop the terror once and for all." He sat back in his chair. "That's all I wanted to say," he concluded.

"Thank you, Jim," Greg said, smiling. "I appreciate your candor and respect your position. I'll keep that option open as we move forward."

Chiapas, Mexico

After waiting two hours, which they hoped would be enough time for things to cool down in the Mexican camp, Alpha Three and Alpha Four snuck back to the clearing, to a point a hundred yards from the office building. As they approached, they heard truck engines chug to life. One backfired, sounding like a gunshot. Worried that it meant they had waited too long, they hurried, as stealthily as they could, the rest of the way to the clearing. The two rusty Ford pickups were just moving away from the building in the opposite direction.

"Should we try to take them out from here?" Alpha Four asked quietly.

"No good," Alpha Three replied. "Better to signal the helo to get a fix and track them. Let's go."

As they turned to head back into the trees, they were confronted by four Mexicans with rifles. Their training kicked in instinctively and they rolled, one to each side. They came up shooting, each taking out the two Mexicans closest to them, as the drug lord's men fired into the empty space where the operatives had been moments before. Then they ran. They could hear footfalls and shouting coming from the clearing. They knew they had to either outrun their pursuers or get far enough ahead to set up an ambush. Their choice would depend on how many men chased them, and for how long.

As they ran, Alpha Four heard bullets hissing past his head and thumping into nearby trees. He watched as Alpha Three went down with a bullet in the leg. Alpha Four slid to a stop, but Alpha Three wasn't having it.

"Keep going," he yelled. "I'll slow them down. Get a message to the helo."

Alpha Three rolled into the undergrowth and turned to face the oncoming Mexicans—he'd been shot before, but they'd been trained to block out the pain so they could continue the mission. Alpha Four knew his friend would be prepared to confront the Mexicans, and he began running again. He could hear shooting behind him, which meant the Mexicans were still coming. The gunshots dwindled, then stopped. Alpha Four didn't know if it meant Alpha Three had killed all his pursuers, or they had killed him. He ran for thirty minutes, then stopped and called in his report. The radioman in the helicopter promised to forward the report, then come and pick him up. He declined, saying he had to go back and check on Alpha Three. He would let them know when he was ready for a pickup.

Alpha Four never called back.

Oval Office, meeting of 'The Panel'

"You asked for an update on the situation in Mexico," Jim said.

President McCormick nodded. Jim told him as much as he knew, as relayed by the helo operator.

"We got a fix on the two trucks. They stopped in a small town and pulled into a building. Shortly thereafter, four trucks left the building, headed in different directions. We followed each of them until they stopped again. One doubled back, the others continued on. We're still following."

"They know they're being watched," the president stated.

"That's our take on it."

"Can we get to any of them? Are they headed toward the border?"

"Yes, and yes. But it will take time, and I don't think we want to tell the Mexican government what we're doing. That presents its own set of risks."

"Do it," the president said. "I'll give you one week to find and stop the bomb, then we consider going public with what we know."

"Aren't you concerned about the panic a public statement would cause?" Tom asked.

"Tom," the president said, "if we have to raise the DEF-CON threat level, the public will know anyway. We're better off telling them ourselves, before they hear it from our enemies." Thinking about Art leaking information, he quickly added, "And before the press finds an inside source and spills the beans."

He looked from Tom to Jim.

"Anything new on Al-Qaeda's dealings with North Korea?"

"The navy has increased shipping intercepts," Jim said. "If they're shipping bomb components, we're not seeing it."

"Yeah," Greg said, "Ambassador Porter at the United Nations is getting complaints about the intercepts."

Tom joined in.

"Israel reports that they're seeing increased activity to their north, between Iran and the Russian states. They're trying to determine what's going on, but it's difficult. So, we have limited intel there."

He sounded apologetic.

"What you're saying," the president said, "is that there may be a link between Al-Qaeda and North Korea, and Russia may be that link."

Tom and Jim looked at each other for a moment.

"That's about the size of it, Greg." Jim said.

Situation Room, emergency meeting of 'The Panel', 12 June

" . . . if the United States of America does not release two hundred and seventeen of our brothers, illegally detained in their prisons, by the 4th of July at 3:00 p.m., eastern time, we will take nuclear war to the U.S. and her evil Western allies. We will deliver a list of names of our brave soldiers to the U.S. embassy in Istanbul, Turkey, a neutral state . . . "

"Shut it off," Greg fumed.

The president was normally unflappable, but he was becoming more agitated with each new revelation. He had now watched the video three times, and he didn't want to see it again—ever. There was nothing new to be gleaned from it, anyway. *With each new twist of the knife,* he thought. Greg stared at the big screen on the wall, even after Tom reached in front of him—making him flinch—and pushed the button on the control panel that turned off the video. The screen went blank.

The president sat in disbelief, still attempting to digest the terrorists' message. The recording was a copy of a transmission that had been broadcast by Al Jazeera TV in Iran about fifteen minutes earlier.

"Did our operations in Russia and Mexico totally fail?"

Greg asked, looking at Jim, then Tom. It was the latter who answered.

"In the last week, the chatter has tripled between Russia, the Middle East, and Mexico. Then, as of yesterday, nothing."

"Which means . . ."

Tom looked at Jim before answering.

"Historically, when terrorists stop talking, it means that discussions are over and the operation is to proceed as planned—everyone's on their own from that point. What we think it means this time is that, whether they have bombs or not, they're close enough to their deadline that they want us to *think* they're ready to go."

"But *are* they ready to go? I mean, do they have bombs and the means to deliver them?"

Greg could tell Jim was struggling with what to say.

"Don't tell me you need more facts, Jim," Greg said. "I want to know what you think."

Jim stared at the president.

"We still don't know but . . . what I think is . . . I think they have a bomb and they're ready to go."

Greg frowned.

"But we haven't stopped looking and listening," Jim added.

"All of our assets are actively working their contacts, everywhere," Tom added, "and not just the obvious ones. We are full-out chasing down leads. I've passed the word to look for ways Los Zetas could transport more volume." Tom suddenly had trouble finding words, as if he, too, was having trouble sharing his opinion. "I think—well, I think that they *don't* have any bombs, or the means to deliver them, but they don't want to wait another year. They don't want to wait for another fourth of July before pulling our chain."

The president was surprised that his DNI and SecDef disagreed. For some reason—maybe because they agreed so often—he thought they discussed everything before they brought it to him.

"If we release the Islamists, will Al-Qaeda back off?"

Greg asked the question, but it was rhetorical—he knew Al-Qaeda would never back off. If they had a bomb and the means to deliver it, they would, even if their demands were met. But as president, he had to consider all the options. He looked at the faces of his most trusted advisers and saw the answer there that he'd known he'd get.

Greg had recently decided to add his chief of staff, Eric Epstein, to the Panel to help with the public interface. He knew that Eric must be worrying about the impact on the public. Not having participated before, Eric seemed surprised at the details and opinions being shared. Up until this point, the chief of staff had been sitting, wide-eyed and silent, at the end of the couch. He spoke now, his voice little more than a whisper.

"Have they ever bluffed before?" he asked, nervously clicking his pen with his thumb. He *looked* scared.

"Not that I know of, Eric," Tom replied.

Eric nearly exploded, which was out of character for him.

"So what makes you think they could be now?"

Tom looked shocked by Eric's reaction.

Eric's right, Greg thought. *Why does Tom think Al-Qaeda is bluffing?*

"Alright," Greg interjected, trying to avoid an unproductive argument, "what do we do now? The media will want a response to this video from the White House. I've called a press conference for an hour from now." He banged the tabletop with his fist. "If I'd held the press conference yesterday, like I said last week that I would . . . " He banged on the table again, not finishing the thought. "Instead of being proactive, this is going to look like we've been caught flat-footed."

Eric spoke frantically, looking at the serious expressions on each of their faces.

"You're not thinking of telling the country that we believe the terrorists have a nuclear bomb, are you?"

Greg looked from Tom to Jim and back again, struggling to maintain his composure. He really needed their input on this.

"What's your recommendation?"

"Considering the panic that would result in major cities," Tom replied, quietly, "I have to agree with Eric on this one. We need to downplay the impact while we continue investigating."

Greg looked at Jim.

"What do you say?"

"You know how I feel about Al-Qaeda," Jim said. "If I had my way, we'd be tearing up the desert trying to ferret them out." He paused for a moment, then added, "If we confirm that Russia's complicit in this for political reasons, I'm going to be very unhappy."

The president stared at Jim. He knew his SecDef thought diplomacy was a waste of time and that most politicians were a waste of space. "Just let the military handle things," Jim had suggested seriously on more than one occasion in the past week.

Greg finally tore his gaze away from Jim and looked at Tom again.

"What else can the Intelligence Community do to help?" he asked his DNI.

"The FBI is already moving agents from outlying areas into the capital, and to the border with Mexico, to help. They've been interrogating known drug traffickers for information about anything unusual coming in through known and suspected drug routes. Nothing so far, but there's a lot of territory to cover. I think we need to buy more time. Besides, the fourth of July is still weeks away."

"*Three* weeks," Eric clarified loudly, still nervously clicking his pen.

"Okay. Eric, come with me. We'll listen to the recording again and work out what to say at the press conference. Thank you, gentlemen."

He started to rise, then an idea came to him.

"Tom, we may need local help. Get with Cy Hutchison at State. Tell him I want him to contact all the governors, starting with those in the Northeast. Let them know we want them to prepare to call up their national guard units."

6

A good show for the masses

The Blund home, Logan, Utah, 12 June

Dr. Amos Blund and his business partner, Dr. Terry Stephens, stood in front of their work table—a six-foot-long solid wood table scattered with blueprints, pads of paper full of notes, and half-empty water bottles. It was surrounded by aluminum-framed chairs with plastic seats and backs. They were staring at a clear image projected onto the lab wall six feet in front of them. Between them, on the table, stood a metal box about two feet square and three feet tall. A cable protruded from one side of the box and plugged into a special outlet in the floor. There was a circular opening, covered by a glass lens, on the side of the box facing the wall, where Amos and Terry were looking.

Amos was fifty years old, six-foot-two in height, with a medium build. He had a full head of unruly hair hanging below the collar that was graying at the fringes. He was a brilliant surgeon, a scientist, and an inventor. He didn't have a high profile in the scientific community, but only because he intentionally avoided attention—his mind was as capable as those of the greatest scientists of the twenty-first century.

Amos's eyes were sharp, and focused in concentration, but

his hands, hanging at his sides, were clenching and unclench-
ing, as if constant motion could somehow solve his dilemma.
Relax, he told himself, *there's a logical explanation for what we're
seeing.*

Terry was forty-five, five-foot-six, and heavyset, with dark
hair cut just above his collar and balding on top. He was also a
medical doctor with a scientific bent, but his expertise was in
finding ways to execute Amos's brilliant plans. He was wring-
ing his hands behind his back, shifting his considerable weight
from one foot to the other in apparent agitation—he lacked
the self-control of his older partner.

As medical doctors and scientists, Amos and Terry had been
conducting research for years, trying to find a nonintrusive way
to accurately observe and diagnose the condition of internal
organs and tissue—something that went beyond MRIs, FLIR,
nuclear imaging, and arterial and intestinal cameras. With
their latest development, the Blund Observer, they knew they
could observe things at a distance—at that moment they were
looking at a hillside above the Weber State University campus
in Ogden, forty-eight miles away. Whether they would ever
be able to look inside the human body was speculation at this
point and would require a lot more research. But something
wasn't right with the image. Amos finally broke the silence.

"Calm down Terry. We'll figure it out."

"What? Oh! Well, that looks like the hillside all right, but
where's the *building?* What on Earth have we got here, Amos?"

"I don't know." Amos said cautiously. "But it should definitely be there. We've checked the coordinates, and the orien-

tation is set correctly. You can tell by the angle of the shadows. It's just not the right image."

He ran his fingers through his hair, something he did whenever he was concentrating, which helped to explain his disorderly appearance whenever he was working on one of his projects.

On the wall was a landscape image, six feet in diameter, showing wild grass, pale scrub oak, and a few cottonwood and maple trees in full bloom. A narrow, hard-packed, dirt trail meandered across the hillside. A large, black-and-white bird—probably a magpie—fluttered into one of the trees and settled on a limb. The bird's screeching song seemed to come from the wall, but the sound was likely bouncing off the wall from the speaker on the front of the box, creating the illusion.

"How can this be?" Terry asked his partner and good friend. "Maybe we're off by a block and the building is behind us, or to one side. This is the farthest we've tried to extend the Observer."

"Mike, are you still at the controls?" Amos asked distractedly, without turning.

Michael Blund was Amos's twenty-three-year-old son. He was the spitting image of his father and almost as brilliant. He had degrees in geology and structural engineering, an unusual combination that made him useful in his dad's research and indispensable in the construction of the Preserve. Mike stood at a sophisticated control panel mounted on the wall. He turned to look at his father.

"Still here, Dad. You want me to back it up a bit?"

"Make it half a mile. Let's get our bearings straight."

Mike manipulated the controls smoothly and efficiently. He'd helped Amos and Terry build the Observer, so he knew the equipment intimately. The objects in the image began to shrink, more landscape entering the image from all sides, as if the lab were suddenly thrust backward away from the hillside. It was disorienting, like riding an amusement park while sitting backward. Amos reached behind him and placed a hand on the edge of the table to steady himself. Terry took a step back and leaned his backside against the table.

As more mountainous desert landscape moved in from around the edges of the scene, they saw a large jackrabbit hop into a bush. Other objects—a road, a parking lot, and a shed—appeared from the right side. Then it looked like they were backing through the wall of a building, with lab equipment, empty desks, and chairs arranged in rows across the room. They backed through another wall, across a hallway, then through another classroom. Then they were looking at the building from the outside, an ivy-covered wall blocking the entire view, but the building they'd been expecting was nowhere to be seen.

Terry turned and stared at Amos, his mouth open, disbelief on his face. Amos's brows wrinkled as he thought. Terry swallowed hard, but he couldn't speak. It wasn't the fact that they were able to move the image through the walls of a building without disrupting any of the objects they encountered—not disturbing even a leaf of the ivy—that amazed Terry. It would have amazed any *other* scientist, but Amos and Terry had been working with the Observer for months now and thought nothing of it.

"I don't know," Amos repeated. "That looks like the old science lab, but where's the new medical research building?"

Abruptly, Amos turned and started shuffling through the papers on the work table. Terry turned around to help him.

"I'll review our assumptions and conclusions again," Terry said. "There's *got* to be something we missed."

"Michael, will you work with Terry?"

Mike nodded and moved quickly toward the bench.

"Review the schematics again," Amos continued. "See if there's something in the controls that could account for this. I'd like to move the Observer to the Preserve, but we should try to investigate this discrepancy before we dismantle it."

"Dad!" Mike cried out later that day, as he threw open the door and rushed into the lab.

Amos and Terry had their heads together at the work table. They looked up simultaneously at the disturbance.

"Mom said to turn on the TV, Channel Four. Quick, before it's over."

Mike continued across the lab and seated himself at the work table. Terry, who was closest to the TV control, picked it up and pointed it at the TV. He hit the power button and switched to Channel Four. A news anchor was just completing her report.

" . . . to summarize, the United States has received an ultimatum to release two hundred and seventeen Islamists who are being detained in three U.S. penitentiaries. There's irony in the July fourth deadline," she said, looking at her co-anchor. "We're switching to Washington now, where the White House press secretary, Lisa Appleton, is responding to questions from the media."

The scene on the TV switched to a striking woman in her thirties, with short brown hair and an expensive pantsuit. As she stood behind a podium, straight-faced and alert, she looked into the camera amid a cacophony of voices calling *"Ms. Appleton"* repeatedly. There was a banner at the bottom of the screen that read: Lisa Appleton, White House Press Secretary.

White House Press Room

"Mr. Clements?" Lisa Appleton said, trying to hide her nervousness and pointing to a man in the second row. On the podium in front of her were microphones bearing the insignias of every major network and cable news service in the country. There were about forty chairs set up in the Press Briefing Room, and reporters took up about two thirds of them. Cameramen stood around the perimeter of the room, their equipment focused on Lisa.

"What makes the president think this threat isn't credible?" Mr. Clements asked.

"As I said, the president and his advisers have been reviewing a copy of the video that appeared on Al Jazeera TV a little more than an hour ago. Our intelligence services tell us that the terrorists don't have the nuclear weapons they claim to have, nor do they have a means to deliver them."

"Ms. Dickens?" she said, pointing to a woman on the front row.

"What's the possibility that the terrorists have obtained a Soviet missile on the black market without our intelligence services being aware of it?"

"We don't believe that's happened. Mr. Sandborn?"

She pointed to a man in the third row.

"Is the president planning to take any measures to increase security at home and abroad in case our intelligence services have missed something?"

Ms. Appleton's mouth turned up almost imperceptibly at the corners, then straightened again quickly. This was the question she'd prepared for and was hoping would be asked.

"As a precaution, the president has raised our Defense Readiness Condition, or DEFCON, from Level 4, Green, where it's been for some time now, to DEFCON Level 3, Yellow. If you'll look at the monitors, you'll see a copy of the Defense Condition ladder."

A chart appeared on the monitors in the press room showing DEFCON Level 5, color coded Blue, at the bottom, representing the lowest state of readiness—an ordinary day. Above that was Level 4, coded Green, representing increased intelligence watch and strengthened security measures—an elevated level of readiness. Then came Level 3, coded Yellow, representing an increase in military force readiness above that required for normal preparedness, meaning that the air force could be ready to mobilize within fifteen minutes. Then came Level 2, coded

Red, representing a further increase in force readiness, requiring the air force to be ready to deploy and actually engage in less than six hours. Finally, there was Level 1, coded White, at the very top, representing maximum readiness, meaning that a nuclear war was imminent.

"Where we've been, at Green, means that we're already taking security precautions at all domestic transportation facilities, National Defense systems, and overseas facilities where U.S. citizens are working. The Yellow category means an increase in force readiness, or that the military can mobilize within fifteen minutes, if needed."

She knew the president was on his way, but she needed to buy time until he arrived, which was why she'd requested this slide.

Just then, a voice spoke in her earpiece. She put her hands to her ears and looked down, to block out the distraction of the questions from the reporters, concentrating on what she was hearing. When she looked up again, she looked relieved.

"The president is here to make a statement. He will not answer questions at this time. Then this meeting will adjourn until we have additional information to share."

The president of the United States, Gregory McCormick, back straight and head tall, entered the room and approached the podium. Ms. Appleton moved out of the way, her manner relaxing. There was a smattering of applause, and a few reporters called out, trying to attract his attention so they could ask a question. The president raised both hands and smiled apologetically, indicating that he wasn't going to answer questions at the moment. The reporters gave up then and settled in to hear what he had to say. Becoming serious, he began.

"My fellow countrymen, those of you safely in your homes, as well as those abroad, constantly in harm's way. The United States has, for close to two and a half centuries, been the strongest and most secure nation in the world. Amid global crises, we here at home have enjoyed near uninterrupted peace and prosperity.

"In recent years, though, cowardly terrorists have attempted to disturb that peace, as with the attacks in New York, Virginia, and Pennsylvania in 2001. The United States, in cooperation with our allies, have countered this threat at home and abroad, through a vast intelligence network and with significant military action. That intelligence network now assures us that this latest threat is unfounded. The terrorists have neither the bombs, nor the means of delivery, that they claim."

He smiled and raised his hands, palms outward, preempting any interruptions—it was a polite and friendly gesture his chief of staff told him would appease the public and win him votes.

"Nevertheless, we will not sit back idly and wait for a surprise. As Ms. Appleton has explained, we have elevated the DEFCON level to Yellow to raise our preparedness around the globe."

The Blund home, Logan, Utah

The president dropped the smile and the camera zoomed in on his serious face, so that he was staring right into the camera.

"Let me make it clear to the terrorist cowards who hide behind women and children as they threaten the innocent citizens of the United States and our allies. We will not be intimidated by you. We will find you in your holes and under the rocks where you hide . . . "

Amos turned down the volume and set the TV control on the table. The others turned to look at him.

"Dad," Mike blurted out, "don't you want to hear what the president has to say?"

Amos's heart was racing.

"We can read the full text on the internet in a few minutes. What we need to do now is get the family together to discuss this. We've been preparing for this day for years, ever since 9/11 and the increase in global terrorist activity. Now it's time to act. We've got less than three weeks. Michael, tell your mother to get the girls home if they're out, and let's meet in the family room in one hour for a family council."

"On it," Mike said quietly, disappointment on his face. He stood quickly and left. Amos suspected that he was upset at not being allowed to hear the president's remarks but Amos was sure he would get on his laptop and find a recording of the president's press conference before the family meeting.

"Terry, you're welcome to get your family over here to go over the plan with us."

"On it," Terry said, mimicked Mike with a broad smile to

cover his concern. "What else do we need to do?"

Amos's mind was automatically organizing and prioritizing as he answered.

"I'll get copies of the evacuation plan and lists of supplies and meet you in the family room. We need to back the truck up to the trailer in the trailer bay. We'll do that as soon as the family meeting is over and start loading equipment and supplies."

Terry nodded, then got up and strode out.

"Hello?"

"Kevin, this is Amos." There was silence on the line. "Did you see the president's press conference?"

"Mandy told me about it." Kevin said indifferently.

"What do you think?"

"About what?"

"Kevin, this is what I've been talking about for the last few years. This is what I've been preparing for. It's here."

"You're full of it, Amos. The president said there's no threat. Are you smarter than the president of the United States?"

Amos sighed.

"I spoke with the president . . . "

"Ha. Ha. Ha. Right," Kevin said sarcastically. "You and the president are buddies, huh?"

"Listen Kev . . . "

"No, you listen. You've been spouting this doomsday crap

for years, and nothing's happened. Nothing's going to happen now, either. The government's got it under control."

"Kevin, the Preserve is finished and we can accommodate your family . . . "

"Oh, great! Your bomb shelter is big enough to cram in all your relatives, and you've got enough toothbrushes for everyone! Just because you're my big brother and some genius inventor doesn't mean you know everything. For your information, we've got enough corn growing in the fields to feed half the county. I've got a well with enough natural pressure to last years without electricity. We're close enough to Denver to walk there if we need anything. We—"

"Kevin," Amos interrupted, "you won't be able to leave your house if they drop a nuclear bomb on Denver."

"Oh, that's right, Russia's going to start World War III because they believe a nuclear war is winnable. Sorry to disappoint you Amos, but I know enough about history to know that the Cold War proved no one was stupid enough to use a nuclear weapon and risk nuclear war."

"This is different. Al-Qaeda—"

"Oh yeah. Al-Qaeda is stupid enough to use a nuclear weapon because they don't care how many people they kill. But they're not stupid enough to kill themselves in the process. Hah! So much for your Al-Qaeda theory."

Kevin had always had a chip on his shoulder, resenting Amos's educational and professional accomplishments. They'd fought when they were young, but Amos always won because he was bigger and stronger. *Maybe I should have let him win sometimes,* he thought. *Maybe he'd listen to me now.*

"Okay, Kevin, this is the last time I'll say anything about it."

"Good!"

"If you change your mind, pack an overnight bag for each of you and get to our house in Logan before the end of June. After that, we'll be gone."

"Don't hold your breath, big brother. Goodbye."

In the Blund backyard, behind a vinyl fence with a wide gate, stood the lab. It held an office, where Amos and Terry worked on their projects, and an attached trailer bay. The office was equipped with a work table; state of the art video, audio and recording equipment; a kitchenette with a well-stocked refrigerator, pantry, and microwave; as well as a restroom and cots. The cots were for nights when they worked so late that they didn't want to disturb their families by going home.

The trailer bay was thirty-four feet wide by forty feet long, with a sixteen-foot ceiling. A set of double doors—eight feet across when open—allowed them to move equipment and tools between the two rooms without having to take things apart. Two overhead doors, one sixteen feet wide by twelve feet high, the other twelve feet wide by nine feet high, accommodated their truck and trailer, with room to move around them. All the windows in the office and trailer bay had been fitted with blackout curtains to allow them to work without worrying about nosey neighbors, or, as Lillie politely put it, "so we don't disturb the neighbors."

As Amos prepared for the family meeting, he thought about his conversations with the president. *You put on a good show for the masses, Greg,* he thought. *Now, can you stop the bomb?*

7

"Is this threat real, Dad?"

The Blund home, Logan, Utah, 12 June

Amos was looking through a sheaf of papers when Lillie came into the office. She leaned against the door frame for a moment, watching him set another page face down on the pile, and a smile spread across her face as she thought about how much she loved this complicated man.

They had met when she'd been a volunteer at the hospital during his residency. Amos, then only twenty-three years old, had fallen madly in love with the cheeky nineteen-year-old—at least, that's what he'd told her. She'd been amused by how easily he was distracted by her, and he often had to be paged by the nurses to get him to continue his rounds. Most of the nurses thought their budding love affair was cute—they were a handsome couple—so Amos never got in trouble for his lapses. It was a whirlwind romance that hadn't diminished with the years.

Lillie walked up behind Amos and ran the fingers of one hand through his hair. With the other, she picked up the overturned pages on the table.

"Are these the ones you need copied?"

"Oh, hi honey," Amos said, stopping to look at her. "Have I told you lately that I love you?"

It was a line from one of his favorite songs, and she laughed easily—quoting lines from old love songs was one of his eccentricities. Lillie never had to wonder about Amos's feelings for her.

"Can I copy these for you, lover boy?" she asked, still amused.

"That would be great," Amos said distractedly. "Oh, here's one more." He added a page he'd just finished reviewing to the pile. "Thank you."

He put his arm around her waist and hugged her, already focused on the next page.

Not so easy to distract now, Lillie thought. She deciding not to say what she was thinking. She would tease him later when he didn't have so much on his mind.

The atmosphere was subdued as the Blund and Stephens families settled into the Blund family room for what Amos called Family Council. Everyone had heard the news reports and had some idea of what this meeting meant for the families.

Amos sat on a folding chair facing the couch where Lillie, his wife of twenty-six years, now sat. Lillie had completed her training to become a registered nurse just before their son Michael had been born. Amos, still a young doctor at the time, had done all he could to help with the baby, taking night shifts whenever possible so that Lillie could work days. It had been a struggle for the first few years, until they'd established themselves in their professions. What Amos loved most about Lillie was how aware she always was of those around her, and the way she always seemed to know what people needed. Now he made eye contact with her and she winked, the corners of her mouth turning up in a smile.

To Lillie's left sat Terry and Rebecca Stephens. At forty-one, Becca, as her friends called her, was slender and active, like Lillie. The two were alike in temperament and abilities, as well: calm, compassionate, understanding, and excellent caregivers.

But that's where the similarities ended. Where Lillie had retained her youthful beauty, Becca had aged. She'd given up a career as a botanist to raise her two children, and ever since Chris, her youngest, had gone off to college the year before, Becca spent most of her time on her hobbies: raising fruits and vegetables and cooking. She loved to get her hands into the soil and make things grow, and she was an excellent cook. Although she was four years younger than Terry, she was more like a mother to him than a partner. When he was working, he became so focused that she had to remind him to eat and sleep.

The Stephens children, Katie and Chris, were sitting on chairs to Amos's right. Twenty-one-year-old Katie, a former college gymnast with a degree in elementary education, was now teaching school.

Chris, at nineteen, was a political science student at Utah State University. He was learning Russian in school and considering an advanced degree in international relations. He hoped to land a job with the State Department after graduation and thought a poli-sci degree would help. He'd already corresponded through social media with several people at the State Department whom he thought might help him reach his goal. Amos wondered what Chris would do if he found out that Amos was good friends with President McCormick.

Amos's daughters, Emily and Rachel, sat on a loveseat to the left of the couch, with Mike sprawled out on his back on the floor in front of them, his head resting on a couch pillow. Emily, at twenty-one, was studying to be a veterinarian at Utah State University. She was as beautiful as her mother had been at her age, with long blonde hair and delicate features. She embraced life and wanted to do something to make the world a better place. She admired the work of Mother Teresa and held the same philosophy. "It's about love, not statistics," Emily would say. "We need to serve those within our reach." She always thought the best of people and tried to excuse their faults. She particularly loved animals, and had decided that helping them was her calling in life.

Rachel was eighteen, with jet-black, shoulder-length hair, an almond-shaped face, and her mother's slender build. She was working on a degree in literature at Utah State. She was a romantic, wrote poetry, and wanted to teach high school students to appreciate reading, particularly the classics. Amos was grateful that both of his daughters had inherited their mother's good looks, not his rugged features.

The Blund and Stephens children had known each other for most of their lives. They'd lived one street apart in Logan for longer than Amos and Terry had been business and research partners, and they'd all been up Logan Canyon to the Preserve that Amos and Terry had built as an emergency underground retreat. Looking at them now, Amos had little doubt that they would do well stuck together in the Preserve, their relationships solidifying rather than straining under the stress.

Amos passed around stapled copies of a document several pages thick and returned to his seat. He'd just opened his mouth to speak when Mike beat him to it.

"Is this threat real, Dad?"

Amos looked down at his son and smiled. Mike's casual pose belied the stress of the situation they were facing.

"I think so, Michael. I reviewed the full text of the threat and the response from the government. This looks like what we've been preparing for. The terrorists say they have nuclear weapons, and if their demands aren't met they're prepared to use them on the United States—and possibly Israel, England, and other countries in Western Europe."

Chris Stephens raised his hand and waited for Amos to notice and acknowledge him.

"You have a question Chris?" Amos asked, trying to keep the mood light as much as he could in the circumstances.

"Mr. Blund, Muslims have been moving into Europe in pretty big numbers for years now. I read that at the current rate of immigration from Muslim countries, by the end of the twenty-first century Western Europe will *be* Muslim. And most Muslims are peaceful—they're like anyone else. I can understand the terrorists threatening the United States and their allies, but would they really use nuclear weapons on other

Muslims?"

"That's true, Chris," Amos said. "Al-Qaeda *does not* represent mainstream Muslim philosophy or behavior, and I certainly don't pretend to understand the mind of a terrorist." There was a tightness in his chest that he always seemed to feel when he thought about the pain and suffering caused by violence. "As we've seen in France, the U.K., Israel, and even in Muslim countries like Iraq and Syria, the terrorists seem to have no reservations about killing other Muslims."

An image of a bomb, strapped around the waist of a young Muslim girl, exploding in a crowded bus station in France, flitted through his mind. Amos stopped speaking and made eye contact with Lillie. She knew he always got emotional when he read or watched a report of a terrorist attack, usually involving innocent bystanders. Lillie smiled encouragingly, and he took a deep breath. He became angry as his thoughts moved to *why* the bombings upset him so much.

"It's their twisted interpretation of the words of the Prophet in the Quran," he continued. "They believe that those who die in the battle against the Great Satan, as they call the United States, earn favored status in the hereafter."

"I sure don't want to be in *their* hereafter," Emily said quietly, her voice full of melancholy.

"Doesn't sound like a very nice place, does it?" Amos smiled sadly at his daughter.

"How likely is it that a bomb is going to affect us in Logan?" Rachel asked.

She'd already told her dad that she was hoping he wasn't

going to suggest they move to the Preserve permanently, given how it would disrupt their busy lives. Amos was about to answer when Chris spoke up from across the room.

"Why, do you have a hot date on the fourth of July?"

Chris had teased Rachel since they were in grade school, and was the reason Amos and Terry had first met. Chris had been bothering Rachel on the playground and had made her cry. Amos and Lillie had taken Rachel to the Stephens' home to speak to Chris and his parents. That was when Amos and Terry had discovered that they had a lot of common interests, which led to their eventual partnership. Lillie and Becca had become fast friends, too, and Rachel had been frustrated that her parents had gotten distracted and let Chris off so easily.

Chris's comment caused chuckling around the room. Rachel's response was the usual: a red face, an indignant look, and silence. Amos had often thought that, given time and opportunity, Chris and Rachel's flirtations would turn into a serious and lasting relationship.

Despite the good-natured ribbing, Amos was concerned by Chris's apparent lack of sensitivity. He wondered if the boy was joking because he didn't believe the terrorist threat, or to hide his own fear. *Does Chris understand the impact a nuclear explosion would have on the country?*

"I'm glad to see we haven't lost our sense of humor," Amos went on. "We'll need to stay positive if we're going to keep our sanity through this."

"Rachel," Amos addressed his daughter, "assuming the terrorists have bombs, and assuming they can deliver them, the most likely targets will be major cities, like Washington, D.C., New York, Chicago, or Los Angeles. Their objective will be to cause as much harm, damage, and confusion as possible." He started to choke up again. "Can you imagine the death and destruction that would result from a nucl . . . ?" He couldn't quite finish his sentence, so he swallowed hard and started again. "Think of the loss of faith in the government that one nuclear explosion on U.S. soil would cause."

Rachel nodded, even though Amos suspected she didn't truly understand. Chris, meanwhile, just watched Rachel. It occurred to Amos that it might be easier to talk about the subject if he treated it clinically, like a doctor, rather than personally, like a father and husband. He coughed into his hand and cleared his throat, then tried again.

"One or two bombs, even nuclear, would have a limited physical impact," he said. "There would be destruction within a few miles of the explosion and radioactive fallout downwind from the site. If that was all we had to deal with then the country—and the world—could probably handle it."

"What about the social impact?" Emily asked.

"What we know about the impact on people is limited to the two bombs dropped on Japan in 1945, the nuclear testing in Nevada in the 1950s, and a few nuclear reactor disasters since then. We've learned that nuclear fallout causes sores on any exposed epidermis—the skin—and damage to internal organs, primarily the thyroid gland, leading eventually to cancer and early death."

The images that Amos had seen in medical school were

etched into his memory, threatening to surface each time he thought about a nuclear weapon in the hands of terrorists. He fought for control yet again.

"Would the government respond by firing nuclear missiles at Al-Qaeda?" Chris asked.

"They could. Or, they could choose to retaliate with *conventional* weapons. They could focus on Al-Qaeda strongholds. Unfortunately, I don't think the government knows where the Al-Qaeda leadership is hiding, or they would have done something about it before now. The terrorist leaders most likely spread themselves out to make it harder for us to find them. The military has been trying to ferret them out for a long time now."

He looked Chris in the eye as he spoke, but Chris didn't flinch or look away. *He's trying to understand how this impacts him,* Amos thought. He went on, addressing the family more generally now.

"My concern is that, if the government were to retaliate with nuclear weapons, it could result in global thermonuclear war."

"Heaven forbid," Becca said.

Chris looked at his mother blankly, as if wondering what her concern was. *He still doesn't understand,* Amos concluded silently.

"I agree Becca. The reason this concerns *us* is that, should it come to war, secondary locations could also be targeted. The nearest strategic location to us is Hill Air Force Base, south of Ogden. We're northeast of Ogden, so there's a good chance we'd be in the path of any radioactive fallout."

"And the Preserve is northeast of here, up the canyon," Mike added, awareness and concern in his expression.

"That's true Michael," Amos responded. "But Aspen Valley is somewhat sheltered from the winds, and the Preserve is *fully* protected, so that's our best chance of protection from fallout."

Amos paused to look around the room with raised eyebrows, inviting other questions, but none came. Mike waved a hand in a circular motion, telling him to keep going. Being a goal-oriented engineer, he always wanted to get to the conclusion in a hurry, Amos thought, then continued.

"A second scenario is that a bomb could be detonated in the atmosphere above the U.S. That could affect an entire region of the country. There wouldn't be so much physical damage to the infrastructure, and not much immediate death, but the EMP would take out every microchip in the region that wasn't hardened. EMP stands for Electromagnetic Pulse, which is a burst of electromagnetic energy, similar to lightning, that overheats and breaks the delicate circuitry that we have these days in just about everything we use, including phones and cars."

"Everything? Like even computers and tablets?" Chris asked, sounding panicked.

That drew some smiles and a little polite laughter. Chris had grown up with technology, and much of his interaction with the world was through his laptop, tablet, and smartphone. It was so automatic to him, that he might run an internet search to answer a question while you were still in the process of asking it. He had social media accounts on Facebook, Twitter, Instagram, Pinterest, Tinder, and who knew where else. He used LinkedIn to interact with other engineering students, as well as teachers and a host of Russian speaking associates and government officials.

"Sorry Chris," Amos said. *He's finally beginning to see the impact this will have on him,* he thought. "Everything electronic—whether it's for communication, transportation, water management, or whatever—would shut down. Anything that has a microchip that isn't hardened against EMP. Even power lines could be damaged. The heat from a nuclear explosion is hotter than the Sun."

"Really?" Several people asked at once, then looked embarrassed at their shared reaction.

"Now the good news," Amos said. "If there's anything good about this situation. Because we've been anticipating this possibility for close to fifteen years, and because Terry and I have sold some of our patents, we've been able to acquire—or, in some cases, develop—what we think we'll need to survive indefinitely. You've all been to the Preserve near Garden City, but since our last visit as a group, we've made substantial improvements.

"The Preserve is shielded against an EMP, and we have our own power source, so we'll be able to receive government communications as long as the government chooses to communicate with the outside from their hardened bunkers." Amos had a fleeting image of Greg McCormick in a bunker, trying to run a war, losing contact with a dying country, then finally giving up on trying to communicate with the world.

"Does that mean we'll try to communicate with others, too?" Emily interrupted anxiously.

Amos looked quickly at his wife, to see that she had also noticed Emily's anxiety. Amos looked back at Emily, keeping his expression neutral.

"Well, that depends, Emily. Initially, I don't think we want the government to know where we are. We'll be safer that way." Turning back to the group, he continued. "We have medicine and other supplies to last quite a few years. Between us, we have the medical, technical, engineering, and farming skills to produce whatever we might need. If there's going to be a problem," he tried out a sarcastic grin, "it'll be claustrophobia from being stuck underground together, 24/7, until we can determine that it's safe to leave the Preserve to go above ground."

He waited for a reaction, but was disappointed—not a groan or chuckle. After a sympathetic shrug from Lillie, who understood his quirky sense of humor, Amos continued.

"To help with that, we have recently added a huge library of books, videos, music, and games—everything we could think of. We even have a gym."

"Alright!" Chris exclaimed, punching the air with a fist.

He was working out with free weights these days, three times a week. He flexed both arms to show off his muscles, and Lillie and Becca looked at each other and smiled—proud, knowing, motherly smiles. Rachel gave him a furtive, admiring glance, quickly looking away again.

"That must have cost a lot," Katie Stephens said, clearly impressed.

"Well, we sold a *lot* of patents," Terry Stephens said to his daughter.

Amos glanced at Lillie, who raised an eyebrow and tilted her head to Amos's left. Scanning left, Amos noticed that Emily was frowning. He shook his head slightly at Lillie, letting her know that he didn't understand her message.

"Okay, now it's time for questions from the peanut gallery," Amos said. "After that, we'll need to talk about next steps and individual assignments."

"How long do you think we'll have to stay in the Preserve?" Emily asked, still frowning. "And how will we know when we can leave?"

"Great questions, Emily. We'll be able to monitor communications, including radio, TV, the internet, and social media, as long as the satellites are broadcasting and our antenna is working. We also have sensors set up for monitoring conditions in the Valley. Terry, Mike, and I mounted wireless cameras, speakers, audio receivers, and environmental sensors on trees and rocks in Aspen Valley to monitor local conditions and traffic. When we determine that the threat is over, either because it didn't affect our region or it didn't happen, then we'll be able to come home. Anything else?"

"What about our friends?" Emily asked.

"That's an important question, Emily. I think we need to get this out in the open for everyone. We figured this would be a sticking point for some of you." Amos looked around the room before continuing. "Our goal is to survive whatever catastrophe is coming our way. If it doesn't occur, we all come home in a few days, nothing lost except a few days of work and classes that can be made up. If the worst happens," he closed his eyes momentarily, trying to block out the images of global thermonuclear war that threatened to immobilize him, "we have enough immediate supplies for this group to survive for thirty years. We also have seeds, medicines, raw chemicals, and other supplies to continue for many more years after that. Each of you is going to have to notify your employer or school, and anybody else who depends on you, that you'll be gone for a few days. But not just yet—that can wait a few days until we're ready to leave.

"Some of you may want to take friends along. I get that—I might want to, too, in your place. But even if we each invited just one person to come along, our supplies would be spread over twice as many people and last only half as long. The more likely scenario is that each person we invite would result in an entire family wanting to come along. There are nine of us now, but we could easily end up with fifty or a hundred people in the Preserve if that happened, and quite likely it'd be three, four, or even five times our present number. We'd be sharing beds and toothbrushes."

There was scattered laughter around the room. Amos smiled, and let the mood lighten a bit before going on.

"No joke," he continued. "Our supplies could dwindle to a three-year supply, easily. If that's what we're going to do, then why go to all this trouble? Let's just stay home and take our chances along with everyone else."

"Three years is a long time," Emily said wistfully.

"Three years may *seem* like a long time, Emily," Amos agreed, "but it's not nearly long enough if we have to survive the aftermath of a nuclear war."

Amid general grumbling and whispering, Terry spoke up, quietly but forcefully.

"Hey everyone, this is serious! The only way to keep a secret is to tell *no one!* I mean it! Human nature is to want to tell *just one person.* We convince ourselves that it won't hurt to tell our best friend, that he or she will understand. But they *won't* understand. They'll want to know why they're not invited. And each person you tell will want to tell just one other person. Worst case, there will be an uprising—a stampede of people who don't want to be left behind. By the time we're ready to leave, we could have half the community camping on the front lawn saying that they want to go, too."

Amos appreciated the support and picked up where Terry had left off.

"If you haven't seen people who are under extreme stress, or really frightened, you may not be able to appreciate how dangerous they can be. People who are normally kind and gentle can turn on you like feral cats."

He had a sudden memory—one that came to him from time to time—of furious, desperate parents at the hospital, demanding to know why he hadn't saved their severely burned, innocent child from death, their faces turned savage with emotion, when the truth was he simply couldn't. It was one of many memories that kept him awake at night.

"Like in a zombie movie where people fight each other to

get away from the zombies," Chris said. "Only the strongest ones succeed. I watched a movie where one really big man watched his wife and daughter get attacked and turned into zombies rather than give them his place in the car. It gave me chills."

He shivered at the image he'd conjured up.

"Thanks, Chris," Rachel said, rolling her eyes. "That really helps."

Then Emily spoke up in a quivering voice.

"Maybe some of us would rather stay with our friends. Maybe that would be better than living without them."

Amos finally understood what his daughter was talking about—why she'd asked so many questions. Emily was dating Matthew Green. It was serious, and she'd been hoping that Matt would ask her to marry him. In the two seconds it took Amos to come to this realization, Lillie gave Emily a stern but loving look.

"Emily," she said. "You have less than three weeks to decide if that relationship is going where you want it to go."

Amos could tell that Matt must have been the subject of several conversations between the two of them. Emily teared up, while most of the others in the room just looked on, not privy to what the issue was. After a few moments of awkward silence, Amos continued more sympathetically.

"I'm hopeful that each of us understands how important we are to each other. We will already be with our best friends in the Preserve." He paused to let them think about that and to assess their reactions, then continued. "Okay, any other questions or comments?

"Yeah, what about Uncle Kevin and his family?" Rachel asked.

"Thank you for asking, Rachel. I've talked to Kevin repeatedly, including just a few minutes ago. Terry's spoken with his extended family as well. They're not interested. They either don't believe it or can't believe it. Like almost everyone around us, they see the way things are now—our prosperity, or technology, our stability—and they can't imagine circumstances coming to a point where they won't be able to drive to the supermarket and buy whatever they need with plastic money."

"You spoke to Kevin today?" Lillie asked.

"Yeah. Sorry I didn't tell you. Got a lot on my mind. Nothing's changed with him. I thought that the Al-Qaeda threat would make him think seriously about joining us, but he just doesn't want to hear it."

"I feel sorry for Mandy and the children," Lillie said, shaking her head.

So did Amos, but he'd done everything he could think of to convince Kevin.

"Most people expect the government to preserve our way of life forever," Amos's voice rose as he continued. "We thought the economic crisis in 2001, or the one in 2008, would be a wakeup call, and some people actually did start thinking about preparedness, buying up food storage and emergency supplies. But the economy recovered fairly quickly, so most of them settled right back into their stupor—including Uncle Kevin. It's killing your mother and me, but I haven't been able to convince him of anything."

Amos's realized he was getting emotional. *How am I going to get the family through this if I can't even control my own feelings?* he wondered.

"Sorry," he said. "It's a sensitive subject for me. Now, can everyone agree to keep what we're doing *just between us?*"

After getting a nod or a word or two in the affirmative from each family member, he continued.

"Okay, we have less than three weeks to be out of here. The papers we handed out list the items each of you needs to gather for yourself, and the group tasks that need to be completed. Make sure to look at the last page, which is a list of suggested optional items, like things for hobbies—musical instruments, and so on. We'll go over the task list in a minute and make assignments. Everything needs to be brought to the lab. We'll load up the trailer and make a trip to the Preserve each time it's full. I expect that to be every other night, initially, then every three or four nights after that, as needed. When you bring a load, drive right into the lab trailer bay. And try to be discreet, don't draw the neighbors' attention if you can help it.

"Let's look at the task list . . ."

Amos asked Terry and Mike to stay for a few minutes after the others left. When they were alone, he told them about his conversations with the president and his fears about what might be happening in the world.

"The *president* is the Greg you always talk about, the one that was best man at your wedding?" Terry asked, incredulous.

"How does the president have time to talk to you when he has a national crisis to deal with?" Mike asked

"We have a unique relationship, Mike. Greg—the president—seems to think I can help him solve some of the nation's problems." Amos chuckled and shook his head, thinking about some of the things Greg had asked him over the years. Then he sobered. "In this case, I don't think I've been a lot of help. What he needs is to find that bomb . . . or bombs."

"Why are you telling us this now?" Terry asked.

"Because the situation is much more serious than Greg is telling the public. It's very likely that Al-Qaeda is building a bomb in Mexico to smuggle into the country and set off in Washington, D.C. It's also entirely possible that North Korea is getting help from Russia to launch a missile with a nuclear warhead at the United States."

Amos paused a moment to take a deep breath. At their questioning looks, he ran his fingers through his hair and continued.

"North Korea claims to have nuclear weapons and the missiles to deliver them here. We don't think they've figured out how to marry the warheads to the missiles, or they would have done it already. But if Russia is helping them now, the U.S. could be attacked on two fronts. If Greg asks me, I'll tell him to retaliate without restraint. Al-Qaeda will never stop until someone stops them."

"That's why you were so emotional during the family meeting," Terry said. "You're the confident *in control* side of our partnership. If you're having trouble keeping it together, how can we manage this?"

Mike stared at his dad and shook his head.

"I've seen you excited about a scientific breakthrough," he said. "And I've heard you swear over a failed experiment." When it looked like Amos was about to argue, he added quickly "though not often. I've seen you calmly challenge a schoolteacher over lost homework. But I've never seen you so worked up that you would seriously say, 'drop a bomb on your enemies.'"

Terry nodded.

"I think you're right, Amos. This war with the terrorists is unlike anything we've ever seen. I don't condone violence. But if we have to fight, we should take the offensive. This country's never been afraid to defend its principles."

8

"Should people evacuate?"

Situation Room, emergency meeting of 'The Panel', 18 June
"What's the latest from the CIA, Tom?" President McCormick asked DNI Tom Mitchell.

"We're keeping in touch with intelligence services in the U.K., Canada, and Israel. Britain's concerned about all the Muslims who have immigrated to Europe in recent years. Israel's primary concern is an increase in traffic between Iran and the Russian satellite countries between them."

"What are they doing about it?"

"Britain's been meeting with their EU counterparts to raise awareness. France wants to be included in future discussions. Israel is just monitoring, so far."

"Thanks Tom. Anything new from Mexico or North Korea?"

It was SecDef Jim Seymour who spoke up.

"North Korea's conducting ICBM firing tests, as you know. They recently sent one out into the Sea of Japan that stayed up for more than forty-five minutes. That's long enough to reach Hawaii, maybe even the west coast with the right trajectory. In addition, we believe they've detonated at least three bombs underground in the last two weeks. One of them was large enough that it may have been nuclear."

"Where are they getting the bombs? Are they making them themselves?"

Greg was just thinking out loud, and his advisers knew it. He'd read all the intelligence on North Korea, how they didn't have the ability to mate their nuclear capability to their missiles. But with Russian help, they could jump that hurdle in short order. *But how would the Russians benefit from such an alliance?* he wondered.

"Greg," Tom replied, "We don't know for sure that they have nuclear technology, or could put a nuclear warhead on their ICBMs. It's—"

"But we don't know that they can't, do we Tom?" Greg demanded, cutting him off.

"No. Everything's speculative at this point," Tom said apologetically.

"We need to consider our response in case they really do have the capability," Jim added. "And we need to consider what to tell the public in either event."

"Our computers have been listening to millions of phone conversations over the last few weeks, all over the world," Tom said. "We're monitoring keywords and phrases that would alert us to any threat. We've even been listening to back traffic. If the American public finds out what we're doing, there'll be riots in the streets . . . "

"There may be riots shortly, either way," Greg muttered, then waved for Tom to continue.

"We haven't heard anything that we can nail down as nuclear weapons discussions. Either it isn't there, or they're better at encrypting their messages than we've supposed."

"Okay, okay," a frustrated President McCormick snarled, slapping the table, hard, with his open palm. It stung, and he shook his hand in the air and tried to calm himself. "Thanks Tom. Any ideas?" he said, looking at each of his advisers.

"We need to accept the possibility that they have a bomb or bombs and that they intend to use them against us," Tom said flatly.

"What are our options if they do, besides mass evacuations?" Greg asked. "Russia will think we're too reasonable to retaliate with nuclear weapons—that we'll take our lumps and go after Al-Qaeda with conventional weapons. What do you think we should do?"

"You know what I think," Jim answered.

Greg stared at his SecDef, knowing perfectly well that Jim wanted to take the offensive.

"Press conference in twenty minutes, Mr. President," Eric Epstein cut in.

As always, the president's chief of staff was keenly aware of the president's schedule, although up to now he'd been silently listening to the others.

"Okay Eric. Cy, what news from the governors?"

The president had invited Secretary of State Cyril Hutchison to this meeting without disclosing the function of the Panel. He needed to know what Cy had done about getting the states prepared for an emergency.

"I've spoken with New York, New Jersey, Connecticut, and

Massachusetts," Cy said. "They represent almost forty million citizens. We've agreed to call an emergency governors' conference for next week. We'll get as many as we can to come here and the rest by teleconference, if possible. I'd appreciate your help deciding exactly what to tell them."

"No problem," Greg said, thinking, *I have no idea what to say to them.* "Let's go, Eric." He looked around the room one last time. "Think on it, gentlemen. I'm going to raise DEFCON to Level 2. Any objections?"

There were none.

Logan, Utah

" . . . and we are raising the DEFCON threat index to Red, based upon information coming from Europe," the president said seriously, staring into the camera. "While the terrorists' threat clearly includes the United States, we have no reason to suspect that the United States is in any real danger at this time. Of course, we're taking this precaution to raise preparedness, both here and overseas."

A cacophony of voices began calling out to get his attention. The president pointed, and a female voice asked from offscreen.

"Are you planning to issue evacuation orders for any of the cities that could be affected?"

"As I stated, there is no reason to believe the danger extends to the United States. If that changes, we will outline a plan. In the meantime, of course, we are considering what direction to take if that should become necessary."

More yelling. The president pointed again.

"Should people evacuate voluntarily?" a male voice asked. "And if so, where should they go?"

An obviously frustrated president shook his head to show what he thought of the question. Then he took a deep breath and answered anyway.

"We are not recommending an evacuation. If citizens choose, on their own, to leave their homes, their best option would be to take temporary shelter upwind from any major population center, perhaps put a mountain range between themselves and the city. But let me be very clear on one thing. Do not panic. Do not break any laws. Law enforcement is currently at heightened security and will take swift action against anyone breaking the law. When you find that there really was no threat, you can . . ."

Amos turned the volume down a bit and shook his head as the president continued to field the same questions, over and over, albeit stated in different ways, from the reporters.

"He as much as told everyone to evacuate the large cities," he said.

Lillie and Mike, who were watching with him, turned to look at him, concern on their faces. Lillie took his hand in both of hers, and when they made eye contact Amos could see his own concerns mirrored in her eyes.

"So, what do we do?" Mike asked.

Amos was deep in thought and didn't answer. Lillie looked from Amos to Mike.

"We stick to the plan," she said. "After this announcement,

we may have to be a little more careful that people don't see us packing up to leave."

Amos smiled at her. *That's my Lillie*, he thought.

Logan, Utah, 19 June

"Mom," Rachel Blund called as she closed the front door behind her and walked quickly into the kitchen, where Lillie was preparing lunch. "Mrs. McKensie, across the street, just asked me what's going on."

"What did you tell her?" Lillie asked quietly, wondering what *she* would have said.

"I told her I didn't know what she was talking about."

"So how did she respond"

"She cackled, put her finger to the side of nose like a witch, and said she has insomnia and saw us moving around two nights ago, in the middle of the night. She said it looked like we were packing up to move, or something. She wondered if we were behind on the mortgage and had decided to skip out without paying. I said, 'Well duh, wouldn't you?' So she cackled again and went back inside. What do we do?"

Lillie smiled at Rachel's quick thinking.

"Very clever," she said proudly. "I'll talk with your father about it. You handled that nicely. Just keep being careful."

Logan, Utah, 21 June

"Mom, that snot-nosed kid, Joshua Parker, saw me in the front yard just now and asked what's going on at the Blunds," Chris Stephens said with obvious concern. "He said he was playing night games with his friends when he was sure he saw us drive into the Blunds' lab. Well, he called it 'that big building in their backyard.' Did I blow our secret?"

"What did you say to him?" Becca asked, concerned.

"I told him it wasn't us and I didn't know what he was talking about."

"Did he believe you?"

"I doubt it. He said he was going to find out what we're up to and tell everyone. I felt like telling him to mind his own business. But I thought that would just make him more curious. So instead I told him he was crazy and came in the house."

"Anything else?

"No. What should I do if he asks again?"

Becca smiled.

"Stick to 'you're crazy.' I know dad's been talking to Amos about it. A similar thing happened with them two days ago. I'm sure your dad and Amos are coming up with a plan."

Logan, Utah, 23 June

"Mom, I can't hide it anymore," Emily Blund cried. "Matt can tell something's wrong. Last night he asked me why I was so moody lately. I broke down and cried. I told him we were moving and I might not see him again. He put his arms around me and said of course we could still see each other. He asked where we're moving to and I just cried harder because I couldn't tell him."

"What do you want to do?" Lillie asked sympathetically.

With tears running down her cheeks, Emily could only

speak in a whisper.

"I want to tell him what we're doing and see if he'll come with us."

Lillie smiled.

"Let's go talk to your dad, okay?"

She turned to leave. Emily didn't immediately follow, so Lillie took her startled daughter by the elbow and led her into the kitchen where Amos was sitting at the table reading the news on his tablet.

"Amos," Lillie began, "Emily needs to speak with you."

"What is it, honey?" Amos asked, concern pulling at the corners of his mouth as he saw Emily's tears. He set his tablet on the table and gave her his full attention.

Emily sat in the chair next to her father, knees almost touching, and spent the next few moments relating what she'd just told her mother. As she went on, it seemed to Lillie that her daughter's courage grew, and her voice rose, until finally her father held up his hand and interrupted her.

"Okay," Amos said.

He looked at Lillie and got a nod of approval. They'd already discussed this possibility and come to an agreement on how they should respond. Lillie hoped Amos would get it right.

"Have Matt come over tonight and we'll talk to him," he said. "We'd like to know his intentions anyway."

Emily threw her arms around her father's neck, giving him an enthusiastic hug.

"Thank you, Daddy! Mom!"

Amos tried desperately to keep his tablet from flying off

the table as he was crushed in her embrace. Emily giggled quietly as she jumped up, startled her mother with a kiss on the cheek, and then bounded out of the room, wiping tears from her cheeks.

Lillie smiled at Amos as she retrieved his tablet from across the table, where his flailing arm had pushed it. When he thanked her, Lilly responded with a wink. She understood that it was her who kept the family together, and Amos had often told her that it was her strength and his love for her that drove him during bad times. Lillie saw, for the thousandth time, how wonderful Amos could be with his children, and she loved him for it.

Emily practically floated through the kitchen entryway, leading Matt by the hand.

"Daddy, Mom, Matt's here," she called out enthusiastically. "Is this a good time?"

Amos and Lillie were sitting at the table talking quietly and reviewing papers. They both looked up as Emily and Matt walked into the kitchen, Matt's face revealing his confusion. He looked worried.

Amos discreetly turned the papers on the table over to hide their contents and then stood. Both parents smiled, and Lillie rose, too, to greet the young couple. A roast and vegetables cooked in a Crock-pot on the counter and the kitchen smelled wonderful.

"Wow," Matt said, clearly nervous. "Um, that smells delicious."

"Hello Matt. How are you?" Amos said, as he met them partway and shook Matt's hand.

Emily gave her dad a hug.

"He's great!" she said, then reached over to give her mom a hug as both Amos and Lillie laughed.

"I'm sure he is," Lillie said with a smile.

Matt, his expression betraying his obvious uncertainty, looked first at Amos, then at Lillie.

"Actually, I'm a bit confused. Em has been mysterious and a bit . . . uh . . . moody for days. Then, suddenly, today, she's all smiles and wants me to talk to you. She said you'll explain everything. What's going on Mr. and Mrs. Blund? I kind of just hope you invited me over for dinner."

He laughed awkwardly.

Matthew Green was twenty-three, two years older than Emily. He stood straight and tall, almost eye to eye with Amos. He was in medical school, and it took up almost all of his time, but when he wasn't in school, he was with Emily. Matt stifled a yawn.

"Excuse me. I'm not getting a lot of sleep this semester."

"I've been there Matt," Amos said. "No apology necessary."

"Dinner won't be ready for a few more minutes," Lillie said.

"Then why don't we go into the family room and sit down?" Amos said. "We have some important things to talk about."

"Can I get you something to drink, Matthew?" Lillie asked.

Even though Emily had asked her to call him Matt, Lillie

persisted in using his full name. "*Matthew* sounds so much more mature, don't you think?" she'd said more than once.

"A glass of water would be great, thanks."

Lillie walked into the living room carrying a glass of cold water with two ice cubes floating on the surface. Emily snuggled close to Matt on the couch. Amos sat in his favorite recliner. After handing Matt the water, Lillie sat on the arm of the recliner and draped her arm across Amos's shoulders.

Amos spent a few minutes talking about the importance of trust in relationships—how important it was that he and Lillie be able to trust Matt, and for Emily to be able to trust him if ever they were going to have a long-term relationship. Matt glanced questioningly at Emily several times, as if he expected her to explain what her dad was talking about, but she was quiet, looking almost as confused as Matt. Amos was hoping the next topic would clarify things.

"What I'm going to share next requires that we be able to trust you to keep it a secret. That means you don't discuss it with anybody—not your parents, your friends, or anybody outside of this room. Do we have your word that you'll keep this conversation private, Matt?" Amos asked.

"Yes, of course," Matt said confidently. "You can trust me." He still looked confused, though.

After a short pause to gather his thoughts, Amos began to discuss the news from Washington—the possibility of a nuclear attack and the talk of evacuation. Then he outlined the plan developed by the Blund and Stephens families to stock up on emergency supplies in preparation for a crisis. Several times,

Matt opened his mouth to speak, but each time he quickly shut it, apparently choosing to wait until Amos was finished.

Several minutes later, without divulging the location of the Preserve, Amos concluded by explaining that they intended to avoid the fourth of July deadline by moving to a sanctuary they had built in the mountains. He told Matt that they would stay there for however long it took to be sure they were safe—perhaps years if a nuclear explosion occurred nearby. He paused to let Matt absorb what he'd said—he could see the wheels turning in Matt's head.

"Any questions, Matt?"

"Let me see if I understand this," Matt said. "You believe the terrorist threat is legitimate, and you've been preparing this . . . this sanctuary for several years for just this kind of thing, this emergency. Now that it seems to be happening, you want to go into hiding until the threat is gone?"

There was no animosity or incredulity in his voice.

"Essentially, yes. There's a lot more to it, but those are the basics. So, what do you think?"

"That's why Em told me we wouldn't be able to see each other again, right? So, why are you telling me this now?"

He was still missing the point.

"Emily asked us to," Amos said.

Matt turned to look at Emily, who was holding tightly to his right arm. Her eyes were moist and her lips quivered. That was when it sunk in.

"Are you inviting me to go with you . . . to be with Em?"

Lillie smiled. Emily attempted a smile through her tears.

"Oh Em, I so want to be with you. But I've got to think about this. The guys at school think the threat isn't real. The government's been telling us that the terrorists don't have a bomb. What your dad is talking about is . . . well, it would interrupt my education. If I drop out of school now, I could lose an entire year. I might not even get back in."

Emily released Matt's arm and ran from the room.

"Em?"

Matt stood so quickly he tipped over the small table next to the couch where his untouched glass of water sat. He stumbled, almost falling down in the process, spilling water on himself, the couch, and the carpet. He stared after Emily. Amos could hear her rapid retreat up the stairs and her sobbing by the time she slammed the bedroom door behind her. Matt's face fell—he looked like a lost puppy. He picked up the table and now-empty glass, shook water off his jeans, and sat back down, putting his head in his hands. Amos and Lilly watched without intervening.

"Matt?" Amos finally said. He could see Matt was upset and regretted having to say more. "I want to remind you that you promised to not share this with anyone. Not your family, your friends, people at school, or the people you work with. We took a big risk in telling you these things. Can we still trust you on this?"

"Huh? Of course. I don't think anyone would believe me anyway. *I* wouldn't believe me."

Matt looked distractedly toward the stairs, probably hoping that Emily would reappear.

"Matthew!" Amos said more sternly, getting his attention. "I'm serious about this. No one can know. We need to be able to trust you not to tell *anyone*. We don't know how people will react. You could put Emily and the rest of our family in harm's way with a careless word to someone you think you can trust. Do we still have your word that you won't tell anyone, not even your family, about this?"

"My family?" Matt snorted, "Not much going on there. I haven't spoken to my parents since I decided to go to medical school instead of law school. Dad wanted me to join him at the firm. Mom would call me if Dad would let her, but . . . " He ran out of words, chuckling self-consciously. "Okay. I won't say a word. But does Em have to go with you? She has a choice, doesn't she?" At Amos's glare, Matt changed his approach. "I mean, does this mean that if I don't go with you, I won't be able to visit Em?

"Matthew."

Lillie spoke in a quiet voice, and was more successful in getting Matt's attention than Amos, with his demanding tone, maybe because she sounded so much like Emily. His head jerked over to look at the stairs, then back at Lillie.

"Matthew, Emily loves you and wants to be with you, but she also loves her family and trusts her parents to know what is best for her. You're both adults and have the right to make your own choices. Please don't make the wrong one, for both your sakes."

Amos reached up and patted Lillie's hand, which was resting on his shoulder. They smiled at each other, then looked back at Matt, expectantly.

"Thanks Mrs. Blund. I'll think seriously about what you said. You too, Mr. Blund."

Amos smiled, although he was still concerned about whether Matt would make the right choice.

"I'd better go," Matt said. "Please say good night to Em for me. Sorry about the spilled water."

Lillie walked him to the door, but his eyes kept returning to the stairs. He sighed as Lillie closed the door behind him.

The Blunds had a delicious pot roast dinner—Amos said it was the best roast beef he'd ever tasted, which got him a pat on the head and a pinched cheek from Lillie. Then the family held their regular Family Council and began loading the trailer. Emily didn't join them for dinner or the discussion that night, nor did she help with the loading.

"I wish we'd eaten before our discussion with Matthew," Lillie said. "He looked like he could use a home-cooked meal."

As they were loading the trailer, Mike approached his parents, speaking quietly.

"I'm concerned about the neighbors asking questions."

"Are you worried someone might figure out what's going on and cause a problem?" Amos asked, and Mike nodded.

"I agree," Amos said with a sigh. "We'll need to be ready for a confrontation if any neighbors come knocking."

"Hard to say whether they would laugh at us for taking

the threat seriously, try to understand what we know that they don't, or be angry that we didn't invite them to join us," Mike said.

"Thinking we're crazy would be the best we could hope for," Lillie said. "If that's their view then they probably won't bother to come by—unless they just want to gawk at the loonies, I guess."

"If someone gets angry, maybe violent," Amos said, "we may have to defend ourselves. That's why we're keeping the guns with us."

"Would you really threaten our neighbors with guns?" Lillie asked. "None of them has ever been violent as far I've seen."

"That's not the same thing," Amos said, running his hand through his hair. "People act differently under stress than they do normally. If someone's really afraid for their safety, or for their family, who knows what they might do?"

"Even you, apparently," Lillie replied.

Amos sighed and pulled back on the handle of the hand truck he'd loaded with boxes prior to the meeting, then stopped.

"You know, pulling a gun is a last resort—it's for if and when all else fails. But at the same time, I was always taught that if you stop to wonder whether you should pull your gun, it's going to be too late. It has to be reflexive. If the situation's bad enough that you have to bring out a gun, you'd better be prepared to use it. But I hope I wouldn't fall into the trap of acting out of fear and stress, rather than logic."

Amidst the stares from his family, Amos wheeled the hand truck into the trailer bay where the trailer sat, half-filled. The blackout curtains were closed.

"Amos."

Lillie approached him, holding out the ringing sat phone, but it stopped before Amos could get to it. He moved back into the office with Lillie following, and pressed the speed dial number for the president.

"Amos," Greg McCormick said, "thanks for calling back."

"What's up, Greg?"

He held the phone so that Lillie could hear Greg's side of the conversation.

"You saw my press conference?"

"The one where you told us not to evacuate, but if we do, go to the mountains?"

"Yeah, that one," Greg sighed. "What am I going to do, Amos?"

"Does Al-Qaeda have a bomb?" Amos asked seriously.

"I think so."

"North Korea?"

"I don't know—maybe."

"You know they'll use them if they have them."

"I know."

Amos looked at Lillie before continuing. He didn't know how she was going to react to what he planned to say.

"Then take them head-on, Greg. Let them know how irresponsible it is and threaten to retaliate."

"Al-Qaeda won't care. Death makes them martyrs."

"But Russia will. If they don't back down, then they're part of the problem. You can't let the terrorists win. They'll never go away."

Lillie nodded—Amos needn't have worried.

"So, I go to the U.N.?"

"If that's what it takes. You could try calling Putin first, if you think it might help. I'd think that the president of the Russian Federation might be interested in avoiding a full-scale nuclear war."

"I don't know whether it would make a difference."

The president sighed again. Amos could hear the stress in Greg's voice.

"Tell me what you're working on, Amos. Take my mind off this for a few minutes."

Amos looked at Lillie questioningly, but she shook her head. When Amos didn't respond right away, Greg continued.

"Are you still developing that viewer? What did you call it?"

"The Observer," Amos answered cautiously. "Haven't had much time for it lately."

"Does it work?"

Amos had to say something, just to keep Greg from becoming suspicious.

"We've had some success—we can see things a few miles away. Got a bug though, so we'll need to troubleshoot when we have more time."

"I'm sure you'll figure it out. You still preparing for a crisis? We have one hell of a beauty in the works now."

Amos wasn't sure how to answer and decided to redirect.

"You're doing the best you can, Greg. Everyone will see that."

"Not everyone agrees with you, but I don't want to talk about it. I remember you used to talk about preparing for an emergency, building a hideaway of some kind. Did you do it?"

Lillie nodded reluctantly. Although unsure, Amos decided he couldn't lie.

"We did. We have a retreat in the mountains. If things get much worse, we may have to use it."

Amos tried to laugh, but it fell flat. Greg didn't laugh.

"Any chance you can get your family to safety before the fourth?" Greg sounded sad.

"We're going to try."

"You do that, Amos. Will you take the phone with you?"

He'd been dreading this question. *This is going to be touchy,* he thought. He wasn't positive how Greg would feel about what he'd done.

"And let you track us?"

Lillie was startled and looked at Amos questioningly. Greg didn't answer for a few moments. Amos knew what he was thinking—he could tell Amos how to disable the GPS in the phone so Amos would take it, or he could claim ignorance and Amos would leave the phone behind. Greg responded the way Amos had hoped he would.

"There's a way to disable the GPS."

Amos waited a beat.

"I know, Greg. We disabled it today. I just wanted to know

where you stood."

Lillie punched Amos in the shoulder, frowning as she realized that he'd been testing the president—she didn't like it.

"You're always one step ahead of me, aren't you?" Greg sounded upset.

"You've got a lot on your mind," Amos said politely, trying to make up for his trick.

"Have you thought of anything else you could share with me . . . about the global situation, I mean?"

"Actually, your press conference reminded me of a report from the Hurricane Katrina incident."

"Katrina was handled by FEMA," Greg said.

"Yes and no. The major difficulty in getting relief to the people who were affected was that the communication from the top was too slow. Mayors declared a state of emergency. Governors contacted the federal government for relief. Washington was restricted by law from sending in military help, and FEMA was understaffed. The governors were left with only their national guard units to manage the crisis. The bottom line was that Washington and the states should have had an agreement in place ahead of time on the military's role in a disaster. This time, you have a chance to get ahead of the curve."

There was silence for several moments. Amos was sure Greg was reviewing what he knew about how Katrina had played out, and the things he'd done so far to deal with the current crisis.

"You know Amos," Greg said, "we decided to have Secretary of State Cy Hutchison talk to the governors, though at the time I really didn't know what I wanted them to do. But you may have just shown me the way forward. I'm going to do some background work on Katrina, then sit down with the Panel and brainstorm. Thank you. And let me know when you're safely away."

"Will do. Good luck."

Greg hung up first.

"Was that necessary?" Lillie demanded. "He *is* your friend."

"*He* called *me*," Amos replied defensively, then pursed his lips the way he always did when he thought he was being funny.

Lillie slugged him again, harder this time.

"Ouch."

9

"An imminent threat of nuclear war"

Logan, Utah, 24 June

"Hey Amos, you worried about the terrorist threat?" Jason Carlsen asked loudly.

Amos wasn't surprised Jason was bringing this up now. His next-door neighbor had zero tact when it came to social situations. Now, after church on Sunday, Jason had decided to basically announce to all of their neighbors that Amos was up to something. This was the same guy who couldn't hold the attention of the teenagers in his Sunday School class, despite his attempt at grandiose sermons.

"No Jason," Amos said blandly, his heart skipping a beat. "The president said we don't have anything to worry about." He tried to change the subject. "Did you sign up to help with the service project on Saturday?"

But Jason wasn't going to be derailed. He continued, amiably, but loudly.

"I hear you're packing up to move. Where're you moving to?"

Several heads turned, wanting to hear what Amos would say.

"Nah," he said, thinking quickly. "We're not moving. How could I leave such wonderful next-door neighbors?" He chuckled at his own joke as several people around him laughed. "We're just moving some stuff out of the lab to make room for more projects."

Amos was doing his best to act as though nothing was wrong, but inside he was worried that Jason wouldn't be deflected, and that others might begin to wonder about what he was up to. In a desperate attempt to change the subject, he turned to talk to another neighbor, Tyler Parker, who lived one street over.

"Hey Tyler, did you get the SUV sold? Lillie said she's seen a couple of people come by to look at it."

"Not yet," Tyler replied with a smile. "You need it to help with your move?"

Tyler laughed.

Not what I was hoping for, Amos thought.

"Yeah, just ignore Jason. We're not moving. There's nothing like a juicy rumor to keep the gossip mill turning, right?"

He forced another good-natured chuckle. Then, seeing Lillie, he excused himself and walked off. As he went, out of the corner of his eye, he saw Jason walk over to Tyler and begin talking animatedly, gesturing with his hands, and a few of the others turned to see what had Jason so agitated.

Oval Office

The president entered the room with a spring in his step and a smile on his face, taking his usual chair. Eric Epstein, Tom, Jim, Secretary of State Cy Hutchison, and Secretary of Homeland Security Charles Dickson, who had been impatiently milling around the room, took seats quickly, looking at each other a little quizzically. The president had asked Eric to invite Secretary Hutchison and Secretary Dickson to this meeting since the topics at hand would involve their respective areas of expertise.

Homeland Security—or HomeSec, as the president referred to it—was the body concerned with protecting the United States and its citizens, and had become a cabinet-level position following the September 11 terrorist attack. Functionally, it was a consolidation of Customs, Border Patrol, Immigration, the Secret Service, FEMA, and similar groups. Greg had only met Chuck after he became president, when Chuck's name showed up on a shortlist of candidates for the HomeSec position, but he'd been pleased with his performance so far.

Greg tossed copies of a document across the table to each of them. It was a report: *Civil–Military Relations in Hurricane Katrina: A Case Study on Crisis Management in Natural Disaster Response,* by Jean-Loup Samaan and Laurent Verneuil.

Five faces looked up at the president, four of them clearly confused. HomeSec Dickson smiled and nodded, making it clear that he understood why he'd been invited to this meeting, and the president smiled back.

"What are we looking at, Greg?" Jim asked.

"Chuck, do you want to handle the explanation?" Greg asked.

"Certainly," Chuck said. "The main lesson we learned in the aftermath of Hurricane Katrina was that the government's crisis management plan needed to be improved. For various reasons, most of them legal, the federal government was slow to respond to state requests for assistance. Later, laws were passed that strengthened FEMA's authority to act and required the different layers of government to plan ahead for emergencies."

"So, why are we just hearing about this now?" Jim asked.

HomeSec Dickson looked embarrassed and turned to the president for support.

"FEMA's historical role has been in the context of hurricanes, tornadoes, floods—that sort of thing," the president explained. "There have only been a couple of crises since Katrina that required this level of coordination between Washington and multiple states. None of us were in our present positions when they occurred. When you read the report—and I want you to read it and give me your suggestions—I think you'll see that there are things we can do now, today, to get ahead of the curve on the current crisis."

Amos had used that same expression, Greg remembered, smiling again. Now he had something the National Security Council could sink its teeth into.

"I've called an NSC meeting for tomorrow morning, and Cy has the governors' conference after that. I want to have a plan that Cy can present to the governors. Can we meet back here in three hours?"

There were nods of agreement, the men already leafing through the report.

Situation Room, NSC meeting, 25 June

The members of the NSC were seated in their usual places

around the situation room, clearly anticipating important news. The president hadn't called them to a meeting in three weeks. Now, he looked around the room and began.

"Who wants to go first? What is this I saw in the Daily about the Mexico bomb?"

After a long pause, DNI Tom Mitchell spoke.

"Our agents believe they have credible evidence that a weapon has entered the U.S. from Mexico, but we were too late to stop it. We don't know where it is now."

"What's the *credible evidence*, Tom?"

Tom took a deep breath, then slowly let it out.

"If something is outside the country, but on its way, our sources say one thing. If it's already in the country, the way they talk about it is slightly different. It's subtle differences in the way something is said, but our agents have the experience to tell the difference."

"But we have no hard facts."

It was a statement rather than a question.

"No facts," Tom agreed.

"Where do you think the bomb is headed?"

"The logical place would be Washington, D.C., but, we haven't been able to pick up its trail."

The president sighed.

"What about North Korea?"

"Still flexing their muscles. Another ICBM test, but no indication there's a bomb."

"Okay. We're going to assume the possible existence of a bomb and implement the evacuation plan for the northeast.

I'm going to have Ryan Jamison announce it in the press conference—"

"Why Jamison?" Eric Epstein interrupted. "What happened to Lisa?"

Greg knew Eric had a soft spot for Lisa and felt bad that he'd had to let her go. She had what it took to be a great press secretary someday, but she had found it too hard to adjust to the stress of the situation.

"Lisa was having trouble handling the press conferences. She's asked not to be involved until this crisis is over."

Eric would put the pieces together, and Greg was fairly sure that Eric would check up on her, just to make sure she was okay. That was good—Greg liked her as much as anyone, apart from Eric.

"In any event," he continued, "I've spoken with the prime minister in Ottawa, and he agrees with my plan to open the border with Canada and allow people to move freely in both directions. I've written an executive order to make it happen.

"You should all know that Secretary Hutchison has called a governors' conference for later this morning. We've compiled a list of suggestions for the governors, which Cy will present with help from Jim. We need to keep order, protect stores and businesses that sell emergency supplies, water, that sort of thing. That means we need the states to have police and national guard units on call for immediate response. We'll ask the governors to keep Cy informed of their whereabouts at all times, since we'll need state permission in order for military units to move to critical locations to assist. We'll also need

FEMA, the Red Cross, and other relief agencies to be on call. We'll make government stockpiles of emergency equipment available to dispense to local authorities and relief agencies. The military can help with that . . . "

"Greg, are you saying that we're going to war?" Vice President Art Klemp asked, interrupting the president.

"No Art," Greg replied. "In case you weren't listening, we're asking the governors to place their police and national guard units on call *in case* there is a national emergency."

"What's the difference?" the vice president asked sarcastically.

"The difference is defensive versus offensive actions. Did you play sports, Art? You *do* know the difference, don't you?"

Art stared at him, saying nothing, his face turning red.

"No, I guess you don't."

Greg was tired of Art's interruptions. There was a risk that Art would go to the press with this information and it would be spun out of control, and he briefly considered having Art locked up to prevent a leak. He put the thought aside and looked around the room again.

"Everyone, listen. We're already seeing vandalism and hoarding. People are scared. The state governments are the first line of defense against this type of problem. They control the resources: the police and national guard. But we need to be available to assist. And we need to provide that assistance through strictly legal channels. Is that understood?"

There were a few nods, but also some questioning looks.

"If you don't understand, do a little research on how the

government handled Hurricane Katrina. You represent the organizations that will need to be involved in relief efforts if we have a national crisis. I want all of you to prepare your people to assist when asked. But above all, *do not* share this information with anyone except on an absolute need-to-know basis. Is that clear?"

There were several people in the room who didn't make eye contact, and he made a mental note of who they were. One was Art. Greg turned to his chief of staff.

"Eric, get in touch with Ambassador Daniel Porter at the UN and have him call an emergency session of the General Assembly. I'm going to confront this head-on."

"Are you sure that's wise, sir?" DNI Tom Mitchell asked. "It could interfere with our investigation."

"I don't see much choice, Tom. I really don't see our investigation getting us anywhere. I'll go down in history as bold, for confronting it, or as a pariah, for being in this situation in the first place. We'll continue to look for the bomb, but we're going to DEFCON 1."

Oval Office, follow-up meeting

"How did the governors respond, Cy?" President McCormick asked his secretary of state.

"Well, most of the northeast bought in. We have written agreements to activate military units with a single phone call or text from the governor, or his or her delegated representative. The others are thinking about it—they want to talk to their political leaders."

"Did you give them a deadline?"

"We told them about your press conference this afternoon. That made them nervous. Some are downright panicky—they think raising the DEFCON level will incite riots and violence. Even some of the western governors were concerned about the announcement. It doesn't take much to get a good riot going in Los Angeles."

"Do I need to declare martial law?"

"I suggest we look at that on a state by state basis when we see how the states handle their problems."

"Fine."

"Mr. President," Eric spoke hesitantly, "the press conference is in an hour and we still need to brief Mr. Jamison."

"Okay, Eric, let's go."

Logan, Utah

"Amos, there's another press conference in five minutes."

Lillie knew Amos wanted to have as much information as was available so they could adjust their plans, if needed.

"Ryan Jamison, the president's adviser on terrorism, and a member of the United States Department of Counter-Terrorism, will address the latest news on the terrorist threat and answer questions from the press," a narrator said in a quiet voice over an image of reporters milling around the press room, finding their seats.

The podium was still vacant.

White House Press Room

Ryan Jamison, a small man in a rumpled suit, with thinning hair and a nose that looked like it had been broken sometime in the past, walked into the press room. He was a veteran when it came to dealing with terrorism, and it showed in his confident demeanor as he approached the podium. Without looking at his notes, he addressed the reporters in the room and the millions of people he knew were watching from their living rooms.

"Ladies and gentlemen, on the advice of the United States Department of Counter-Terrorism, the president is raising the DEFCON Level to 1, White, meaning that there is an imminent threat of nuclear war."

He was interrupted by insistent shouts from the reporters wanting to ask questions. Jamison held up one hand, palm out, in an effort to get them to settle, then waited. He'd known his announcement would get a rise out of the reporters, but he'd chosen to begin his address boldly, without fear. That was his style.

Just as he'd expected, dozens of reporters shouted questions—some mild, others bordering on the obscene. He ignored them, looking at his notes instead. It took several minutes before quiet was restored, the reporters finally accepting that they wouldn't be heard at this time. He continued.

"This decision has been made after much deliberation, the president's primary focus being his concern for the safety of the citizens of the United States. I'll be blunt. We now have credible evidence that a nuclear device has entered the country from Mexico through a previously undetected drug route."

Again, the reporters began angrily clamoring for attention. Jamison raised both hands this time, his patience wearing thin.

"Please, please. Can I please have your cooperation to get this message out quickly? I'm not going to answer your questions individually. Listen to me, and your questions will be answered. If not, I'm sorry."

His tone was both authoritative and a little condescending. He waited until the reporters settled down again, then went on.

"We *do not* want anyone to panic. We still believe the threat can be neutralized before the deadline. However, to err on the side of caution, the president is working with governors to call up national guard units in specific locations—backed up by federal military units—to assist with a voluntary and orderly evacuation."

Jamison continued, more loudly now so as to be heard over the angry shouting of some members of the press.

"We have a list of the most likely targets and have developed plans for an orderly evacuation. Those plans are being distributed to governments and media outlets in the affected states as we speak, and a copy is being provided to the reporters in this room now."

There was a sudden hush in the audience, and the shuffling of paper was the only sound in the room until Jamison resumed speaking.

"We're asking the media to make this information available

immediately by radio, television, internet, social media, and print, and you'll see that it will answer all your questions.

"I'm going to summarize the material briefly. We believe that the most likely target is Washington, D.C. Citizens of Washington, D.C., and areas north and east of D.C., including the eastern portions of Maryland, New York, Pennsylvania, and Virginia, and the entire states of Connecticut, Delaware, Maine, Massachusetts, New Hampshire, New Jersey, Rhode Island, and Vermont, should begin a calm evacuation away from that area. Those who are unable or unwilling to leave the area for whatever reason, should shelter in place or go to one of the public shelters that are being set up for this purpose. A searchable list of shelters is being prepared now and you'll find it on the website listed in the handout before the end of the day.

"Our counterparts in Canada are sharing this same message with their citizens in Quebec and the eastern provinces. We have agreed to open the border between our two countries to aid in the orderly evacuation of citizens to points further south and west. If you can put a mountain range between you and the targeted area, so much the better. After you've reviewed the handouts, if you have questions, you may contact our office at the phone number or website listed in the handout.

"One last thing. We're receiving reports of rioting and violence in isolated locations. The police, national guard, and military are being called out to those areas and will deal with the violators, with force if necessary. We advise sensible citizens to avoid being part of the problem. Thank you."

With that, Jamison picked up his notes and walked out, amid dozens of shouted questions.

Logan, Utah

"That was brief," Lillie said sarcastically, as Mike turned down the volume on the TV.

"They're worried about public panic," Mike said.

"The way they handled that briefing," Lillie said, "they just about guaranteed panic. But it was no-nonsense, that's good."

"I'm just glad they're finally going public," Amos said. "It'll probably save lives." He sighed. "Okay, let's get some dinner and then get everyone together for Family Council."

Logan, Utah, 26 June

The three men met on the sidewalk, walking side by side to the Blunds' front porch. The smallest one of the three, Patrick McKensie, lived across the street and was in his seventies. He was a quiet man who generally kept to himself, but today was different. After his wife—Kathy, though Patrick called her Kitty—had confronted Rachel Blund, Patrick had heard rumors about the Blunds. He'd finally contacted Jason Carlsen, the Blunds' next door neighbor, to see if he knew anything. Patrick had to walk on the lawn because the other two took up the entire sidewalk, but he was determined to keep up and show his solidarity with the others.

Jason Carlsen, who had confronted Amos at church, and Tyler Parker, who lived two doors down from the Stephens family on the next street, were both large, muscular men. Jason was in his forties, Tyler in his late thirties. Neither of them had really believed Amos's denials during their conversation with him at church, and both were sure that Amos was up to something. All three wore sour expressions as they approached the Blunds' door. None of them spoke until Lillie answered the door.

"Hi Lillie," Jason began. "Is Amos at home?"

Seeing their expressions, Lillie saw in a flash that Amos might well have been right about scared people becoming violent, but she put a cautious smile on her face and invited them in.

"He's in the back. Have a seat in the family room and I'll go get him. Would you like something to drink?"

Patrick opened his mouth to speak, but Jason beat him to it, speaking bluntly.

"Don't need a drink, Lillie. Just need to talk to Amos, thanks."

Patrick looked disappointed and more than a little nervous. As the men entered the family room, Patrick headed toward the couch, but a sharp look from Jason stopped him and he moved over to stand by the others.

When Amos and Lillie came in, all three men were still standing. Amos noted the frowns and tense postures of the men, but he faked a friendly smile and put on a casual tone.

"Hi Tyler, Jason, Patrick. What can I do for you?"

"You can tell us what's going on," Jason blurted.

Amos chuckled, hiding his nervousness behind a calm facade. He avoided looking at Lillie so he wouldn't give himself away.

"You'll have to be a little more specific, Jason."

It was Patrick who spoke up.

"Ma' Kitty said she saw yoo folks out in da' middle uv' da' night wanderin''round the yard, movin' stuff."

Amos barked a laugh.

"Is that what has you three so uptight?" Maybe he could talk his way out of this mess. "Our Michael works long hours. It's hard for him to find time to work with us. We have to take his help when we can get it."

"Well, whatcha movin''round all 'spicious like in da' middle uv' da' night?" Patrick continued.

"Come on, Patrick," Amos said in a teasing tone. Maybe he could keep them off balance by taking the offensive. "When's the last time I came across the street and asked to check out the projects you always seem to be working on in the basement behind drawn shades?"

"Never yoo min' what ah do in ma' basemen'," Patrick huffed, but the response seemed to take the wind out of his sails.

Amos was about to relax when Tyler Parker spoke up.

"My boy, Joshua, saw you loading stuff into that building . . ."

"Into my *lab*," Amos interrupted, trying to fluster Tyler.

Tyler sputtered and started again.

" . . . into your lab, then leaving the yard with a full trailer in the middle of the night. He said it looked like some of the Stephens family were out there helping.”

“Well, Tyler, you may not know it, but Terry Stephens and I are business partners. We’ve been working on several projects, some of which are pretty absorbing. Sometimes Terry’s family has to come over and remind him where he lives.”

He laughed gently again, trying to lighten the mood. Tyler didn’t respond and didn’t seem to have a follow-up question.

Amos was afraid to let his guard down—Jason Carlsen hadn’t had a run at him yet. He had the urge to run his fingers through his hair, but resisted it, keeping his arms at his sides. Finally, Jason spoke.

“Being your neighbor for the last few years, I’ve seen you moving stuff in and out of that . . . lab and have to wonder what you two are up to.”

That’s enough, Amos thought. He dropped the smile and looked Jason in the eye.

“Jason, we’ve been neighbors for close to fifteen years and we’ve always had a friendly, over-the-fence relationship with your family. Our children don’t play together because of their different interests and ages, so we don’t have a lot in common, but we don’t interrogate you about what you do in your home, and we’ve never felt a need to tell you what goes on in ours.”

Lillie took Amos’s hand in hers. He looked at her briefly, calmed by her reassuring smile.

“However, since you asked, I’ll tell you this much. The things Terry and I are working on involve medical and scientific research, some of it patentable. We don’t advertise exactly what we're doing because that way no one can beat us to the patent office."

Jason looked surprised. He hadn't anticipated something like this and it was probably forcing him to reassess everything he'd noticed, and assumed, in the last few days. Amos watched as the expression on each of their faces changed from confrontational to slightly embarrassed. *Good,* he thought. He waited a few seconds, then started wrapping things up, using the same serious tone.

"Was there anything else you wanted to know?"

All three shook their heads.

"No," Jason said. "I guess that covers it. Sorry we interrupted your evening."

"No problem, Jason," Amos said, the smile back on his face. "We like having all of you as neighbors," he added, hoping this was the last they would hear from the three of them, but fearing that it wouldn't be. "If anything else comes to mind, don't hesitate to give me a call."

The three men filed out of the family room, and Lillie opened the front door with a friendly smile.

"Come again, anytime, gentlemen," she said. Once the door was shut, she let her smile drop and added, sarcastically, "Well, that went well."

"I wish I hadn't had to do that to them," Amos said.

"I know. I hate lying, even if it's the only thing we can do," she agreed, reaching her arms around Amos's waist and pulling him close.

Logan, Utah, 27 June

Emily charged into the house, dragging Matt after her.

"Mom? Dad?" she called out. "Matt has decided to go with us. Isn't that great?"

"That's wonderful," Lillie said, as Emily and Matt burst into the kitchen. She was just lifting a casserole out of the oven while Rachel set the table. "You'll stay for dinner, won't you Matthew?"

"Of course he will," Emily said for him. "That's why we came now, so you and Dad can answer Matt's questions while we eat."

Over dinner, they discussed their impending departure. Matt's questions were mostly about what he should pack and when he should be ready to go. Amos knew that, as a nearly destitute medical student, Matt wouldn't have much to contribute financially, but he could see that Matt wanted to help as much as possible.

"Dad refused to fund my education," Matt said, rubbing the back of his neck self-consciously, "because I'm not studying law. But Mom sends me a little money on holidays and birthdays, and any other excuse she can find, to help me stay in school."

Amos smiled, remembering how difficult it had been to pay his way through medical school. He hadn't had time for a job, and he'd also had to pay for the privilege of working in the hospital during his residency. Lillie had commented one time, when Amos had gone close to seventy-two hours without sleep and then crawled into the apartment, that maybe that was why doctors charged so much. Amos had responded without missing a beat.

"And they deserve every penny of it!" he'd said.

After they finished eating and clearing the table, Amos handed Matt a list of personal supplies. Matt skimmed it briefly, then looked up.

"I'm planning to withdraw the money I saved for tuition," he said. "I'll use it to buy whatever you tell me to get. If I have any left, you can have it."

"Bring it along," Amos said, impressed. "Do you have to work tonight?"

"No," Matt said, rubbing his neck again. Amos could tell he was struggling with how to explain what he'd done, to another doctor. "I called in sick. I told my supervisor I didn't think I would be in for a few days."

Amos smiled. *That was brave* he thought—*brave to do and brave to confess to me.*

"Good," he said. "Since you're here, you can help with tonight's load. I have an extra pair of work clothes that should fit you well enough."

After dinner, Emily and Matt sat on the back porch swing waiting for instructions. Rachel and Mike had gone off separately to take care of personal business until it was time to start loading. Amos helped Lillie clean up after dinner and do the dishes, and Lillie finally worked up the courage to ask the question that had been on her mind since they'd invited Matt to go with them.

"Amos, what will we do if Emily and Matthew want to get married after we're at the Preserve?"

He took the dish towel from her and set it on the counter. With a loving expression that still took her breath away, he put his arms around her waist, giving her a hug, and she responded, putting her arms around his neck.

"Always the practical one," he said. Then he surprised her. "It's already taken care of."

He pursed his lips in that annoying way that said he thought he was being funny.

"What do you mean?"

She put her hands on his chest and pushed away from him so she could look him in the eye. She didn't see anything funny in what he'd said.

"I didn't think of it until just now."

He laughed—it welled up from his belly and shook his whole upper body. His brilliant smile usually melted her resolve, but this time she fought off the reaction and glared at him, challenging him to explain himself.

"Okay," he said, regaining his composure after a moment's effort. "With the way international tensions have increased, and with more and more weather-related emergencies, it looked to me like we might actually move to the Preserve some day. So, I filled out some papers and took a cheap course from an online church. And I created our own church. I'm the religious leader, with the legal right to perform civil marriages. The Church of

Aspen Valley—that's the name."

Lillie's mouth dropped open in surprise.

"You didn't."

Amos went on hurriedly.

"It was either that or get Aspen Valley incorporated as a town, with me as mayor. I didn't want our hideout being added to maps of the area just so that I could perform marriages."

As he spoke, Lillie's resolve slipped. She smiled, shaking her head in disbelief at his forethought.

"You never cease to amaze me."

She put her arms back around his neck, drew his head down to hers and kissed him deeply.

10

"Caught ya'!"

Logan, Utah, 28 June, about 2:00 am

Mike drove the truck with its heavy trailer out of the lab, keeping the headlights off. As usual, the trailer was loaded to the brim and covered with tarps. Terry sat in the cab next to Mike. Amos and the others, now including Matt, were just headed back to the house from the lab, when a bright floodlight lit up the yard from the driveway and an angry, male voice called out.

"Caught ya'!"

Amos was startled.

"That sounds like Jason Carlson," he said quietly.

He recognized Jason's voice despite it being distorted with anger. Willing his heart to be still, and shielding his eyes with one hand, he replied in his calmest, doctor-telling-a-patient-they-have-cancer, voice.

"Who's there? Can you move the light out of our eyes?"

The light shifted down slightly and the voice came again.

"You thought you could fool us, but we figured out what you're up to."

Amos turned to Lillie, his heart pounding, and spoke quietly but urgently.

"Get everyone in the house."

Then he turned back toward the light. Out of the corner of his eye, Amos could see Mike and Terry peering from the windows of the now-stopped truck. He knew they would be ready to step in if necessary. It was one of many possibilities they'd talked about, with their responses agreed on in advance. With false bravado, Amos walked toward the light.

"Is that you, Jason? What are you talking about?"

He visualized himself as Daniel, walking into the lion's den.

"The other night," Jason said, his voice tense and strained, "after you embarrassed us at your house, I started watching you, comparing notes with Tyler and Patrick. You hauled a load out that night and another one again tonight. You're moving."

Jason's voice was getting louder as he worked himself up.

"At first," he said, "we couldn't figure out the secrecy. Then Tyler remembered the president's press conference and the nuclear threat. Well, the deadline's almost here and you're trying to skip town without any of us knowing."

It was clear that the situation could easily spiral out of control. He tried to think quickly so he could defuse a dangerous escalation.

"Interesting story, Jason. Who's with you, anyway? Is that Tyler and Patrick?"

"Among others," Jason growled. "We want some answers Amos."

"Answers to what? It seems to me as though you think I owe you something. How can that be when all I've ever done is be a good neighbor? I've never criticized any of you, borrowed things from any of you, or failed to be kind to a single person in this neighborhood. So, Jason, why is it that I owe you an explanation for anything I do?"

"That's . . . that isn't what I mean," Jason said, stumbling on his words. "I mean, we'd like to know what's going on. That's all."

"Oh, *that's* all. Well, Jason, again, I'm struggling to think of why I need to explain myself to you. But if you'll please lower the light from my face and calm down, I'd be happy to have a sensible, adult conversation with you and anyone else who's hiding behind your spotlight."

"Fine."

The floodlight went off, and its absence left everyone blind for a moment. Amos closed his eyes to get them to adjust to the change.

"Thank you," he said. "Now, you want to know if what we're doing here has something to do with the potential nuclear threat. Is that right?"

"Yes."

"The answer is no. Why would we go to all that trouble? It's not like Logan would be a high-value target for terrorists. And even if it was, where could we go to get away from a nuclear explosion?"

"That's exactly what we want to know," Jason said, belligerent again. "Where are you going?"

The others had moved up to stand behind him, apparently in a show of force.

"We're cleaning out the lab and moving old projects to a storage unit, like I told you on Sunday."

"Yeah, but it was a bunch of bunk then too, wasn't it? Just like it is now."

Jason's voice was rising again. Lillie had told Amos after their last encounter with Jason and the others, that Jason took medication for high blood pressure and had been warned by his doctor to control his stress—his wife had told her about it one day at church. Thinking that Jason's stress level at the moment might lead to a stroke or heart attack, Amos's medical training kicked in.

"You're upset, Jason," Amos said calmly. "Maybe you should calm down so you . . . "

"Damn right I'm upset," Jason bellowed, interrupting, his demeanor changing from merely self-righteous to indignant. "And don't you worry about my heart, Amos. You're not *my* doctor."

The group of visitors closed in as Jason moved toward him. Amos's eyes had adjusted to the meager light from the front porch, and he was close enough to watch as Tyler Parker laid a cautioning hand on Jason's arm, but Jason shook him off and continued.

"We think you've been stocking up on emergency supplies, and now you're taking them to some secret hidey-hole in the mountains."

He knew better than to antagonize an angry man with a heart condition, but Amos had reached his limit for politeness and his temper began to get the better of him.

"Oh my goodness, you've found me out, Jason," he said sarcastically. *Let Jason worry about his own damned heart.* "We've dug a big hole in the ground and we're going to go bury ourselves for a thousand years until the nuclear fallout degrades enough for us to dig ourselves out."

Lillie had stepped onto the porch in time to hear, and she moved quickly toward him. They'd agreed after the last confrontation that Jason seemed to have no restraint whatsoever, and that if Amos ever lost his own temper, things could escalate quickly. She didn't reach him in time to stop his next comment, though.

"Use your head, Jason."

Amos and Jason stood only a few feet apart, and Amos looked him in the eye as he spoke. In the dim glow from the porch light, he could see the crimson color of Jason's face and a large vein standing out on his neck, threatening to burst. He wanted to say more, but his medical instincts held him in check.

"Jason, you've got to calm down. You're on the verge of—"

Jason swung the light to his left, toward Patrick, who wasn't ready for it, and it fell to the ground with a crash as Jason took a swing at Amos with his right fist. Amos, distracted by the movement of the light, only saw the blow coming at the last second—he turned his head, catching the blow behind the ear. It was enough to knock him to the ground.

Suddenly, everyone was in motion. Those who'd come with Jason tried to keep him from going after Amos on the ground, but before they could stop him, he'd kicked Amos in the shoulder, causing an agonizing moan to escape Amos's lips. The crowd dragged Jason away, cursing and screaming. In the confusion, nobody heard exactly what Jason said. Lillie thought later that it might have been something about them not leaving without his family.

Lillie was close enough to see the attack. Terry and Mike, from their vantage point in the truck down the driveway, saw Amos go down, but everything happened so quickly that by the time they could react, it was over. As Jason was hustled away, Terry and Mike climbed quickly out of the truck and rushed over.

Lillie reached Amos first and knelt down next to him, checking his pulse, then looked at his head to see if there was any obvious injury. The dim light of the porch lamp cast shadows, making it impossible to tell whether he needed medical help. Mike stood in a defensive position between Amos and the crowd. Terry knelt down opposite Lillie.

"I can't tell anything in this light," Lillie complained, leaning back to let Terry have a look. She took Amos's hand between hers and said a silent prayer.

Terry flipped on a flashlight he'd brought with him from the truck and shone it on Amos's scalp and shoulder. After a cursory check to see that nothing was broken, he called to Mike.

"Help me get your dad into the lab."

The meeting was held in the lab office, so Amos wouldn't have to get off the cot. Lillie had propped him up on some pillows so he could participate, but he'd asked Terry to lead the discussion this time. Lillie sat next to Amos, running her hand over his forehead and neck affectionately. She smoothed his unruly hair and occasionally touched the bandage behind his ear, needing reassurance that Amos was still with her and was going to be okay.

The lab had limited furnishings by this point—a folding table, four chairs, and two cots—so some of the family stood, leaning against the walls. They went over the lists and talked about the tasks that remained to be done.

"I still want that load to go out tonight," Amos said. "And we should move the departure date up."

"I'll drive the truck tonight," Terry said. "We'll go a roundabout way in case we're followed. I'd like Mike and Rachel to come with me because they're already packed. I need Mike to help me check out the Preserve to make sure everything is working properly before the rest of you arrive, and we'll have Rachel drive the truck back. Becca can stay here to make sure Katie's ready for the next ride."

"I'm ready," Katie said defensively. Then, with a glance at her mother, and seeing Becca's doubtful look, added. "Well, almost."

Lillie laughed lightly.

"It's okay, Katie. I have two daughters, so I know how it is."

"I'll make sure Katie and I are ready to come with the next load," Becca said, still looking at her daughter.

"Thanks," Terry said, patting Becca's arm affectionately.

"I want the last load to leave in two days," Amos said, lifting his head slightly, then sinking back onto the pillow with a moan.

"Well then," Mike said. "We've got work to do. Let's get to it."

Logan, Utah, 28 June, about midday

The doorbell startled Lillie, whose mind was on Amos. He was in the lab, working, though he should have been lying down and resting.

She wasn't expecting anyone. Opening the door, she was surprised to see Jason Carlsen, his eyes downcast and his hands folded loosely in front of him. Behind him, his wife, Brittany, stood with her arms folded in front of her, a stern expression aimed at the back of her husband's head. Tyler Parker, his wife Megan, and the McKensies from across the street, were all crowded on the front porch behind the Carlsens. *Now what?* Lillie wondered. She folded her arms and waited for Jason to speak.

Jason glanced up at Lillie, then back at his wife, then back down.

"Lillie, how's Amos?" He paused. When Lillie didn't immediately respond, he continued, the words coming out in a rush. "I'm sorry for last night. I was stupid and let my temper get the best of me. I hope you will forgive me?"

He made it a question. He was about to go on, but another quick turn to look at his wife stopped him. Lillie had never seen him cowed by Brittany, and part of her wanted to laugh at the thought of little Brittany, who put up with so much, standing up to him. After a few moments getting her vacillating emotions under control, she took a deep breath and responded.

"Well, he's going to be okay, no thanks to you. He doesn't have a concussion, but you did cut his head. He's got a pretty bad headache and his neck and shoulder are very sore." Uncharacteristically, she spoke without thinking beforehand about what she would say. "I guess as good Christians we have to forgive you, so I accept your apology—but I'm not happy about it."

Brittany Carlsen, half the size of her husband, shouldered him out of the way so she could stand face-to-face with Lillie. Lillie knew that Brittany had, of necessity, become strong willed and independent. Jason worked too many hours to be of any help at home. He was a corporate controller with a lot of responsibility—that's how he described it, anyway. Brittany had told Lillie, several months earlier, that she thought it was just his way of getting out of doing his part to help manage their home and family. Brittany was left to raise her three children by herself.

Their oldest boy, Aaron, had grown up mostly unsupervised. Brittany said he was intelligent and headstrong, like his father, so when he started running with a tough crowd at school, Brittany couldn't handle him anymore. She tried to get Jason to follow up with Aaron, but he said he didn't have the time. Aaron was eighteen now, and seldom home except to eat and sleep, usually during the day.

Their second son, Nathan, was seventeen, and he'd been polite and obedient as a child. Lillie had always been impressed by how well he handled himself at church and in the neighborhood. But lately he'd taken to idolizing his older brother and had begun to follow him around. As Aaron became more independent, Nathan stopped listening to his mother and started staying out late with his older brother.

The Carlsens' daughter, Sydney, was fourteen and a really wonderful girl, well-mannered and polite. Brittany raved about Sydney being on the honor roll at school, playing piano, running track—and knowing her own worth. She encouraged her daughter to be the best at whatever she chose to do, then supported her by going with her to recitals, competitions, school assemblies, and parent-teacher conferences. It was something she regretted not having done with the boys, an oversight she seemed to be paying for now.

Lillie and Brittany weren't close friends, but they knew each other and each other's children well enough for Lillie to believe what Brittany said about the kids. She also knew Brittany to be a quiet, reserved, and mostly submissive woman—but right now she was angrier and more indignant than Lillie had ever seen her

"Lillie, please accept my apology for letting Jason out without a leash."

She aimed a dirty look at her husband, who seemed oblivious to it. She smiled, but Lillie just stared mutely, her anger not subsiding yet.

"He doesn't have a way with words," Brittany said. "So

he never got around to saying what we all wanted to say last night." She paused, an anxious expression on her face. When Lillie didn't seem moved, she sighed and plowed ahead quickly. "We're scared. We want to go with you."

Lillie stood there for several moments, trying to think through the request. She looked at each of the people on her porch, considering what to say. She and Amos had discussed this possibility after the previous night's attack, and they'd agreed that sending their neighbors away wouldn't resolve anything—it would just provoke another confrontation. Amos had asked Lillie to let him do the talking if it came to that, because he was worried that Jason might attack her too. So, Lillie opened the door wider.

"Come in. I'll get Amos."

Amos sat across the room from his neighbors. He'd made them squeeze together on the long sofa by failing to offer any additional seating. Patrick McKensie was perched on the arm of the sofa at one end, with Megan Parker in the same spot on the other. He didn't want them to be comfortable.

Lillie had judged correctly. They couldn't postpone dealing with this any longer now that these people had come crawling to the Blunds' door seeking, not only forgiveness, but an invitation. He wondered if he could convince them to *just go away,* so he didn't have to turn them down. After several minutes of nervous squirming, Jason coughed self-consciously into his hand. Amos, still considering how to begin, turned his head in that direction, then winced at the pain in his neck.

"Who else was with you last night and how many people know what you're doing here today?" Amos asked abruptly.

All six of them began speaking at once and Jason held out both arms, outstretched, so that Brittany on one side and Kitty McKensie on the other had to lean back to avoid being hit in the head. It had the desired effect—everyone stopped talking.

"No one else was with us and no one knows we're here," Jason stated emphatically. "But you have to understand that your behavior has people wondering and talking."

"You mean *your* behavior has people wondering and talking, don't you?" Amos demanded, trying to control his temper. His aching head and shoulder were making it hard to be polite.

Jason's face contorted in anger and he started to get up. Patrick and Brittany tried unsuccessfully to restrain him, but it wasn't working.

"Jason, get a grip on yourself!" Brittany shouted.

To Jason's surprise, as he took a step toward Amos, his neighbor sat calmly, simply watching. Jason stopped suddenly, looking into Amos's calm face, and realized that he'd let the man upset him again. He forced himself to calm down, not wanting to spoil their chance of being invited into the hidey-hole.

Jason had been listening to the reports from the government, reading the speculation in the newspapers, and discussing various rumors, almost nonstop for the past several days. If even half of it was true, the country was in real trouble. He collapsed back onto the sofa, half-sitting on Kitty's lap, then shifting away as Kitty squawked in surprise. Amos and Lillie were watching him quietly as he collected himself, his head bowed. He shook his head side-to-side a few times, then looked up. He had to see if he could save the situation.

"Amos, I'm sorry," he said, trying to sound contrite. "I'm just scared."

There were murmurs of agreement from the others.

"Well, sorry for baiting you, Jason," Amos said. "But you need to understand that your behavior doesn't give me a lot of confidence that you can control your temper long enough to listen to what I have to say."

"I can . . . "

"Words, Jason. Only words. Your actions tell me otherwise."

"But you lied to us," Jason cried, exasperated. Jason had never met anyone he couldn't manipulate. How could Amos do this to him?

"What makes you think I lied?"

"We know what you're doing Amos. You're leaving all of us here, to die."

"To be truthful, Jason, yes, we're leaving. But that has nothing to do with you, does it?"

"No, I guess not," Jason admitted honestly. "But we want to go with you," he pleaded.

He had to find a way to break down the wall Amos had placed in his path.

"You can leave anytime you want. Why do we have an obligation to help you with whatever it is you think is coming?"

"I think . . ." Jason began.

He'd been about to say that he thought Amos was being selfish, then changed his mind when he saw the other man's expression. He had to go along with Amos until he saw where this was going.

" . . . I think we can help each other," he concluded.

11

"The ant and the grasshopper"

The Blund home, Logan, Utah, 28 June

Amos thought, *Oh, this ought to be good.* He'd been watching Jason carefully: the changes in his expression, his fluctuating attitude, his eyes flitting here and there—looking at Amos, then looking away suddenly. It was as if there were two people inside Jason's head—more likely, Jason was trying to manipulate him.

"Look, Jason—in fact, all of you," Amos said as he looked from one to another of their visitors. "We've been preparing for a natural disaster or crisis for close to fifteen years. I don't know whether something like that is going to happen—probably not. But we've worked very hard to put together everything we might need, while many people have dismissed the need to be prepared."

"Aesop's fable of the ant and the grasshopper," Megan Parker said quietly.

"What's that?" Jason swung around to look at Megan, obviously upset.

"Aesop's fable," Megan repeated. "The ant warned the grasshopper that he should be storing food for winter, but the grasshopper was enjoying the summer weather and there was still plenty to eat. When the weather turned cold, the grasshopper realized the ant had been right, but it was too late. The grasshopper hadn't prepared and didn't survive the winter."

Everyone went still—the impact of Megan's story apparent. She took her husband's hand and started to cry. Tyler put his arm around her and patted her shoulder.

"I'm one of those," Tyler said sadly, "that started to collect food, water, and emergency supplies back in 2008, but I lost interest when the economy recovered. I thought we were past the problem."

Amos watched the interaction between Megan and Tyler. It was consistent with everything Lillie had told him, after seeing them at church. This was a couple who loved each other deeply. Tyler managed a grocery store, worked regular hours, and spent his spare time with his wife and two kids. They were outside whenever they could be—camping, skiing, and fishing.

Now Brittany choked out a sob.

"We're the grasshopper, aren't we? And you don't have room for us in your ant hill."

Amos watched as Jason rolled his eyes and turned away.

"Brittany, Jason, all of you, listen," Amos said. "I don't know if the reports of a terrorist bomb are true or not. If they are, I don't know if it'll be a danger to us, here in Logan. But, as I told you once before, we're leaving and going far away from here. If it turns out that there's no crisis, we'll be back in a few days looking foolish.

"If, on the slim chance this valley becomes unsafe, I don't

know when we'll be coming out. It could be in a week or in a hundred years. We don't know. But we're going to be stuck with each other, in a small, closed space, twenty-four hours a day, seven days a week, until it's over.

"We've gathered enough supplies for our family to last for a while, but if we let you, or anyone join us, we reduce our chance to outlast the emergency. It's not that we don't want to share, it's just that you have nothing to contribute."

"So yur really leavin'?" Patrick McKensie asked. "Where ya goin'?"

"Well, I'm not really inclined to tell you. It's a special place we've found. There isn't really room for anyone else."

Megan sobbed louder. Tyler looked at her with concern, then turned to Amos.

"Were you serious about the hole in the ground?" he asked.

Megan looked at her husband, disbelief written on her face, and Tyler noticed the look.

"Well, he *did* tell us, last night," he said apologetically. "We thought he was just blowing us off."

"Yes," Amos said. "I was serious."

"Surely this thing will be over within a few weeks at worst, won't it?" Brittany said, with a scowl aimed at Jason.

Amos paused, trying to decide what to tell them. He didn't want to lie, but he didn't think they could handle the whole truth, either. Besides, he wanted them to decide to stay home or go to a local shelter. He spoke as calmly as he could.

"Listen. *We've* heard the reports, too. We don't know if the terrorists have a bomb—we don't know any more than you do.

There's no way to tell if they have a way to deliver a bomb to the United States. The government is trying to neutralize any threat. Even if they do have a bomb, and can deliver it, I don't think Logan will be the most likely place to drop it. I'd guess Washington, D.C. Or maybe New York, Chicago, or somewhere on the West Coast.

"Most likely, nothing will happen and we'll come home in a few weeks with our tails between our legs. I don't know. But this much I *do* know. Being stuck in close quarters, twenty-four hours a day, will put a strain on even the best relationships."

Amos paused, making eye contact with each of their visitors in turn. He needed to make a point—without coming right out and saying it—that they didn't have a *good* relationship to start with.

"We'll be hiding, while you're enjoying the freedom of going to the store when you want. If you have to go to a public shelter for a few days until this blows over," Amos shrugged, "you can think of it as a campout."

Jason stirred restlessly, and Brittany spoke up.

"What if we just stay with you, wherever you're going, for a few days, until the worst is over, then come back here? Wouldn't that work?"

Amos looked at Brittany thoughtfully for a few moments before speaking. She smiled at his hesitation, her eyes moist, but when he finally spoke her face fell and she started to cry.

"Brittany, thank you for your suggestion, and it would be great if it would work. The problem is that, as I said, we're leaving the valley. Our hole doesn't have the room for you. But more importantly, once I close the doors, I don't plan to open them again until I can be sure that any threat, however remote and unlikely it seems now, has passed—for good reason.

"Assume we did let you come along, and then later, let you out," Amos continued, "either because we thought the emergency was over or, more likely, because you couldn't handle the isolation and cramped living conditions. If a real threat came along later, you would want to get back in. But we wouldn't be able to let you in, in case you were contaminated. And, I don't want anyone to know where we are. Bottom line: no one goes out, or in, until this thing is resolved."

Jason cut in, frustration in his voice.

"But if you have a way to verify that there's no disaster, or that the threat has passed, that'd be different, wouldn't it?"

The stoic look on his neighbor's face gave him his answer even before Amos spoke, and he dropped his head into his hands.

"Look, Jason, based on what we've heard so far, the worst I'd expect to see in Logan is a little fallout from the West Coast. The effects would be minimal if you went to a shelter. But my plan for my family is to stay in our hole in cramped living conditions for a long time. Personally, Jason, I don't believe that you—any of you," he said, looking at each of them without turning his head, "would do well under those conditions."

For several minutes, everyone sat quietly, looking around at each other or staring at the floor. Finally, Amos spoke again.

"How much do you know about nuclear fallout?"

There were only shrugs and shaking of heads, then Brittany

answered, looking at her husband.

"Not much, I guess."

"Let me make this simple. Radioactive fallout is like volcanic ash. Some of you are old enough to remember when Mt. Saint Helens erupted back in 1980. The eruption blew the top off the mountain and sent volcanic ash up into the atmosphere. The ash floated on the prevailing wind and settled downwind. In some places it was several inches thick. The amount and distribution of the fallout depended on the force behind the explosion and local weather conditions. The worst it did was disrupt farming for a while and melt the paint off some cars. People in Washington and Idaho wore painter's masks until the rain washed the ash away.

"Most of what we know about the effects of nuclear fallout on people and animals came from the Nevada testing back in the fifties. Most of the downwinders—that's what they called the people in southern Utah who were affected by the fallout—lived for many years. Some of them had medical problems later in life, I won't minimize that, but my point is that nuclear fallout is survivable."

"Yoo min' if me and Kitty talk a bit?" Patrick asked, looking at Amos.

"Go ahead, of course," Amos said. "Feel free to step into the kitchen if you'd like."

Patrick and Kathy stopped just inside the living room and

looked at each other as they held hands. Now in his seventies, Patrick had grown up in rural Arkansas, where he'd had very little formal education. He loved his country, so while he'd been too young to serve in the Korean War, he'd lied about his age when he was seventeen so he could join the army and fight in Vietnam. He had seen the horrors of war and didn't want to live through another one, especially a nuclear conflict. He'd often thought he would rather be among the first to die if war ever reached the U.S.

Patrick and Kathy had been married for nearly forty-five years. Only three years into their marriage, they'd discovered that they wouldn't be able to have children. They'd considered adopting, but had never got around to it, and had ended up being happy with just the two of them. Kathy liked to knit, although her arthritis made it difficult now, and liked to walk, even if she sometimes had to use a cane or a walker. Life wasn't as fun these days as it had once been. They were glad they had each other, but they decided that they really couldn't see a reason to hide in a hole—as Amos had described it—just to extend their lives by a few years. Kathy nodded to Patrick, who bobbed back and forth from one foot to the other, then cleared his throat to speak.

"Kitty an' me, we have a understandin' and we agree we wouldn' do well in the kinda' isolation yer talkin' abou'. We'd be better off stayin' ome or goin' ta one uh them shelters. We're through here. We promise we won' say anythin' to anyone. And we'll deny knowin' where ya' went if anyone asks." He chuckled, then added, "Hey, we don' *know* where yer goin' anyways, so that shouldn' be hard, shouldit?"

Lillie smiled sadly as they walked past her toward the door, still holding hands, Kathy shuffling along next to Patrick. Everyone watched them go.

"Well, we may be back in a couple of weeks, feeling silly," Amos said as Patrick opened the door for his wife. "You two take care."

"We'll do tha'," Patrick replied, looking back, before closing the door behind them.

Amos had been trying to limit his neck motion, but when he turned back to look at the remaining four, he forgot, and winced at the pain. Lillie squeezed his hand and took over.

"Anyone else?" she asked.

"Are you saying we can't go with you? Because, we'd like to go if you'll let us," Brittany said.

"After everything I've said?" Amos asked. "I think you'd hate every minute of it, and we'd all regret that."

"But you'll consider it?" Jason added, hopefully.

Without speaking, Amos made eye contact with Tyler. Tyler cleared his throat and looked at Megan.

"Same here, I guess," he said. "If you'll have us."

Amos tried to look at Lillie, his hand on his neck. He wanted to know what she thought they should do. She patted him on the shoulder—her way of saying that she'd support whatever he decided.

"I'll consider it," Amos said. "But I'm not guaranteeing anything. If—and I really do mean *if*—we decide to invite you to join us, there are going to have to be some strict conditions."

He still hoped that he could scare them off, but if he couldn't then he wanted the rules to come from him, not his family more generally, so that he would be the sole focus of Jason's anger. He had no doubt that Jason would have trouble with some of the conditions.

"First, whether we invite you or not, you will not say anything, to anyone, about what we're doing."

"I thought this was a condition of *being* invited," Jason said irritably. "If we're not invited, what's to keep us from telling people?"

"If I find out that you've spoken to anyone, any possible invitation will be off the table. I need you to promise me now that, no matter what I decide, you will never speak to anyone about this. Do you make that promise?"

He looked around the room, and each of them said they did, including a reluctant Jason.

"Second, if we decide to invite you, we'll provide you with a list of supplies—that list is the minimum that you'll need to get and bring with you. The list will be substantial, so you'll have to take money from your savings."

They all nodded.

"Third, you and any of your children who have jobs or school, will be required to notify your employer or school—on the day that I tell you to—that you'll be away for a few days."

Jason was slow to agree this time, but he eventually joined

the others in nodding his acceptance.

"Fourth, and this is the most important condition. If you're invited and you end up joining us, you have to understand that our group is going to function less like a family and more like a company. I'll be the boss. In effect, our community will be a dictatorship, with me making the decisions and everyone following them without any questioning or debate."

Jason opened his mouth to say something, then shut it again.

"Fifth, everyone will have tasks assigned to them on a rotating basis, like cooking, cleaning—and that includes cleaning toilets—gardening, and so on. I'll decide, fairly, who does what and for how long, based on each person's skills and strengths."

With that, Jason reached his limit.

"Look Amos, I'm an accountant, a corporate controller, not some house cleaner."

"What's your point?" Amos asked. *Maybe Jason will back out.* He could only hope.

"My point is that I can do your books and keep your records, things like that, instead of cleaning toilets and gardening."

He spit the last words out as if just saying them left a bitter taste in his mouth.

"Jason, we don't need an accountant. We *will* need house cleaners and gardeners."

Jason started to get up, but Brittany grabbed him by the arm and pulled him off his feet with a dirty look. He landed back on the couch with an *umph.*

"If I go, I'll be doing it for my family," he said, indignantly.

"If it were just me, I wouldn't bother."

That's a lousy reason for making such a huge commitment, Amos thought.

"I hope your family appreciates the sacrifice you're making," was what he said instead, though even this earned him a dirty look from Jason.

Amos turned to Tyler with a questioning expression, inviting him to say what was on his mind.

"I suppose I'd like to know more about what we'd need to contribute to this operation before we make a decision," Tyler said. "After that, we'll just hope and pray you invite us to join you."

Amos reached up and patted Lillie's hand. He wanted to look at her, but the pain in his neck wouldn't let him.

"Will you get a couple of lists for them?" he asked her. "While Lillie gets a list, remember that this version is based on the needs of my family, not yours. You can take a look at it, but if we invite you to join us then the list you get may not be exactly the same."

Everyone sat silently while Lillie was gone. She returned a few minutes later with two stapled stacks of paper containing copies of their lists of supplies and assignments. Amos looked through one, then tore off a couple of pages from the back of each. He returned them to Lillie, who handed one each to Jason and Tyler.

"The first pages are personal supplies. The others are group supplies. *If* we invite you to join us, you'll need to get as many of those things as you can in the time that's left before we leave."

Tyler, who had been looking over the list with his wife, Megan, silently pointed to a couple of things on the list.

"What if we don't have a lot of the things on the list?"

Brittany was trying to look over Jason's arm to see the list, but Jason, oblivious, wasn't making it easy, and in the end she stood up and leaned over him. He finally noticed and turned the paper so she could see it.

"We liquidated almost all of our assets to buy the things we needed," Amos said. "You can't eat your money. And you can't brush your teeth with it—though I guess you could try."

The last comment came with a chuckle, and Tyler and Megan smiled. Brittany joined in a moment later, but Jason didn't even acknowledge the attempt at humor, and Amos moved along.

"Tell you what, take the lists and look them over. Decide whether or not you can come up with everything on the lists *and* whether or not you can live with my conditions. You have twenty-four hours to make a decision about whether you think it would be in your best interest to join us. In the meantime, Lillie and I will decide whether we're extending any invitations. We'll talk again tomorrow with each family individually. If your children are going to have input into your decision, then they have to agree to my conditions first. Then, if you decide you want to go with us, and if we offer an invitation, you'll have until July second to get everything ready to go."

"July second?" Jason complained. "I've got a job with deadlines, I can't just drop everything to prepare for this."

"I told you that was one of the conditions, Jason. And I'm not the one setting the timetable. Today's June twenty-eighth. The terrorists' deadline is July fourth, next Wednesday—by then, we have to be gone. If you can't accept that, just let me know. I'm not going to be offended, and I have no problem leaving you off the guest list. As I said, we don't have that much room."

Jason looked like he wanted to protest again, and opened his mouth, but shut it again without saying anything. His expression made it clear that he wasn't happy.

"We've already notified our jobs that we're taking some vacation starting Monday, and we'll be telling the university tomorrow that we'll be out of town for a few days. After that, we'll either come back or we won't, depending on events. You need to decide whether you can do the same, but you obviously wouldn't want to quit your job before we've decided whether or not to extend an invitation."

Jason glared at Amos, but said nothing. *Just say forget it,* Amos thought, *that you're not going. Make this easy on all of us.*

Tyler and Megan got up, excusing themselves.

"We have a lot to think about," Tyler said. "Thanks for the information—and thank you very much for at least considering letting our family join yours. We'll get back to you tomorrow."

Lillie showed them out. Meanwhile, Jason huffed as Brittany rose from the couch and pulled on his arm.

"Come on. We can talk at home," she said, then turned to Amos. "Thank you for being direct with us. We'll have a serious discussion about this and get back to you tomorrow, too. I really hope you'll believe in us and let us come with you."

Lillie held the door open.

"Thanks Lillie," Brittany said as they passed.

Jason jerked his arm away from his wife as they left, and they'd started arguing before they reached the sidewalk. Amos and Lillie looked at each other, letting out a breath they had each been holding. Lillie laughed quietly.

"Well, that went well."

"Where have I heard that recently?" Amos wondered aloud with a nervous laugh.

Shaking her head, Lillie returned to the living room and sat carefully on Amos's lap. She laid her head on his good shoulder and sighed, hugging him as he tickled her back affectionately.

"And I thought I had a headache *before*," he said.

At the family council that night, Rachel confirmed that Terry and Mike were safely at the Preserve, setting things up.

Amos explained about their visitors, and that their final departure, originally planned for the next night, might now have to be spread over the next several days. He stretched his stiff neck cautiously as he spoke.

"I told them I still needed to decide whether to invite them, but actually, if they agree to my conditions, I can't in good conscience leave them behind. So, if they decide to join us, I'll need some help loading up their stuff. We won't know until they get back to us tomorrow how much stuff that'll be, if any. I'm going to insist that we use only our vehicles, though, because of the limited space at the Preserve."

"I don't like it," Emily complained.

"Well, I don't like it either," Amos said. "But we knew that if word got out, there was a risk we might have to let others come along."

"No, I mean I don't like the idea of us splitting up or delaying our departure. What if something goes wrong and we can't all get to the Preserve in time? What if someone follows them over here or sees us hauling out their stuff? We could be followed and confronted—or worse."

Amos knew she was thinking about Jason's attack on him the night before.

"What if we just leave tonight?" Emily continued. "We could ditch them."

"I understand your concern," Amos said. "But we can't ditch them. We told them we'd give them until tomorrow to let us know if they would accept my conditions. I'm not going to break my word. Plus, we aren't quite ready to leave."

Emily frowned, pulling Matt's arm tighter around her. Amos's integrity meant a lot to him, and his family knew it.

"We'll just have to be extra careful," Amos continued. "So far, no one has tried to follow us that we've been able to detect. If someone *does* follow, we follow the plan. First, take a roundabout route through the city to the mouth of the canyon. If they're still following, we try to shake them in the canyon. If they stay on our tail, we bypass the turnoff to the Preserve and go into Garden City. The keys to the Bear Lake condo we rented should be on the truck key chain."

"They are," Rachel said.

"Good. That way, we can go straight to the condo and see if whoever's tailing us follows. About your other concern, we carry guns and be prepared to use them."

"I don't know, Amos," Lillie sighed. "About the guns, I mean. We know how to use them, but, I'm not sure if I can really shoot someone."

"You will if they have a gun pointed at you," Matt said, looking at Emily.

"Okay," Amos said calmly, putting an arm around Lillie's waist. He knew she couldn't shoot anyone. He wasn't even sure that he could. "I'm sure we'll all be able to do what needs to be done. Anything else? Emily and Matt, how are you coming on your supplies?"

"Good Dad," Emily said. "Does this mean we have until next week to get everything ready?"

"No. I want you two out of here as soon as possible—tomorrow preferably. Can you make it happen?"

"We're trying," Matt replied. "Is it more important for me to get everything on the list or to be ready to go tomorrow?"

Amos thought for a moment.

"Be ready to go tomorrow night if you can."

He'd be happiest if he could get his whole family out of the valley tomorrow, but he needed help with the moving until his neck improved.

"Okay Dad," Emily said, looking at Matt, who smiled at her.

"Let's get the rest of the supplies loaded tonight so we'll

have room for the Parkers' and Carlsens' stuff to go tomorrow, if necessary," Amos said.

"And we'll have a family prayer tonight," Lillie added. "For your protection, before you leave."

Amos started to stand. He flinched at a sharp pain in his neck and stopped. Lillie went to him immediately, sitting him back down.

"I've got it Dad," Rachel said. "You take it easy for a day or two."

"Lousy timing," Amos said, scowling.

12

"We've decided you can go"

Logan, Utah, 29 June

"Hello, Lillie? It's Megan."

"Hi Megan."

Even though Lillie was expecting the call, she still hadn't decided quite what to say, so they both waited an awkward minute until Megan spoke again.

"We've decided to go with you, if you'll have us. Tyler is out shopping, just in case. The kids and I are getting ready to pack. Have you and Amos made up your mind?"

The words, "yes, we decided you can't come," crossed Lillie's mind, but she knew she couldn't say them. They had already decided the Parkers and Carlsens would be invited if they could live with Amos's rules. There were already ten people going to the Preserve, including Matthew. Megan's family would add four more. They would have to make a few changes at the Preserve to handle the extra load.

Lillie thought that Amos should do most of the talking, but she didn't want to keep their neighbors in suspense, either, so she gave her the bottom line.

"We've decided that your family would be a welcome addition. When Tyler gets home, have him call and talk to Amos. The details will depend on how much you have that needs to be loaded into the trailer."

"That's wonderful Lillie! Thank you so much. This means so much to me and my family."

"You're welcome, Megan," Lillie said, trying to keep the frustration out of her voice as she hung up the phone.

At the Carlsens' house next door, Jason, Brittany, and their daughter, Sydney, were sitting in the family room, waiting for Nathan and Aaron to make an appearance. Sydney was playing a game on her phone, and Brittany was envious of her ignorant bliss. Jason was on his phone, probably checking his work email. He was oblivious, as usual, to both Brittany and Sydney.

Brittany thought about her conversation with Jason the night before. Her main concern had been whether or not they could get ready in time, if they were even invited, and whether the children would accept the change in lifestyle. Then Jason had made the mistake of announcing that there was no way he'd ever allow Amos to control his life—they'd argued for hours after that, and Brittany had shed a lot of tears. Now she was just trying to save her family from disintegrating.

"Did you wake them?" Brittany finally asked.

"Yes," Jason replied impatiently without looking up from his phone. "Apparently, they had a long, hard night out with friends."

There was nothing more to say, so Brittany simply sat and worried. The boys finally sauntered into the room, shooing their sister off the couch and dropping onto it, barely awake. Sydney relocated to the floor—being evicted from the sofa by her brothers was nothing new.

"What's so important that you couldn't let us sleep?" Aaron grumbled.

He was bare-chested, barefoot, and his pants hung so low that three inches of his plaid boxers were showing. He had dark shaggy hair hanging in his eyes and several inches down his back. He was tanned and strong, and he obviously loved to show it off. The tattoos on his arms and upper chest rippled as his muscles flexed. Nathan was a skinnier version of his brother, without the tattoos.

"Can't you at least wear clothes when your sister is in the room?" Brittany asked.

She was embarrassed and irritated, but Sydney, sitting cross-legged on the carpet, didn't seem surprised by her brothers' appearance. She didn't even look up. Aaron just glared at his mother.

"Sorr . . . " Nathan began, but stopped when Aaron turned the glare in his direction. Brittany rolled her eyes.

"We have a proposition for you," Jason began. "One of our neighbors has a secret hiding place somewhere around here. They've been stashing emergency supplies, preparing for an evacuation."

That got Sydney's attention. Brittany gasped, turning on her husband.

"Jason, that's no way to explain it."

Jason motioned with one hand for her to take the floor, so she took a deep breath and started talking, her eyes not straying from Jason's.

"These neighbors have been preparing for many years for any type of emergency, like this terrorist threat—"

Aaron interrupted, his tone blasé.

"What terrorist threat?"

Brittany was astonished.

"What do you mean 'what terrorist threat'? Haven't you seen the news? Terrorists have threatened to detonate a nuclear bomb somewhere in the United States on July fourth."

"Psshhh," Aaron said, exhaling rudely but looking a little more tuned in. "It'd serve us right, the way we treat the rest of the world. So, what do you mean by a stash of emergency supplies."

Sydney was looking back and forth between them now, as if she were watching a ping-pong match.

"It's not a 'stash,'" Brittany said. "They've supplied and stocked their emergency retreat and they're considering inviting us to join them, if we can follow a few rules."

Jason snorted, and Brittany turned to give him a dirty look.

"What?" Jason asked, pretending innocence. "They aren't inviting us. They all but told us we couldn't go."

Brittany was still staring at Jason when Aaron spoke up again.

"What do we have to do?"

"Well, *if* we're invited—"

She paused, thinking about how she would answer the question. She wanted to be enthusiastic, to get Sydney to think of it as an adventure, but Aaron's responses kept putting her on the defensive. She finally continued, trying to sound encouraging.

"We'll buy our supplies, take them to the neighbors, then go—"

"You have to give them your stuff?" Aaron demanded, interrupting her. "You trust them not to take your stuff, then stiff you?"

"What?" Brittany asked, off-balance again. "What are you talking about? These are good people who care about their family and neighbors."

Aaron's attitude was frustrating her, and Jason wasn't helping. He started to laugh, and they all turned toward him.

"What's so funny, Jason?" she demanded, furious. She had to fight back tears.

"You make it sound like they spoke to us out of the kindness of their hearts, and that they're really considering inviting us." Jason looked at Aaron. "The truth is that they lied to us to keep us from finding out—they were keeping it a secret. We confronted them, and they had no choice any more—they had to consider inviting us so we wouldn't tell anyone. And we still don't know if we're even invited."

"Jason!" Brittany exclaimed, tears coming to her eyes finally. "How dare you! They're being very generous."

Jason just snorted again.

"Who are these neighbors?" Aaron asked.

He tried to downplay his interest, but he had immediately

focused on news of a *stash*, wondering what was in it. Jason opened his mouth to tell Aaron, but Brittany stopped him with a shout.

"*Jason!* You promised!"

Jason shrugged, but he kept quiet. Brittany blinked tears out of her eyes—she refused to wipe them as they rolled down her cheeks. Aaron looked back and forth at his parents, trying to figure out what was going on. Brittany continued to glare at Jason for a spell, while Jason smirked. Finally, Brittany looked back at the children and continued.

"The decision we have to make is whether or not we can live with certain rules—"

Aaron interrupted again, jumping ahead of his mother. He really was quite intelligent, just poorly motivated.

"What's the downside?"

Brittany didn't trust herself to answer—she was too close to losing control of her emotions. After a moment Jason answered.

"We have to agree to live underground, twenty-four seven, and follow orders from a dictator."

"Jason!"

Brittany was shouting now, pulling a tissue out of her pocket to wipe her eyes and blow her nose, all eyes on her. She glared at Jason through her tears.

"Okay, okay."

Jason put on a sincere tone, both hands up, palms facing Brittany as if fending off an attack, but he was still grinning.

"Not interested," Aaron said after a moment.

"Me neither," Nathan said, following his brother's lead.

Brittany looked from Aaron to Nathan, then at Jason. She was afraid she knew where this was leading. Their marriage had been shaky for some time now, beginning three years earlier when Jason had gone to Las Vegas for a week without telling her. He'd said it was a business trip, but their relationship hadn't been the same since. She'd never found out what Jason had done there, but she had her suspicions, and ever since it had been hard to trust anything he said. Jason had never mistreated her physically, but his attitude toward their marriage and her interests showed just how little he still cared. She had hoped this crisis might bridge the gap and bring them closer together, but now she had to wonder. *Maybe Jason sees this as his way out of a marriage that no longer makes him happy,* she thought. *And maybe it's the best thing for me, too.*

"I guess I'll have to stay and watch these two," Jason said, trying to wipe the grin off his face, but failing. "But I'll go get the supplies you need later today assuming, ol' A—um, I mean—assuming the neighbors extend a warm invitation." Turning toward the boys, he added, "You two want to help me shop for supplies for your mom and sister?"

"I'm going back to bed."

Aaron got up and sauntered out of the room, a tattoo of an eagle—with it wings spread across his back from shoulder to shoulder—stretching taut as he walked.

"Me too," Nathan added quickly, rushing to catch up with Aaron.

Sydney watched her mother, concern etched across her face.

Jason seemed indifferent to her quiet sobbing. Brittany took a deep breath, exhaled, wiped her eyes again, then handed Jason and Sydney copies of the supply list Amos had given them. They looked at it in silence as Brittany wept.

Aaron thought about his dad's comments and his mom's reaction. It was clear that there was a rift between his parents over going to the crazy neighbors' retreat. That didn't interest him, but the stash of emergency supplies did. *Definitely worth looking into,* he thought.

He knew he'd frustrated his mom with all his interruptions and questions. *Whatever.* He wasn't going to lead his mother on if she was serious about going. He would have to get his dad alone to find out what was really happening.

He smiled, thinking of his mom's reaction to the way he dressed. Years earlier they'd argued about his clothes, his hair, and his tattoos, but she'd finally given up trying to correct his 'bad behavior,' as she called it. He knew she'd been glaring at his eagle as he sauntered out of the room, and he reveled in it. He liked his lifestyle—it suited him.

Lillie answered the door, wiping her flour-covered hands self-consciously on her apron.

"Hello, Lillie. Can I come in?"

Brittany's voice was shaky, she looked worried, and she'd clearly been crying.

"Of course, Brittany."

Lillie reached out to touch Brittany's arm, trying to comfort her a little, then led her into the kitchen, where she'd been rolling out bread dough.

"Sit down," Lillie said, pointing to a chair at the table. She washed her hands at the sink, dried them on a towel, and sat down next to her neighbor, taking some time to decide how to handle the situation. It was clear that Brittany and Jason had argued. *Maybe they've decided not to go,* she thought hopefully.

"You look upset. Problem with the family?"

"Jason and I talked about our options for a long time last night. We noticed when the Stephens arrived at your house. We were still talking when the trailer pulled out in the middle of the night."

Brittany paused, and Lillie waited, suspecting that she wasn't sure how much she should say. She might be embarrassed by how difficult Jason was being, or how poorly the conversation had gone. Finally, Brittany squirmed a little, then continued.

"We kept our daughter home from her art class this morning to talk to her along with the boys." She stopped again and took a quivering breath before going on. "Aaron, you know, is eighteen. He runs with a tough crowd. Nathan follows his brother around like a sheep, and Aaron encourages it. Nathan even skips school. A lot. I think that's why they've never really gotten to know your Rachel, or Rebecca Stephens's son Chris. I think they've lost interest in anything to do with the family and they don't spend much time at home. To them it's nothing but a bed and a pantry. Jason says he can relate to them—he was a little wild in his youth, I guess—but he's never spent much time with them or tried to correct their behavior. He thinks they'll grow out of it."

Brittany tried to smile, but it looked awkward—she was clearly embarrassment.

Yeah, look how Jason turned out, Lillie thought. She was curious about what decision Brittany and Jason had reached the night before, if any, but decided not to ask. Instead, she continued to wait patiently and soon Brittany's mind returned from wherever her thoughts had taken her. She spoke with more conviction now.

"The bottom line is that I want to go with you and bring my daughter, if you'll have us. Aaron and Nathan refuse to leave their friends, and Jason thinks he needs to stay to watch out for them. I personally think he has other issues . . . " She paused, then made herself go on. "I just let it go because I agree that the boys need him, if only to keep the house open and stocked with food. Have you and Amos decided about whether you'll let us go with you?"

Lillie thought about how to reply. She had mixed feelings. She'd hoped the Carlsens would decide not to go, but she really liked Brittany and would be fine if Brittany went as long as she left Jason behind. She felt torn between being disappointed and pleased.

"We've decided you can go," she finally said. "Assuming you can obey the rules and comply with Amos's instructions from last night."

Brittany's eyes lit up.

"Oh, thank you Lillie!"

"What does Sydney think of it?"

"Well, I think she's excited for the adventure of it. She's concerned for Jason and her brothers but she's smart enough to figure this out, I know it."

"Do you think you'll have any problem getting the supplies?"

"Jason is planning to go shopping and take Sydney with him. They're ready to leave as soon as I tell them we can go. You'll want to know how much we're packing, won't you?"

"Yes. Will you call me when Jason is through with the shopping and give me an idea of what to expect?"

"Of course. Thank you. I'd better get back now. I need to start packing."

Brittany got up to leave, and Lillie walked her to the door.

"Are you going to be okay?"

That was when Brittany broke down and cried.

"I don't know, Lillie. This is not how I wanted things to go."

Lillie put an arm around her shoulder, pulling her close. *Poor woman, she's made the decision to leave part of her family behind, maybe forever.* Brittany buried her face in Lillie's shoulder and cried for a few moments, then backed up, sniffling. She pulled a clean tissue out of her pocket and blew her nose. Lillie patted her on the shoulder, but couldn't think of anything to say that would make things any better, so she just smiled. Brittany forced a smile in return as she wiped her eyes, then took another shuttering breath.

"It won't do for Sydney to see me with weepy eyes." She sniffed. "Thank you again. I'll get back to you as soon as I can."

When she was gone, Lillie closed the door, leaned her back against it, and sighed.

Aaron walked into the kitchen, his strut telling anyone who might be watching that he was in charge. He wore a gray tank top, faded jeans, and Nike Air Jordans with ankle socks. He opened the fridge, looked around inside, then lifted a covered plate of leftover fried chicken with one hand. He grabbed a carton of milk with the other and took both to the counter. Nathan followed, waiting until Aaron had moved away from the fridge. He tended to stay out of Aaron's way, a habit that Aaron actively encouraged. Nathan went to the cupboards to get a bowl and box of cold cereal, closing the fridge door on his way past.

While Aaron was eating a breaded chicken leg with both hands, crumbs dropping onto the counter and floor, Nathan poured his cereal then added milk.

Aaron, watching Nathan out of the corner of his eye, threw the chicken bone at the kitchen sink, where it bounced in, then out again, and onto the counter. He lifted the milk carton and took a couple of large swallows. Then he dropped the carton to the counter hard enough that milk from the half-full box splashed out onto the counter. He turned toward the fridge and wiped his greasy hands on a dish towel hanging on the fridge door. He was testing Nathan. Would Nathan blindly follow, or did he still have a brain in that tiny little head of his? Nathan looked back to his bowl and took a bite of cereal.

Aaron grunted in disgust at his younger brother's weakness. He was just opening the fridge to see what else he could find, when Jason came in, Sydney following on his heels. Both of them carried shopping bags filled to the brim. Sydney was smiling and talking animatedly to her dad's back, oblivious to the fact that Jason wasn't holding up his end of the conversation. Sydney quieted as soon as she saw Aaron and Nathan.

"Boys." Jason acknowledged his sons with a nod, then called out loudly. "Brittany?"

"In the family room."

After setting heavy bags filled with packaged goods on the counter, Jason continued on into the family room. Sydney followed, hanging on to her bags possessively. Nathan finished his cereal, rinsed the bowl, and left it in the sink, then opened the cupboard under the sink and dropped Aaron's chicken bone into the garbage can. Finally, he covered the plate of chicken and put the lid on the milk carton. Aaron grumbled without bothering to turn and look.

"I saw that."

But he moved out of the way so Nathan could return the chicken and milk to the fridge—he had more important things on his mind. Shifting closer to the family room, he tried to hear what was going on. He hadn't had a chance to talk to his dad, but maybe he could learn something eavesdropping.

" . . . and we got most of the clothes on the list from the thrift store, like you said. I sure as hell hope no one I know saw me there. I'd never live it down if someone from work saw me in a *thrift store*."

Aaron couldn't hear his mother's response.

"Yes, Sydney's excited about the clothes she found. Lots of t-shirts and jeans, sturdy shoes, just like you said. Plus, we got the coats, hats, and gloves. I did everything you wanted, so calm down."

"Look what I found," Sydney said breathlessly.

Aaron could hear rustling of the shopping bags and Sydney squealing with excitement as she showed her mother her new treasures, but once again couldn't hear what his mother said.

"Yes *dear*," Jason continued, sarcastically. "I stopped at the Family Store and bought the underwear. I wasn't going to have her wearing someone else's discarded panties. We unloaded the cases of food and the rest of the clothes and stacked them in the garage. I couldn't find all the equipment on the list, but what I could find, is stacked with the rest. Now my back hurts. Are you happy?"

Aaron had moved closer to the door and thought he heard his mother say something about money, which piqued his interest.

"Fine. I'll go out again and look for the rest of the stuff. Money? Here's six thousand in small bills. You're robbing me blind here, you know. I stopped at a coin shop on the way home and gave them five hundred down on some junk coins and silver and gold bullion. Beats me why Amos wants that worthless crap. The dealer has about twelve thousand in junk coins and as much bullion as you need. He said he would hold it for me for one hour while I get a cashier's check for the balance. Now, I need to get going or I won't make it."

Aaron backed up suddenly when he heard his dad's footsteps on the hardwood floor. He bumped into Nathan who was leaning over his shoulder, also trying to hear, nearly knocking him over. Nathan scrambled out of the way and Aaron moved to the sink, bending his head under the tap to get a drink of water. Nathan leaned against the counter. He looked guiltily at his father as Jason hurried back through the kitchen, absentmindedly nodding to them as he went.

"Stupid!"

Aaron hissed the word in his brother's ear as he pulled him outside by the arm. Making certain Jason had gone, Aaron walked quickly to his restored, 1958, powder-blue Impala, with the distinctive red-and-yellow flames painted on the hood and down both sides.

"Get in," he told Nathan, who obeyed without question.

As they were pulling away, Nathan finally spoke up.

"Where are we going?"

Aaron smirked.

"To get rich."

13

"We just need to follow them"

The low lighting in the bar left their faces mostly in shadow. Aaron moved his beer bottle around in the pool of moisture dripping off the cold bottle, then looked up at the two men seated across the table from him. They were both dressed in t-shirts, jeans, and sneakers, and both looked to be in their late teens or early twenties. Jordan—Aaron called him Jord—had greasy blond hair than hung limply against his head and so many tattoos that his pale skin looked black in places. He was working on his second beer, moving unnaturally, like he was drunk or high, and tapping his foot nervously on the floor. Deshaun—Aaron called him Duke—had dreadlocks, and a scar on his left cheek that gave him a dimple—it looked incongruous with his sour expression. He was calmly nursing his first beer, the look in his eyes reminding Nathan that he was dangerous. The sparse clientele at this time of the afternoon made Bicardo's Tavern a good place to meet anonymously and talk without being overheard. Bicardo's was also notorious, at least among the younger crowd, for its laxity with drinking laws.

Nathan sat next to Aaron, peering out the window. He had a beer but was only pretending to drink it. He also had a glass of water that he sipped from time to time. The neon beer logo in the window flickered sporadically, the sound of static from its tubes making Nathan jump. He didn't know these guys very well, and he didn't like the looks of them.

"They have a stash somewhere close by. We just need to follow them and take it," Aaron said.

That brought Nathan back from his ruminations. Across the table, Jordan took a swig from his bottle with a shaky hand.

"What kinda stash?" he asked.

"Mostly stupid stuff, like food and clothes," Aaron said. "But there's also cash, plus silver and gold."

That got their attention. Duke looked up from the table, where he'd been doodling with his index finger in the condensation from his beer bottle.

"Are you thinking of robbing Mom?" Nathan asked, startled.

Aaron gave him a look.

"Weren't you paying attention, lamebrain? There are other families going with them, so multiply that by at least three or four."

Their parents hadn't said how many families were going, so Nathan knew Aaron was making that part up—but these guys had no idea, so Aaron could say whatever he wanted. Turning to Jordan, Aaron continued laying out his plan.

"We'll need your ride to follow them tonight. They might recognize mine."

"Well, duh, you moron," Duke said. "If you hadn't put those

stupid flames on it, it wouldn't be so easy to spot."

"Too late to worry about that now, Duke, but we still need Jord's car since you can't drive."

"I drive when I want," Duke said defensively.

"Illegally," Jordan said with a snort, tapping furiously with his foot.

"Enough. Are you guys in?" Aaron asked.

"What's the take and what do we have to do?" Jordan asked.

"My old man," Aaron said, "was talkin' about six Gs cash and at least double that in gold and silver. Multiply that by three families, and I'd say the take is at least sixty thou'. That's fifteen each. If my mom's involved, this is probably a simple case of following them to the stash and waiting until they leave to get another load of stuff to hide away. While they're gone, we grab it."

"That's too simple man," Duke said. "It's never that simple, which means it's the wrong way. We need to find the target, stake it out for a while, and then decide how to do it."

"Okay, Duke, you're the expert. I'm sure you learned more about this kind of thing during your time in the clink than I'll ever know. You tell us what we should do. But I don't think there's time to stake it out. They have a deadline."

Duke stiffened at the mention of his jail time—he still had nightmares about it. It had been six months of hell, but he forced himself to put on a proud face and snorted.

"You softenin' me up or what?"

He paused while they studied each other, and Jordan took the opportunity to ask a question.

"What if something goes south? This is your mom and sister we're talking about."

"Yeah, Jord. Well, if we decide it's worth the effort, then we try not to hurt the women and children."

Aaron smiled, but the smile didn't reach his eyes.

"Meaning what?" Duke asked. "Are you talkin' about beating on these people? Bringing guns? What?"

"Come on Duke. This is a bunch of turn-the-other-cheek Christians we're talkin' about. Still, if it comes to it, we better have some kind of weapons with us. What do you have?"

"I prefer a knife. It's quiet and scary. It flashes in the light."

Duke's face lit up with an evil grin and he laughed. He could see that Aaron's kid brother was bug-eyed at the image of a knife flashing in the light. Or, maybe it was the idea of using a knife on his mom and kid sister. The truth was, the one time he had been caught during a break-in, all he'd had was a knife, while the homeowner, who'd showed up unexpectedly, had had a gun. If he ever did a break-in again, he was going to take his gun.

"But you can take whatever you want man," he said to the others.

"Let's talk about tonight," Aaron said.

"As you know, the Parkers want to go. So that's four more," Amos said during the family council that night.

"Brittany Carlsen and her daughter want to go, too," Lillie added. "That's two more, plus their supplies."

Most of the family was prepared for this, but there were a few groans as others thought about it.

"That's sixteen people," Emily said, frustration in her voice. "It means another trip and another couple of days of being split up."

"And that much more time for problems," Katie Stephens added.

Katie was sitting next to Mike, their thighs touching. Mike kept glancing at her hand which rested against his leg, warming it—it felt good. He didn't move or speak, he almost didn't breathe, for fear she'd move her hand if he drew attention to himself.

"It's been straightforward so far," Katie continued.

"And we want it to stay that way," Lillie said. "Emily, we need to deal with this. Maybe you should work out a schedule to get everyone there by Monday night."

"Sure," Emily said, then added, mostly to herself, "What a pain."

Lillie smiled, and a couple of the others chuckled.

"We were already planning on you and Matt bringing an extra car," Lillie said. "We can do that, or Tyler Parker has offered to take his SUV, which might be a better option if we need the extra car."

Emily nodded, whispering to Matt and making notes on

the back of her stack of papers.

"I'd rather take Terry's SUV than Tyler's, Lillie," Amos said. "Emily, let us know what works."

"How much space do we need on the trailer for their supplies?" Emily asked distractedly, still talking to Matt and writing.

"Can't say," Lillie replied. "We haven't seen their supplies, and so far they only have part of what they need to get. They'll gather the rest tomorrow . . . or not. I think we should give them a cutoff time."

"Can we load up *some* of their stuff on the trailer for tonight's trip?" Emily asked.

"And can we take some of them up to the Preserve tonight?" Katie Stephens added.

"The Parkers are probably okay with us taking some of their stuff, but Brittany's concerned about Jason's attitude. We'll ask while you're finishing loading. Who's ready to go—and to stay?"

Amos walked into the lab trailer bay to find his daughter, Rachel, and Chris Stephens tying down the load on the trailer.

"How much room do you still have?" he asked. "Both families said we can pick up their stuff. Brittany, next door, said she'd like to see her daughter go tonight. Her boys have been acting strange and she wants Sydney out of the house."

"Do you want us to drive the trailer over?" Rachel asked.

"No," Amos said. "But it wouldn't hurt to take the pickup

over so you don't have to walk everything back. Your mother's gone over to talk to Brittany and Sydney so that Sydney will feel more comfortable about going with us. Talk to your mother when you get there to see how you can help."

"Okay," Rachel said. "Come on, Chris."

They quickly disconnected the trailer from the pickup, climbed in, and drove next door.

Brittany led Lillie into the living room to talk with Sydney. Aaron and Nathan were sitting at the kitchen table, eating leftovers. Sydney wanted to know everything about where they were going, how long they would be there, what there was to do, and when her mom would be joining them. Brittany knew Lillie was being intentionally vague because the boys were within earshot and she didn't want them to have details since they weren't going along. The less said, the less that could go wrong in the next few days.

When Rachel and Chris arrived, Brittany led them through the kitchen to the family room, pausing momentarily to say something to the boys about cleaning up after themselves—and in that moment she detected a real tension in the room. It seemed to her that Aaron was sizing up Rachel and Chris in some way, and Chris appeared to be doing the same with Aaron and Nathan. Chris and Aaron had played together when they were much younger, but they'd had little to do with each other in the years since then.

After a few tense moments, Brittany led Rachel and Chris into the living room, where Lillie was still talking to Sydney. They waited patiently while Lillie finished answering a few more questions. Then Brittany led them into Sydney's bedroom to disassemble some of her furniture and move it out to the truck. She also showed them where the supplies were in the garage. She didn't bother asking Aaron or Nathan to help.

As soon as Aaron saw Rachel and Chris, he realized who the turn-the-other-cheek Christians were that his mother was joining. *Rachel Blund and Chris Stephens,* he thought with a smirk. *No problem.* He couldn't remember their parents all that well, but he decided that his plan would work—they'd be easy to follow now that he knew who they were.

Logan, Utah, 30 June, 2:00 am

At 2:00 a.m., Rachel pulled out of the garage with Chris next to her in the front seat of the cab. Sleepy-eyed, Sydney Carlsen was belted into the back seat with Katie and Becca Stephens. Becca had tried—successfully, or so it seemed—to help Sydney feel better about leaving her mother at home, making the trip seem like a fun adventure, and until Sydney realized she would be away from mom, staying in a strange place overnight with people she didn't know very well, everything had worked out as planned. She'd had a near panic attack for a few moments when they'd first climbed into the truck, but now, tucked into the cab with her tablet, earbuds, and favorite music, she began to doze. Rachel and Chris planned to leave the others at the Preserve before returning home in the early hours of the morning.

Down the street from the Blund home, Aaron Carlsen sat in the passenger seat of Jordan's dark gray Nissan, with Nathan and Duke in the back. Knowing that someone was headed out tonight, they hoped to see where the truck and trailer would go. The quarter moon would give them a little light, so Duke told Jordan to drive without headlights as long as possible.

Duke knew that there was no traffic on the roads at this time of night, which meant they'd stick out like a sore thumb as soon as they turned on their headlights. But with his police record, he couldn't afford to be pulled over by a cop hiding along the way somewhere. So, lights on or off, this was going to be tricky.

The truck, pulling the trailer, turned right on Mendon Road and headed east. Jordan let it get half a mile up the road, then started the engine and followed with the lights off. The truck turned left on Park Avenue and followed as the road ambled first right, then left.

"Hit the lights," Duke said. "Cops like to hide out around

that bend up ahead.”

Jordan glanced in the rearview mirror, and in the light from a passing street lamp he saw a look on Duke's face that he'd never seen before: Duke was scared.

Looking in her rearview mirror, Rachel noticed headlights behind them. There was nothing unusual about that in itself—it stood out simply because it was two in the morning. Someone had, more than likely, just turned in from a side street. She knew there was construction ahead, so she turned right onto Center Street to avoid it. The car behind her followed. Knowing this was the most direct route into town, made sense for the car to turn the same way she had, but her dad had warned them to be on the lookout, so, to satisfy her curiosity, Rachel turned left at the next intersection rather than going on toward Main. Chris looked at Rachel, surprised.

“Why didn't you go straight on to Main?”

“Just a precaution,” Rachel said.

When the car turned to follow, Rachel spoke again, this time enunciating carefully.

“Call Dad.”

Her phone was paired with the truck by Bluetooth, and the phone automatically called Amos's mobile phone.

“Hi Rachel, what's up?” Amos asked.

“I think we have a tail,” Rachel said quietly.

Chris turned in his seat to look out the rear window, Becca

and Katie following his lead

"Are they following us?" Becca asked, her voice shaky. But Rachel was too preoccupied to answer.

"Hmm. Where are you?" Amos asked.

"We just turned off Center onto Third West."

"Third West?"

"Yeah. I got suspicious, so I turned to see if they would follow us, and they did."

"What do you want to do?

"I'm not sure, Dad. Maybe it's nothing."

"If they follow you all the way to Main, why don't you go north on Main, far enough that it looks like you're headed out of town, but then pull over to the curb before you get to Tenth North. If they're not following you, they'll turn off or keep going. If they're following you, they'll probably keep going to try to make it look like they're not. You can turn on Tenth and lose them through the neighborhoods."

"Okay, hang on a minute. Just turning east on Second North now. Hmm, they didn't follow us on the turn," Rachel told her dad. "But they also didn't pass by the street. They either stopped or turned another direction. Maybe it was nothing after all."

"I hate to sound paranoid, but keep an eye open when you turn onto Main. I'll stay on the line."

"You think maybe they turned a street early and they're trying to get ahead of us?"

"Or follow you at a distance. You'll be easy to find again on Main."

In the Nissan, Jordan followed the truck onto Third West.

"Why did they turn on Third West?" Aaron thought out loud. "Where are they going?"

"Maybe they're going to double back on Second North and go west?" Jordan suggested.

Ahead of them, the truck turned onto Second North—also known as state Highway 30—but it turned right instead of left.

"Should I follow them?" Jordan asked, unwilling to make a decision that Aaron or Duke might counter.

Aaron made a snap decision. If they'd been spotted, they needed it to look like they weren't following. *That trailer will be easy enough to find again,* he thought.

"Turn right here and parallel them. Speed up so we can see if they turn again."

Rachel slowed at the light, which turned green before she could come to a complete stop. She turned north onto Main, where she saw just three vehicles—including the car she thought had been tailing them.

"You may be right." she said into the phone. "A car just turned onto Main a block south of us. I'll pull over in a bit. What do we do if they stop behind us?"

"Let's hope they don't," Amos replied. "We don't want a confrontation if we can avoid it."

"No, but I won't let anyone here get hurt."

She pointed at the glove compartment and Chris opened it.

"You know how to handle a gun?"

Chris just raised his eyebrows.

"Hand me the gun, please," Rachel said.

She was an excellent marksman. She'd never tested her skills against a person, of course, but she wasn't afraid. As Chris gingerly handed her the gun, Rachel spoke aloud to her dad again.

"I'll give it a minute, then turn up Tenth North and zigzag our way through town until we get to the highway."

"Remember that Seventh East is a dead end," Amos said. "Use Sixth or Twelfth. If they figure out where you've gone, use the backup plan—the condo at Garden City."

"Thanks Dad, I remember. If we have to go to the condo, we'll wait there a couple of hours before heading back to the Preserve."

"If they follow you that far, try to get a description of the car and a plate number. And maybe you should get a couple of hours sleep before you head back. It's been a long day."

"Good idea," Rachel said. She'd already thought of it, but appreciated her dad reminding her—she had a lot on her mind at the moment. "We pulled over a minute ago and they went past. I'm turning onto Tenth North. I'll text you when we get to the Preserve."

"Thanks, Rachel. Your mom will appreciate that."

Chris stared at Rachel's profile, watching the outside lights play across her features. He'd always liked her, but he'd had no idea how self-confident and capable she was. *She handled that situation as if it happened every day,* he thought. *She's amazing.* Rachel turned suddenly and made eye contact with him. She smiled, making her whole face light up. *She's beautiful.* He smiled back.

"Can we quit now?" Jordan asked. "I've been drivin' for over an hour and we haven't seen even a glimpse of that trailer. We lost 'em."

"Quit your whinin'." Duke grumbled from the back seat, but he was worried too. He was sure they'd been seen. Thankfully, Jordan's car wasn't distinctive, and they'd only passed close the one time, so he didn't think they could be identified later. But he had to make sure that riding with these morons didn't end up with him being caught. Last time he'd been a minor—this time he'd go to prison.

"He's right," Aaron sighed. "Let's go back to the 'Cardo and have a beer before we call it a night. Maybe we can figure out our next step."

"Next?" Duke demanded. "You said the stash was around here. We looked all over this part of town for nothin'. We don't have a clue where they went. I say forget the whole thing."

"I second that," Jordan agreed. "And who's gonna' pay for my tank of gas?"

Jordan was shaking so badly he was either freezing to death or needed a fix.

"I'll pay for your gas," Aaron blurted in anger, then calmed himself. "Look, I'll buy the drinks too, while we think about this for a few minutes. Maybe there's something we didn't consider."

Jordan took the next right and deadheaded it back to Bicardo's on Main.

When they entered the darkened, all-night bar, the barkeeper was the only one there. They lumbered to a table in the back, with Aaron in the lead and Nathan bringing up the rear. The younger Carlsen brother was half asleep, and he had an upset stomach from riding in the back seat half the night, but he didn't dare say anything. As they crossed the dark room, he noticed a newspaper on one of the tables, and the huge headline caught his interest: **PRESIDENT DECLARES MARTIAL LAW, CALLS FOR MORE EVACUATIONS.**

Nathan picked up the paper and took it with him to the table, reading the subheading. Aaron slid into the seat against the window, and Nathan sat absentmindedly next to him, trying to read the text of the article in the dim light. Duke held up four fingers to the barkeeper, who quickly brought four cold beers and opened them at the table. After he left, everyone but Nathan took a swallow and settled back to relax.

"Where's the most logical—" Aaron started, but he was interrupted by a tired, angry Duke.

"Stop right there," Duke leaned across the table and demanded quietly. "You said the stash was somewhere around here."

"What if they intentionally misled us? We followed 'em until they pulled over, then we lost 'em. What if they pulled over 'cause they knew we were behind 'em?"

Duke snorted.

"It wouldn't have been hard. We were the only two cars on the road until we got to Main."

"Exactly," Aaron agreed, getting excited again. "Where did they pick us up?

"Well, that turn onto Third West was a surprise," Jordan said. "They should have taken the direct route to Main, instead of making that turn."

Aaron noticed that Jordan was smiling and tapping his foot, apparently beginning to enjoy the puzzle. He was looking steadier too, now that he had a quick half a bottle in him. The pills he'd taken when they sat down were probably helping too, whatever they were.

"Okay, where were they headed if they got that far before spotting us?" Aaron asked, trying to keep everyone engaged.

"They could have turned left on Highway 30 and gone west," Jordan said. "That's what I thought they were doin', but from Main you can go any direction."

Aaron finally noticed Nathan reading the paper. He shook his head and plunged on.

"But if they were goin' south, wouldn't they have gone south out of the subdivision, not north? So, we can assume they were goin' somewhere north of Highway 30, right?"

"Unless they take different routes just to confuse anyone watchin' 'em," Duke said flatly.

He was doodling with his finger in the condensation from his beer bottle again, which pissed Aaron off. Duke wasn't paying attention. Aaron's nostrils flared in anger, but he checked his temper and spoke slowly.

"We can't anticipate everything. We have to make some assumptions or we'll get nowhere."

"We're already nowhere, my friend." Duke replied, looking up briefly at Aaron, then back down at his doodling.

"Humor me for a minute. You're drinkin' my beer."

To that, Duke raised his beer bottle in a salute, looked up, and motioned for Aaron to continue, so he resumed his train of thought.

"So, they're either in the north part of the city or somewhere that they can only get to from there. Where can they hide? Some place they can get to without too much trouble?"

Nathan spoke, drawing Aaron's attention and making Jordan jump in surprise.

"Logan Canyon."

That was all he said. He kept his head down but watched them surreptitiously. The others looked at him as if he had suddenly appeared out of a magician's hat. Aaron's mouth was open as he stared at his little brother, who'd had no input whatsoever up until then, except to question them.

"What do you know?" Jordan asked.

Nathan held up the newspaper shakily so that they could see the headline. He was so nervous around these guys, he didn't really trust his voice. **PRESIDENT DECLARES MARTIAL LAW, CALLS FOR MORE EVACUATIONS**.

"So?" Jordan demanded.

"It says here that—" Nathan said, with a slight quiver in his voice, then broke off. He turned to Aaron, who motioned impatiently for him to continue. "It says here that on June twenty-fifth—that's last Monday. On Monday, the president called for an evacuation of the Northeast."

He paused to swallow. Their glaring was making him more nervous than usual.

"You talkin' about the New England states, like Maine and Boston?" Duke asked impatiently.

Nathan nodded, forcing himself not to correct Duke by pointing out that Boston wasn't a state. He swallowed again, then continued slowly, with a dry throat.

"In the last two days, he's added the Chicago area, Los Angeles, San Francisco, Seattle, and Hawaii to the evacuation order and declared martial law in several major cities to, um, to stop looting and violence. The governors have—they called up the national guard and the military is being deployed to those cities."

Nathan's throat was rough as sandpaper. He was choking on his words, but he made himself go on.

"He told everyone to—to move upwind. To cross a mountain range if they could."

Nathan's throat closed up for good. He needed to drink something, but all he had was the beer he'd been avoiding. He could barely breathe and knew that if he told them he needed a glass of water they'd just laugh at him. He thought he might pass out, so he grabbed the beer in desperation and took a swallow, coughing as the bitter flavor coated his tongue and slid down his throat. When it reached his upset stomach, the organ tried to rebel, and Nathan had to swallow several times just to keep it down. Aaron slapped him on the back a couple of times, laughing, until Nathan could breathe again. He was in agony and hoped Aaron wouldn't think he was a pussy.

"Nathan, you're a genius!" Aaron declared

He was still laughing as he turned to the others. Nathan would have explained his thinking, but it seemed he didn't need to—Aaron had caught on immediately. Nathan was as surprised by Aaron's praise as he was by his own action gulping down the beer. He decided he was proud of himself. He was one of the guys now, he'd made a contribution.

"What's so genius about him?" Jordan asked. "He's hardly said a word since we started."

"The answer. *The answer,*" Aaron repeated.

There was surprise and admiration in his voice as he patted Nathan on the back to help his brother stop coughing. He grabbed the paper from Nathan's hand, laying it on the table and turning it so the others could see the headline.

"The answer, gents, is Logan Canyon. It's not upwind, but it's close and it's in the mountains. We follow them up the canyon and see where they go."

"You sure about that?" Duke asked.

Aaron was already thinking ahead.

"They could be going west on Highway 30, but that's just a gentle drive over the hills, ending at Riverside and the freeway. Not likely. No, they're going up Logan Canyon somewhere. So yeah, I'm sure—I'd bet my life on it.

"We need to split up, do a two-car stakeout, like in the movies. We station one car on Main near the Fourth North turn onto Highway 89. The other car waits near the mouth of the canyon—right by the college campus—and waits for them to pass, then follows them up the canyon. The first car turns off and the second car picks them up. They won't question a car following them up the canyon. They could be going to Garden City. This is beautiful."

Aaron was ecstatic.

"We don't have a second car," Jordan said straight-faced.

That brought Aaron up short, but not for long. His grin

came back and he looked at Duke, leaned over the table and said conspiratorially, just above a whisper.

"We steal a car. Take it from one of the parking lots on campus, near the mouth of the canyon. You can do that, can't you Duke?"

"Harder on the newer cars, but I'm sure we can find one I can move easy enough." A grin spread across Duke's face. Aaron had one to match—he knew *this* was the stuff Duke loved.

Rachel and Chris arrived home just as the morning sun was peeking over the eastern mountains, casting long shadows across the valley. Chris was driving while Rachel slept, her head leaning against his shoulder. Opening the overhead door to the lab woke her, and she stretched, covering a yawn with her hand.

"Thanks for driving," she said quietly into Chris's ear, holding onto his arm. "I can't believe I'm so tired."

Chris laughed, then yawned. She noticed and jabbed him in the ribs. Amos, who was sleeping on a cot in the office, woke as they entered the lab. He rubbed his eyes and yawned.

"Everything okay at the Preserve?" he asked, stretching his neck.

"Great," Rachel said. "Winding through the city put Sydney to sleep. Katie and Mrs. Stephens put her right to bed once we arrived. We got a couple hours of sleep before heading back."

"But we're starved." Chris added.

Amos smiled.

"Let's go tell Lillie—and get something to eat."

Amos was trying to hold a meeting with Lillie, Emily, and Matt. Rachel and Chris lay on the couch, their eyes closed. Chris had his arms wrapped around Rachel, who was backed against him so they would both fit. Amos wasn't sure they were awake. Emily and Matt, as usual, were paying more attention to each other than their surroundings. Lillie, at least, seemed to appreciate the difficult position they were in. They still had eleven people to get to the Preserve, along with all the Parkers' supplies and furniture, and the remainder of the Carlsens' supplies, and time was running out. Plus, there was the new concern that Rachel might have been tailed. Someone might be watching them.

"I told Tyler Parker that we want them to go tonight with whatever supplies they've been able to get," Amos said. "He's out shopping this morning, so we'll take the truck over this afternoon to collect everything. We can't get everyone that's left in one trip, so we'll take everything we can tonight and make one final run, hopefully tomorrow night. I've been telling everyone Monday night, but I want to be ready to go tomorrow, if possible. Emily, do you have a plan for getting everyone out?"

"Yeah. If we take the Parkers and their gear tonight, assuming we can fit it all in the trailer, and we use the Parkers' SUV to carry people, all we'll have left tomorrow are five people and whatever gear we can't get on the trailer tonight."

"Jason is buying the rest of their supplies today," Lillie added. "But Brittany wants to keep it low-key because of the stress in the house."

"Okay, let's have Emily and Matt go tonight," Amos said. "Rachel, are you with us?"

"Yes," came the groggy reply from the couch.

Rachel didn't open her eyes. Amos smiled.

"Emily, maybe you and Matt need to drive the truck. You can leave Rachel and Chris at the Preserve. If we can fit the remainder of the Carlsens' stuff in the back of the truck tomorrow, we'll leave the trailer at the Preserve tonight. So, the last to go will be Mrs. Carlsen, Emily, Matt, Mom, and me. Any questions?"

"Yeah," Rachel said, opening her eyes to look at her dad. "How are you feeling? Maybe you and Mom should go to the Preserve and we'll stay here."

"Thanks for the offer. I'll be fine."

That afternoon, Lillie, Emily, and Matt took the truck and trailer over to the Parkers and loaded the furniture, equipment, clothes, and food the Parkers had collected. It all fit, but just barely. Tyler loaded a few things he thought his family would need during the day into his SUV. Then the Parkers piled into the SUV and went into town for dinner and a movie. They weren't planning to go home before leaving for the Preserve. Instead, they would meet at the Blunds' house at ten o'clock that evening for the Family Council.

When the Parkers arrived, Emily directed them to pull their SUV into the trailer bay, next to the loaded truck and trailer. Now that they were actually leaving, the Parkers seemed a little self-conscious, likely because they had basically invited themselves. Lillie, assuming that to be the case, had asked Rachel and Chris to sit with sixteen-year-old Joshua and his fifteen-year-old sister, Rylee, and make conversation with them. To make the Parkers feel at home—a part of this new, larger family—she brought out homemade cookies and milk. Soon Megan was all smiles and Tyler was chatting happily with the others. Once everyone had settled in and quieted down, Amos got to the point.

"All of our departures so far have been at 2:00 a.m. or later but, as we thought could happen, it seems Rachel might have been followed last night. She had to do some fancy maneuvering to lose the tail before leaving town."

"And she was great!"

Chris had interrupted quietly, but everyone heard, and he cringed a little when all eyes turned to him. Rachel, sitting next to him, smiled and squeezed his thigh. Amos paused before continuing.

"Anyway, tonight, we want you to leave at 12:30 instead of

2:00. That should throw off anyone who's planning to follow you. Tyler," he said a little more quietly, "are you comfortable carrying and using a gun, if there's no way around it?"

"Do you really think it'll come to that?" Tyler asked.

"I hope nothing happens," Amos said. "But we have a lot riding on this. We need to protect ourselves. I'd hate to see us lose anyone out of carelessness."

"Well, I have my handgun, and I've had a lot of practice on a range. I don't know what it's like to shoot at a person, though."

"Neither do I. Think of it as a *shoot or be shot* situation and it might be easier. Think about how important your family is to you."

"I guess that puts it in a perspective I can understand."

Their smiles were grim.

14

"Aaron Carlsen. Is that you?"

Logan, Utah, 1 July, 12:30 am

Matt drove the truck, with the trailer attached, out of the lab and into the street. Emily sat in front with him, while Chris and Rachel took the back seat. Chris looked out the rear windshield to make sure the Parkers were behind them and was relieved to see Tyler pull into the street and begin to follow.

With his only job taken care of for the time being, Chris turned his attention to a more pressing matter. He'd been trying to get up the courage to hold Rachel's hand, and now was the time. He knew that Matt and Emily would be focused on the road ahead, so he slid his hand over and placed it on top of one of Rachel's, which was resting on her leg. Rachel turned her hand and intertwined her fingers with his. She looked at him, smiled, and leaned her head against his shoulder. Next on his list—the kiss. For that, he would need a bit more confidence than he had just now. _Soon,_ he thought.

Aaron and Duke walked through a student parking lot on campus, making an effort to seem casual, looking for a car Duke felt comfortable hot-wiring. Aaron kept a nervous lookout for anyone coming out of student housing. Duke had forgotten his previous concerns—he was in his element.

"Hurry and find something already," Aaron complained, looking around.

"Don't get a knot in your undies. Here's a good candidate."

Duke stepped between two cars, pulled a long, flat bar from inside his pants, and threaded it down between the window glass and the door body. He looked at Aaron and smiled when he heard the satisfying click he'd anticipated. Then he popped the door open, his fingers slipping from the handle as Aaron's phone rang.

"What? Can't talk now," Aaron whispered angrily, looking around self-consciously.

"We've got a problem," came Nathan's voice from the phone.

Jordan and Nathan sat in Jordan's gray Nissan in the shadow of a building, just inside an alley, facing onto Main. They'd bought coffee at an all-night drive-through moments before and then settled in to wait. Nathan was tipping the coffee cup to his lips when the truck and trailer went by at about 12:40 am. He spilled the hot coffee down his front as he frantically pulled out his phone and called Aaron in a panic.

"We've got a problem," Nathan whispered when Aaron answered.

"What?"

"The truck just passed us. They're early."

Aaron swore, using words Nathan had never heard from him before—he was taking this way too seriously. And, after reading about the terrorist threat in the newspaper, Nathan had begun to wonder if he'd made a mistake hitching his cart to Aaron instead of leaving town with his mom. Nathan could hear Aaron's frustration through the phone as he called out to Duke.

"Duke, ya' gotta hurry. What? Then forget it. We gotta go."

Aaron came back on the line with Nathan, who was blotting coffee off his shirt and pants with a napkin.

"Get up to the mouth of the canyon, quick as you can," he commanded.

Jordan took off so fast, turning onto Main, that he almost sideswiped an SUV that was headed in the same direction. He swung into the left lane, passed the trailer, which had stopped at a red light, and kept going. He was just turning at Fourth North, without stopping, when Aaron changed the plan.

"Wait, wait. Follow 'em that far, then pass 'em and wait a few miles up the canyon. We'll get to the mouth of the canyon and follow 'em after you pass. Maybe we can still do the two-car tag team. Keep your phone handy in case I need to give you more instructions."

"You got a car?" Nathan asked.

Aaron swore some more.

"We're using mine."

Aaron's good at planning and making quick decisions, Nathan thought, *but how's the plan going to work now that he's in his very recognizable ride?*

Jordan pulled over to the side of the road, waiting for the trailer to pass so he could follow it.

Following instructions, Tyler Parker had taken a different route to Main, so they were just catching up to Matt when an old, gray sedan pulled out of the shadows from an alley. The car nearly sideswiped the Parkers' SUV before racing north. Tyler slammed on his brakes—he didn't even have time to honk before the car was gone. He apologized to his wife, then picked up speed again. He could see the trailer up ahead, stopped at a red light. They had caught up to Matt and Emily.

The truck and trailer were in the right-hand lane. Tyler watched the car that had cut him off swerve into the left lane and run the red light. Tyler pulled into the left lane and stopped alongside Matt. Megan rolled down her window and Matt followed suit.

"What do you think his problem is?" Matt asked, laughing.

"Don't know. He cut me off a block back. Came out of the shadows in a hurry. We should probably keep an eye out for him. Might be drunk."

Tyler was staring after the car's taillights as it sped away.

"Hmm. Why don't you back off a bit?" Matt said. "Maybe he's the tail from last night. If he's only watching for the trailer, maybe you can get behind him and get a plate number. If he's not trying to follow us, and we see him again, then we can both try to ID them."

"Sounds good. I'll leave some room between us."

The light changed and they picked up speed. Tyler dropped behind Matt in the right lane to make the turn ahead, at the same time letting the distance between them increase.

Duke put Aaron's phone on speaker so they could both hear what Nathan was saying.

"We're parked on the side of the road, waiting for them to pass," Duke said with a smirk.

"Okay. They're just passing us," Nathan said. "We'll pull out behind them and follow them to the mouth of the canyon, then we'll pass 'em. That's still the plan, right?"

Aaron looked in his side view mirror as Duke looked back over his shoulder. Aaron fidgeted, tapping his hands on the steering wheel. Something bothered him about what Nathan had just said: *we'll pass 'em.*

Aaron tried to hide his agitation as Duke stared at him from the passenger seat. *I'm losing it,* he thought. *Maybe Duke was right. Maybe this is a bad plan.* But he tried not to show his own nervousness at the risk they were taking. He knew this was an adrenaline rush for Duke, but Aaron preferred to have more control over the situation.

"Maybe I should drive," Duke said, still looking at Aaron.

"Why?"

"I think you're losing it."

"I'm not. This is my plan, and it's going to work."

"Well," Duke replied, "you've never done this before. You amateurs are going to get me caught. And if you do, you'll regret all of this. You can be sure of that."

"Why don't you just shut it and let me drive. Nobody's gonna' get caught."

"Alright *boss*, but I warned you."

"Jord needs to stay behind them," Aaron said, ignoring Duke's last comment. He was thinking frantically. *Jord was spotted last night and already passed them once tonight. They may already know they're being followed. He shouldn't pass them again.*

"Huh?" Duke said, just as the truck appeared around the curve—with Jordan passing it.

"That boy's lucky there isn't a car coming the other direction," Aaron thought aloud.

Duke swore, then spoke into the phone.

"We see ya'. Yeah, let's stick to that plan for now."

Matt had seen the dark Nissan pull out behind him, quickly catch up, and pass. He called Tyler, who said that he'd seen it pull out between them, too.

"Keep an eye open," Matt said into the phone. "We don't know what to expect."

He cut the connection.

"Emily," Matt said. "Will you open the glove box and hand

me my gun?"

A little surprised, Emily did as he'd asked, passing it over still in its holster. Matt removed it, letting the holster drop into Emily's lap, and she made a small, surprised sound. Matt liked the feel of his Springfield Armory's .40 Smith and Wesson—it was like a natural extension of his arm. Using his knee to keep the steering wheel steady, he pulled back, then released the slide, which loaded a hollow point cartridge into the chamber with a loud *ka-chunk*. He laid the gun in his lap with the barrel pointed out the left side of the cab. It was ready to fire and had *stopping power*. He hoped Tyler would be able to do the same if it came to it.

Joshua Parker, sitting behind his mother on the passenger side of the SUV, was very aware of the gun his father had just laid in his lap. Looking out through the front window, he noticed the light blue car ahead as Matt's headlights passed over it.

"That looks like Aaron Carlsen's car."

"What?" his dad asked, alert to the name *Carlsen.*

"That's Aaron Carlsen's car," Joshua said, certain now. "I can tell from the flames on the side."

"Didn't Lillie say there was some kind of problem at the Carlsens'?" Tyler asked his wife. "About having trouble with their boys?"

"I don't think this is a coincidence," Megan said, a concerned look on her face. "Aaron being here at the exact moment that we're heading to the Preserve."

Tyler called Matt and told him what Joshua had said.

Matt relayed the new information to Emily.

"Call Dad," she said aloud, and the truck paired with her phone, dialing Amos.

"I can take care of this," Matt said, as the phone began to ring. "We don't need to get your dad involved."

"Maybe, but Dad knows the Carlsens a lot better than we do. He might have an idea about what to do if they give us trouble."

When Amos answered, she repeated what Joshua had said.

"Just a minute," Amos told Emily. "Lillie, are you awake? Can you think of any reason why Aaron Carlsen would just happen to be at the mouth of the canyon when the truck passed?"

Emily could hear her mom in the background, answering drowsily.

"Well, I'd call Brittany, but that might upset things at their house. The only thing I can think of is that Brittany had us take Sydney early because her boys have been acting up, staying out late and running with a bad crowd."

"That's good enough for me, thanks. Go back to sleep."

"Right. Like that's going to happen. Tell me what's going on."

Emily could hear in her mom's voice that she was wide

awake now, and she pictured her throwing the covers back and climbing out of bed in her pajamas. The familiar image made her smile, but it didn't last.

"When I'm finished talking to Emily." Amos said, then spoke into the phone again. "Emily, keep going. We'll catch up to you."

After hanging up with her dad, Emily called Tyler. They were already in the canyon.

"We're at a good place to pass," Tyler told Emily. "We're going to try to talk to whoever's driving the blue car."

"No! Don't!" Emily shouted.

"Too late," Tyler said.

They were on a straight length of highway, with no oncoming traffic, so it was safe to pass, and Tyler had crossed over into the oncoming traffic lane, pulling even with the light blue car. Megan powered down her window.

Aaron had noticed the SUV coming up on his left side but refused to look. *Maintain your distance from the trailer,* he told himself. Nathan's comment—*we're passing 'em*—replayed in his mind. *They may have recognized Jord's ride, but they haven't seen mine yet,* he thought.

He'd just convinced himself that everything might be okay,

when someone called his name. He reacted automatically, before he had a chance to think. Looking out the window to his left, he saw a woman he thought he'd seen before, her head out the window of her car. Her voice was muffled by his own closed window, but she had definitely yelled his name.

Everything that happened next seemed to happen at once.

Emily yelled at Tyler, through the phone, to back away.

Megan called out again.

"Aaron. Aaron Carlsen. Is that you?"

Aaron panicked. He'd been recognized! Suddenly, he had trouble keeping the car in the lane.

Duke yelled at Aaron to lower his window.

Aaron jerked his head back and forth between Megan and Duke, who were both yelling at him. With so many people yelling, and so much at stake, what Duke said didn't really register in his brain.

Duke gave up trying to talk to Aaron and raised the 9mm handgun he'd been holding against his right leg, pointing it at the SUV. He fired three times through Aaron's closed window into the cab of the SUV.

Seeing a gun suddenly pointed at her, Megan shouted in a panicky voice.

"He's got a gun!"

Tyler's reacted immediately, lifting his foot from the gas pedal and applied the brake, quickly slowing the car as it tried to climb the canyon road.

The explosion of the handgun, so close to Aaron's face, blinded and deafened him. He didn't see or hear anything after that.

The bullets shattered Aaron's window, and glass sprayed in the open window of the SUV, showering Megan. The first bullet hit Megan in the back of her head as she turned away, and exited out the front. With the SUV already slowing, however, the other two bullets passed in front of Megan and Tyler. The first passed through the cab, shattering the closed window on the driver side. The second passed through the passenger-side window frame and through the windshield, blowing a spray of shattered glass outward, over the hood of the car.

As Tyler hit the brakes, Aaron's involuntary reaction, flinching away from the gun in his face, caused him to turn away, to his left, taking the car with him. The car slammed into the right front fender of the SUV, causing it to veer off the highway and into a tree on the left side of the road.

The impact with the SUV forced the Impala back to the right, where it careened off the highway and dropped down a steep embankment. It smashed into a large boulder halfway down the incline, rolled twice, and landed upside down in a river that lay thirty feet below. Neither of the young men inside had been wearing a seatbelt, and both were thrown from the car. Aaron flew across the river, crumpling as he hit the ground. Duke's body fell through a broken window on the near side of the river as the car rolled. He was dead before he hit the ground.

The explosion of the Impala's gas tank could have been seen and heard up and down the canyon for more than a mile, had there been anyone in the area at that time of night. Matt had slowed the truck, listening to the commotion through the phone, which was still connected. He could see the car lights fading behind them, but there was no place to turn around. He continued up the canyon until he found a spot wide enough to do a hasty three-point turn. It was awkward with the trailer attached.

Tyler didn't respond to Emily's repeated calls, as Matt finally managed to get the truck turned around and headed back down the canyon. She got her mom on the phone.

"I think there's been an accident."

She filled Lillie in on what they'd heard over the phone. They feared the worst.

"We're already on our way, Emily," her mom said. "See what you can do until we get there."

"On your way?" Emily asked.

"We weren't going to get any more sleep after you called. A voice in my head said we should get to you. We should be there in five minutes or so."

As Matt steered the vehicle around a bend, headed back down the canyon, he saw smoke drifting up from the river, ahead on their left.

"You see that Em?"

"Yeah," Emily said. "That doesn't look good at all."

As they neared the scene, headlights shone through the undergrowth ahead on the right. Soon they could see that there was one headlight on either side of a large tree, and steam came from under a crumpled hood.

"That's Tyler's SUV," Matt said. "But I can't see the other car. It must be down in the river, where all that smoke is coming from."

"This is very bad," Emily said, choking on her words.

"This is serious," Chris chimed in from the back seat. "I hope everyone's okay."

Matt nodded as he slowed the truck and trailer, but he had his doubts. He pulled off the right side of the road, just past the SUV, unbuckled his seatbelt, grabbed a flashlight from the storage compartment in his door, and climbed out of the truck. Emily followed from the passenger side, and Chris and Rachel joined them.

"Stay back for a minute, okay?" Matt said. "Let me just make sure there are no safety hazards around the SUV."

His powerful flashlight traced a systematic path over the ground, and up and over the SUV, as he walked all the way around. He knew that Emily, Rachel, and Chris were anxious to check on the Parkers, but he was glad they respected his warning in case the site was unsafe. Only after Matt was certain that there were no fallen power lines, broken tree limbs that might fall on them, or other safety concerns, did he approach the SUV with the others following. He shone his light in the front passenger window. Unlike the other windows, which were shattered, this one had been rolled most of the way down. What he saw made his stomach lurch.

"A car's coming," Chris said.

Matt turned away and saw a car coming toward them down the canyon. It slowed, then pulled over just short of the SUV.

"Chris! Go deal with them. Keep them away, okay? Tell them we've got it under control here and that we've called an ambulance."

"Did we call an ambulance?" Chris asked.

"Just do it," Matt said.

Chris turned and walked quickly toward the small car that had just pulled over.

Matt was still in his residency, but his medical training kicked in as he turned back to Megan's window. She had fallen forward against her shoulder restraint, and she was clearly dead. A bullet had entered through the back of her head and exited out the front, leaving blood and brain matted in her hair and running down the front of her blouse. He swallowed several times, trying to keep his dinner down. He turned the light off at the same time Emily looked in the driver-side window.

Matt shouted, "Don't open the door!"

He didn't want her seeing what he'd just witnessed. She looked at him, surprised.

"You don't want to see this," he added. He felt bad that he'd raised his voice, and he went on more quietly. "Will you please check on the kids in back?"

Emily looked at Matt questioningly, but took her hand off the door handle without opening the door. Matt hurried around the car to check on Tyler. His light reflected off bits of safety glass both inside and outside the car. Forgetting his own warning, he opened the driver-side door, making the overhead light come on.

"Oh," Emily said, taking in a sharp breath.

Matt looked over the driver's seat at Emily. She was staring at the back of Megan's head.

"I'm going to . . . " Emily started to say.

She didn't get to finish, turning quickly away from the car and vomiting. Matt wanted to help her, but there wasn't much he could do. She'd just be embarrassed by his attention, and he needed to check on the rest of the family. He turned his attention back to Tyler, whose head leaned back on the headrest at an awkward angle. There was blood and tissue splattered all over his right side from Megan's gunshot wound. His neck was broken, and he was dead.

"Joshua. Wake up, Josh," Rachel said from the other side of the car.

Matt looked up to see Rachel gently shaking Josh, who'd been sitting behind his mother. The boy had a large concave area on his forehead where he'd hit the seat in front of him—it must have been a solid impact. It looked like the skull had been fractured, and blood was running down his face from a gash in the wound. Just then, he fell sideways, hanging out of the car, held in place only by his seat belt. Rachel screamed and jumped back.

"Rachel," Matt said, softly but emphatically. *I don't have time to treat Rachel for shock,* he thought. *I'm just glad she didn't look at Megan.* "Rachel, go sit in the truck, please?"

Rachel looked stricken, but with a last look at Josh, she moved toward the truck.

Matt left the driver-side door open so he'd have some light and moved to check on Rylee, who had been sitting behind her dad. While he was checking her pulse and breathing, Emily spoke up from behind him.

"Ooh, that tasted disgusting. How is she?"

Normally Matt would have tried to comfort Emily, but it wasn't a priority now—and there wasn't time. Someone might have heard the accident and would come to investigate. They couldn't be here when the police arrived, or there would be a lot of questions and a huge delay in getting to the Preserve. Rylee moaned and took a deep, shuddering breath.

"Hey Rylee, you're gonna' be okay. Em, will you stay with her?"

"Sure," Emily said, moving to take Matt's place. "Rylee, you wanna' sing a song?"

Rylee's voice barely rose above a whisper.

"What? What song?"

Rylee started to look around, but Emily placed a hand on her face and turned her head so they were looking at each other and began to sing a lullaby her mom had sung to her as a child. Rylee closed her eyes and appeared to fall asleep. As

Emily sang, she looked Rylee over. There was blood and other matter staining Rylee's blouse and jeans. Emily pulled a tissue from her pocket and wiped at the spots she could see.

Matt stepped back, then heard gravel crunching and a voice came from his left.

"What can we do to help?"

He looked up to see two young men dressed in casual button-up shirts, corduroy slacks, and loafers—college students, he guessed. Chris stood behind them. Matt looked pointedly at Chris, but Chris lifted his shoulders and eyebrows in a what-could-I-do shrug. The two men looked into the front windshield to see what was going on inside the car. Thinking quickly, Matt closed the driver-side door so the interior light would turn off.

"I'm a doctor," he said. "I have things under control here. I think I saw smoke coming from the river a few seconds ago. There may be a problem over there." He pointed across the road, and they turned to look. "If you want to help, go check that out."

They nodded and started back toward the road, but Matt called out to them.

"Here, take my flashlight. It's a steep drop. Be careful over there and take it slow."

He smiled as he held out the flashlight. One of them took it and they hurried across the road.

"Are you trying to get them out of the way?" Chris asked quietly.

"I'm hoping it'll slow them down a little. We can't still be here when the police arrive." Matt moved around the car to check on Josh, though he was afraid he already knew what the verdict would be. He had little hope that Josh had survived the head injury.

"That's why you had me tell them that we'd already called an ambulance?"

Chris followed Matt around the car.

"Yep," Matt said.

He shook his head as he checked for Joshua's pulse and breathing.

"That's what I'm worried about," Chris said. "How are the Parkers?"

Matt turned away from the car and spoke quietly to Chris.

"Em is with Rylee. We lost the others."

"All three of them?" Chris said, looking shocked. His usual enthusiasm disappeared.

"Shh," Matt said, looking across the car at Rylee and Emily. "Chris, I sent Rachel to the truck. Go see that she's okay."

Chris turned toward the truck while Matt turned to speak to Em across the car.

At a turnout about five miles up the canyon from the accident, Nathan and Jordan sat in the Nissan, the engine running. Nathan was more nervous with every passing minute.

"Aaron should have passed by now."

"You think something happened to them?" Jordan asked.

"Maybe we should go back and see."

"Naw, they'll call if there's a problem."

After a few more minutes, Nathan took out his phone and called Aaron. There was no answer.

"Why don't you try Duke on your phone?"

Jordan laughed.

"You afraid of him?"

"Aren't you?"

"Naw. He's a pussycat." But Jordan made the call. After a few moments, he disconnected. "Went to voice mail," he said, looking over at Nathan nervously.

Jordan put the car in gear, pulled out onto the highway, and headed back down the canyon. Minutes later, Nathan saw headlights in the bushes on the right. He hadn't seen anything there on their way up the canyon. Thinking it was Aaron's car, he started to panic.

"Oh no. Is that them? Aaron can't be hurt. I hope he's not hurt. It looks like they've had an accident. What do you think? Should we . . . "

"Nathan . . . shuddup," Jordan said.

Nathan stared at Jordan, but he stopped blubbering. As they neared the scene, Nathan made out the Honda that had passed them a few minutes earlier going down the canyon. It looked like they'd stopped to help. Then Nathan saw the SUV and he let out a breath he'd been holding.

"That's not Aaron's car," Nathan said. "But who are all those people?"

"Where's Aaron's car? Where's Duke." Jordan asked, looking around.

Nathan began to panic as he saw Jordan's face turn pale. Aaron's car wasn't there.

"Dammit," Nathan said quietly, as they slowly approached two men standing by the side of the road. "Some of those people are Blunds."

"You mean the people we're supposed to be robbing right now?" Jordan asked sarcastically. Then he pointed to the truck and trailer just beyond. "Isn't that the trailer we were following?"

Jordan slowed down more so they could get a better look. Nathan made eye contact with one of the Blunds. *I can't let them recognize me,* he thought, panicking, and turned his head quickly.

"Speed up man. I can't let them see me."

Chris had just turned toward the truck to go check on Rachel when he saw a dark Nissan approaching slowly, traveling down the canyon. He stepped back to get out of its path. It slowed more as it approached and Chris made eye contact with the passenger, who quickly turned his head and said something to the driver. Then the car sped away. He turned to Matt.

"The guy in that car looked like he'd seen a ghost. Maybe he's never seen an accident before."

"There was something familiar about him," Matt said. "And the car."

He watched the car speed away for a moment before turning back to talk to Emily.

"Em," Matt said to her across the car, "we need to get Rylee to the truck."

"What are we going to do?"

Emily turned away from Rylee to talk to Matt.

"How's Rylee?" he said, not answering her question.

"A little shaken. She has a bump on her forehead, maybe a concussion. She doesn't know about . . . you know."

Emily looked at her boyfriend, admiration in her eyes. She loved the way he'd taken charge of the situation, doing exactly what needed to be done.

"Let's leave it that way for now. Maybe you should get her to walk, keep her awake."

"I'll walk her to the truck," Emily said, then spotted a car coming uphill toward them. "I think that's Dad," she said, indicating with a nod.

"Change of plan," Matt said as he reached the truck. Chris was leaning in the passenger-side door, talking quietly to Rachel. "How is she?" Matt asked.

"I'm upset," Rachel said angrily, then forced herself to be calmer. "I'm fine."

"Good," Matt said. "Chris, can you get the truck turned around? After I talk to Amos, I want you two to get out of here. Get to the Preserve as quickly as you can and stay there."

"You're worried about the police?" Chris asked.

"Yes, I am," Matt said. "If they follow you up the canyon, you need to be off the road."

"Okay," Chris said. "But what about the Parkers?"

"We'll take Rylee to your house to take care of her," Matt said.

"We're not going to wait for an ambulance," Emily said flatly.

She'd come up behind them, helping fifteen-year-old Rylee walk. Rylee was moving erratically and looked dazed.

"We'll check her out. We have medical supplies at the house. We can't go to a hospital or we'll never get out of there. We'll have to leave the others here. I wish there was another way, but there's nothing we can do for them."

"What's wrong with Mom and Dad?"

Rylee's voice was loud and had an edge, and her eyes were wide. Matt looked down for a moment to gather his thoughts, kicking himself for not being more careful about what he said.

"It's okay Rylee," Emily said soothingly. "You're going to be okay."

But Rylee wasn't going to be placated.

"What's wrong with Mom and Dad," she asked again more frantically, looking around. "And Josh! Where's Josh?"

Emily held Rylee's arms, trying to get her attention.

"Rylee. Rylee. Look at me."

Rylee raised her arms, trying to break free of Emily's hold.

"Let go of me. I want to see," she wailed.

Emily lost her grip and Rylee tried to back away and turn toward the SUV, but Emily threw her arms around her and pulled her into a bear hug.

"They're dead, aren't they?" Rylee bawled, still struggling to break free of Emily's hold.

Emily looked over Rylee's shoulder at Matt, pleading for help. He didn't know what to do, so he just shrugged.

"Mom . . . ?" Rylee wailed. "Dad . . . ?" She continued to bawl, but she gradually lost steam, her sobs becoming quieter, her struggles losing strength. "Josh . . . ?"

Emily placed one hand behind Rylee's head and pulled the girl against her. Rylee didn't resist. Emily started rocking back and forth, humming softly. Rylee's cries dwindled into whimpers. She hiccupped. Her eyes glazed over, and she leaned heavily against Emily. Matt watched, impressed with the almost magical effect of Emily's ministrations. He smiled, and she smiled back.

"What about their stuff in the back?" Chris asked quietly from behind Matt.

"Casualty of the accident," Matt said. "We don't have much time. Grab what you can, fast, then, *get out of here.*"

Chris turned to help Katie out of the truck. They jogged over to the SUV and opened the back, and several backpacks and other items fell out. They were piled chaotically, scrambled by the accident. They took as much as they could carry and hurried back to the truck.

Meanwhile, Amos had pulled his car to the side of the road. He approached Matt, his eye on Emily and Rylee, and Lillie followed.

"What's the situation?"

Matt gave Amos a quick summary, including the two young men he'd sent to check on the car in the river.

"We should take Rylee to your house to check her condition," he concluded.

Emily had struggled over to them, dragging Rylee, who was still leaning heavily on her—it took all of Emily's strength to hold her up. Lillie helped Emily get her into the back seat of the car and climbed in beside her.

Chris had turned the truck and trailer around, and now slowed to wave goodbye, when Amos stopped him, holding up one hand.

"Wait Chris," Amos said, then turned to Matt and Emily. "You two go with them. We can handle it from here."

"Are you sure?" Matt asked.

"Positive. Get out of here."

Matt helped Emily into the back seat of the truck and climbed in beside her. They all waved, and Chris pulled away.

"I'll clean up the scene and be right back," Amos told Lillie.

"You need to hurry," she said. "We don't want to be here when those two young men come back from the river."

Amos hurried over to the SUV and looked inside. Even

though Matt had told him what to expect, he was still shocked by the violence of the scene. He was always amazed at how fragile life was. Pulling his shirttail out of his pants, he quickly wiped the door handles as he closed the doors, then turned and ran back to the car. Lillie was waiting, both arms around Rylee, rocking her and singing softly. Rylee sat perfectly still, her eyes closed, either listening quietly, asleep, or in shock. As Amos put the car in gear, he looked around for the best place to turn around.

"I see a flashlight beam," Lillie said, pointing toward the opposite side of the road.

The college students were coming back up the hill. Amos quickly turned the car around, with barely enough room on the roadway and sped off the way they had come, before the two young men arrived at the roadway.

"Here they come," Lillie said.

The flashing lights of emergency vehicles reflected off trees and bushes below them in the canyon.

"I was hoping to get out of the canyon before they got here," Amos said.

"Too late now," Lillie said. "Better pull over like a good citizen."

Amos glanced at her in the rearview mirror, then slowed the car, using his right-turn signal and pulling to the side of the road just as a police car, then an ambulance, and then a fire engine sped past.

"If those college kids saw us, it would only have been as we drove away," Lillie said, "but they *did* see the truck and trailer."

"The truck was pointed down the canyon when they saw it," Amos said. "With any luck they'll think Matt drove into town, not up the canyon."

Lillie was thinking about the impact the accident was going to have on the family and their plans, when Amos spoke up again.

"It'll only take a few minutes for the police to get to the scene and talk to the students. They'll figure out pretty fast that we might be witnesses and come looking for us. I'll turn off into the university campus as soon as we get out of the canyon."

"Leaving the SUV at the scene could lead them right to us." Lillie said. She'd been about to say, 'the SUV and the bodies,' but she'd realized that Rylee might be awake and hear.

"I cleaned up the accident scene," Amos said, his jaw tight with anxiety. "Still, it's almost impossible to get everything. With modern forensics, I'm sure they can tell a lot from even a scrap of evidence." He thought for a few moments. "We'll go to the lab and hide while we figure out what to do."

Amos took the first right turn that would lead them off the main highway and into the labyrinth of Logan at night.

15

"Where are my mom and dad?"

Amos drove into the lab parking bay and closed the overhead door. He made sure all the shades in the bay and the lab were closed, while Lillie helped Rylee out of the car. As she stood, Rylee became alert again and looked around.

"Where are we?" she asked. "Where are my mom and dad? And Josh?"

"It's okay Rylee," Lillie said soothingly. "We're at my house. You have a bump on your head that we need to check out. We'll get you cleaned up and get a good night's sleep. Then we'll talk about it."

"Lillie," Amos said, "why don't you take Rylee to the bathroom and check to make sure she doesn't have any other injuries. I'll find some food and set up the cots for the two of you."

Lillie nodded and helped Rylee into the restroom. She looked the girl over carefully, all the while watching for signs of physical injury as Rylee moved. Then she had Rylee strip down to her underwear to check for other injuries, but Rylee was able to move her arms, legs, and neck without apparent pain.

"You have a bump on your head, and there's a bruise on your chest where your seat belt was," Lillie said with a smile, trying to be reassuring.

Rylee was quiet throughout the process, and Lillie worried that the impact to her head might have given her a concussion, which often happened in auto accidents. But her eyes looked fine, and she said she had no nausea or dizziness. She reached up and felt the bump, wincing as she touched it.

"Your seat belt kept you from getting hurt more seriously."

"You mean like Mom and Dad and Josh?" Rylee asked forlornly.

Lillie's smile vanished as she realized that they hadn't been careful enough about what they said around Rylee, and she'd figured out what happened. Lillie chided herself for not protecting the girl better from the painful truth. That said, she wasn't going to lie. Finally, she swallowed hard and spoke as gently as she knew how, tears in her eyes before she said the first word.

"Rylee, I'm sorry. I'm *so* sorry. Your mom and dad, and Josh, they weren't . . . " she wasn't sure what to say. "Your car ran into a tree and they . . . they . . . well, we weren't able to save them."

Lillie wiped away a tear as she looked to Rylee for a reaction. Rylee stared at her for several seconds before her face crumpled. Seconds later, a quiet whine began, quickly escalating into loud sobbing. She buried her face in her fists as she continued to cry.

Lillie placed her hand on Rylee's shoulder just as she began to list to one side—her eyes closed, and she fainted. Amos carried Rylee to one of the cots he'd just set up, covered her with a light blanket, and stayed with her while Lillie went to the house to find pajamas for her. When Lillie came back a few minutes later, Amos was kneeling by the cot, holding a cool cloth on Rylee's forehead. Rylee was crying, but it was more controlled than before.

"She knows," Amos said—it was more a statement than a question.

"Yes," Lillie replied.

Amos touched Rylee on the arm gently.

"Rylee?" he said softly.

She turned her head and looked into Amos's eyes. Lillie swallowed hard again as she watched her husband in his element. His bedside manner had endeared him to many patients over the years. When the news was bad, Amos had a gift. He couldn't take away the pain, of course, but his patients, or their surviving families, were usually able to at least understand what had happened. Lillie hadn't heard of a single instance where anyone blamed Amos for the result, though it was a common reaction. Still, this would be a real test. Rylee had just lost her whole family.

"Rylee," Amos began quietly, "do you know what happened to your family?"

Rylee's cheeks were wet with tears, and she sniffled before she answered.

"Yes. They're dead."

"That's true Rylee. I'm so sorry that we couldn't be there to help them or protect them. Do you understand what happens to a person when they die?"

"Yes," Rylee replied. "If they were good, they go to heaven."

"That's right. Your mom and dad, and your brother Josh—they were very good people. You know that, right?"

"Yes. But Josh was mean to me sometimes. Is he in heaven too?"

"What do you think?" Amos asked.

"I think he is. And my grandma and grandpa are with them. And my dog, Watson. He was a good dog, even though he chased birds."

Lillie smiled from behind Rylee as they talked, and she fell in love with Amos all over again as she watched. Her own reaction to the accident, which she'd kept tamped down, threatened to surface, and her throat constricted so she couldn't speak. She wanted to cry, and thought her heart might break for this beautiful young girl who had lost her entire family. They couldn't even let Rylee go home to the familiar surroundings that might comfort her because of the risk of running into police.

Lillie was just regaining control of her emotions as Amos wound down his talk with the girl. She watched as her husband leaned in and gave Rylee a tender hug, and Rylee pulled her arms out from under the quilt and wrapped them around Amos's neck, giving him a brief squeeze. Lillie took a few deep breaths to calm herself and give her time to get herself back under control.

"Does anything else hurt?" she asked Rylee when she was able to speak again.

The response was a shake of the head, and Lillie suspected that the emotional pain might be far worse than the physical.

"Here are some pajamas you can wear while I clean your clothes," she said with a sad smile, holding out a pair she'd fetched from the house. "We'll ask Amos to leave the room while you change, then you can sleep right here next to me. Does that sound okay?"

Rylee nodded and Amos stepped out.

Logan Canyon, Utah

"It was a black Ram 1500 Crew Cab, pulling a long trailer full of stuff," one of the college boys told Officer Ahlstrom. "They said they called an ambulance, but nobody was here when we got back from checking the car in the river. That's when we called you."

"And the guy said he was a doctor?" Officer Ahlstrom asked again, as he wrote down the detail in his notebook. "Did he look or act like a doctor?"

"Well, he was pretty young for a doctor. And the others who were with him looked even younger. All of them were around our age."

Ahlstrom's partner, Officer Dooley, walked up and pulled Ahlstrom to one side.

"What do you think?" Dooley asked.

"Well, it looks like one of the victims was shot, and the other two died in the collision with the tree. A family of three, maybe on a late-night drive up the canyon. There was an impact to the right front fender of their SUV. A good bet that the shots that killed the woman and destroyed the windshield came from the car that rammed into them, the one down in the river. If this was a drug deal gone bad or a road rage incident, the people in the SUV didn't have a chance to defend themselves. The gun I found on the floor of the SUV hadn't been fired. The two officers walked back over to their witnesses.

"Did either of you get a look at what was in the trailer?" Ahlstrom asked. "You say they were headed into town?"

"That's the direction they were pointed, but I couldn't tell what was in the trailer. Everything was covered with a tarp."

Ahlstrom turned to his partner.

"Dooley, put out an APB on the truck and trailer. Tell everyone what to watch for. Make sure the bulletin goes north to the Idaho border, east to the Wyoming border, and west to Ogden. If anyone finds them, I want them detained for questioning. They probably just happened by, saw the accident, and stopped. We need to know why they didn't call it in and stay until we got here."

Dooley turned and hurried back to the patrol car, while Ahlstrom turned back to the two students.

"Now. Tell me about the people you saw."

Logan, Utah

Amos spoke quietly to Lillie, as they listened to Rylee whimpering in her sleep.

"Let's spend the rest of the night in the lab. The police will follow up on the car. With guns involved, and at least three people dead, they'll be taking this seriously. If they figure out that Rylee's missing, they'll be looking for her."

"Will they come here looking for us?" Lillie asked.

"Who knows how thoroughly they'll search," Amos said. "Let me think about it. We need to be ready for anything."

As Lillie walked quietly toward the cots, Amos checked the door locks, turned off all the lights, and made sure both of their cell phones were off. He wasn't sure whether the police could track their phones, but he didn't want to take any chances.

A couple of hours later, unable to sleep on the hard floor with just a coat under his sore neck, Amos finally stood and walked to the small kitchen in the lab to get a drink of water. He noticed the reflection of flashing lights out in the street. Stretching his neck to loosen it, he peeked out the window. He wasn't surprised to see a police car in front of the Carlsens' house. Lillie walked up behind Amos and wrapped her arms around his waist. She laid her head on his back and spoke drowsily.

"What's going on out there?"

He dropped the curtain back into place and turned to face her, his arms going around her back. Without opening her eyes, she rested her head against his chest.

"The police are at the Carlsens'. If it was Aaron Carlsen's car down in the river, as Matt said, then I'm guessing Aaron didn't survive."

"I wonder how Jason and Brittany are handling the news," Lillie said quietly.

She pulled her husband in tighter, and he kissed the top of her head.

"How's Rylee?" he asked.

"Sleeping."

"What are we going to do with her?"

"She needs a mother"

"Are you ready for that?"

"Does it matter?" she asked.

They stood together a few moments longer before Amos walked Lillie back to her cot.

"I'm going to stay up a bit longer," Amos said. "The police might decide to come here next. I'll wake you if you want."

"Only if we need to move quickly."

Jason sat stoically in his robe and slippers, his hairy legs exposed. Brittany, in an old housecoat, sat in a nearby chair sobbing inconsolably into a tissue—she'd gone through several already. Officers Ahlstrom and Dooley remained standing.

"We identified the family in the SUV," Officer Ahlstrom said. "We need to notify their next of kin before releasing their names. They all died when their car hit a tree.

"How'd it happen?" Jason asked impatiently.

"It looked like the cars collided. Your son's car was in the river. He and his passenger—"

He stopped when Jason and Brittany both looked up sharply.

"His passenger?" Jason asked. He had a sudden terror that the passenger was Nathan.

"Yes, a black man about the same age," Ahlstrom replied. "They were both thrown from the car. It looks like both of them died on impact. Is there anything you can tell us about why your son was in the canyon?"

"You're sure it was Aaron?"

It was the second time Jason had asked, trying to control his shaky voice. At least the passenger hadn't been Nathan. Officer Ahlstrom nodded, referring to the iPhone in his hand.

"The car was burned pretty badly, but we found the VIN number on the dash. Both men were thrown from the car, but . . . " he looked at his notepad to be sure of his facts. "But Aaron had his wallet, with his ID, on him. We'll need one of you to come down and confirm his identity—whenever you're ready, of course."

Jason looked over at Brittany, who was still sobbing. He wanted to be anywhere but here. He didn't think he could deal with Brittany's emotions.

"I can go over this morning, in a couple of hours," he said.

"If you can look at the other man, and identify him, we'd appreciate that as well," Ahlstrom added. "He didn't have any ID on him. When was the last time you saw Aaron?"

Ahlstrom looked at his iPhone again and typed in a note with an index finger.

"He left here yesterday afternoon with Nat . . . " Jason could have kicked himself for mentioning Nathan. Officer Ahlstrom looked up sharply, then made another note in his phone. *Great, now the police will want to talk to Nathan, too,* Jason thought. He looked down and noticed a discolored spot on the carpet.

He focused on that rather than the policemen. He'd have to find some way to make it easier on Nathan.

"Who's Nathan?"

"Nathan is Aaron's younger brother."

Ahlstrom made a note.

"Do you know where Nate is now?"

"No. We don't usually know where they go or what they do," Jason said, then went on quickly. "We try to keep tabs on them. Typical youngsters, you know."

"But they're usually together?"

Maybe Jason could make up for his mistake now. He looked up at Ahlstrom.

"We don't know. I think he drops Nathan off at a friend's house. They leave together because Nathan doesn't have a car."

Jason paused, thinking furiously about how to help Nathan avoid being questioned. He made a mental note to tell Nathan what he'd said to the cop, in case Nathan needed an alibi. Officer Ahlstrom seemed about to speak, when Jason cut in hastily.

"Nathan doesn't really like Aaron's lifestyle, but sometimes he tags along."

Brittany had calmed down some as Jason spoke, but this last comment set her off sobbing again and Jason realized his explanation wasn't helping much. He didn't know what to say that *would* help.

"They're getting too old for us to control what they do," he added in frustration, lowering his head.

Brittany's sobs got even louder at that, and she blew her nose again. Jason looked at her. Since she'd decided to leave with the

Blunds, he'd had plenty of time to think about what his life would be like without her. They hadn't been intimate for some time, but he still leaned on her when things were stressful. In that way, he needed her, not to mention all the housework and the cooking. The boys, well, Nathan was going to be more of a burden than a help. Even with all her emotional outbursts, he realized that he needed Brittany much more than he'd thought just a few days before. He wondered if he could convince her to stay. If not, he might have to overlook his dislike of Amos and go with her to the hidey-hole. He was brought back from his thoughts when Officer Ahlstrom spoke again.

"Here's my business card. Please call me when you hear from . . . " He looked at his notes, " . . .Nathan. Or if you think of anything else that might help us. I've also written the address where you can see Aaron's body. If you'll excuse us, we're going to talk to some of the neighbors to see if they can add anything."

They let themselves out and closed the door quietly as they left.

Jason sat for a long time watching Brittany, trying to understand her pain. This was her firstborn. Aaron had made some bad choices in his short life, but he was still her son. She loved him unconditionally, and had sacrificed a lot for him. Eventually, Brittany cried herself out. Jason helped her to her feet and into the bedroom. He couldn't bring himself to console her physically, even though he wanted to and knew she would like it, or, at least, appreciate the gesture. Their relationship was already too strained.

Jason realized that he hadn't told the officers about Amos Blund, next door. He wondered why. It was too much of a coincidence that the accident had happened while Amos's family was trying to leave town. Had Amos really had nothing to do with Aaron's death, or did he just need to believe that? Maybe he was subconsciously trying to preserve Amos's plan for some other reason? Jason didn't know, and maybe it didn't matter. The police would probably talk to Amos while canvassing the street, anyway.

Amos's head drooped repeatedly in exhaustion as he sat waiting for the police to show up or the sun to rise, whichever came first. He jerked awake when he heard banging on the outside door of the lab, but he decided not to answer it. The knocking came twice more, and a flashlight beam shone against the blackout curtains but didn't penetrate. Eventually, whoever it was went away. It was Sunday morning and just getting light outside.

"I think we should stay here until we know the coast is clear," Lillie said to Amos quietly, as they watched Rylee eat an energy bar. "The police could be watching the house."

Amos put the last bite of his energy bar in his mouth and finished off his punch. He hesitated briefly before turning on his phone. There were four voicemail messages and several emails waiting for him.

"I think we need to take a chance and listen to some of these messages. There may be something important, and we can't stay here forever without information."

Lillie nodded, then went to sit on the cot by Rylee. The first message was from Rachel.

Dad, we arrived safely. Call when you can.

The next one was from Jason.

Amos, this is Jason. The police were here. Aaron and his friend are dead. I'm going to claim his body. Brittany is a wreck. Call me.

Jason was curt, but Amos couldn't tell if he was angry or just grieving. He didn't recognize the next number.

Mr. Blund. This is Officer Ahlstrom of the Logan City Police Department. We would like to talk to your daughter, Emily. If you know where she is, please have her call me.

He left a number where he could be reached at any hour. The last message, in a tired, gravelly voice, surprised Amos.

Amos, this is Patrick McKensie. The cops woke us ta' smornin'. They was goin' door to door lookin' for any sign uh yer family or Nathan Carlsen. Wherever ya' are, stay there . . . an' call if ya' need anythin'.

Amos turned off his phone. He noticed Lillie talking to Rylee. When she saw that he was off the phone, she stood and went to him.

"How is she?" Amos asked.

"She says she wishes that she'd died, too."

"I've heard that before."

"I told her we're going to stay here for a while. It's too bad I don't have anything to entertain her with."

"Maybe you can sing to her. Isn't that what Rachel said she did to calm Rylee after the accident?"

"I can try that, but she's not a little girl. She'll need something more entertaining than a song. Maybe I'll try to check her injuries, too. She said the bruise on her chest hurts."

Amos smiled. Lillie looked like she hadn't slept much or well, but he wasn't going to say anything about it.

"You look like you haven't slept," she said tiredly.

Amos couldn't help a quiet laugh.

"What?" she asked.

"I was just thinking the same about you, but I wasn't going to say so."

She slapped him, open handed, on the chest.

"Oh, stop your laughing," she said. "What did your messages say?"

Amos told her what he'd heard.

"With the police looking for us, I don't know how safe we are here," he said.

"I say we leave as quickly as we can," Lillie said. "Any kind of police investigation will hold us up. It'll be complicated and messy and it'll drag on too long for what we need to do."

"I agree, especially since we could be accused of withholding evidence. But we agreed to take Brittany Carlsen with us, so we can't go before we find out where she stands. Aaron's dead and Nathan's missing, with the police looking for him."

"You said they were asking about Emily. Why would they?"

"She must have left something at the scene—fingerprints, you'd think, but I don't know how they could have processed fingerprints this quickly. Anyway, our first priority is to talk to Brittany, or Jason, before deciding what to do next."

Lillie turned on her phone to check for messages.

"A message from Rachel, but nothing from Brittany."

She turned the phone off again. Amos sighed.

"I'll go talk to Jason," he said.

He really didn't want to talk to Jason, especially not in person, but it had to be done, and a phone call—which might be traced—was out of the question.

"Jason, I'm so sorry."

Amos stood on the back-porch steps of the Carlsens' home. He'd checked the street out front for police cars before going out the side gate and around to the back of the house. It was early Sunday morning and no one was on the street, but he wanted to be careful. After a long pause, Jason finally answered.

"Come on in and sit down, Amos. The police just called us back. They said it looked like—" Jason choked back a sob before being able to go on. "They said it looked like Aaron's car and the Parkers' SUV had a collision. Aaron went off the cliff into the river. I mean his car went into the river, he was thrown out of it, they found him on the other side. They also said Rylee Parker's missing and they wanted to know if we knew anything about that. Were you there? Is Rylee with you?"

Amos didn't want to lie, but he needed Jason's cooperation. Jason was emotional, and he'd always been difficult and unpredictable even when he wasn't.

"I arrived after the accident. It didn't look like we could do anything for Aaron or Rylee's parents, so we helped Rylee get out. She needed medical treatment."

"I wanted to blame you. That's why I called earlier. But I finally realized that Aaron did this to himself. I'm the one who's sorry—for Aaron's bad choices, for messing up your plans. What are you going to do now?"

This was where it got sticky.

"We still intend to leave, and we promised we'd take Brittany, assuming she still wants to go. That's why I'm here."

Jason didn't answer. Amos waited as long as he dared, but he was anxious to get back to Lillie and Rylee.

"Jason, I have to go, I'll get back to you in a little while."

He stood up and walked to the back door.

Jason sat, staring at his back door as it closed behind Amos, wondering what he should do. He thought about what Brittany had told him, and what *he* really wanted. He couldn't imagine being able to live by Amos's rules. But Nathan wanted to get away, see if he could change his way of life. Jason didn't know what he would do if he lost all of them.

Amos was frustrated at not getting an answer from Jason, but he could see that he had to give Jason a little more time to work through his feelings.

"What did he say?" Lillie asked.

She was gazing across the room at Rylee, who was still lying quietly on her cot, staring at the ceiling.

"He didn't really say much of anything. He's sorry that Aaron messed up our plans. But nothing about what Brittany, or he, want to do now. I didn't want to stay over there too long in case the police came back, or the neighbors started leaving for church, so I left. He's probably sitting there thinking about what he should have said."

"So, what do we do now?"

"Well, we have the same two options we talked about earlier. We can hide out until evening before leaving or make a run for it now. We don't know what the police will do, but I'm sure they'll keep looking for Rylee, thinking she's been kidnapped. They'll probably get a subpoena to check out Tyler's house. When they find a lot of furniture missing, they'll think this is bigger than just an automobile accident and shooting."

"Will they want to search our home too, because of Emily?" Lillie asked.

"They might," Amos said. "But I say we give Jason and Brittany a little more time before we decide."

Lillie nodded.

Part of the solution came an hour later, when Amos checked his phone again. There was a text message from Jason.

Amos, Jason. Please call. Nathan came home and told us the whole story. Details later. Bottom line is that he's changed his mind and wants to go with you . . . and I do too. We accept all your conditions. Please tell me it's not too late. I'm sure the reason you left here in a hurry is that you think the police may be watching our house. We haven't told the police any of this, honest. Please call me back and tell me what we have to do.

The police had called Jason earlier to let him know that the Parkers' next of kin in New Jersey had given them permission to release their names. They now knew that the Parkers had a daughter, Rylee, who was missing, and wanted to know if Jason knew where Rylee was. The police also suspected that it was more than just a coincidence that Aaron had had a gunfight and collision with a neighbor. After talking to Jason and Brittany, they suspected that Aaron's lifestyle was at least partly to blame for the incident.

Jason had decided not to tell the police about Amos, or that Amos had Rylee, because Brittany wanted to go with Amos, and Jason was still deciding what he wanted for himself. He'd decided to tell Amos about it now because it would help his story, help him get what he wanted.

"Amos, if they come along, that makes fifteen of us in the Preserve," Lillie said. "That's too many people."

"We expected to have sixteen people before the accident. We can make it work."

"Yes, we can. But trading the Parkers for Jason and Nathan isn't a fair trade. You know Jason could change his mind again—and probably will—especially once we're in the Preserve and he comes face-to-face with all the things he didn't like the sound of at the beginning."

Amos put his arms around Lillie and hugged her.

"I know, but we need to give him the benefit of the doubt."

"Look, I know people can have a genuine change of heart, and we're not in a position to judge another person's sincerity, but I just don't buy it. Jason can't be trusted. He's already attacked you once. What's he going to do the next time he loses his temper?"

"I know. But a promise is a promise. We'll have to deal with it." Seeing Lillie's stern look, Amos was about to continue. "Lillie—" he said, but she cut him off.

"Never mind," Lillie said quietly, but forcefully. "We've lost Tyler's SUV and we still have six people and the rest of the Carlsens' supplies to take to the Preserve. We need other transportation. Didn't you say Jason has an SUV?"

"He does," Amos said, "but it won't fit everything."

"Then we have to take Terry's SUV, too."

"What we need is a van," Amos said at almost the same time.

"Both good ideas," Amos added diplomatically, "but I don't

think we should go out to get Terry's SUV or to rent a van. The police might be watching for us. Maybe we can get Jason—"

Lillie shook her head at him.

"You're right," he said. "Same problem. The police might be watching for the Carlsens to do something unusual."

"What about Patrick McKensie?" Lillie asked. "He offered to help."

"The police interviewed the McKensies," Amos said. "That might not be good either."

"But they've probably interviewed the whole block," Lillie said. "Maybe they won't make the connection if Patrick rents a van."

It was a long shot, but the first one they'd come up with that looked like it had a chance of success.

"I'll call Patrick," Amos said. "Gotta be quick though."

"Be careful, honey," Lillie said, as Amos started to dial.

16

"Patrick, we need transportation"

"Patrick, it's Amos. Thanks for the call and the information."

"Ya' okay? The cops said there was a' accident an' sev'ral people died, one of 'em Jason Carlsen's boy. They said yer family was involved but disappeared. Well, what they said was ya' left the scene. That true?"

"Unfortunately, true. We can't get tied up with the police right now. You understand?"

"O'course . . . yer gone then?"

Was that disappointment in Patrick's voice?

"Not yet. Patrick, were you serious about your offer to help?" Amos held his breath, afraid of missing Patrick's response. The phone was on its speaker setting so Lillie could listen.

"O'course. Whadaya need?"

Patrick spoke rapidly, his voice taking on a sharp tone, as if he were back in the army, responding to a senior officer. Amos would have laughed if the situation weren't so serious, and he let out his breath in a rush, cautiously optimistic about getting out of town before the deadline.

"Patrick, we need transportation. We need you to rent a van

that will hold at least six people, plus supplies. I'll pay for it, if you'll put it in your name."

It felt like he was pleading, which he guessed he was. Patrick hesitated.

"If it's in ma' name an' you take it, how'm I gonna' return it?"

"That's the rub, isn't it?" Amos was thinking furiously about how to make this work. "We'll try to get it back to you . . . But, if you don't see it in your driveway within a day or two, you'll have to call in a stolen vehicle report to the police . . . If we can't get it to you, we'll try to leave it somewhere the police are sure to find it. They won't hold you responsible."

Amos could tell Patrick had his hand over the phone while he explained to Kathy. He was almost ready to hang up when Patrick spoke again.

"I have 'nother idea. What if I rent a van fer eight an' we go wit' ya'?"

Amos was speechless. This was a twist he hadn't counted on. "Are you serious?"

"Ah would be, if we was younger," Patrick said good-naturedly, and Amos realized he'd been having fun with him. Patrick continued, more seriously, "Had some time ta' think 'bout it. Been watchin' the news, too. Me an' Kitty, we know ya' was right 'bout there bein' a war comin'. It's gonna be ugly, ahm bettin'. But no, we made our 'cision. We're gonna stay here, maybe go ta' a shelter. Kitty foun' one not far 'way. Ahl rent ya' a van. Whadaya need?"

Amos was surprised by Patrick's talkativeness. He was also relieved that Patrick and Kathy hadn't changed their mind about going with them. He was already trying to figure out how to handle fifteen people in the Preserve.

"Patrick, we've been on the phone too long," Amos said. "Let me get right back to you."

"Understood." It was Patrick who hung up first.

When Amos returned, Rylee was working on a book of sudoku puzzles with a pencil. Lillie had been sitting, watching, but she got up as soon as she saw Amos and went to him. Amos told her what he had in mind, and they mapped out a rough strategy that depended mostly on Jason. For that, he would need to talk to Jason again. Lillie called Brittany on her cell to minimize the time Amos's phone was in use.

"Hello."

Brittany sounded like she'd been crying and was on the verge of crying again.

"Brittany, it's Lillie. How are you holding up?"

"It's hard Lillie."

"You're sure you still want to leave with this going on?"

Brittany's voice changed, becoming firmer.

"Absolutely sure. The sooner we get out of here, the better. Didn't somebody famous say, 'let the dead bury the dead'?" Her voice changed again, weary this time. "Jason arranged for the mortuary to have Aaron's remains cremated and his ashes held until we pick them up. He's paid for everything in advance. Jason and Nathan are packing now. We're just waiting for your word."

"Can Jason stop for a minute to talk to Amos?"

"I'll get him."

Lillie handed the phone to Amos.

"Hello?" Jason said.

"Jason, Amos here."

No response. Amos wondered if Jason were already having second thoughts. He decided to find out.

"Do you have any questions?" he said.

Jason choked out his response.

"Only question is when and where. You were right and I was wrong. I hope you'll let us come."

"And your boy, Nathan?"

Jason let out a strangled laugh.

"Nathan, yeah. He was so scared when he came home this morning, he spent over an hour apologizing for things he'd done with Aaron. I had no idea some of the things they'd gotten up to. He begged his mother to take him away, where he could think about what he wanted his life to be like."

"Hmm . . . .." Amos said noncommittally, thinking that Nathan's reason for wanting to join them was far from ideal. "Did you explain my conditions to him? Does he understand what the living situation will be like?"

"You're asking if Nathan should stay in Logan. And if maybe I should." It was a statement, not a question. "I had a long talk with him. We both know it'll be difficult, but neither of us will do well without Brittany."

"Okay," Amos said. "I still need to work out the details with Patrick McKensie, but I need you to watch for Patrick to come home with a van. He'll back it into his driveway and he'll need help taking out the rear bench seat. Then you can back it into your driveway and load your stuff into the back."

They talked for a minute about how much gear Jason and Nathan had that needed to go.

"We'll get a fairly large van, since there'll be six of us plus your gear. We'll have Patrick and Kathy watch the street to let us know if there's anyone there who shouldn't be. Once we have your gear loaded and we know the coast is clear, we'll come out and get in the van."

Jason laughed sarcastically.

"Why not? Okay, I'll have Brittany watch while I finish packing. Thanks again, really."

"You're welcome, Jason." Amos hung up wondering whether he'd done the right thing. Letting Jason into the Preserve might be the worst mistake he'd made in a long time. But it was the right decision, right now. *That's going to have to be good enough*, he thought.

"Patrick, it's Amos."

"Been waitin' fer yer call. What'll it be?"

Amos suggested a place where Patrick could rent the van.

"Make it a twelve passenger, I already verified they have one. Think you can back it into your driveway?"

"Humph! Use ta' drive the buses all o'er the base. They're lots bigger than a twelve-seater."

"Great," Amos said, then repeated what he'd told Jason.

"After Jason takes the van, do you think Kathy could spend some time watching for any unusual activity on the street?"

"Hah! Ya' mean like a stakeout by the cops? Saw that on TV. Cops in plain, unmark'd car, but they din't belong an' the guy they was stakin' out spotted 'em. Kitty'll luv it. I'll tell her ta' tek her knittin' out on the porch, maybe even tek a walk down the street. She does that sometimes. Won't be 'spicious lookin'. She can do that while ahm gettin' the van. Ya' can coun' on *us*."

Amos had to restrain himself from laughing out loud. This was a side of Patrick he'd never seen in all the years they'd been neighbors. But he couldn't laugh—Patrick was taking his request seriously.

"We'll watch for you," he said instead. "Thanks Patrick."

Lillie watched out the window as Patrick, true to his word, pushed Kathy out the front door, her arms full of knitting, as she awkwardly pulled on a sweater. Patrick whispered instructions in her ear and Kathy shooed him away, then sat in the rocking chair on the enclosed porch, organized herself, and started knitting. The garage door opened, and Patrick backed the car out, stopping in the driveway. He opened the door and called to Kathy, waving her over. With her arms full of knitting, she hobbled awkwardly down the front porch steps and over to the car, Patrick hurrying to meet her partway. After a few words, Patrick grabbed the knitting out of her arms and threw it into the back seat. He was backing out of the driveway before she had the door closed.

Lillie started laughing.

"What's so funny," Amos asked as he came up behind her.

"Patrick and Kitty," Lillie said, as Amos peeked out the window to see. "Patrick must have realized he needed Kitty to drive the car home, otherwise he'd have to leave it at the rental agency. He's so anxious to do what you asked that he's running around like a Keystone Cop."

Jason helped Patrick remove some seats, then the three of them climbed into the van and drove across the street, backing into the Carlsens' driveway.

"Come on inside," Jason said.

Brittany and Nathan were stacking things in the mud room, waiting to load them into the van.

"Kitty, Patrick," Brittany said. "Thank you for getting the van."

Patrick addressed Brittany proudly.

"We're here ta' help ya' load yer gear an' ta' watch fer the cops."

Brittany knew the basic plan, but looked at Jason questioningly. Jason shrugged, lifting a duffel bag in one hand and a pile of blankets in the other, and looked at Nathan.

"Let's get this stuff out to the van," he said.

Nathan nodded mutely, his expression showing just how profoundly Aaron's death had upset him.

"How can we help?" Kathy asked Brittany.

"All these need to go to the van," Brittany said, motioning to the pile of supplies.

Jason walked up to the van for the second time, with Nathan following, their arms full of bags, just as a police car pulled up and stopped, blocking the driveway. Officer Ahlstrom stepped from the car and walked over. Officer Dooley got out, too, but stayed on the far side of the vehicle. Jason walked to the front of the van to meet Ahlstrom.

"Hello, Mr. Carlsen. Going somewhere?"

Nathan's head came up at the sound of Ahlstrom's voice. Seeing the police uniforms, he quickly retreated into the house, but not before Ahlstrom saw him and looked that way. Jason followed Ahlstrom's eyes.

Nathan backed right into Brittany. She yelped.

"What's the matter with you?" she asked.

"Shhh, Mom," Nathan whispered. "The police are here. They're talking to Dad. I'm just trying to hide."

"That probably looks very suspicious Nathan. Go back out there and load your stuff. Then walk over and say hi."

Nathan reluctantly went out again, his head down. He was followed by his mother and the McKensies.

"Looks like your son got back," Ahlstrom said, nodding in Nathan's direction.

"Yeah. He's already given his statement at the station."

Jason wanted to be angry, but knew it would be counterproductive.

"Uh, we've got to get away or go crazy," he went on. "Our good friends from across the street are going with us."

Kathy started to say something, but a nudge from Patrick stopped her. When the policemen didn't leave, Jason set down the bags he was carrying. Patrick walked over and picked them up and, with a nod to Officer Ahlstrom, took them to the back of the van to load them. Ahlstrom nodded back.

"I saw the report your son gave. No funeral?"

"We're having his body cremated. We asked them to hold the ashes until we get back."

"Where're you going?"

Jason thought as quickly as he could about how to answer without giving too much away. He knew he should've had an answer planned, just in case, and chided himself for the oversight. He decided on misdirection. After all, they were loading bedding and clothes into the van.

"Yellowstone . . . camping."

"Nice place. Do you have a reservation? I understand the campgrounds fill up quickly."

"Last minute decision. You understand. But there are a few campgrounds between Yellowstone and Jackson, just in case."

Am I ever going to get rid of this guy? he wondered.

"Why a twelve-seater? There are only, what? Five of you?"

More misdirection.

"Actually, there are eight of us. Our daughter's taking friends. She's with them now. Plus, we have a lot of gear. Patrick and Kathy will probably have to sleep in the van. Old bones, you know," he added conspiratorially.

"Sure you're not trying to escape?"

Jason's heart skipped a beat, but a moment later, Ahlstrom went on.

"You know, the terrorist threat?"

He grinned to show he was kidding.

"Maybe we should," Jason said, making himself smile back. "But where the heck would we go to get away from a nuclear explosion?"

Jason remembered Amos using the same argument on him, and surprised himself by feeling a pang of empathy for the man.

"Good point. Well, you take care. Don't go playing with the bears or bison in the park." With that, he turned and nodded to his partner. They got back into their patrol car and drove off. Jason watched them go, feeling like he'd just aged ten years. When Patrick walked up behind him and spoke, Jason nearly jumped out of his skin.

"Thin' they'll be watchin'?"

"I don't know. I think that maybe Brittany and Kathy should go for a walk around the block, just to make sure, while we finish loading."

"Good idea," Patrick said, with a twinkle in his eye and hop in his step. "Ahl go tell 'em. They can say they're gettin' ready for tha long car ride—if they're asked."

Jason nodded, then smiled and shook his head at Patrick's exuberance. The old coot was okay. Looking back the way the police car had gone, he got on the phone with Amos to bring him up to speed. An idea was forming in his head.

Everyone moved quickly, and by early afternoon they were putting their final departure plan into action. While the women walked slowly around the block, looking for any sign of a stakeout, Jason, Patrick, and Nathan walked out to the front sidewalk to get an idea of which neighbors might be able to see what they were doing.

The Blunds' vinyl fence and gate reached from the property line to the garage, so no one would be able to see into their backyard from a main floor window—a second-floor window, maybe. The house directly across the street was the McKensies'—no problem there. There was no worry about someone seeing them from the back, either, because the nearest subdivision was more than a quarter of a mile away, with a stream and an undeveloped field in between. They wouldn't be seen from that direction unless someone had field glasses and stood high enough to clear the fences. That left the six-foot gap between the property line and the Carlsens' garage, where there was no fence. That determined, Jason moved the van to the side of the driveway that partially obscured the view to the backyard. Then Patrick and Nathan went back and removed a section of the vinyl fence between the Carlsens' and the Blunds' backyards.

The women returned, Kathy hobbling, Brittany walking slowly to stay with her.

"Will you and Kathy stand at the front of the van and just talk—you know, pretending you have nothing better to do?" Jason asked Patrick.

"Shur, but wha' for?" Patrick asked.

"Mostly, I just need you to watch the street. Let us know if the police come back, or if you see anyone else looking this way. Signal us if you see anything."

"Tha' we cun do."

"Jason," Brittany said. "Kitty brought up a good point. What if the police come back and find the McKensies at home when they're supposed to be camping with us?"

Patrick looked at Kathy and smiled.

"Tha's ma' Kitty," he said quietly.

He looked at Jason to see how he would respond. Jason thought about it, but it was Kathy herself who came up with the solution.

"We can say we decided we're too old to go camping and turned down your invitation at the last minute. *Old bones, you know*." She said in a deep voice, mimicking Jason.

Jason frowned. Was she making fun of him?

"Perfect," Brittany said with a smile. "And we decided to take the van anyway because we'd already rented it."

"So, if the cops thin' you 'ave the van in Wyomin'," Patrick thought out loud, pleased with himself, "and it don't come bak, we can say we don' know where t'is."

Brittany laughed, Jason frowned, and Kitty smiled proudly

at her Patrick for coming up with that bit of reasoning.

While the McKensies stood watch out front, the Carlsens moved around the van as if they were still loading it. Amos, Lillie, and Rylee slipped through the break in the fence. They mingled briefly with the others, then slid into the van through the rear doors, climbing awkwardly over the gear. Once they were in the seats farthest back, the Carlsens got in, Jason driving and Brittany riding shotgun.

"Patrick," Amos called through the side door before it closed. Patrick stuck his head in the open doorway, and Amos handed him a wad of cash to pay for the van.

"Tha's too much," Patrick said, looking through the stack of bills and trying to return some of them.

"We won't need it Patrick," Amos said, pushing Patrick's hand away. "We appreciate all you've done. You take care."

"Yoo, too," Patrick said with a sad smile. "Besta luck to ya'."

"I'd like to say a prayer, for protection," Amos said. There was grumbling from somewhere in the front of the van, but they bowed their heads as Amos began. When he finished there was a round of "amens."

"All right everyone, let's turn off the phones now," Amos said. "Completely off. We can't have anyone, like the police, tracking us."

"You think they'd do that?" Jason asked, turning his head to face the back.

"Probably not," Amos said. "But I don't want to take a chance. I just sent a text message to Terry at the Preserve, so he knows we're coming. We should have no other reason to be on our phones now."

The small group drove away, waving to Patrick and Kathy. A small tear formed in the corners of Lillie's eyes. As Amos and Lillie had discussed earlier, they might not be back for a very long time.

17

"This is home"

Logan Canyon, Utah, 1 July

They played musical chairs in the van a couple of blocks away from their home so that Amos, in the front passenger seat, didn't have to backseat drive Jason. As they approached the mouth of the canyon a few minutes later, Amos remembered a concern Patrick had raised a couple of hours earlier.

"Ya' should 'ave a plan for gettin' past a roadblock, in case the cops 'ave one set up in the canyon . . . to catch ya'," Patrick had said.

"I don't think the police are looking for us," Jason had replied. "They've already talked to us and they know we're leaving town."

"Din't ya' say that cop . . . "

"Officer Ahlstrom."

"Yeah, Ahlstrom was questionin' ya' like he din't believe ya'? I say ya need ta be ready to run a roadblock. I saw that on the TV once. There was a chase an' everythin' . . .."

"There's not going to be a roadblock." Jason had gotten a little exasperated with Patrick. "We're not going to have to run from the police."

"Ah da' know. Ah think ya' shood 'ave a plan," Patrick had insisted.

Brittany had seen that Jason was reaching the limit of his patience, and had jumped into the conversation.

"Patrick, I put some blankets in the back. They're on top. If we see any police, we'll have everyone—except the driver, of course—pull them over their heads and pretend to be asleep. They'll just think it's Sydney and her girlfriends."

"Maybe you should go that far with us, Patrick," Jason had added sarcastically. "If they want to know who's under the blankets, we'll say it's you, and you can pretend you just woke up, real grouchy, and scare them off."

Brittany had given him a look that said the sarcasm wasn't constructive.

"Yeah, I like tha'," Patrick had replied, missing the sarcasm. "Maybe we should go wit' ya' tha' far, Amos."

"Yes," Kathy had added. "Patrick can do *grouchy* real well."

They'd all laughed except Patrick, who didn't get the joke.

"Thanks Patrick," Amos had said laughing, "but I think we'll be fine. Remember what I said about calling the police if the van doesn't get back."

"Yessir," Patrick had replied with a sharp salute.

Now, approaching the mouth of the canyon, Amos began to worry. But there was no roadblock and they all settled in for the ride.

The ride up the canyon should have been delightful. The distance they had to travel wasn't far, but the narrow, winding roads of the canyon would take some time to navigate. The trees were every shade of green, the color of life. Flowers of all colors were in bloom on the sides of the road and on the surrounding hills. The river was running high, due to a wet winter and late thaw. By all appearances, they were out for a Sunday afternoon ride in nature. But Lillie was the only one who took time to notice and appreciate the beauty. She had done everything she knew how to do. The rest was up to God—and the government.

No one spoke in the van. Jason had the radio tuned to a business news report, which played quietly, but no one was listening, not even him. He'd received an email from the office just before leaving home that made him angry. *Bloody executive committee—that was a dumb move*, he thought. *It's completely illogical. I need to get in touch with Tom and the other board members and make sure they understand it can't go forward.*

Brittany, sitting in the second row of the van behind Amos, wrestled with thoughts about her dysfunctional family. *What could Jason and I have done differently to save Aaron?* No answer came to her. *How is Aaron's death going to affect Nathan's behav-*

ior? Again, she had no answer. *What can I possibly do to make Jason respect Amos Blund's rules. I don't believe for a minute that Jason has actually become humble.* She knew him too well.

Nathan sat next to his mother, oblivious to the presence of the others. He thought about all the stupid things he'd done, following Aaron around for more than a year. *My old man didn't seem surprised by most of it,* he thought shaking his head. *Of all the dumb things I've done, I wonder if going to this retreat might be the dumbest. It's not like it's going to be a vacation, like sitting on the beach thinking about what I want my life to be like. It's going to be more like a prison, where I have to do what someone else tells me to do all the time, at least if what my old man said is true.* He had just started thinking of himself as an adult, and now he was going to be one of the children again.

Rylee, sitting in the third row, behind and to the right of Nathan, noticed him, but for now was so devastated by the death of her family that she paid no attention. *I'm an orphan with no say in what happens to me for the rest of my life,* she thought desperately. *Why did I live when they all died? What do I have to live for?* Each time she glanced in Nathan's direction, which was more and more often as they drove, she was more intrigued by and attracted to his sober expression and roguish looks. Each time she looked at Nathan, she thought, *he knows what this feels like. He could understand me.*

Amos trusted Terry, but he thought about all of the things that needed to be checked when he got to the Preserve and wondered how much Terry had accomplished. *Has he checked out the Observer,* he wondered?

Lillie noticed Rylee turning to look at Nathan—again. *They've both lost someone close to them,* she thought. *Rylee's at an impressionable age and still dependent on adults for direction. She needs someone to take her parents' place. How do I make sure it's me and not Nathan, when I have the rest of the family to take care of, too?* She was starting to feel responsible for Rylee, *as if she were my own daughter,* she thought. *I wonder if I'll have to protect her from Nathan.*

Being protective of the Preserve, Amos had misled Jason into thinking they were headed to Garden City. The fewer people who knew their ultimate destination, the better, at least until they arrived. Now, as Amos started looking around, Jason noticed.

"What are you looking for?"

"I don't want anyone to see where we turn off the highway," Amos said, "so I need to make sure there's no traffic."

"What do you mean?" Jason's voice betrayed his confusion

"Watch for a dirt road on the right about a hundred yards past mile marker 488, just ahead. If there's no traffic, turn there."

"What? I thought we were going to Garden City."

Now Jason was upset.

"We're almost to Garden City," Amos explained. "It was easier to tell you to go to Garden City, than to give you directions to the exact spot where we were going to turn off."

"What you mean," Jason said angrily, "is that you were afraid we might give away the location of your ultra top secret hidden base if we knew any sooner,"

He immediately regretted his outburst. *Why do I let him get to me like that?* He really was trying to cooperate. He just didn't like the secrecy. *I said I was in,* he thought. *My word should be worth something. Then again, I haven't given Amos any reason to trust me.* When Amos didn't reply, Jason was contrite.

"I'm sorry, Amos. I had no right to say that."

They were quiet after that. Jason began to slow down, checking his mirrors.

"There it is," he said, spotting the turnoff. "There's no traffic. Should I make the turn?"

Everyone looked around, trying to find some sign of the Preserve.

"Yes, thanks Jason," Amos said.

Jason slowed the big van further, then turned onto a trail that was no more than two dirt ruts with wild grasses growing between them and to either side. Almost immediately, they were surrounded by trees and undergrowth that hid the trail—and the van—from the highway. The rutted and uneven track led into a beautiful wooded valley, where dappled afternoon sunlight filtered down through the trees, shining on flowers of various colors amid the grasses.

Seeing the beautiful valley made Lillie smile. She fell in love with it all over again, as she did every time they visited.

"It's gorgeous," Brittany said.

"Umm-hmm," Lillie agreed.

Looking at it this time, though, it saddened her, too—it might never look this way again, spoiled by the violence of war.

The trail took them along the base of a hill and around the southern edge of the valley, abruptly ending next to a large rock outcropping about half a mile from the highway as the crow flies. The rock face rose a hundred and fifty feet above them, with sheer rock wall directly ahead. As the trail disappeared, Jason slowed to a stop. Those who hadn't been there before continued to look around for anything that appeared man-made. It was still daylight, so that it seemed like there should be some indication that the rest of the family was nearby.

"Where is it?" Jason asked.

"You'll see," Amos said, smiling. "Drive another twenty

yards toward the cliff face."

As the van approached, the rock wall in front of them split along a natural crevice in the rock, the two sides opening inward, away from them, along an irregular, vertical seam. Jason turned and stared at Amos.

"What is this?" Jason asked.

"This is home," Amos replied. "Go ahead and drive in. Park on the right side of the truck so we can unload."

The Preserve, Aspen Valley, 1 July, 3:35 p.m.

When the van had passed through the opening in the rock wall, the doors closed behind them. Lights came on, and they could see that they were in a vast, cavernous room. The rest of the family—those who'd already arrived—appeared through a set of double doors that slid open on their right. Sydney Carlsen was in the lead, and she hurried toward the van, a big smile on her face. As Brittany opened the cargo door and climbed out, Sydney wrapped her in a warm bear hug. She might not be a child anymore, but she still missed her mom. Sydney quieted suddenly, though, when Nathan got out after his mother.

"What's he doing here?" she asked her mother quietly.

Brittany wrapped her arm around her daughter and walked away from the van, talking quietly to Sydney.

"Nathan and Dad decided to join us," she said.

"Why?" Sydney whined. "I don't want him here. He'll spoil everything."

Brittany hadn't heard Sydney whine in this tone since she was a little girl—she'd always tolerated her brothers' behavior.

Rylee didn't leave the van immediately—she watched Nathan walk away first. Her heart beat faster at the way his shaggy, dark, shoulder-length hair moved as he walked, and at his cool indifference to his surroundings. He seemed dangerous and exciting. Lillie, waiting behind Rylee, cleared her throat to break Nathan's spell. Rylee didn't look at Lillie, but she did move, getting out of the van with Lillie following close behind.

Mike and Terry had been hanging back as everyone greeted each other, but moved forward when Lillie finally appeared.

"Welcome to your new home," Mike called to the newcomers.

He threw his arms wide, and Lillie laughed when he came over and gave her a bear hug, lifting her off the ground. She hugged him back and gave him a kiss on the cheek. Amos smiled at the display of mother and son affection, then turned to Terry.

"Should we start the tour here?" Amos asked.

"Everyone else has already heard it," Terry said. "You may as well lead the newcomers." Amos smiled and clapped his hands to get everyone's attention.

"Okay, everyone. It's good to be back together. Thanks for the friendly welcome. Let's get the gear out of the van and you can show us our new home. Everyone grab an armful of supplies from the back of the van, please. Don't worry about what you grab or whose it is. We'll sort that out later."

Everyone gathered to the back of the van.

"Most of this stuff is ours, so maybe I can help sort it out now," Jason said. "Might be easier that way."

"Okay, Jason," Amos said, backing away to avoid any sort of confrontation.

As Jason pulled each bundle out and handed it to the next person in line, he identified the family member it belonged to or said, "Group supplies." Nathan insisted on taking his own backpack, tearing it wordlessly from Rachel's arm. Rachel gave him a dirty look, but he didn't notice—he was already moving away. Rylee stood off to the side, never taking her eyes off Nathan. He didn't notice, but Lillie did.

"Let's take all the gear to the community center, where we can regroup," Mike said.

Those who were already familiar with the layout of the Preserve started off in that direction, and the others followed.

Jason looked around at the cave walls and ceiling, which looked like they'd been covered with gunite. Metal conduit ran between bright LED lights. The drive-through doors seemed to have disappeared when they closed. The wheel tracks on the concrete floor were the only way he could tell where the doors were.

"Did you blast this cavern out of the rock," he asked, "or was it here before?"

"We did the blasting," Amos said. "It took some time and a lot of research on how to use explosives safely." He laughed. "Actually, Michael is the engineer, so he gets the credit for doing such a professional job with the blasting and the electrical and mechanical work."

"The government let you use explosives here?" Jason asked suspiciously.

"Well, it *is* private property and I *do* have a permit." Amos was obviously trying to control his temper, and Jason savored his discomfort. "The wiring is in conduit, the lighting is explosion proof, everything is according to code."

"It's amazing," Brittany said admiringly. "It looks like a professional did it."

Amos laughed.

"Well, Michael's an engineer, so a professional *did* do it."

"It looks like you covered everything in gunite," Jason said, to show his knowledge. "Were you afraid of it caving in?"

"Actually, the gunite is to keep the EMP shielding in place," Amos said.

Jason was wracking his brain to figure out what EMP shielding was, when he realized that Amos had just forced him to be quiet or admit his ignorance by asking what he meant. He wanted to know, but he also didn't want to look stupid.

"I guess we should get going," Amos said.

He moved toward the exit and Jason followed. Most of the family had left the garage already, and the only bags left were the ones they were holding.

"Just a minute," Terry said, approaching Amos and Lillie. He was about to go on, but Jason interrupted.

"What's the setup, Amos?" Jason asked. *Best to assert myself early, so Amos knows I won't be pushed around,* he thought.

Terry jumped in, smiling.

"We'll show you part of the Preserve as we make our way through to the bedrooms. We'll let you settle in, then show you the rest later, or even tomorrow. No hurry. It's been a long day. Becca's been working on dinner, so that's the main thing on the schedule for the rest of the day."

"Exactly what Terry said," Amos told Jason. "If you'll follow the others, we'll be right along."

Jason hadn't met Mike or Terry, but assumed they were the two men who had welcomed them. He hesitated, watching Terry.

"Jason, this is Terry Stephens, my business partner," Amos said. "And this is my son, Michael. Terry and Michael, Jason Carlsen, his wife, Brittany, and their son Nathan."

Terry stuck out his hand.

"Nice to meet you, Jason," he said with a friendly smile. "I'm sure we'll become good friends in time."

"Thank you," Jason replied formally. *I doubt it,* he thought to himself. He ignored Terry's hand, picking up his bags so that his hands were full. He moved toward the sliding doors, leaving the others to catch up, and Brittany and Nathan followed.

☢

Terry spoke quietly to Amos, watching Jason's retreating back.

"He's going to be fun to have around. We need to talk after you settle in, maybe after dinner. Mike and I have been monitoring C-SPAN. It's not a pretty picture."

"Fine," Amos said. "We've been in hiding since early this morning." At Terry's questioning look, he added, "I'll tell you later."

Amos, Terry, and Mike approached the double doors, where Lillie had one arm around Rylee's shoulders and was talking to Brittany. Jason and Nathan were standing to the side, looking at nothing in particular and avoiding eye contact with each other. The doors opened.

"There's an elevator!" Brittany said, surprised.

Jason and Nathan tried to look disinterested, but couldn't resist craning their necks to look.

"Yup," Lillie said with a smile as they entered. "See the second set of doors in the back? That's where we'll exit into the Preserve."

Amos picked up the narrative as they got in.

"This is a state of the art elevator: polished stainless-steel walls, industrial carpeting, recessed LED lighting, and a simple control panel," he said.

There were buttons and a keyhole on the panel, but only two floors were listed: "Garage" and "Home." The seven of them, plus their bags, fit comfortably.

"The garage is carved out of the natural rock of the mountain, but the rest of the Preserve was excavated into the floor of the valley," Amos told them as the elevator descended smoothly and quietly. "We'll be descending twelve feet into the ground. There are other ways to get into the Preserve, but this is the easiest since our arms are full of supplies. We'll meet the others in the community center."

"What other ways?" Jason asked.

Amos was instantly on alert, wondering why Jason was so interested in the ways into and out of the Preserve, but he forced himself to sound casual.

"Well, there's a staircase to the side of the elevator, but you don't want to carry the bags down that."

Amos smiled, trying to keep his voice conversational. He wasn't about to tell them about the other entrances yet—and he wasn't sure that he'd ever tell Jason. When Jason turned away, Amos made meaningful eye contact with Terry, who nodded subtly. When the elevator stopped moving, the doors at the back opened.

"Please exit out the back and take the tunnel to the right," Amos said.

The tunnel before them ran to the left and the right.

"This tunnel," Amos said, "like all the connecting tunnels, is constructed out of corrugated steel, six feet wide and seven feet high. The walls are actually eight feet high, but they're embedded a foot deep in concrete to hold them in place. You'll be relieved to know that this is the only tunnel painted utility gray."

The walls were vertical, rounded at the top, with a flat, unpainted concrete floor. To the left, the tunnel took a sharp bend a few feet away. That portion of the tunnel was dark. To the right, the brightly lit tunnel ended at a set of open double doors taking up most of the metal wall.

"Where's that staircase?" Jason asked.

"Just to the left of the elevator," Amos said, "but the community center's to the right. That's where we're going."

Amos extended his arm to the right to show them, but Jason was still staring down the tunnel on the left. *Why is Jason so interested in that?* Amos wondered, once again uncertain about Jason's intentions.

"Good to know where the exits are in case of an emergency," Jason said conversationally, as if it would be an obvious concern for anyone.

"Michael, why don't you play tour guide for us," Amos said.

He wanted to stay back and see what else drew Jason's attention.

"Sure," Mike said and motioned for everyone to follow him, turning to face them and walking backward. "If you'll follow me, through these double doors is the airlock. It's a twenty-foot-long room with another set of doors at the other end."

There were metal cabinets and drawers against the left wall and full height metal lockers on the right. Everything was gray. The doors at the far end were open.

"The lockers contain hazmat suits," Mike said. "They protect the wearer from airborne contamination. The drawers and cabinets hold specialized equipment and supplies used with the hazmat suits, like Self Contained Breathing Apparatus—or SCBA—tanks, which are a lot like the scuba tanks used by divers. There are also radiation dosimeters that anyone leaving the Preserve will have to wear if we detect excess radiation in the valley."

"What do you mean, *excess radiation?*" Brittany asked.

"Well, there are always naturally occurring radioactive particles around us. They come from certain types of rock. That's called background radiation. If the radiation level increases beyond the background level, that's a sign of an abnormal situation—like nuclear fallout."

Brittany nodded.

"You'll see that there's a control panel by each set of doors." Mike continued. "Right now, everything is unlocked and open so we can move freely in and out with our luggage. When we lock down, only those with keys and a passcode will be able to get through the doors."

He rattled the keychain attached to his belt loop. As they continued the tour, he noticed Jason glancing at the keys several times over the next few minutes.

"This airlock is the only thing keeping us safe from any contamination that the valley's exposed to," Mike said. "We don't want anyone inadvertently opening the doors at the wrong time. You'll also notice what looks like a shower head in the corner, with a floor drain. That's exactly what it is."

Mike chuckled as he watched their expressions go from awe to disappointment.

"If anyone is returning from outside when the air is contaminated, they'll have to decontaminate their hazmat suit before removing it. There's a detailed procedure on the wall in the corner."

He pointed to a laminated notice.

"The control panels also direct the scrubbers that cycle and clean the air when needed." He chuckled again. "It's like standing in a wind tunnel. This room is made from sixteen-foot diameter corrugated steel pipe, split lengthwise, like all the rooms in the Preserve. That means this space is actually wider than it looks—there's dead space behind the cabinets and lockers."

"For the mice," Terry added with a laugh.

Brittany and Lillie laughed with him. Jason looked at Terry with disgust.

"Are you serious? Mice?"

"Not that we know of," Terry said. "It was a joke."

Jason just scowled at him.

"And it's embedded in concrete, like the tunnels?" Brittany asked to change the subject.

"That's right," Mike said, as he led them through the second set of airlock doors, into another tunnel. "All the tunnels and rooms in the Preserve are made from corrugated steel embedded in a foot of concrete. There's EMP shielding, a foot of concrete, and at least two feet of soil over the top of everything. That's to protect against radiation contamination."

"So," Brittany calculated, "That makes them seven feet high in the middle . . . "

" . . . tapering to the floor on the sides," Mike finished for her. "As I said, all the rooms are made from sixteen-foot diameter pipe, so, they're about sixteen feet wide and seven feet tall. But the seven-foot dimension is in the middle of the room. There's not as much head room on the sides of the room, and that can take some time to get used to. You'll see that in the community center in just a minute."

They came to another set of double doors, closed this time, with a large *C* painted in the center of one of them.

"The tunnels and rooms are separated by these bulkheads. They're not airtight, but they're insulated against sound. All the doors lock from both sides except the bedrooms. They only lock from the inside."

He rattled his keychain again. When they opened the doors to pass through into the community center, the noise of laughter and talking hit them full force.

"Maybe we should have dampened the acoustics in here," Terry said to Amos quietly.

"Can't get everything right," Amos said.

"And now we're in the community center," Mike said.

Chris Stephens and Rachel Blund were sitting on one of three couches on the right side of the room, and their voices reverberated off the walls. Sydney stood quietly at the far end of the room, looking in their direction. When they came in, she waved her arms and called out to them.

"This is the way to the bedrooms. Come on. I'll show you."

"Where are the others?" Lillie asked, smiling at Sydney's enthusiasm.

"Becca, Emily, and Katie are working on dinner," Mike said.

"Becca told me dinner will be at six, so you should have time to unpack, wash up, and relax before she calls us to eat."

The newcomers were looking around the community center. There were various pieces of furniture scattered around, arranged in small groupings. The ceiling and walls were cream colored. The floor was covered in industrial-grade carpet which, while it wasn't pretty, was functional and it would last. The entire room was turned about thirty degrees to the left with respect to the tunnel. There was a set of double doors at the far end, one door standing open, and another set halfway down the left side. An entertainment center sat against the wall at the far end of the room next to a large screen for a projection TV that hung from the ceiling, and other electronics were arranged on the nearby shelves. Durable brown couches were set up in front of the screen. Partway down the right side, there was an electronic keyboard, with other musical instruments arranged on shelves.

"It's big, but feels smaller because of the curved walls, doesn't it?" Brittany said.

"Yeah," Terry said. "We moved the furniture away from the walls because we kept bumping our heads when we stood up." He laughed, rubbing the back of his head. "Something to watch."

"The community center is what we call a hub," Mike said. "It's like the hub of a wheel, with tunnels leading off to other rooms and other hubs. At the far end of the room, where Sydney's waving at us, is the tunnel to the bedroom clusters. Looks like she's anxious to show them to you."

Rylee plopped down on the nearest couch, placed her face in her hands and started to cry. Lillie sat next to her, placed an arm around her shoulders and hugged her. "It's alright, Rylee," she said. "Everything will be fine."

"Nothing will be fine!" Rylee bawled angrily, turning to glare at Lillie, "ever again."

Lillie didn't know what to say, in the face of Rylee's anger and grief, until she noticed Sydney waving for everyone to follow her. "Would you like Sydney to show you your room?" she finally asked Rylee.

Rylee paused in her crying, long enough to look toward Sydney, then pulled a tissue out of her pocket and blew her nose. She wiped her eyes with the back of her hand, stood, and walked to the other end of the room—to where Sydney stood. "Will you show me my room?" she asked softly.

"Sure!" Sydney said loudly. "Anyone else ready to see the bedrooms? This is the way," she said loudly. "That's why there's a *B* on the door. Guess what the *D* and *E* stand for."

A large *D* and *E* were visible under the *C*. She didn't wait for anyone to respond. "Dinner and exercise," she shouted.

Lillie noticed that Rylee kept her head down, looking at the floor. Then Mike clapped his hands loudly to get everyone's attention.

"Let's help the Carlsens take their stuff to their rooms."

Chris and Rachel stood and picked up the bags that were

at their feet, and Sydney turned and started through the door. When Rylee didn't follow immediately, Sydney took her by the arm, and she allowed herself to be pulled into the tunnel. Mike and the others followed.

"Looks like Sydney's already taken over the place," Amos whispered to Lillie.

They had slowed to create space between them and the rest of the group.

"And she doesn't want Nathan to *ruin* it," Lillie said. "I hope Rylee will be okay."

"Keep an eye on her and let me know if I need to do anything."

18

"Welcome to the Preserve"

The Preserve, Logan Canyon, 1 July

"This is the bedroom wing," Mike explained

He led them down the main tunnel, away from the community center, speaking loudly so everyone could hear.

"All the bedrooms are on your right. As Sydney pointed out, the dining and exercise areas are on your left. We'll meet in the dining room later. Feel free to check out the exercise area on your own if you want, and I'll be available to answer any questions.

"Is this all there is to the Preserve?" Brittany asked.

"Well, no," Mike said. "You've seen the airlock and the community center, and we'll see the bedrooms now, but the Preserve is big. It's kind of like an ant hill with a lot of rooms connected by tunnels, and we want you to know your way around, so feel free to look around, try things out, and ask questions."

He stopped as he reached the first side tunnel on the right.

"We had to rearrange the bedroom assignments from our original plan. Putting fifteen people in a space designed for nine makes it pretty tight, but we managed."

Mike pointed down the side tunnel.

"These are the Stephenses rooms. Terry and Becca, along with their children and some of the Blunds, have their rooms here."

"This tunnel on the left goes to the dining cluster," he said, pointing to a tunnel with a *D* painted on the wall next to it. "That's where we'll meet for dinner later."

When they reached the next tunnel on the right, Mike had them turn into it.

"These are the Carlsens' rooms. There are three bedrooms surrounding a central common area. That's true for each of the bedroom wings."

They entered the common area, which was about twenty feet from end to end. There were three doors, one at the far end and one midway on each side. Mismatched furniture was arranged around the room to allow the family to sit and visit.

"We already had furniture in the rooms," Mike said. "But we replaced some of it with your own furniture, when we got it, so you'd feel more at home. We were in a hurry, though, to get everything ready, so we didn't worry too much about matching furniture, as you can see. If there's anything you don't like, just let me know. The rest of the furniture is in a storage room."

Sydney stood in the doorway at the far end with Rylee behind her.

"This is my room," she said. "I don't have a roommate, but Rachel said I can invite Rylee to sleep over sometimes. Mom and Dad get that room." She pointed to her left. "And Nathan has that one," she added, pointing the other way. "Mom, come and see my room."

"Okay, dear," Brittany said, sharing an amused smile with Lillie.

"We tried to keep parents and children together as much as possible," Mike explained. "I hope everyone's okay with the arrangement, but if not we can adjust it later."

Mike allowed the Carlsens, and anyone who'd helped carry the Carlsens' luggage, to pass.

"Drop the bags here," Jason said pointing to a spot in the middle of the common area. Everyone did. Nathan grabbed his duffle bag and went into his room, closing the door without speaking. Sydney and Rylee watched him go, Sydney with a disapproving look on her face and Rylee with a curious look on hers, before disappearing into Sydney's room.

"Look, Mom," Sydney said, "they taped our names on the doors."

"The names are just there until everyone's more familiar with the layout," Mike said. "You can take them off any time you want. The couples' rooms have queen beds, the others have two double beds. The double beds can be converted into bunk beds, but the ceiling gets in the way unless you put the bed right in the middle of the room."

Brittany stood in the doorway to Sydney's room, looking around.

"It's so nice to see some furniture from home," she said. "Thank you for that."

She smiled at the failed attempt to match the bed covers and furniture in each room.

"Well," Mike said apologetically, "just let me know if you want to change something."

"It'll do just fine," Brittany said, following Sydney into her room. "I think it makes them look homey."

Mike spoke a little louder so that everyone could still hear despite spreading out.

"All the beds, dressers, desks, and chairs can be moved, but we need to be careful. We don't have a lot of spare furniture, so if anything breaks, someone has to fix it, if possible."

Jason, who'd been waiting impatiently for a break in the monologue, bent over and picked up a couple of backpacks and took them into his room, closing the door behind him.

"We'll remind you when dinner's ready," Mike said as Jason closed the bedroom door.

We just got here, Jason thought, *and I'm already regretting it. Underground tunnels, Amos running the show—what's next?*

"Let's continue the tour," Mike said as he led the way back out to the main tunnel. Brittany came out of Sydney's room, holding hands with Sydney and Rylee, to follow Mike.

Brittany was disappointed. She'd really hoped that Jason

had had a change of heart and would want to be part of this adventure. She looked from his closed door to the luggage on the floor, then to Nathan's closed door, feeling torn between staying with Jason and Nathan and being part of this new family.

Lillie watched Brittany's expression, thinking that she understood what was going through her mind and smiling sympathetically. Brittany gave a half-hearted smile, then followed the others, still holding onto Sydney and Rylee.

Lillie started to follow Brittany and the girls, then noticed that Rylee was still staring at the floor. She reached out and touched Rylee affectionately on the top of the head. Rylee turned and looked at Lillie, but her expression was blank, like she was suffering emotionally.

"This next tunnel on the left—the one with an E painted on the wall—is the exercise rooms. Feel free to use the equipment, but if you have any questions about their proper use, please ask for a demonstration. We don't want anyone to get injured. The last tunnel is the Blund family bedrooms, but Rylee will share a room with Rachel, and Matt Green has a room there, too."

Sydney walked past him, pulling Rylee behind her and talking nonstop.

"Mike let me decide which furniture you got," she said excitedly, as if trying to say everything before someone could stop her. "I picked the one with the prettiest headboard. Then Rachel let me help set up your room. We left your clothes in your suitcases on the bed."

She leaned close and whispered conspiratorially as she led Rylee through the common area.

"I didn't think you would want anyone seeing your private things, you know."

She was still talking when they turned right, into Rylee's room. Rylee just stared at Sydney—she looked overwhelmed.

Matt Green came out of his room at the end of the common area and spotted Mike. "Is this the end of the tour?"

"Yup," Mike laughed, "this is it. I was just going to see how they're coming with dinner. Want to tag along?"

"Sure," Matt said. "I only heard female voices. The men cut out early?"

"Yeah. I think Terry captured Dad. Jason and Nathan turned down the tour."

"You never were good at attracting men."

"Thank goodness," Mike said, and they both laughed as they walked away.

Just before six o'clock, Mike and Matt did a circuit, reminding everyone to go to the dining room for dinner.

"The plan is to have dinner at 6:00 each night, so put that on your schedules," Mike said several times as they rounded people up.

"Lillie, the table decorations are beautiful," Brittany said as they entered the dining room together.

Folding tables extended down the middle of the room, surrounded by fifteen folding chairs, so that everyone could eat together. The tables were decorated with white lace tablecloths and live flower centerpieces, and the place settings consisted of three sets of china dishes, crystal stemware, and silverware.

"I recognize my china," Brittany continued. "The other dishes are . . . ?"

"They're mine and Becca's," Lillie said.

"Are we going to eat on china every meal?" Jason asked, walking up behind Lillie and his wife.

"No. We have plastic place settings that'll be easier to clean and less likely to break," Lillie said. It was clear by her voice that Lillie had decided not to be offended by Jason's brusque manner. "All the furniture's the folding kind, so the room can be used for other activities. The live flowers, well—they're not going to be too common."

"Well, obviously," Jason said bluntly. "You can only have live flowers during the spring and summer."

"Feel free to tour the gardens and see if that changes your opinion," Lillie said. Jason and Brittany both stopped and stared after Lillie, confused, but she'd turned away, not wanting them to see her disgust at Jason's constant provocation.

"You have to tell me more," Brittany said as she hurried to catch up to Lillie.

"Let's find a seat and then I'll tell you all about the dining

area," Lillie said. "It looks like Amos wants to say something."

Amos stood at the end of the table, opposite the main doors. When everyone was seated, mostly by family, he raised both hands briefly and spoke to the group.

"I know everyone's hungry, so I won't take long. I just have a couple of things to say."

There was impatient stirring around the room, and Mike motioned for his dad to speed things along.

"Welcome to the Preserve. Through an unusual set of circumstances, which none of us envisioned a few weeks ago, we are here together, in our own little world, safe and sound. Formerly four separate families . . . "

"Four families?" Jason turned to Brittany. "Who's the fourth?"

"Shh," Brittany hissed, seeing people turn. "Rylee Parker," she said quietly.

Amos continued, ignoring the interruption.

"We hope that you'll consider yourselves members of a single family from now on and treat each other like family—with love and understanding."

He looked around the room to see their reactions. Most were smiling, looking around at each other. Jason, Nathan, and Rylee were the only exceptions. Jason was staring at Rylee down on the next table, who until now had been staring at the plate in front of her, but who'd looked up long enough to see

Jason's look of disapproval, then looked down again and begun to cry. Nathan, meanwhile, ignored everyone, staring off into space.

"Before we eat," Amos went on, "I want to point out that tonight's meal is exceptional compared to most of the meals we'll have here. This is a special occasion, so enjoy the food but don't get too used to it."

He smiled, and a few people chuckled good-naturedly.

"I've asked Lillie to pray, thanking God for our safe arrival, and to bless the food we're about to eat. I ask you all to include in your personal prayers a request to protect the innocent, who are at the mercy of the world's governments, for their safety. Also, to ask that the governments of the world will seek a peaceful resolution to their differences. Lillie?"

Lillie prayed. Then several family members, who'd prepared the meal or been asked to help serve, got up and went to the kitchen. The servers returned with large bowls of fresh green salad and steaming hot soup, which they passed down the center of each table. They went back to the kitchen, returning with plates of cooked vegetables and fresh fruits, then did another round with platters of ham and turkey and pitchers of several different juices. Finally, the servers brought out several kinds of cakes and pies, and set them on a table in one corner of the room.

"What a spread!" Mike said. "You really outdid yourself Becca."

"I had a lot of help," Becca said, smiling at those who'd been in the kitchen with her.

While they ate, Lillie explained the layout of the dining area to Brittany. As others realized what they were talking about, they stopped talking and listened.

"The dining area is arranged like the others, with a central common room and three other rooms surrounding it. Obviously, this room is divided into a kitchen and a dining room, separated by that bulkhead over there."

She pointed to the end of the room, where Amos had been standing and where the meal had come from. There was a pair of swinging doors centered in the wall.

"The other three rooms are pantries. There's one opening from the dining room side, over there," she said, pointing, "and the other two open from the kitchen."

"Are these floors actual wood?" Brittany asked.

"No. They're laminate, which means they're easy to clean," Lillie said.

"Good idea," Brittany said, then continued more quietly. "You must have seen my husband eat."

When it looked like Lillie had finished what she had to say, and everyone had eaten their fill, Mike stood and clinked his spoon on a crystal goblet to get their attention.

"We would appreciate everyone taking their dirty dishes to

the cleaning area in the kitchen," he said. "If you haven't tried the desserts on the side table, be sure to do that before you leave. There are clean dishes on the dessert table. Also, before you leave, we want you to know that, as with all the activities in the Preserve, we'll take turns with food preparation and meal cleanup. Becca will be in charge of those activities and she'll tell everyone what help she needs. We should have a schedule in place by tomorrow, but for tonight Mom and I will clean up. The rest of you can go relax after you clear your dishes."

He smiled when some of them patted him on the back as they passed, headed for the kitchen or the dessert table. After the cleanup, some of the adults hung around to talk. Brittany put a hand to her stomach

"Now I know what Amos was talking about," she said to Lillie. "I guess we won't be able to eat like this all the time."

"Well, this is a special occasion," Lillie said. "A welcome home celebration of sorts."

"What I mean is, all the fresh fruits and vegetables. Living underground, we're not going to have the fresh foods."

Lillie smiled. "You can see the gardens tomorrow," she said. "You'll be surprised."

This caught the attention of several of the adults.

"You have gardens?" Matt asked. "Underground?"

Lillie raised her voice so more of them could hear.

"We started gardening underground about two years ago. We have a large vegetable garden, and even some dwarf fruit trees—including citrus, which don't normally grow in this part of the country. We planted a few fruit trees topside, but we don't hold out much hope for them if the air quality gets bad."

"Do you have grapefruit trees?" Matt asked. "When we lived in Arizona we had some. I love grapefruit."

"Yes, and oranges, lemons, and limes," Lillie said, laughing at Matt's enthusiasm.

Terry motioned for Amos to follow him.

Amos nudged Lillie with his elbow.

"If you'll excuse me," he said, "Terry needs to show me something."

Lillie nodded as she looked around to see who was still in the room. As Amos and Terry left, Brittany started to get up.

"You're welcome to stay and talk, or wander around the Preserve," Lillie said, loud enough for everyone still in the room to hear. Brittany sat back down and turned toward her.

"I like to wind down with a good movie after dinner," Brittany said. "I saw the video equipment in the community center. What kind of selection do you have?"

"Oh, we have a lot to choose from," Lillie said. "Emily, will you show Brittany the video library."

"Sure Mom," Emily said, taking Matt's hand and motioning for Brittany to follow them.

Jason turned to Nathan.

"You want to check out the exercise equipment? I think I can find my way back there."

Nathan nodded, then followed his dad out of the room. That left Mike, Katie, Becca, and Lillie to finish cleaning up the dining room.

"You go," Lillie said, shooing Becca away. "You cooked.

Michael and I will take care of cleanup. I'll work on an assignment list tomorrow."

"Oh, I couldn't do that to you. There are too many dishes for you two to do. Besides, you've had a long day."

"I'll help," Katie said, making eye contact with Mike and smiling.

Mike returned the smile and took her hand.

"Thanks Katie. I'll show you where the cleaning supplies are."

She followed him to the kitchen. Lillie thought for a moment. It really had been a long, difficult day

"Thanks, Becca. I really am tired. I'd love the help."

They both laughed.

19

"*You* are the devil, not us"

The Preserve, Aspen Valley, 1 July

Terry led the way into the office, with Amos on his heels.

"Mike and I have been taking turns monitoring C-SPAN and other news channels since we got here," Terry said. "Becca insisted that I help her get everyone settled in as they showed up, so we've been trading off duties. We wanted to get some of the lab equipment set up, but also monitor what's going on in the world."

"So, where are we?" Amos asked.

"All life-support systems and utilities are working properly," Terry said. "I haven't been able to assess the impact of the extra bodies on the water and sewage systems yet, but the septic tank will fill sooner than we planned. I guess we'll have to decide what to do about all of that, but as long as the lines leading into the drain field don't clog up, we should be okay. The extra water filters and chemicals you sent will extend the life of the water treatment system, but for how long?" Terry shrugged. "I'll run some calculations," he said when he saw Amos's expression. "The security system in the valley is working properly. We were alerted as soon as you left the highway. We have both video and audio. I think you should take away everyone's phones, tablets, and any other electronic devices, so we can turn off the interrupters. Even though cell signals don't get through the walls, they're using energy we can't afford to waste."

"I'll wait a bit to bring that up," Amos said. "Don't want to hit them with too much at once. Speaking of using power, how does the power grid look?"

"The reactor's working and it's being monitored. The power grid's fine. We tested the backup generators in both automatic and manual mode. The interface is working as designed."

"Have you checked the satellite TV and radio reception?"

"They work, but we still get interference because of the way we camouflaged the dish. No help for that. I still wish we could have added solar power as a backup."

Amos opened his mouth to explain again why they couldn't use solar, but Terry held up a hand to stop him.

"I know," Terry said. "Solar panels could create a reflection that would be visible to satellites and planes."

"If the satellites keep working," Amos said. "What about the lab equipment?"

"We haven't had a lot of time yet," Terry said. "That was next on my list. You being here will help."

"Okay," Amos said, "I'm anxious to get the Observer up and running so we can figure out what we saw, or rather, didn't see on the university campus, before all this started. I can't imagine why we couldn't find that new medical building. Tell me what's going on out in the world."

"The UN started an emergency session yesterday at the request of Daniel Porter, the U.S. Ambassador, who sits on the Security Council."

Terry said this as he was turning on the TV and DVR.

"There's been lots of finger pointing and denial. President McCormick made an appearance, so I recorded it. You'll find this interesting."

He turned on the recording and Daniel Porter appeared on the screen, standing at a podium. He was speaking.

" . . . and I will turn my time over to President Gregory McCormick, president of the United States of America, to address the General Assembly. Mr. President?"

United Nations General Assembly Hall in New York City, 30 June, prerecorded

U.S. Ambassador to the UN, Daniel Porter, moved away from the podium as President Gregory McCormick walked onto the stage and stopped at the lectern, leaving his nervous, ever-vigilant, security detail at the edge of the stage and around the perimeter of the auditorium. McCormick turned to look at the president of this emergency session of the United Nations, Peder Jorgensen of Denmark.

"President Jorgensen, esteemed members of the Security Council, representatives of member states, ladies and gentle-men, thank you for allowing me these few minutes to address the General Assembly of the United Nations. The United States of America has hosted the United Nations since its inception because we believe in the founding principles that unite us. The United Nations gives all of us a place to air our grievances and a guarantee that we will be heard and treated fairly. In return, as member states, we each have a responsibility to every other state to be fair and honest. When any one state takes advantage of another, the Security Council makes every effort to level the playing field for the aggrieved state. I'm here today to tell you that some of our members have violated the trust that we place in them."

A murmur spread through the auditorium. President McCormick knew it was a bold and confrontational statement. The General Assembly delegates weren't unaccustomed to confrontation—it happened all the time. What surprised them was that it was coming from him. He continued.

"The United States security services have obtained evidence that Al-Qaeda does, indeed, have a nuclear weapon, and is intent on detonating it within the borders of the United States."

There was louder murmuring now. This was a very specific accusation. The president raised his voice to be heard over the noise.

"Our evidence indicates that Al-Qaeda is using source funding from Saudi Arabia to build a nuclear device in Mexico with the help of the Los Zetas drug cartel. The cartel plans to help Al-Qaeda smuggle the bomb into the United States using one of its as-yet-undiscovered drug routes, to be detonated somewhere near Washington, D.C."

The Saudi representative to the UN, seated in the second row of the auditorium, stood, pointed a finger at the president and yelled.

"That is a lie. We do not fund Al-Qaeda and we do not

build bombs."

The president laughed a little bitterly.

"Mr. Halabi, your denial is the lie. You have been sponsoring terrorist training camps and indoctrinating young people in fundamentalist Wahhabi doctrines for years, and everyone knows it. Your country *created* Al-Qaeda."

The noise level in the room got so loud that the president had to nearly yell the last sentence. President Jorgensen stood and moved to a position next to President McCormick. He pounded his gavel on the podium until the noise level decreased to a reasonable level. Then he turned to President McCormick with subdued anger.

"Do you have to do this? This is highly unsatisfactory."

President McCormick spoke into the microphone again.

"President Jorgensen has asked me if this accusation is necessary. I will answer to all of you. Any state that deems nuclear war as an acceptable means of obtaining its objectives, is a threat to all of us, not just the target of their aggression. You should all be incensed by Al-Qaeda's crass ignorance of, or carelessness about, the real harm—that one nuclear bomb can ignite a global thermonuclear war that will end the world as we know it. This is not just ignorance, not carelessness—it is of the devil."

He knew using that term would incite, at a minimum, all the radical Arabs. He wanted to see the reaction.

The auditorium exploded again, with Mr. Halabi standing, pointing at the president and shouting.

"*You* are the devil, not us."

The president had to yell to be heard, even with the micro-phone.

"Mr. Halabi, do you deny that the Al Saud family provided funding to build a bomb for the purpose of detonating it in Washington, D.C.?"

"I have already denied it and I deny it again."

Mr. Halabi was seated again now, so he could use his micro-phone, but he had to yell as well, his voice barely carrying above the raucous noise in the room. President Jorgensen pounded his gavel on the lectern again, trying to return the auditorium to some semblance of order. President McCormick didn't wait for the noise to subside, but spoke over it.

"Then tell me, Mr. Halabi," the president yelled, "why have two thirds of your staff and their families left the United States in the last week, and why do you, personally, have a one-way ticket out of John F. Kennedy International Airport for tomor-row afternoon? Are you afraid to be in New York on Wednes-day afternoon? What do you know that you're not telling this august international body?"

As he spoke, the noise in the room again rose to a roar. President Jorgensen pounded on the podium again, then asked President McCormick to excuse him and took over the micro-phone.

"Mr. Halabi, are you lying to this assembly? Does Saudi Arabia intend to detonate a nuclear device in the United States?"

But Mr. Halabi wasn't listening, he had gone white and was hunched at his desk, talking on his mobile phone. President

McCormick grabbed the microphone again.

"*Mister* Halabi!" he bellowed.

Halabi reflexively looked up, and the auditorium quieted, shocked at hearing the president of the United States raise his voice so raucously. In a quieter voice, the president resumed.

"Since you're talking to the Al Saud family at the moment, you can pass along the rest of my message. If a nuclear device is detonated in the United States, whether in Washington or elsewhere, whether this Wednesday or any other day, we will drop a larger bomb right on Riyadh. In fact, I'll tell the military to paint your name on the side of it, so that King Salmon knows who is responsible for delivering it to him."

Mr. Halabi's mouth hung open. He lowered his phone to the desk and stared, dumbfounded, at the president. But McCormick was done with him. He turned to the Russian member of the Security Council, sitting on the podium.

"Mr. Sokolov . . . " He shook his head. "Mr. Sokolov, where did Al-Qaeda get the nuclear material to build their bomb?"

The Russian just shrugged, straight-faced, appearing disinterested. President McCormick continued, shaking his head.

"Russia has been supplying arms to the Middle East for years and has a history of selling nuclear material to other countries through the Siloviki—your former KGB, turned mafia, turned industrialists. If we find that you sold nuclear materials to Al-Qaeda, either directly or through an intermediary, like Iran or Syria, we will be very unhappy. What we *do* know, Mr. Sokolov, is that your country very recently shipped a weapon to North Korea, a country that has *insisted* that if they get a nuclear weapon, they will launch it against the United States on one of their ICBMs, which, by the way, they are currently testing again."

The room had gone unusually quiet. Only murmuring could be heard as delegates got on their cell phones to talk to their respective government contacts. Mr. Sokolov smiled, but the smile didn't reach his eyes.

"We have done no such thing," he said into his microphone, then leaned confidently back in his cushioned chair. His arrogance was palpable.

President McCormick turned back to the General Assembly.

"In case you didn't hear him, let the record show that Mr. Sokolov said 'we have done no such thing'. My response to Mr. Sokolov, and to the Russian President, is *if not, then why did our Special Forces locate a bomb in Vladivostok last week?*"

Sokolov jumped up at that, looked threateningly at the president, and spoke, quietly, but with great fervor.

"You violated Russian territory by sending troops into Vladivostok? That is an act of war."

"An act of war, you say? And you supplying nuclear weapons to North Korea, a state with an unstable head—a man with a God complex—knowing they intend to use it on the United States—that's not an act of war?"

"You cannot prove it was nuclear," Sokolov said.

His slip of the tongue wasn't lost on those seated in the General Assembly room—he had all but admitted that the Russians *had* sent bomb materials to North Korea. Every eye turned to Sokolov, the unanswered questions threatening to spill over.

"Ah, you are right. We can't prove it was nuclear. But, you know what? We don't need to. I'll give you the same message I gave the Al Saud family. If North Korea fires an ICBM aimed at the United States, we will blow North Korea off the map, and we will send a nuclear warhead to the Kremlin with your name painted on the side."

"You wouldn't dare. Russia still has a large arsenal of ICBMs."

Sokolov sat down slowly. He didn't look as confident as he had moments earlier. President McCormick spoke to the General Assembly again.

"Mr. Sokolov just said the United States wouldn't dare send a nuclear weapon against Russia because Russia still has a large arsenal of ICBMs. Sir, you don't have as many as you used to have, since you started selling them on the black market. President Jorgensen?"

President McCormick turned to face the president of the United Nations.

"I'm tired of listening to all the lies." He turned around to face the room again. "Ladies and gentlemen, here is my ultimatum. Russia and Saudi Arabia will stop the nuclear weapons that are intended for the United States. If they do not, the United States will respond with a *nuclear* retaliation on any state that we believe is responsible for, or complicit in, this attack. And I may as well say, Mr. Montes," the president looked at the Mexican ambassador to the UN, "that Mexico needs to ferret out the terrorists who are working with the Los Zetas drug cartel. We need you to see if you can stop the bomb. You don't want the United States to feel obligated to send troops into Mexico to handle this."

Montes, seated in the third row of the auditorium, looked like he was going to be sick. The president knew there was no way Mexico wanted the U.S. to send troops across the border.

"Thank you, President Jorgensen," McCormick said, "for allowing me this time at the podium."

He gave a nod to Ambassador Porter, then strode from the platform, headed for his security detail and the exit. His security team continued scanning the auditorium for any overt act of hostility. The noise level in the room rose to fever pitch as the president left the stage.

A badly-shaken President Jorgensen stared for a few moments at the retreating figure of President McCormick, then walked to the microphone. He pounded his gavel on the podium until the noise decreased enough for him to be heard.

"China has asked for time to respond. Mr. Chung."

The Chinese member of the Security Council stood and walked proudly to the podium. He leaned into the microphone and spoke loudly.

"President McCormick," Mr. Chung said with a heavy accent. The president had not yet reached the exit, and he turned around. "Do *not* launch a nuclear missile toward Asia."

The room went silent in anticipation of the president's response. He called from across the room, loudly enough that everyone could hear—in that moment the hall was nearly silent.

"Even if North Korea fires first and our response is aimed

at them?"

"We will respond to any act of aggression aimed in our direction," Mr. Chung said into the microphone.

"Then we have to deal with China as well?" President McCormick asked.

"Do not launch a nuclear missile in our direction," Mr. Chung repeated.

"Then I suggest, Mr. Chung, that you take that up with the kid playing God in North Korea."

With that, the president left the auditorium. Mr. Chung had said what he had to say, so he sat down. The noise in the auditorium reignited—nearly every person in the room had a phone to his or her ear, talking frantically.

President Jorgensen stood again, pounding his gavel on the podium until the noise level dropped a few decibels. He knew it would be difficult to control the assembly now. He recognized the British member of the security council, Horace Blakesley, who'd been trying to get his attention for several seconds. As Mr. Blakesley approached the podium, the noise level once again dropped to near silence, although the phones hadn't been turned off.

"I have to say," Mr. Blakesley said, "that it would not only be irresponsible for someone to use a nuclear weapon in this day and age, it would be suicidal. Do you realize that there are between ten and fifteen *thousand* nuclear missiles in the world today, with multiple warheads? The United States and former Soviet Union, between them, have about that many. Then there are those in China, the United Kingdom, France, Pakistan, and

India, not to mention other states that claim the capability.

"Who do you think would survive a global thermonuclear war of that magnitude? Well, I'll tell you. The only survivors will be the government officials who have hardened bunkers to hide in until the earth warms up from a nuclear winter that kills the other ninety-eight percent of the world population over the next five years or so. And at that point the few noble souls who started the whole bloody thing can come out of their holes, sharpen their swords, paddle across the oceans, and spit on each other.

"Global nuclear war won't change ideologies, theologies, or feelings between the peoples of the world. What it *will* do is force the surviving leaders, who today are so casual about sending innocent men, women, and children to do their fighting, to do their own fighting.

"I call upon the good people of the world, wherever you are, to force your political leaders to stop this madness—immediately. In this age of social media, where you can let your feelings be known around the world instantaneously, we should see a positive *firestorm* of indignation against any government that believes it can use nuclear weapons to solve its problems. Let it start right here, right now.

"Nuclear war . . ." he stopped talking long enough to shake his head, "if we can't come up with a better way to solve our problems, then maybe that's what we deserve after all."

Ambassador Porter noticed that many people in the crowd had gone back to their phones the moment Blakesley planted the idea of using social media to stop the madness. He got on his own phone and sent a text to the president.

Mr. Blakesley sat down and President Jorgensen recognized the French member of the Security Council, Jean-Luc Denis. He began hesitantly.

"Not knowing what President McCormick was going to say, my government has not authorized me to speak in support of the United States in this thing. France has, for many years now, welcomed and tried to live peacefully with our Muslim immigrants and neighbors, many of whom are now French citizens."

His face made a transition from one of concern to one of determination.

"But from the evidence provided by President McCormick, and the responses from Saudi Arabia, Russia, China, and the United Kingdom, I will encourage my government to stand with the United States and the United Kingdom in defending our rights as free states to protect ourselves from aggression and tyranny, in whatever form. We have been patiently waiting for the Islamist radicals to come to their senses and see that the only way to live in today's world is to live *together*—to work toward peaceful coexistence. We, too, are tired of the terrorists, with their suicide bombings in our restaurants, airports, and stadiums. I agree with Mr. Blakesley. If we can't have peace, then we will have war. It is the way of this world."

The auditorium erupted in noise again, and many delegates stood up and left the room in a hurry. President Jorgensen sat back in his chair, placed his hand over his eyes, and shook his head. The session was effectively over. He had lost control. But worse than that, it appeared the world had lost control.

The Preserve, Aspen Valley, 1 July

Terry turned off the recorded chaos of the UN auditorium and looked at Amos.

"As Lillie would say," he said, "*that went well.*"

Amos chuckled humorlessly at Terry's joke.

"What's next?" Terry asked.

Staring at the blank TV screen, Amos thought.

"What is it with politicians? Do they check their brains at the door?"

He looked around the room at nothing in particular, then turned back to Terry.

"Batten down the hatches and take us down."

"How much do we tell everyone?" Terry asked.

"Nothing's changed. Anything we say will just upset people," Amos said. "It's certainly upset me."

"Yeah, me too," Terry agreed. "But everyone here knows we have satellite communications. They're going to ask."

Terry had been quietly considering the implications of the recording they'd just watched.

"Make sure communications are interrupted everywhere in

the Preserve except here in the office," Amos said. "Let's try to keep everyone too busy to ask what's going on outside."

"They won't be happy, Amos."

"Well, if they haven't already, they're going to figure out soon that their cell phones are no good in here. If anyone asks for news, send them to me. Terry, are you still okay trading off with Mike, monitoring C-SPAN in your free time?"

Terry nodded.

"It won't be often. We've got to get the rest of the equipment operational. You can give me the CliffsNotes version."

"Should we lock the airlock doors?" Terry asked.

"Yeah, Terry. I think it's time."

Amos was just coming into the community center, Terry right behind him, when Jason hailed him from across the room.

"So, Amos, what's going on in the outside world? I can't get a cell signal."

That didn't take long, Amos thought. He tried to deflect the conversation.

"Hi everyone, have you figured out your way around?"

They kept walking, as if they were headed for the bedroom tunnel. There was a round of nods, although some members of the family were elsewhere. Lillie gave Amos a concerned look that Amos hoped the others didn't see. He'd have to ask her about it later. As Amos passed Jason, he spoke quietly.

"Walk with me."

Jason fell into step with Amos. Terry had split off to be with his family. They walked slowly down the bedroom tunnel until they arrived at Jason's bedroom area.

"You know we have communications with the outside, right?"

"That's why I asked," Jason said. "I figured you went somewhere to check things out."

"That's right . . . in part," Amos said. "We have communications, but that wasn't the primary reason for meeting with Terry. We're stressing this facility by housing fifteen people when it was designed for nine."

"Plus growth, no doubt," Jason added.

" . . . plus growth," Amos agreed. "However, now, we not only have no room for growth, we're over capacity."

"You want us to leave?" Jason asked, sarcasm in his voice.

"No," Amos replied, emphatically. "That's not what I'm getting at, at all. But I want you to understand. Nothing has changed outside. The governments are still making accusations and world war is still a possibility. The deadline is still over two days away. What we need from you is to help keep everyone calm."

"And submissive?" Jason asked snidely.

Jason's expression challenged Amos to explain, but Amos stared him down until Jason looked away, self-consciously. Finally, Amos answered him.

"No, Jason. Just preoccupied. There's a lot to do here. Mike and Lillie are working on a task schedule. If everyone's pitching in, they won't have too much time to worry about what's going on out in the world. We want each person to find something they like to do—a hobby—and get involved with it. Right now, I'm thinking about the long day we've had. I suggest we encourage everyone to get a good night's rest and we'll start fresh tomorrow. Can you accept that?"

"Okay. I'll be a good boy scout, if you'll promise not to keep us in the dark."

"That's a promise," Amos said, trying to control his temper. Afraid of what he might do if he didn't get away from Jason, he turned and went to his own bedroom.

Lillie was waiting for him. She stood and went to him, arms open and they embraced.

"If I knew a few swear words . . . " he said.

"That bad?" she asked, chucking sarcastically.

"You have no idea."

"Tell me."

"You first. Why the concerned look out there?"

"One, we've overloaded the Preserve," Lillie said.

"Um-hmm." Amos waited for Lillie to say more.

"Two, we've been here less than a day and there are already family issues."

"Jason?"

"And Nathan and Rylee."

"Rylee?"

"Have you noticed the way she looks at Nathan?"

"Tell me," Amos said. "My focus must be too narrow again."

"I think she's beginning to identify with Nathan, both having lost close family. I'm afraid she'll become infatuated with him and do something stupid. Tell you what. You watch Jason and I'll watch Nathan and Rylee."

"I'm sorry you got saddled with Rylee, honey."

"And here I thought I was done raising children. Now I have a teenager flush with hormones. Oh well, I'll manage. What are you going to do about Jason?"

"Any suggestions?"

"Keep him busy. And don't let him find out how to get out of the Preserve."

"Ah, you noticed that too," Amos said. "I was beginning to think I was imagining it. As you said, we've been here less than a day. Is he really trying to figure out how to get out already?"

She nodded.

"So, what's going on outside?" she asked.

He told her, watching her beautiful face become lined with concern.

Amos was in the office, reviewing project documents before going to bed, when the sat phone rang. He picked it up.

"That's got to be a first for the UN," he said. "I think you broke every rule of diplomacy in one speech."

"It was your idea," Greg groused.

"And about time, too," Amos said.

"I've had calls from half the world's governments already today, not to mention the response from social media. Half the country wants me to apologize, the other half wants to push the button that fires the first missile."

As expected, Amos thought.

"What are the heads of state saying, and what are you telling them?"

"I haven't taken any of the calls. I gave that assignment to my Chief of Staff, Eric Epstein."

"Eric's good. A little naive, but his heart's in the right place."

Epstein was one of the people Amos had met, and liked, at Greg's son's wedding, two years before.

"He loves his country. I'll look over Eric's notes tomorrow, after I've had a chance to cool down. What's your status?"

"We arrived last night, all battened down and ready for whatever comes. You should consider getting out of town soon. This could get ugly very quickly."

"Tomorrow. Jim compiled a recommendation about where to send everyone, and I'm reviewing it with him in the morning. This is sad, you know."

"Are you referring to the destruction a nuclear war will cause or the political fallout?"

"Both. Why is it that some people can't see how stupid the fighting is?"

"You don't have to retaliate with nuclear weapons, Greg. You have options."

"Yes, we do have options, but actually we do have to do this. We—my advisers and I—have debated this for hours, not to mention the hours I've fought with myself over it. We've been fighting the terrorists for years with conventional weapons. It's not even a stalemate. They're getting bolder. More radical groups are rising. And we're struggling to keep our own people behind us in the fight. There are too many sympathizers, even in our government. It's getting overwhelming. They'll never stop until we stop them."

"You're right, of course, Greg. Al-Qaeda has been brainwashing young people for over a generation to hate the West. They've completely buried that inner voice that tells them right from wrong beneath layers of unnatural feelings—with promises of rewards that appeal to the carnal side of the mind. They can't hear the inner voice anymore."

The president barked out a laugh.

"You make it sound like they're good people who've been fooled into believing the way they do."

"Well, you know, I believe everyone's born with an inner light, a voice, that helps them choose right from wrong. Those who make bad choices gradually lose the light they're born with. The voice stops talking to them. For those who listen to the voice and make good choices, the inner light shines brighter, until you can see it in their eyes. I know you've seen people who seem to sparkle with goodness."

"Yes, and lucky for us, our wives are two of them. Damn, Amos, you make it sound so simple. Life just isn't that straightforward. Look at the mess we're in now."

"It could be that simple, if we could eliminate greed and selfishness. I wish everyone would just love each other. I wish they would just try."

"Not going to happen, my friend."

"I know. What're you going to do now?"

"Follow your example, hunker down in a hardened bunker. Except that while you're hiding out with people you love, I'm going to be directing a war—the biggest and baddest war this world has seen. Maybe Armageddon."

Amos thought about Jason and Nathan. And Rylee. Who knew how many other problems the family was going to have to deal with during the next months or years? But his good friend had enough going on without being burdened with Amos's concerns.

"You're right Greg. We'll be praying for you, and for all the innocent victims of this war."

"Thanks Amos. Take care."

"You too," Amos said, but Greg had already hung up.

20

"I really love this valley"

The Preserve, Aspen Valley, 2 July

Over the course of the next two days, everyone was encouraged to tour the Preserve and ask questions. The garden area consisted of a sixteen-by-forty-foot common room, surrounded by three smaller garden rooms. Like nearly every other room in the Preserve, the common room was painted a cream color, and all the garden rooms had bare concrete floors. There was a large workbench in the center of the common room, with cabinets down both walls and shelves underneath the workbench.

"The cabinets and shelves are full of fertilizers, tools, and seeds," Mike said, opening one of the cabinets under the workbench. Its door creaked quietly as he closed it again. "These two side rooms," Mike continued, pointing to the right and left, "consist mostly of raised planting beds filled with a mixture of compost and potting soil. The air in there is warm and humid, but you'll get used to it. You might even like it."

All eyes were fixed on the beds nestled in boxes under artificial light, in all stages of growth. Some of the beds were deep enough for root crops, while others were shallower. One of them was filled with stalks of corn. A walking path ran down each side of the center, dividing each half of the room again into halves. There were large plastic bottles of liquid fertilizer above each of the beds with tubes running from the bottles down to the rows of plants.

"Liquid fertilizer and water are distributed automatically. Excess water is recycled for reuse. And there are environmental controls at both ends of each room."

"If it's all automated," Sydney Carlsen said, looking confused, "then what are we supposed to do?"

"There's still planting, daily harvesting, mixing the fertilizer, and a few other chores," Mike said with a laugh. "We sterilized the soil before using it, but we still get a weed every once in a while. There must be weed seed mixed in with the plant seeds."

The room at the end was divided in two, with walking paths similar to the other two rooms. But this final room contained miniature fruit trees of all varieties. The larger side was dedicated to cold-weather fruit and the other to warm-weather fruit, and there were environmental controls in this room, too, to maintain proper growing conditions. Brittany laughed when she saw the dwarf citrus trees with tiny fruit. "I love the grapefruit tree," she said. "It's making me hungry, and I just ate breakfast."

Mike identified each tree, including the two apricot trees, which were barren at the moment, their fruit having already been harvested.

"The apricots we had for dinner last night came from this tree," he said.

As they left one of the garden rooms, Chris Stephens called

out to Mike. "What are the other doors we've seen in the tunnels? If I have my directions straight, they're all on the side opposite the living area. Where do they go?"

"There are mechanical rooms, storage rooms, and labs that Amos would prefer we not go into," Lillie said. "In some cases there are hazards, so they could be dangerous, and it wouldn't be necessary for anyone who wasn't properly qualified to go into any of them."

"What's he doing, making a Frankenstein monster?" Nathan Carlsen asked with a snort. It was one of the few times he'd spoken since he'd arrived.

"Yeah, and he's going to take your brain," his sister Sydney replied. "Since you're not using it."

"Sydney!" Brittany scolded.

Nathan's expression turned dark and dangerous. He didn't move or speak, but his jaw clenched and unclenched several times. Brittany wondered where Sydney had suddenly gotten the nerve to talk back to Nathan—that made twice in two days. And she wondered why Jason seemed so indifferent to it—he wasn't even looking at his kids. Rylee, standing behind some of the others, watched Nathan with interest.

"The medical center," Lillie said, "has a common room divided into a waiting room, a medical office, and an examination room, each partitioned off by a bulkhead with a door. The group stood in the waiting room, where a few folding chairs rested against the walls, then followed Lillie through the office and into the examination room.

"I know it won't last," Lillie said, "but I'm hoping that the polished tile in here will stay clean."

There were doors from all three rooms to another room on the right. They entered from the examination room.

"This is a surgical center," Lillie said. "It comes complete with x-ray, cancer screening, and other equipment. Cancer is the most likely long-term physical effect of radiation exposure. Amos and Terry believe the portable cancer screening equipment is essential. Unfortunately, there isn't room for an MRI machine."

"It smells just like a hospital," Brittany said, shivering.

Lillie looked at her questioningly, inviting further explanation.

"I had surgery last year," she explained. "I don't like hospitals."

"You and I will be spending a lot of time in the hospital," Amos said to Matt. "We're going to complete the medical training you're missing by being here instead of at school."

"Hopefully we won't have much need for a hospital," Matt replied.

"Well, we're going to start your training later this week. We'll use family members as mock patients for all types of procedures."

"You're not going to cut us open, are you?" Sydney asked with a grimace.

"Only once in a while," Amos said, laughing.

"Can I be there when you sew up Sydney's mouth?" Nathan asked—it was supposed to sound like a joke, but there was venom in it.

"Nathan!" Brittany scolded, staring at him, while Nathan and Sydney glared at each other.

"What's the room on the other side of the waiting room?" Jason asked, indifferent to the conflict between his children.

"That's a nursery." Lillie replied. "So we can eventually deliver the babies of the next generation. We're prepared for long-term care, in case of complications.

"The nursery's fully stocked," Mike added, "including incubators, for when we have newborns."

Lillie looked at Emily and Matt. Emily blushed and Matt began to fidget, rolling his hands around in his pockets.

"Well, we hope that won't be too soon," she added, deadpan. "It can also be used as a surgical recovery room. The end room is a fully stocked medical supply room. But, access to that is restricted, so no wandering in there."

In the study cluster, there were two schoolrooms. "This is where you'll want to spend most of your time," Amos said to Sydney and Rylee, trying to be funny—he knew the teens would *not* like being reminded that they still had to go to school.

Mike led them into the study common area, which was furnished much like the community center, with tables, chairs, couches, and industrial carpet. The lighting was subdued, and there were electric lamps on the tables that plugged into floor outlets.

"Ugh," Sydney said. "You said we'd like this room. I thought we were getting out of school."

Amos laughed.

"I did say that. I can't believe you don't like school, Sydney."

At the back of the common area were two doors, leading to rooms that were clearly meant to be classrooms. Each was furnished with white boards, cork boards, alphabet and number cards, a world map, desks, and chairs. A teacher's desk and chair sat at one end of each classroom. There were bookcases with various educational tools all around the room, including a globe of the world.

"We've asked Katie to set up a curriculum of study subjects for everyone who doesn't have a high school diploma yet," Lillie said, looking at the younger ones. There were moans and groans. "Rachel will help out with the teaching."

"So you don't feel picked on," Amos said, "Matt will be here studying for his doctorate degree in medicine."

It was Matt's turn to groan, to some laughter and applause.

"It'll be homeschooling," Lillie added. "But it'll be a lot like normal school, with quizzes, tests, and graduation certificates."

She tried to sound enthusiastic, but she wasn't getting much of a response from the teens.

"The rooms on either side of the common room," she said, walking into one of them, "are libraries. This one is full of books for all ages and interests, fiction and non-fiction."

"Look at all the books!" Rylee said. "It's wonderful."

The library was filled floor to ceiling with bookshelves, with over a thousand volumes. They wandered around the room for a few minutes, looking at the books and getting oriented to the layout.

"The library on the other side has e-books, DVDs, and a storage area for spare equipment."

Lillie led the group into the exercise area.

"If you haven't already been in here," she said, "go ahead and look around."

The floor of the common area was covered with exercise mats, with extras piled in a corner. Down the middle of the room was gymnastic equipment that Lillie hoped someone would eventually use. There was a sink and a supply of workout towels at the far end.

The room on the left held several treadmills and exercise bikes. The room to the right was a weight room, with a universal gym, exercise bike, rowing machine, and other exercise equipment. There were free weights and a bench on a rubber mat at one end, and there was a CD player, with a supply of music.

"We're going to let everyone decide what they want to work on," Lillie said. "Katie will help you decide what fits your needs best. Then everyone will have an exercise schedule, that Katie will monitor. Any questions?"

"I thought Katie was going to be the school teacher," Mike said.

"She's going to have help with the teaching," Lillie reminded them. "She's also responsible for physical exercise."

"Well, with all of the gymnastics she used to do, I guess the job fits her."

Mike smiled at Katie.

"Can we learn tumbling?" Sydney asked cautiously, not knowing what to expect and assuming she'd be disappointed.

"If you want to," Katie said, smiling.

"I really do," Sydney said excitedly.

"We'll start with tumbling," Katie said. "Then, if you have an aptitude for it, you can try floor exercises and bars. You too, Rylee."

Rylee looked around, her eyes stopping on Nathan, before responding. He was looking in the weight room. She smiled at Katie and nodded.

With the tour over, everyone left in ones and twos. Lillie watched as Rylee followed a few feet behind Nathan, who didn't seem to notice.

Matt and Emily hung back, holding hands as they looked at each other, a silent message passing between them. Emily nudged Matt encouragingly.

"Mrs. Blund . . . " Matt started.

"Call me Lillie, Matthew. Or mom." Lillie added with a smile.

Matt wasn't sure he was ready to call Lillie "mom" just yet.

"Okay—um, Lillie. Em told me how beautiful Aspen Valley is. Is there any way we can go out and walk for a while?"

"I don't know. Let's ask Amos."

Lillie led Emily and Matt back through the community center, unlocked a door with a key from her pocket, and led them through a network of tunnels splitting off to the right and left. They finally stopped at a locked door. She knocked, and Terry opened it a few moments later.

"Hi Terry. Is Amos in there?"

"Sure. Come on in."

He held the door open and they entered the office, where Amos sat, head down, studying something on his desk. He looked up and smiled, then came around the desk to greet them.

"What's up?"

"Emily and Matthew want to go outside for a walk. Do you think that would be ok?"

"I think that's a great idea." Amos said. Turning to Matt he added, "We want to keep our presence here a secret. Those of us who've been here a fair bit have a sense for the normal sights, sounds, and smells of the valley. In the middle of the day, there's traffic on the highway. It would be difficult for any-one on the highway to see us across the valley, but once in a while someone wanders in. It won't do for us to be out there when that happens."

He turned to Terry, who had walked over and was looking at a group of small screens on the far wall.

"Anything Terry?"

"All clear right now, but I suggest they take a radio."

He picked up two radios from a nearby shelf and turned

them on. He checked to see that they were set to the same frequency, talked into one and then the other to ensure they were working properly, then handed one to Amos who handed it to Emily.

"Thank you, Daddy." Emily said, an enthusiastic smile on her face.

Amos laughed.

"Be alert, and keep the radio on."

"We will."

She hooked the radio on her belt.

Amos turned to Lillie.

"Anyone else asking to go?

"No. But it might be a good idea to take them all out soon. We may never have another chance to see Aspen Valley the way it is now—and it *is* beautiful. I'll schedule tours for this afternoon and tomorrow. Groups of three or four at a time, with strict rules on noise?"

Amos nodded his agreement.

"That may be difficult with Sydney and Rylee," Emily said, smiling. "They really chatter when they're together."

Unless Nathan's around, Lillie thought.

"Then maybe we should split them up," Amos said.

He flashed the smile that always gave Lillie butterflies.

"I'll work on a schedule," she said.

As Matt turned to leave, Emily stepped over and gave

Amos a hug.

"Thanks Dad."

"Yes, thanks Mr—I mean Amos," Matt said.

"You're welcome. You two enjoy yourselves—but not too much," he added with a wink and a smile.

As they left the office, Lillie handed Emily a key, which she put in her pocket.

Emily led Matt through the community center to the airlock. Unlike the night before, when the airlock doors had stood open, Em had to insert a key—*probably the one her mother gave her*, Matt thought—and enter a passcode into the control panel on the wall beside the doors, before they would open. The light came on in the airlock when she opened the door.

"Dad locked down the Preserve after everyone was inside last night," Em explained.

Once inside the airlock, Em relocked the double doors behind them. They passed the cabinets containing the hazmat suits and approached the outer airlock doors. Matt was already familiar with the principles behind hazmat suits and dosimeters before coming to the Preserve. He'd seen the suits as part of his EMT training, and he'd been instructed in the use of dosimeters as part of his medical training. Once they were through the second set of airlock doors, Emily touched a spot on the wall and lights came on overhead in the tunnel. Matt leaned over to get a close look at the button Emily had touched. Emily giggled.

"That's *so* Dad," she said. "It was his idea to make the light switch look like a dark spot in the rock."

"It works really well," Matt said. "I never would've found it."

Emily locked the airlock doors behind them, and they walked on, passing the elevator to the garage and coming to a wide set of stairs.

"That elevator," Emily said, pointing at it as they passed, "is the one we used when we first came. It goes to the garage. These stairs go to the garage, too, but we're going to another exit that's a little smaller—and exits into the valley."

They continued to a spot where the tunnel bent to the right, and Emily touched another button on the wall to light the tunnel ahead of them. Matt had to check this one out too. They reached the end of the tunnel, and Em led Matt up two flights of stairs to a standard-sized passage door. Em inserted her key and touched a button on a control panel on the wall. The door opened inward. Bright afternoon sunlight and warm air spilled into the tunnel from the outside.

As they passed through the doorway, Matt studied the door itself. Its outside face looked like rock, and when it closed Matt had to look closely to tell it apart from the rest of the stone wall. When he turned to look at the valley, Em was smiling at him.

"You're curious about the doors," she said.

"I meant to ask about them when we came in," Matt began. "They're not real rock, are they? Rock would be too heavy."

"They're made of graphite . . . something. Dad says it's like fiberglass, except that it's lighter and stronger than steel. I don't really understand it."

"It's called graphite composite," Matt said, nodding. "I've read about it. It was developed for the aerospace industry—for rocket motors, I think. Now, it's used for race cars, golf clubs, tennis rackets, and who knows what else."

"That sounds right," Em said with a nod. "Dad got involved with graphite composite when he was doing research into medical uses—prosthetic limbs, robotics, that kind of stuff. He and Terry made the designs. They were able to buy the graphite material and rent an auto-something-or-other to cure the parts.

"An autoclave?"

"Yeah, that's it. Once they knew the process, building the doors just meant scaling it up. Dad said the outside is covered with lightweight concrete, or something like that, I think. Then it's painted to look like the rock around it."

"That's amazing." Matt said. "Did they patent any of their designs?"

"Yeah. Those were some of the patents they sold to get the money to build this place."

They had stepped out of the diffused, artificial light of the tunnel into bright midday sunlight. The air was warm, and a slight breeze ruffled Emily's long hair. Matt stared at her. *How I love this beautiful, amazing woman,* he thought.

Apparently self-conscious at Matt's attention, Emily took his hand and started them strolling slowly down what looked like a deer trail. Matt's hand tingled, and he got the same feeling in his stomach that came each time they touched. He realized he probably had a goofy expression on his face and tried to change it to a more natural smile.

They walked through an area of small brush and tall grass.

"This area is above the Preserve," Emily explained. "We had to cut down a lot of the trees for construction and we didn't plant new ones. The soil is pretty shallow, and we don't want tree roots cracking the concrete that covers the rooms."

"The concrete must be part of the radiation barrier," Matt said.

Em smiled at how quickly he caught on to the ins and outs of the Preserve. As they reached the edge of the clearing, they entered a heavily wooded area. Matt stopped, so Em stopped with him. She looked at him, wondering what was going on. His face was a study in emotion, a silly expression on his lips, but an intense look in his eyes. She felt her own eyes get moist.

"I really love this valley," she said. *Almost as much as I love you*, she thought.

"Em, I love you," he said, then swallowed, his Adam's apple bobbing up and down once.

She took his other hand, turning to face him, and gave him a crooked smile—then stood on her toes and leaned in for a quick kiss.

"I love you too, Matt."

They stood looking at each other, then embraced for a long

time. Finally, Matt swallowed again and spoke in a husky voice.

"I guess—I guess maybe we should see the rest of the valley?"

She giggled, pushing away from him and looking up into his eyes, smiling.

"I guess so. Before they send out a rescue team."

They continued down the deer trail, through several varieties of trees and bushes. There were fallen trees decaying in the thick undergrowth, and the ground was thick and spongy with decomposing plant matter.

Em pointed out different types of trees and bushes as they moved along the trail.

"Limber pine . . . spruce . . . fir . . . aspen . . . maple . . . box elder . . . birch . . . do you want me to go on?"

Matt was impressed, then amazed, as Em continued.

"How do you know all that?" he finally asked.

"When I found out that Becca was a botanist, I made her teach me all about the trees and plants in the valley. I can go into a lot more detail if you want—like the genus and species of each tree, or how to tell the difference between a limber pine and a lodgepole pine. The difference is in the shape and spacing of the needles and leaves, or the color and shape of the flowers and cones."

Em spoke quietly, with an awe at the intricacies of nature in her voice.

"Ummm, I don't think that's necessary," Matt said, "but it's cool that you know it."

"I love it here, Matt. I love the fresh smells, the flowers, the animals, the birds. It makes me want to whisper so I don't disturb anything. It's sad to think that it could all be gone in a few days."

Matt saw her expression change, becoming more sober, then sad. He took her in his arms and hugged her. Em shivered in Matt's embrace, even though the air was warm.

"Em," Matt had to clear his throat to go on. "Can I ask you a question?"

"Of course."

"Why do you think all this might not be here in a few days?" he asked.

"Dad explained what could happen if there is a war. It's possible that we could have an earthquake or a fire that would damage or destroy most of this."

"He really thinks that?" he asked.

"It's just one possibility. Hopefully, nothing will happen to our valley."

"Em, this Preserve is really elaborate. It's obvious that your dad spent a fortune to build it. Why did he go to all this trouble?"

Emily seemed taken aback.

"I'm not sure what you mean. Dad loves his family. He wants to protect us from the war."

"I know that, Em. Sorry if the question seems strange. But lots of men love their families—most of them don't end up building underground retreats for them. Why did your dad?"

Emily thought for a minute before answering.

"Well, as long as I can remember Dad has talked about being prepared for emergencies. I think it's the same reason he became a doctor. We've always had a supply of food, clothing, fuel, and other emergency supplies in the house. When he and Terry became partners and started patenting their inventions, I think he saw a way to make a dream come true."

Matt thought about that for a few moments, and Emily waited patiently for him to process it.

"How long do you think we'll have to stay here. Does your dad really think it could be thirty years or more?"

"We certainly have enough supplies to last that long. Well, we did until the Carlsens joined us. Now I don't know. I think Dad took that into account."

"You mean the Carlsens *and me,* don't you? And Rylee?"

"Matthew Green," Emily said sternly, "don't you dare think that your being here is a problem. If you weren't here, I—well, I wouldn't be either."

With that, she teared up and melted into his arms. Matt held her tightly, hoping he hadn't insulted Em or her father. He could tell she was crying from the damp spot on his sleeve. Eventually, he spoke softly.

"It seems more humid right here."

Em swiped at her eyes with the backs of her hands. She took Matt's hand, her smile widening.

"I'll show you," she said, still blinking tears out of her eyes.

She took a cutoff to the left and led him carefully along a narrow trail that soon took them to a bubbling stream that ran over moss-covered rocks. Em pointed out plants that grew near the water.

"Birch . . . willow . . . alder . . . fern . . . clematis," she said, going through them in turn.

They followed the stream, still holding hands, and soon came to a wild thicket of raspberries.

"You have to taste these," she said.

"Mmm, they're great," he said after popping a couple into his mouth.

Matt moaned in mock ecstasy at the flavor, eliciting a laugh from Em. Without thinking, she playfully slapped him on the chest with her open palm, realizing as she did so that it was something she'd seen her mother do to her dad more times than she could count. They moved on, finally coming to a clear pond about twenty-five feet across, that contained small trout and water skaters.

"They're called gerrids or gerridae," Matt said. At Em's look, he explained. "Really. I looked it up one time in one of my medical books."

Emily laughed, hugging him again.

"I don't see an outlet for the water," Matt said. "This pond should be stagnant instead of fresh and clear."

"It sinks into the loamy soil," Em said.

"Do you know where it comes out?" Matt asked.

"No, but there are several lakes and reservoirs down the

canyon from here. It probably goes underground and resurfaces in one of those."

Looking into Matt's face, she could see another question bubbling to the surface.

"What?" she asked.

"Will we ever have a normal life? I mean, get married, buy a home, raise a family?"

Emily started to cry again.

"I'm sorry, Em. I'm asking all the wrong questions. Forget I asked that one."

"No Matt. You're right. I don't know how we can have a normal life. We can't even get married."

"I'm sorry, Em. Maybe I shouldn't have come. Maybe I should leave."

"Stop it, Matt," Emily cried. "I couldn't live without you."

She pounded on his chest softly, in frustration, then collapsed against him, crying again.

"I couldn't live without you either, Em. Hey, tell me about the animals in the valley."

She sniffled, then fought off her tears.

"Well, I've seen a few smaller animals. Some snakes," Em said. "Mike says he's seen deer and bobcat."

Just then, Matt spotted a doe moving between the trees on the other side of the pond, and he turned her so she could see it. Their laughter startled the deer, and it bounded away into the trees.

"I guess I shouldn't ask if there are lions," Matt said.

"Really, don't." Em said, taking a tissue from her pocket and wiping her eyes and nose as they laughed again.

"There are a lot of birds, too," Em said. "Like tanager, thrush, chickadee, Clark's nutcracker . . . "

"That's a real bird?" Matt asked.

"Yes," Em laughed. "The nutcracker is the reason limber pine grows in these mountains. They bury the seeds in the fall, then forget where some of them are."

Matt watched Em closely—the sparkle in her eyes, even through tears, and the energy in her every movement. He realized he might love her more than he did his own mother—and that he would die to protect her. Em noticed Matt's look and turned to face him. Putting her hands around his neck, she pulled his face to hers. He came willingly, placing his hands on her waist and moving them up and down along her sides. She shivered at his touch and kissed him passionately.

Eventually Em lowered her hands and placed her arms around his waist, resting the side of her face against his chest—he was sure she could hear his heart pounding in there. As his hands came down her sides, they continued past her waist, stopping on her backside. Em reached back casually, took Matt's wrists and moved his hands, holding them together in front of her.

"Not in front of the cameras," she said, teasingly.

Matt tried looking around without moving his head.

"Where?" he whispered.

His lips barely moved and his heart skipped a beat.

"I think there's one behind me, to your left, in that big tree."

She laughed quietly. Matt tried looking that way without moving. His contortions finally made her laugh out loud.

"I don't see it," Matt whispered. "And I don't see any wires."

"That's because there aren't any. Everything's wireless."

She dropped one of his hands and took the other in hers. They moved away from the pond, back the way they had come. Matt continued to look around to see if he could spot any cameras, and Em laughed at him all over again.

"What?" Matt asked.

"You don't have to worry about being watched," Em said.

"You mean I can tell my pulse to slow down a little?"

"Unless it's beating for me."

Just before they arrived at the main trail, Matt pulled Em to a stop.

"Are there any cameras right here?" he asked.

Em looked around.

"Not that I know of," she said.

He pulled her into an embrace and kissed her long and hard, and they both came away breathless. Then they strolled slowly back to the Preserve, enjoying the fresh air. They avoided talking about the future. They stopped periodically to hold each other close—and managed to fit in a few kisses, too.

21

"We need to hit them hard."

***Prime bunker, somewhere northwest of Washington, D.C.,
3 July***

President Gregory McCormick sat in the situation room of a hardened bunker, referred to as Prime, looking at a wall of eight video screens, in two rows of four. The screens displayed the situation rooms in eight other hardened bunkers located in different parts of the country. Key advisers, regular NSC attendees, participants and staff, Congressional and Senate leaders, Supreme Court Justices, and military leaders were distributed among the bunkers. They had all left Washington, DC shortly after McCormick's historic—and disturbing—speech to the UN General Assembly.

At the moment, only half the screens were lit. Secretary of Defense General Jim Seymour was seated by himself in the SEC DEF bunker situation room, Secretary of State Cy Hutchison was in STATE, Director of National Intelligence Tom Mitchell was in DNI, and Secretary of Homeland Security Chuck Dickson was in HOME SEC. Above each screen was a small sign showing the name of the bunker.

The president was speaking with King Salmon of Saudi

Arabia on the speakerphone in his bunker. His four advisers were listening in, and he was sure others were listening at the other end of the line as well.

"President McCormick, I agree that there are elements within my government, and within the Al Saud family, that are sympathetic to Al-Qaeda. However, I can assure you that we have, since the terrible incident in New York in 2001, been fighting the terrorists as vigorously as you have."

"How can you say that, King Salmon? Your Wahhabi fundamentalism supports the concept of an evil West that needs to be destroyed. Saudi Arabia funded terrorist training camps and recruited youth from all over the Muslim world to train as suicide bombers. Are you saying that you now denounce Wahhabism and all it stands for?"

King Salmon hesitated before speaking.

"What I am saying is that Saudi Arabia is doing all it can to stop terrorism throughout the world. We are trying to find out who went to Mexico to build a bomb and to stop them."

"I hear a 'but' coming."

"We have not identified who went to Mexico. However, we have located the strongholds of some of the Al-Qaeda leadership, and we are sending that information to your Secretary of State, Mr. Cyril Hutchison."

The president looked at Cy, who nodded.

"And why are you not dealing with the Al-Qaeda leadership? You created this mess. Why have us clean it up for you?"

Silence stretched for a full minute. They could hear heavy breathing on the line. The president was the one to finally break the silence.

"Deniability? In case Al-Qaeda decides to attack the hand that feeds it?"

"You have better weapons and targeting capability," King Salmon said.

"And you don't end up with a bloodbath in the Al Saud family, right? With fifteen thousand members in the family, maybe you could use a little thinning out."

The president could feel a tirade coming on, but he stifled it. There was a long sigh on the line, but King Salmon didn't speak.

"Okay, King Salmon," McCormick said. "You may have just prevented a nuclear missile from redecorating your living room. But we need to see that your future actions reflect genuine remorse over your birthing of Al-Qaeda. Thank you for the information on Al-Qaeda. We will talk again, soon."

The president didn't really know if they would be speaking again—soon or ever. Who could predict what the world would look like twenty-four, or forty-eight, hours from now? He ended the phone call and spoke to the four men who appeared to be sitting in front of him, but were, in reality, hundreds or thousands of miles away.

"Assessment?" he asked.

"Greg," Tom said, "he's telling the truth about Saudi Arabia fighting Al-Qaeda. Al-Qaeda is the perfect example of the dog that bites the hand that feeds it."

"Except in this case," Greg snorted. "Saudi Arabia didn't just feed the dog, they bred it . The question is, can they stop the bomb."

"I doubt it," Tom said. "Maybe there's something in the list he sent Cy that will help us."

The president looked at Cy, who was reviewing the list.

"About fifteen places listed," Cy said moments later. "Most of them are in Iran and Syria. A couple in other Middle East countries. One in Pakistan."

He looked up at the president, a question in his expression.

"Okay," Greg said. "Send it to Jim. Jim, make sure all those sites are targeted as part of our first response. No, on second thought, let's coordinate this with the UK, France, and Israel."

"Yes, sir," Jim replied.

Greg turned to look at Tom again.

"Tom, you spoke with your intelligence counterpart in Israel. What was the outcome?"

Tom's reply was exactly what Greg feared.

"Israel is convinced that Russia—at least the Russian Siloviki—are selling arms, maybe even nuclear weapons, to anyone in the Middle East who has the money to pay for them. They've been watching and listening, as we have, to traffic around the Caspian Sea and the Black Sea, and have come to the same conclusions we have. It looks like Al-Qaeda, in Syria and Iran, are planning to attack Israel. How soon, we don't know. Israel wants to know if we're willing to join them in a preemptive strike."

Cy spoke up. "I'm comparing the list Salmon sent us to the list Tom made from his conversation with Israel. A lot of the locations are the same. I'd say that gives us a high level of confidence in the data."

Greg thought about the consequences of a preemptive strike on the Middle East.

"Tom, tell Israel we're thinking about it and to let us know if anything changes, like a sudden escalation of activity. We can respond pretty quickly if we need to."

"Will do," Tom said, a frown on his usually stoic face.

"You think I'm being too conservative?" Greg asked.

"I have mixed feelings, Greg. Considering the situation with Al-Qaeda and this bomb, I think we need to hit them hard. But I'm opposed to the use of nuclear weapons for any reason. It sets a bad precedent for any state trying to settle a dispute with their neighbor. I wish we could use conventional weapons first. But it's your call."

"I hear you Tom," Greg replied. "We're out of time and out of options. We'll try to limit our nuclear response, but we have to act decisively. We'll try it this way first.

"Cy, did you share my concerns about selling weapons in the Middle East with Russia?"

"Yes, sir," Cy replied, shuffling some papers in front of him. "My contact said, quote: 'Russia is not selling weapons to the Middle East.' When asked if they are making weapons available to Russian industrialists—AKA Russian mafia, AKA Siloviki—to resell to the Middle East, he laughed and said they do not interfere with the business dealings of their industry leaders, just as in the United States."

"Except that we do interfere when national security is involved," Greg said. "Is that an admission of guilt?"

"Sounded like it to me," Tom said.

Cy nodded his agreement.

"Sounds like I'll have to make my threat a little stronger," Greg replied. "Tom, any new intelligence on the situation in Mexico?"

Tom looked briefly at some notes in front of him, then looked up at Greg.

"I reported in yesterday's Daily that the Mexican police captured a member of the Los Zetas cartel, a lieutenant, and were questioning him. They believe he gave them the location where the bomb was assembled—it's the same one Jim sent his special forces team to—but he didn't know where the bomb was going from there."

"They're sure he didn't know?" Greg questioned.

"Uh… he didn't live through the interrogation," Tom said with finality, then continued. "Early this morning, the Mexican police raided the site. They found what appeared to be bomb-making materials, although they may have said that because they knew that's what we wanted them to find—but no bomb, no Arabs, and no drug lord."

He looked back at his notes for a moment.

"They found large fields of poppy and coca plants being worked by peasants, who were overseen by a few guards. They questioned the guards, but they didn't seem to know anything other than that their boss left a few days before in a truck with an Arab and some guards. They're detaining the guards and the peasants until they squeeze everything they can out of them, and they destroyed the crops. It's consistent with what we're hearing through our CIA and FBI contacts. I'm convinced the bomb has been moved, but no one seems to know where it's gone."

"What about the trucks we were following?" Greg asked.

The look on Tom's face told him what he wanted to know even before Tom spoke.

"If the bomb was ever in one of them, it was transferred to another vehicle," Tom said. "They were empty by the time we got to them."

Jim spoke up.

"I spoke to the Coast Guard Monday morning, after our NSC meeting, about possible water routes into the U.S. They've discovered that the drug cartels are starting to use low profile submarines to move drugs into the country. The submarines are difficult to see unless you're right on top of them. Believe it or not, they're one-time use. The cartels are spending a million dollars apiece to have them built, but the subs can carry upwards of two hundred million dollars' worth of drugs. It's a bargain for them, and the Coast Guard thinks they're only catching about one in four."

Greg shook his head in frustration.

"And you think the Los Zetas cartel might be using a submarine to get the bomb into the States?"

"We don't know," Jim said, "but I told the Coast Guard to watch for submarines all along the Gulf coast and the Eastern seaboard. We now have every available boat in the water and every available helicopter in the air, day and night."

"Chuck, what is Homeland Security seeing on the borders?"

Greg asked.

"Same as the other agencies," Chuck said. "It appears the bomb is on its way and may already be in the States, but we can't tell where."

"Let's have the Secret Service activate all available agents to search the Washington, D.C. area for anything unusual."

"That's already happening sir," Chuck said.

"Good. Is there anything else we can do?" Greg asked.

He was met with shaking heads.

"Okay, let's take a break until the NSC meeting tomorrow at one o'clock. But don't hesitate to call me if you hear anything in the meantime."

The four men nodded as Greg stood to leave the room.

The Preserve, Aspen Valley, 3 July

During lunch, there was animated talk about the walks in the valley. It was by far everyone's favorite part of the Preserve.

Several people had seen deer, and a couple saw humming-birds, along with other birds they couldn't identify. One group even saw a red-tailed hawk flying above the valley. Only once was a group warned by radio that a car had stopped on the highway and they should keep to the trees until it was gone.

They saw the few fruit trees that the Blunds had planted, in no discernible pattern, most of which had large numbers of small fruit on their branches.

"They don't look like they've been pruned or thinned," Brittany said. "I thought that was necessary to get the best crop."

"That's true," Lillie said. "But we're not supposed to be here, right? It would look awfully suspicious if trees growing wild here had been pruned. Besides, they bring deer and other animals to the valley."

"Yeah, I noticed the piles of deer scat," Brittany said.

"I hope you didn't step in any of it," Lillie said, a twinkle in her eye.

Sydney giggled, picturing her mom cleaning deer poo off her shoes.

"I'm glad you all enjoyed it," Lillie said to the group. "We may not get another chance to see the valley in this condition. There's a book of photos in the community center, though, to help us remember it."

When Jason's group, the last to visit the valley, had entered the airlock, Jason had been watching closely, trying to work out the procedure for passing through the doors. Mike was careful to hide the keypad when he entered the code, but not careful enough. From his hand motions, Jason had figured it out.

Now all I need to do is get a key and I can get out of this hellhole, he thought.

He didn't know when or how he would manage it, but it was reassuring to confirm that he was smarter than the Blund clan—even if they didn't know it. He would have to watch for an opportunity to get a key.

But then what?

22

"Two hours before the terrorist deadline."

The Preserve, Aspen Valley, 4 July

"So, what's happening out there?" Matt asked. "It's gotta be chaotic, right?"

"That might be an understatement," Amos said. "The United Nations met yesterday, as some of you know, but they adjourned without coming to any consensus on a resolution to condemn the terrorists. Everything proposed by the U.S., the United Kingdom, or France was blocked by China or Russia."

"What resolutions were they trying to get approved?" Jason asked.

"When President McCormick couldn't get Saudi Arabia or Russia to admit they were behind the terrorists . . . "

"The president went to the UN?" Matt interrupted, surprised.

"He did, five days ago. It's not the first time a president has spoken before the UN General Assembly," Amos said. "Though it's a bit unexpected under the circumstances, with all the global tension. He openly accused the Al Saud family of funding Al-Qaeda, who he said were building a bomb in Mexico so they could smuggle it into the U.S. through a drug route. He also accused the Russians of delivering bomb-making materials to Al-Qaeda and North Korea."

"Wow!" Matt said. "North Korea would love to put a nuclear warhead on one of their ICBMs and launch it at the U.S."

"That's what the president accused them of planning. He gave the Saudis and Russians an ultimatum to stop the bombs or the U.S. would retaliate with nuclear weapons."

"Oh—oh my," Brittany said. She seemed to want to say more, but didn't find the words.

"Was he serious?" Jason asked skeptically, not sure he believed Amos. *Amos can say anything he wants. Who's going to contradict him?*

"There's more if you want to hear it," Amos said.

He ignored Jason's question. When nobody spoke, he continued.

"China said it would enter the war on the side of North Korea. England and France said they would come in on the side of the U.S. That was Saturday. Since then, the King of Saudi Arabia, King Salmon, has assured the U.S. that they are doing everything in their power to locate the bomb and the bomb makers."

"You said Saudi Arabia funded the terrorists. Can't they just tell them to stop the bomb?' Matt asked.

"It's not that simple. Years ago, a radical form of Islam, called Wahhabism, evolved in Saudi Arabia. The Wahhabis believe that the West has become godless and decadent."

"They have a point there," Brittany said, under her breath.

"Maybe we have, to an extent. But the Wahhabis have twisted the words of the prophet Mohammed to convince their followers to commit atrocities in the name of their god."

"Like women and children strapping on explosives and blowing themselves up in a crowd of people," Matt added.

"Exactly," Amos said. "Keep in mind that the Wahhabis don't represent mainstream Islam. They're a small splinter group and very radical. They believe it's their duty to kill anyone who doesn't believe as they do. They also believe that any Muslim who sacrifices his own life for the cause, whether intentionally or as an innocent bystander, instantly goes to paradise, where he or she is rewarded."

"That's disgusting," Brittany said, wrinkling her brow. "They really believe that?"

"They do," Amos said. "The worst part is that the Saudis spent millions to set up indoctrination camps to teach young men and women Wahhabism and train them in terrorist tactics. But now the terrorists are out of control, carrying out attacks all over the world, including some in Saudi Arabia. Some of the Al Saud family—the ones currently in control of the country, including King Salmon—want to stop them. In fact, Saudi Arabia's ruling family probably holds the strongest anti-terrorism position in the Middle East. They do what they can to help control the threat of terrorism, or at least that's what we're led to believe. The problem is that the terrorists have gone elsewhere."

"Where?" Matt asked.

"Iran, Syria, other countries," Amos said. "Now they recruit young people all over the world, including England, France, and the U.S. They indoctrinate hundreds of people, usually young men, and then return them to their homes as sleepers, just waiting for Al-Qaeda to call on them. The number of Muslims in Europe is apparently increasing at about ten percent per year. That creates a lot of places for terrorists to hide."

"You included the U.S.," Jason said. He didn't believe everything Amos was saying, but it was an intriguing story.

"That's right," Amos replied. "Since the bombings of September 11, in 2001, the U.S. Intelligence Community has stopped numerous terrorists before they could act. The U.S. has done a better job of stopping the terrorists than other countries."

"But we've had to give up a lot of our freedoms as a result," Matt said. "Like the TSA checkpoints at airports that are so intrusive."

"True," Amos said, "but it's worked so far."

"So, is war inevitable then?" Jason asked. "Was the president serious about retaliating with nuclear weapons?"

"That's what he said. Like I said, our allies tried to pass a resolution condemning Al-Qaeda, with sanctions against any country sympathetic to them. It's questionable whether sanctions would have done any good, anyway. I don't see Al-Qaeda or North Korea standing down without being forced, even if Russia and China went along with the sanctions. The Russians would love to see the U.S. embarrassed on the international scene . . ."

"Come on," Jason said, mockingly, "Russia isn't going to

intentionally push the world toward global nuclear war."

"I wouldn't have thought so either, Jason. But it looks pretty grim. Most, if not all, of the countries with nuclear weapons have begun bringing their weapons online. The majority of the foreign embassies and consulates in the U.S. have shut down. Their diplomats and families have left the country."

"Really?" Chris asked "Maybe I should contact some of my friends in the State Department."

He pulled out his mobile phone and tried to dial, then frowned when he didn't get a signal.

"Watchdog groups estimate that there are over ten thousand nuclear missiles, with multiple warheads, in the world," Amos said. "Maybe as many as fifteen thousand. If the nuclear powers launch them all, we would see a nuclear winter that would change the environment to the point where most life on Earth goes extinct."

"What?" Jason asked, incredulous. "You've got to be joking. We have the greatest technology the world has ever known and you think it's going to be snuffed out just like that?"

He snapped his fingers for emphasis.

"Like the dinosaurs," Brittany said.

It wasn't a question. Jason turned on her, ready to snap at her, but just as he opened his mouth, he saw Amos looking at him and changed his mind. There was silence in the room while they processed this information.

"I can't get a signal," Chris said, alternately punching keys on his mobile phone and putting it up to his ear.

"I couldn't get a signal last night either," Jason said angrily.

"What's going on Amos? Have you blocked outbound calls?"

Jason stood and took a step toward Amos.

Amos debated not answering, but realized the issue wasn't going to go away without an explanation.

"The mountains, and being underground, would normally block all signals, although we have equipment to overcome that problem. Yes, we've blocked all calls. We don't want anyone outside to lock on to a signal and find out where we are."

"So you've isolated us from the outside, and we have nothing but your word as far as what's going on out there. Is that it?"

Jason spit the words out, furious, as he took another step toward Amos. Amos's pulse quickened as he got ready for Jason to lash out physically again. He stood and took a step toward him, to show that he wasn't afraid of him—he wasn't going to be caught off guard a second time.

Lillie saw Amos's reaction and decided she had to jump in now if she was going to prevent another fight.

"Amos is telling the truth, Jason," she said. "Several of us have heard and seen the reports."

Jason turned on Lillie. He didn't speak to her—she hadn't thought he would. He had a contempt for women. It was beneath his dignity to acknowledge them. But she hoped he would back down. He turned back to Amos, breathing hard.

"You're lying, aren't you. There's no war coming. You're saying these things to keep us here against our will."

"Oh, right Jason, sure" Amos spat. "I forced you to come against your will. I tricked you—somehow, I'd love to know how that happened—I tricked you into *wanting* to come so we could have these little fireside chats. They're just so much fun for all of us."

Jason moved another step, but before the confrontation could get physical, Lillie and Brittany moved to stand between the two men. Mike stood as well, and moved toward Amos, clenching his fists, ready to defend his father if he had to.

Lillie pushed against Amos's chest.

"Amos, this isn't the way to deal with it," she said.

Amos slowly relaxed, and she was able to move him away from the confrontation. Brittany did the same with Jason, though it was more work.

"Stop it Jason," she said sternly, but she had to struggle against him, and he was nearly twice her size. He seemed to have lost his senses, and was spoiling for a fight. When the two men were finally several feet apart, with their wives standing between them, Amos turned away and sat back down. Jason was slower to respond, but eventually sat down as well, his face beet red.

"Amos," Becca said slowly, seemingly concerned that her words might stir up his anger again, or perhaps Jason's. "You were telling us about the possibility of there being a nuclear war. We haven't reached the deadline yet. Is it possible they'll prevent it?"

Amos looked at Lillie, then at Becca, without answering.

"You think it's too late, don't you?" Becca said, looking at Lillie.

Lillie nodded. Amos and Lillie had been talking at length about the impact of global thermonuclear war, from a medical standpoint.

"You said a nuclear war could kill most life on earth, didn't you?" Brittany asked quietly.

Amos nodded.

"Then who would be left?"

Amos kept his eyes on Jason as he spoke.

"We know that the U.S. government has hardened bunkers, a lot like this one, although bigger and better constructed. After all, they have access to taxpayer money to build them. I don't know how well stocked they are, though. Probably not as well as ours, because they're older, built during the Cold War. Other governments will have similar facilities."

He looked around at the others, now.

"What a lot of people don't know," Amos said, "is that there's a movement in the U.S. and elsewhere—they call themselves *Preppers.* People who've been building shelters and preparing for this type of emergency. They're the ones who have a chance to survive this for—well, I don't know how long."

He shrugged.

"I guess that makes us Preppers?" Chris asked.

"I guess it does." Amos said, no longer enjoying the discussion, but amused by Chris's observation. "I haven't really participated in the Prepper movement, but we certainly fit the bill."

"So, this afternoon at three o'clock, the world just blows itself up?" Jason demanded sarcastically, still frowning at Amos.

"That's three o'clock Eastern time, one o'clock here," Amos said, keeping his voice even with an effort. "I don't think it will happen all at once, though. If it's going to happen, there'll be the initial explosion, probably in Washington, D.C. Maybe North Korea will launch a rocket at the beginning to add some confusion. NORAD can give the government twenty to thirty minutes of warning. It'll take at least that long for missiles launched from North Korea to get to the U.S."

"Is NORAD still functioning?" Brittany asked. "Isn't that the group that was supposed to provide early warning of an attack from a foreign country back during the Cold War?"

"That's them," Amos said.

"But I haven't heard anything about them for years," Brittany said.

"Isn't NORAD the group that tracks Santa Claus on Christmas Eve?" Katie asked.

"Yes," Amos confirmed, smiling at Katie despite his anger at Jason. "The North American Aerospace Defense Command, NORAD, was in the news a lot during the Cold War years, when we thought a nuclear attack from the former Soviet Union seemed like a real possibility. We don't hear much about them these days—except at Christmas, as Katie pointed out; but they're still around and active. In fact, as recently as 2015, the government funded the Pentagon to move the computer systems to a big bunker under Cheyenne Mountain in Colorado. It was part of an effort to protect the early warning system from EMPs.

"In the thirty minutes of warning that NORAD gives our government, they'll have to decide whether to try to take out the missile in the air, launch U.S. missiles on their predetermined targets, or do nothing."

"Why the hell would the government do nothing?" Jason asked. "That's totally illogical. You're making this stuff up."

"I'm not," Amos said. "But you know, I don't really care if you believe me, Jason." He turned away, speaking to the others. "That's just one of the options. If the government wanted to prevent an all-out war, they might do nothing, hope that Al-Qaeda only had the one bomb, and that North Korea's bomb was a dud or failed to reach U.S. soil. That would limit the destruction to Washington, D.C. and the fallout to the Northeastern States. The rest of the world would be spared, theoretically."

"That's a real gamble," Matt said, clearly upset. "Thousands of lives lost with no one holding Al-Qaeda accountable."

"Al-Qaeda won't quit until they destroy the U.S.," Mike added.

"What would you want the government to do?" Amos asked

He looked back and forth between Mike and Matt. The two young men sat silently for a few moments, faces turned down. Finally, Matt spoke up.

"I think I would try to destroy Al-Qaeda before they could find another bomb. If Russia's behind this, like you said, they could keep supplying bomb materials to Al-Qaeda until the U.S. gets a backbone and retaliates. I hate to say it, because I'm against just about any kind of violence, but I think it's better for a few people to die for the good of the many. I say they should retaliate. Right away."

"Are you serious Matt?" Emily demanded. "Think about how many innocent people would die if the U.S. retaliates."

Matt looked at Emily, his face apologizing for his words.

"But Em, think about how many could die if we *don't* stop the terrorists. I don't see any other reasonable option."

"So, you'd advise the government to retaliate?" Amos asked. "What if it caused a chain reaction with all the nuclear powers launching their missiles?"

Matt didn't answer. Nobody else spoke either. Some stared at Amos, while others looked at the ground, their feet, or the walls, avoiding eye contact.

"Okay," Amos finally said, "back to my speculation on what the U.S. will do. I think the government will retaliate with one or two missiles . . . "

"Not the whole arsenal, like the president said?" Chris interrupted, interested.

"He didn't say he would launch all our missiles," Amos said. "He said he'd retaliate against anyone who fired on the U.S. and any country that was complicit with them. That could even include holding back our nuclear weapons and launching conventional weapons instead."

"But you think he'll launch some nuclear missiles," Matt said.

"Yes, I do," Amos continued. "Then I think he'll wait to see what Russia and China do."

"What do you think they'll do?" Matt asked.

"Hard to tell. If Russia's behind the attack, they may think the president is bluffing about using nuclear weapons. If so, they'll be surprised by the U.S. response and may launch their own missiles, if only to stop ours. I think Russia has between six and seven thousand warheads, about the same as the U.S.

"China said they would respond if the U.S. launched missiles toward Asia. We don't know how many nuclear weapons they have. I've seen an estimate of about four hundred and fifty. It's hard to know what they would do, but I'm guessing they would fire one or more missiles, at a minimum, just like they said they would.

"If missiles are launched from multiple locations, the U.S. has the capability to see where they're coming from and where they're headed. I think the first targets would be the missile silos themselves. Each side will try to destroy the other side's ability to fight back."

"Do you know where the missile silos are in the U.S.?" Chris asked quietly. "Are any of them near here?"

"I know where some of them are. And no, they're not near here," Amos replied.

"Does that mean we're safe?" Chris continued.

"Probably," Amos said, smiling sadly at Chris's earnestness.

"At least in the sense that I don't think we'd see a direct hit, but we could easily get fallout from a near miss. And there are other dangers."

"Like what?" Brittany asked.

"Get back to the missile exchange," Jason insisted impatiently.

Amos glanced at Jason.

"Just a minute, Jason. Brittany asked first."

Amos turned to Brittany and Jason's face went red again.

"It's a good question, Brittany, which you all need to understand."

Brittany gave Jason a dirty look and he groaned and slumped impatiently back in his seat.

"The primary components of a nuclear explosion are the explosive blast, which causes most of the physical damage, and thermal radiation, which is like a giant sun lamp. The winds from the explosive blast can reach hundreds of miles per hour within seconds after the explosion, knocking down steel structures close to ground zero."

Amos could see from their expressions that the group was having difficulty imagining it.

"The reason they call it *thermal* radiation is because of the extreme temperatures—it's literally hotter than the sun. Add heat to the damage caused by the high winds, and anything that can burn, *will* burn. If there's enough kindling, the resulting firestorm can burn entire forests and put enough soot in the air to hide the sun and depress temperatures globally, causing a global winter. Scientists speculate that a permanent temperature drop of even a few degrees would be enough to freeze the oceans and kill off most life on land."

"That's a pretty grim picture," Matt said.

"Ridiculous!" Jason exclaimed.

Amos ignored Jason completely for the moment.

"It is, Matt. One of the possible results of a thermonuclear war is a worldwide power outage—an electrical meltdown, so to speak. I read one Congressional report, from 2008 I think, that detailed what would happen in the United States if we had a total electrical blackout. They estimated that nine out of ten people would die in the first year—from starvation, disease, and social breakdown."

Amos turned his focus to Jason, who still looked disbelieving and defiant. This was a subject Amos had been passionate about for years, and Jason was acting like it was nonsense. Amos knew his explanation might scare some of the people in the room, but he wanted it to hit home with the one person who was causing him so much grief.

"Even if there isn't global winter," Amos continued, his gaze now fixed on Jason, "there are still other effects. Fallout is the one we hear about the most. If a bomb explodes in the air, there's very little fallout. But if the bomb is close enough for the fireball to touch the ground, the particles that are picked up in the explosion become radioactive. Those that enter the atmosphere are then spread on the wind as nuclear fallout. We could also discuss flash burns, flash blindness, ozone depletion, the long-term effects of nuclear fallout . . ."

"Stop!" Brittany cried out. "That's enough."

She was holding her head with both hands, as if trying to force her brains to stay inside her skull.

"Amos," Lillie said, looking around the room. "I think some of us might want to take a break. Including me."

Amos looked at his wife, then at the others in the room. The worried expressions on some faces, and the clear fear on others, gave him pause. He realized that in his zeal to shake Jason, he'd gone too far.

"This is worst case, all speculation and estimates, you understand. The world hasn't done enough nuclear testing to really understand the effects, thank goodness."

His attempt to reduce the impact of what he'd already said didn't do much, but as he turned toward Jason he could see that his original goal had been met: Jason looked sick.

"Anyone want to leave?" Amos asked. "There's no shame in it. I can answer any questions that any of you have, any time."

Lillie stood and grasped Katie's hand.

"Why don't you come with me?" She said, "You too Rachel. Let's go get something to eat."

Rachel moaned, but she stood to follow Lillie and Katie. Nobody else moved. When those who remained had settled back down, Amos continued.

"Do you want to hear more?"

Nobody spoke, but several people nodded. Since those who couldn't take more had left the room, Amos focused on Jason again.

"Getting back to the missile exchange, Jason, I've studied a lot about the medical impact of nuclear war, but I don't claim to be a war strategist. This is just what seems logical to me. I think each side will try to destroy the other side's weapons first. Knowing that the weapons are being targeted, each side will try to get as many of their own weapons into the air as quickly as they can before they can be crippled or destroyed. NORAD will alert the military as soon as there are incoming missiles, and the military will likely decide to try to take out those missiles, the ones that are already in the air, *and* fire on their own predetermined targets. They'll try to hold back some missiles for a second response, I imagine, but if they wait too long to get them out of the silos, some of them might be compromised before they are put to use. And any explosion in the air will likely cause an EMP."

"Does anyone know how many bombs North Korea has?" Mike asked.

"I don't think so. They claimed to have nuclear weapons before this, but if they did, they couldn't figure out how to attach them to their ICBMs. Now, our government believes that Russia has provided whatever technology North Korea needed to give them at least one operational nuclear missile."

"How are people responding?" Emily asked. "I mean, just ordinary people, not leaders."

"Well, that's interesting," Amos said. "There seems to be a lot of confusion about what to do. From what I can gather, at first people were just trying to evacuate the big cities, going in all directions. Now, with the latest from the UN confrontation, reports are that foreign diplomats have left the country, as I said before. But they're not necessarily going home, I guess.

A lot of people, all over the world are headed south, to Central and South America, Africa, Australia, and New Zealand. Planes have been going south, full, and north, virtually empty. Those who can't get on a plane are hitting the highways. The roads into Mexico are jammed. It looks like Florida in the days prior to a hurricane. They're even dedicating all lanes to one direction: south. Obviously, I don't know any of this firsthand, this is just what the news is reporting, but there's video to support the reports."

"Going to the southern hemisphere?" Matt asked. "I guess people think that will be safer?"

"Yes, and it makes some sense. Most of the destruction would likely be in the northern hemisphere, because that's where most of the nuclear powers are located. And the wind currents in the northern hemisphere basically stay in the north, so most of the consequences would have much less impact south of the equator. It's a little surprising, at least to me, how many people seem to know that."

Amos paused to see if there were follow-up questions. From the sour expression on Jason's face, he suspected that the man was nauseated but was reluctant to show any weakness.

In reality, Jason *was* feeling sick. He'd begun to accept that a nuclear exchange was possible.

Damn, I could be stuck in this hole in the ground for a long, long time.

"Let's go get a bite to eat," Amos finally said. "Then we can meet in my office around noon to listen in on the latest reports."

"Sounds good to me," Jason said. He had to see for himself if what Amos was saying was true.

Prime bunker, somewhere northwest of Washington, D.C., 4 July, 1:00 p.m. Eastern Time

All eight screens were lit this time, showing the eight bunkers visible to the president. Each had a similar array of video screens on the wall of its situation room, so everyone could see each other.

In addition to the four members of the NSC that he'd met with earlier, the other statutory members of the National Security Council were in their places. The vice president was in the VEEP bunker, the Secretary of Energy was in ENERGY, the Chairman of the Joint Chiefs of Staff was in JCS, and the Director of National Drug Control Policy was in NDCP.

President McCormick acknowledged the people in the other bunkers with a nod, noting that in each situation room the seats adjacent to and behind the principals were occupied by additional regular and special members and attendees of the NSC. He knew that other support and military personnel were also attending, though out of his view.

The president thought about the sacrifice the government and military leaders in the bunkers had made. Only a few of them were allowed to take family members with them because the group was large even without them, and space was limited. Liz McCormick, their two sons, and their families, were among the select few. Despite the difficult situation he was faced with, and the likelihood that hundreds of thousands, if not millions, of lives might be lost by his actions, or his failure to act, the president was grateful that his wife and family were safe. But he also felt guilty. He was certain that anybody, in his situation, would have done the same things, and felt the same feelings, but it didn't make him feel any better.

"Are you going to be able to prevent war?" Liz had asked earlier.

Greg had known that her concern was for all the innocent people who would be put in danger, but he'd never lied to her and he wasn't about to start.

"I don't think so, Liz," he'd said sadly. "We can try to limit the casualties, which we're doing, but if we don't deal with Al-Qaeda, they'll never go away."

Several of the people who'd been assigned a spot in the bunkers had refused to do so when they were told that they'd have to leave their families behind. President McCormick sympathized. He didn't think he'd have left his family behind either, if he'd been faced with the same choice. Those government officials who preferred to stay with their families were excused by the president, with his blessing.

The families of other key personnel had been shipped off hurriedly to relatives' homes or deposited in secure public shelters near the bunkers. NSC participants who chose to follow their leaders to the bunkers knew they might never see loved ones again—it all depended on how well this NSC team managed the crisis over the next few days.

This distribution of personnel followed a strategy that had been developed during the Cold War. Each successive presidency was aware of the plan, and each hoped that it would never be needed during their stay in the White House. But military leaders had to study the strategy, among many others, familiarizing themselves with them until they became second nature. SecDef General Jim Seymour had shown the plan to the president, along with two alternative strategies, and insisted that his commander in chief select and implement the one that suited him best. To the president, the plan was the lesser of the available evils.

"We have two hours before the terrorist deadline," the president said, finally breaking the awkward silence. "Our intelligence services, the military, the Secret Service, and the Metropolitan Police have scoured the Washington, D.C. area for the bomb. It would seem that it's not there, or perhaps it doesn't exist."

There was stirring in the Prime situation room and the other bunkers. The president held up his hand to prevent questions and discussion.

"Before you ask, I'll tell you, we're not giving up the search. On a volunteer basis, we have people in the area, and they will stay there until shortly before the deadline in case the terrorists use the evacuation as the cover they need to enter the area and plant the bomb.

"In addition, on the chance that the bomb really does exist, we're still doing everything we can to evacuate people from the capital and from everywhere downwind. It's a monumental task, though. There are more than forty million U.S. citizens in the affected area, plus an unknown number of Canadians."

The president paused to consider what else he should say. He was certain this group had questions, but he just didn't want this to turn into a press conference

"What about the people who choose to stay?" someone asked before the president could continue.

"And what about the west coast cities that North Korea could hit?" someone else asked.

"Okay, I'll answer a couple of questions." Greg took a deep breath and let it out. "We've chosen not to force people to leave the area. In the capital, busses have been and still are rounding up anyone who will leave and moving them upwind of the target zone. In the rest of the affected region, we've set up shelters. I'm told most of the shelters are ready and are accepting evacuees. The media are cooperating by broadcasting instructions nonstop. We're also sending vans with loudspeakers through tourist areas and densely populated neighborhoods. That's the best we can do on short notice. In Chicago, and along the west coast, similar measures are in place.

"I'm sure some of you are also wondering what we're going to do if there *is* a bomb and it destroys the capital, or another city. You all know what I told the United Nations General Assembly. We've put Russia and Saudi Arabia on notice to stop the bomb, but we suspect they won't be able to do that. We're prepared to follow through with a limited nuclear response."

The reaction was instantaneous, as he'd expected—mostly

exclamations of surprise and distress. He ignored the quiet comments about how wrong or stupid it was to use nuclear weapons—he felt the same way, but he was committed. He debated cutting it off, but decided to give them a minute to work through their emotions, just as he'd had to do weeks earlier.

"Didn't you tell them you would bomb North Korea, too?" Vice President Art Klemp asked loudly. "And didn't China warn you not to?"

The president stared at him.

"Good memory, Art," he said.

Inside, he was seething. *Trust Art to ask the one question that I didn't want to come up in this meeting,* he thought. But he'd prepared an answer just in case.

"China has an estimated four hundred and fifty nuclear weapons. The U.S. has over seven thousand. The Chinese government will consider that before they decide to retaliate against us for firing on North Korea. Granted, the Chinese leaders are proud, and they're trying to show the world that they're a world power, but, they have to see the downside of that kind of response."

"Then why are we doing it, *Greg?*" Art asked sarcastically.

Greg had told Art to stop using his first name in group meetings. *Seems Art's decided to ignore my directions,* Greg thought, *perhaps to impress the others, show that he's in some sort of privileged position.*

"Because they think we wouldn't dare," Greg said. "Like the Russians, they think we're weak-willed, that we'll take our lumps, roll over, and play dead. The Russian president envies our role in the global community and wants it for Russia. That's not going to happen on my watch—period."

He'd raised his voice in anger, and he saw Jim shaking his head slightly, reminding him that these people needed to see a calm, rational leader. He cranked down his energy level quickly.

"However," the president went on, in an artificially calm voice, his heart pounding in his chest, "on the slim chance that China decides to defend North Korea, instead of following the wiser course, I need all of you to do what you do best: be alert, and professional, and work through your chain of command to keep me informed of what's happening and what needs to be done about it. Thank you."

23

"If there's a nuclear explosion"

The Preserve, Aspen Valley, 4 July, 11:15 a.m. Mountain Time
"I don't think I can handle watching it, Lillie," Becca said. "If what Amos says is true, the news must be awful."

"I feel the same way," Brittany added. "If it's going to be like Amos says, I don't need to see it. I'm upset enough as it is."

Lillie was surprised. She wanted to see as much as she could stand without getting sick. If the world was going to fall apart, she wanted to be a witness. She wasn't fascinated by death and destruction—far from it—but the impact on the world would be so monumental, she didn't see how anyone could look away.

"Okay," Lillie said. "Amos hoped you'd both come in for a few minutes, anyway. He wants to make sure everyone's questions are answered. And he promised to leave out the details."

They both reluctantly agreed.

After lunch, Terry opened the office. Most of the adults in the group were there, but the young adults and children hadn't been invited. They settled into chairs around a table in front of the TV. Amos looked specifically at Brittany and Becca.

"Do you have any questions?"

"You were explaining the impact of a nuclear explosion on the northeastern states," Brittany said.

"That's right," Amos said.

He glanced at Lillie, who shook her head subtly to let him know to keep it simple.

"In the larger cities like New York and Boston, Chicago, LA, and San Francisco, the news channels are reporting general confusion as people try to evacuate. There's also street violence and looting. I don't know what it is about some people, that they have to start looting whenever there's an emergency."

Brittany started crying quietly. Jason ignored her, but Lillie noticed and put her hand on Brittany's shoulder.

"We're perfectly safe here from everything we've seen so far or can anticipate," Amos added.

Jason noticed Lillie trying to comfort Brittany and decided to explain.

"That's not the problem, Amos," he said. "Brittany has a lot of family in the Boston area. Even though she's not close to them, this is a huge blow to her."

"I'm truly sorry, Brittany," Amos said. "I wish we could do more."

"No, Amos. You've done enough," Brittany said. "We appreciate your family taking us in. We can only hope for the best for them."

"You're *our* family now, Brittany," Lillie said with a sad smile, patting her shoulder.

Brittany put her head on Lillie's shoulder, whispering through her sobs.

"Thank you."

Amos turned to Becca and raised his eyebrows.

"Any questions, Becca?"

"No questions," Becca said. "I've heard enough. I think I'll leave now, thank you."

She got up to leave and touched Brittany's arm to get her attention. Brittany stood and the two of them left the office together.

Terry controlled the TV, switching amongst the news reports, which were on every channel. One showed the violence taking place in major cities around the country, with security forces—police, national guard, and military—having varying levels of success controlling it. Men, women and children were looting, destroying store fronts, fighting amongst themselves, and stealing anything they could get their hands on. Security forces in some places fired tear gas at the looters in an attempt to disperse them, but it didn't have much effect.

One camera captured a confrontation between a group of armed soldiers in riot gear and bare-chested looters who wouldn't put down their "treasures."

" . . . put them down now and walk away," came a powerful voice over a speaker.

Three men in their late teens or early twenties looked over

their shoulders at the soldiers and picked up their pace, trying to get away. The camera panned between the soldiers, who were slowly moving forward, and the looters, who were trying to escape with their arms full of electronics.

"This is your last warning," came the same voice. "Put down the merchandise or we will open fire."

The men looked worriedly over their shoulders, but just ran faster. Automatic weapons fire erupted. Tissue erupted in rows across the backs of the three men. Bodies broke and blood flowed, as they fell heavily to the ground. Their stolen goods smashed to the pavement around them.

More shouting and gunfire could be heard. The camera shifted to the other side of the street, where more people fell to the ground, the things they'd been carrying shattering as they fell. Blood spouted from head and body wounds, and screaming pierced the air.

In the background, children peeked around the corner of a building. A boy, maybe ten years old, was hit in the face by a stray bullet, and the left side of his face exploded, blood and tissue flying in all directions. The teen behind him was covered in gore from the explosion. Then he, too, was hit. His arm flew out to the side, shattered just above the elbow, then hung limply. The boy fell over in a dead faint, ignored and bleeding.

Mike stood and hurried to the bathroom, gagging. He closed the door behind him, but the sounds of his vomiting could be heard through the door. Matt tasted bile, and had to swallow several times to keep it down, shivering at the taste. Jason closed his eyes and tried to dislodge the images from his head. He placed a hand on his stomach and his face contorted as though he were in pain.

On the screen, the camera panned back and forth, up and down the street, amid more shouting and gunfire. Emergency medical personnel arrived on the scene and attempted to help the wounded and dying. Some victims held their hands over wounds to stop their bleeding. Some lay still in pools of their own blood.

A few of the looters fired back or threw objects. The cameraman ducked as bullets whistled around him. He stood his ground, but the camera shook a little after that. Curious bystanders became collateral damage, falling to the ground to join the dead and dying.

"That's enough of that," Amos said, his own face twisted in agony.

Terry changed to another channel. It showed the congestion at airports across the nation, where huge mobs of people holding piles of cash clamored for additional planes so they could get out of the country. Harried airline personnel were frantically trying to process people through.

"Why didn't all of those people try to leave days ago?" Mike asked after returning from the bathroom and focusing on the airport scene. "It's not like this situation snuck up on anyone."

Nobody had an answer.

In one scene, a Jetway door began to close. People still in

line at the ticket counter rushed toward it, shoving and trampling anyone in their way. The camera focused on a woman holding a baby girl in her arms. The mother tripped and fell. The baby was ripped from her arms and vanished in the crush of the desperate, angry crowd. Then the mother disappeared. Only the staggering and stumbling of the crowd gave any indication of where she was, as they trampled her underfoot.

Jason closed his eyes again, clearly struggling with the gruesome displays on the screen in front of him.

The reporter, unaware of the terrible scene taking place in the terminal, was reporting on the schedule changes.

"Four major airline companies use this terminal. All of them are adding more flights, as well as hurrying repairs to get more planes out of hangers. Flights are being redirected from east-west routes to north-south routes. According to sources, the major difficulty in moving so many people south has been convincing the Central and South American countries to accept the huge influx of 'immigrants' without requiring visas."

Terry changed the channel again. This report showed a border crossing between Texas and Mexico. Long lines of cars and pedestrians passed slowly through security gates and onto a bridge. The pedestrians carried suitcases and packages.

"Progress was slow yesterday, with no letup after dark. This morning, it's the same continuous stream of bodies and vehicles, headed south into Mexico. Some of the travelers I spoke with," the reporter said, "have come from as far away as Maryland and Pennsylvania. It looks like they took the president seriously when he said to get out of the northeast."

Terry changed the channel once more, landing on a report from a Washington, DC station. A smartly dressed man and woman sat behind a conference table in what looked like a schoolroom.

"Good afternoon. I'm Dennis Spaulding and this is Melanie Kearns, with Channel Eleven News. We're reporting from the Chantilly Elementary School in Chantilly, Virginia, about twenty-five miles from the capital, and our studio in Washington D.C. We have a crew in the Channel Eleven Skycam helicopter as well, currently getting in position for a firsthand report."

"If there's a nuclear explosion," Melanie said, as she took over the narrative, "and we're told it's still *if* and not *when*, the mushroom cloud would spread downwind, with radioactive particles dropping out of the cloud as 'fallout.' With today's weather, we would expect the cloud to spread to the northeast."

"That's right, Melanie," Dennis said, taking over again, "and now we're told that our Skycam team is in position, so we'll hand off our coverage to Mr. Justin Chase, our reporter in the sky. Hello, Justin, what's going on up there?"

The picture on the TV split so that Dennis was on the left side of the screen. The right side now showed a young man with short, unruly hair and a pair of wraparound sunglasses propped on top of his head. The creases from his smile stretched nearly to his ears, and his tanned skin looked wrinkled where his headset touched his cheeks just below his ears. He was holding a microphone and there was a banner under his picture that read: Justin Chase, Channel Eleven Reporter in the Sky.

"Hi Melanie and Dennis," Justin said seriously. "It's beautiful up here. Clear sky. Gentle breeze from the southwest. It's hard to believe we're actually contemplating a nuclear explosion that could totally destroy the Washington, D.C. area. Wow."

"I agree Justin," Dennis said. "Hard to believe."

"Okay," Justin continued, "we're in the Channel Eleven News Skycam helicopter, ten miles west of Washington, D.C., at five thousand feet." He looked briefly at his watch. "It's 2:52 p.m. We're told the military still has teams in the area, checking for a bomb and watching for terrorists who might try to use the confusion of the evacuation to carry a bomb into the area."

"Our pilot says he can see a military helicopter now," Justin continued.

The camera panned away from his face and to look out a side window, where a military helicopter flew rapidly from the right to the left below the news helicopter.

"Wow," Justin said. "He's really hauling. It must be show time."

The camera panned back to Justin's face, which was turned to the military helicopter. He wore an easy grin, a dimple in his cheek. It was obvious that he liked flying and speed, maybe picturing himself at the controls of the military helicopter.

"Can you tell if anyone's still in the city?" Melanie asked.

That brought Justin back to the present. As he turned toward the camera, he dropped the smile and the dimple disappeared, but his eyes still sparkled.

"It's hard to tell, Melanie. It's been eleven days since the president mentioned voluntary evacuation, and nine days since he confirmed that the terrorists have a bomb and plan to set it off in Washington, D.C. We've been watching people stream out of the capital and surrounding cities for days now, but we're told that there are likely thousands of people still in the city for one reason or another."

"That's amazing! Are the police and military helping with the evacuation?"

"We've seen them helping with traffic control, but whether or not they're going door-to-door telling people to get out is hard to say. Remember, they're also trying to find a bomb."

"Thanks Justin. It's 2:57. Do you want to take over and show us what's going on?"

"Thanks Melanie."

The view of Melanie in the schoolroom disappeared, leaving Justin and the helicopter to fill the entire screen. The camera panned right for a view out the side window and zoomed in on the National Mall.

"If you look closely at the spot where our camera is aimed, you can see the National Mall, with the Capitol building and reflecting pool on the left, the Washington Monument on the right, and the Smithsonian buildings running down both sides of the Mall in between."

What the camera couldn't detect from this distance were the people walking on the Mall and working in offices around the city. There were those who didn't believe the threat was real. There were young families on vacation who didn't want to lose their vacation time and the money their trip had cost, who were betting their lives that the bomb wasn't real. There were business men and women who didn't think they could afford to miss a day's work. And there were those who didn't hear the warnings, didn't understand, or didn't care, like many in the homeless population.

"I'll give you a second-by-second rundown of what's happening from our perspective," Justin continued. "We're putting on special dark glasses that we're told can withstand extreme changes in light, just in case we see a fireball. Whoa, it's like I'm in a cave. I can't see anything now." There was muffled laughter in the background. "We're waiting for the 3:00 p.m. deadline, which is coming up right . . . now."

Immediately there was a disturbance in the air around the mall.

"We can see a shimmer in the air. Looks like it's originating in the Mall."

The shimmer expanded into a fireball, the shape of a dome and brighter than the sun. Justin was still talking.

"Wow, that's bright. We're turning our heads, but we'll keep the camera on it."

In the Preserve, those watching the explosion on the TV screen turned their heads as well, but only briefly. It was uncomfortable to look at. Amos wondered why the bright light didn't shut down the camera. *It must have a special lens.*

"Holy cow!" Mike said. "They really did it!"

The fireball spread, engulfing the entire central district in a second, rising over a thousand feet into the air. It continued to spread outward until, after a few seconds, its brightness began to decrease and Justin picked up the narrative again.

"Okay, we're turning back around," Justin Chase said.

The fireball had decreased in intensity, and the destruction on the Mall could be seen through the smoke and debris spreading across the ground ahead of the growing mushroom cloud. There wasn't a building or monument standing, and there were uncountable fires burning.

"Uh, I've never been accused of being speechless, but *wow*."

The video transmission from the camera started to shake as the air around the helicopter got choppy. The pilot could be heard in the background.

"We're being hit by a high wind. I'm taking us out of here."

The camera angle changed as the helicopter rotated away from the explosion. The cameraman tried to stay focused on the mushroom cloud.

"On me! On me!" came Justin's voice offscreen.

The camera panned back to focus on Justin, whose face had gone pale. The dark glasses had slipped to the end of his long nose and reflected in them was the face of his cameraman, eyes wide with terror. Justin spoke rapidly, his own eyes huge with fear.

"This is Justin Chase, your Channel Eleven reporter. We're relocating to a safer location to continue broadcasting the explosion in Washington, DC. We're handing coverage back to Melanie and Dennis, back in the studio, I mean the—"

The scene changed back to the temporary studio where Melanie and Dennis sat behind their table, clearly shaken.

"This is Dennis Spaulding with Channel Eleven. So . . . while Justin and the camera crew in the Skycam helicopter relocate, we'll go to our affiliate at Channel Six in Cheyenne, Wyoming, who have a report for us."

Wyoming, 3:00 p.m. Eastern Time

Unseen by TV cameras, but observed by sensitive U.S. military instruments beneath Cheyenne Mountain, Colorado, an ICBM missile launched from North Korea. The instruments could not only tell its origin, but its eventual destination—Seattle, Washington, the nearest mainland U.S. destination and the one the North Korean government was most confident that its missile could reach.

President's private office, Prime bunker, Somewhere northwest of Washington, D.C.

"They actually did it." President Gregory McCormick shook his head wearily.

He was watching a live helicopter news report on the explosion in Washington, D.C. in his small office in the bunker, wondering what the freedom-loving people of the world were thinking as they watched similar reports from far less secure locations. *If they see that we can't even protect ourselves,* he thought, *how can they possibly hope that we'll protect them?*

"Greg?"

SecDef General James Seymour's voice emanated from a speakerphone on the president's desk, drawing the president back to their conversation.

"Yes, Jim?"

Greg sighed. He felt like he'd aged ten years from the stress of the last few weeks.

"North Korea just launched an ICBM at Seattle. Are you ready to respond?"

"Yes," he said tiredly. "You need authorization codes, don't you?

"Yes, sir," the general said, unsuccessfully masking his enthusiasm. "I have Cheyenne Mountain waiting."

While Jim added the Cheyenne Mountain control center to the call, the president bowed his head and prayed.

Greg and Jim had discussed the catastrophic impact a nuclear war would have on the civilian population and on global infrastructure. They both knew that if Al-Qaeda had found a supplier of nuclear weapons—and they had strong evidence to suggest that the Russian Siloviki were willing suppliers—nuclear war was unavoidable.

Greg knew Jim was sick of the politicians trying to solve

the world's problems by talking. "Talking has rarely worked and it won't now," Jim had said, "because there's so much greed, ambition, and hate in the world—so many special interests and ulterior motives."

Greg couldn't really disagree.

He knew that Jim had served in the first Gulf War—and every war since—and that Jim's experiences in those wars had convinced him that dancing around the issues didn't get things done. He also knew that Jim's hands had been tied by the politicians, him included, and he'd recently come to think that that was the weakness in politics. Greg knew that Jim had wanted a war like this his entire military career, and now that the attack was a *fait accompli*, Jim was asking the president for authorization to implement their response. Greg hoped that Russia would be rational and limit their response to intercepting the missile launched at Moscow, and that China would stay out of the conflict altogether and not defend North Korea as they had threatened.

"Ready when you are, sir," Jim said, pulling the president from his thoughts.

The president felt drained, and had to force himself to remember his part in the authorization process. He identified himself and asked the control center operator if he recognized his voice. The operator identified himself and gave the correct responses. The president read the authorization codes off a small card he'd been holding in his hand, and the operator confirmed them back to him.

"You are authorized to proceed," the president said.

"Yes sir," the control center operator replied and hung up.

"Okay, Jim, let's get with the Security Council and bring them up to speed."

The Preserve, Aspen Valley, 1:02 p.m. Mountain Time

The scene on the TV changed to show a large expanse of flat terrain where flames shot from a hole that had opened in the distance. A banner on the screen read: Shelly Redding, Channel 6 News Special Report.

"Thanks Dennis. This is Shelly Redding, speaking to you from the Channel Six helicopter near Cheyenne, Wyoming. We weren't exactly sure where to look, but you can see in the distance what we believe is an ICBM missile silo that has just opened." The camera zoomed in on the flames. "Alright! Now you can see the nose of a missile exiting the silo. It looks like the United States is going to respond to the situation in Washington, DC."

In the Preserve, those still in the office were riveted to the television screen. A second, then third silo began to open, as the nose of a missile rose out of the first hole. The first missile tilted slightly to the northwest as it left the silo, accelerating, chased by a tail of fire.

"Two other silos have opened. More nuclear weapons must be headed for the United States. Where are they coming from? North Korea? We'll try to find out."

The second and third missiles rose out of their silos and accelerated away, one to the northeast and one to the northwest.

"Okay, we're handing coverage back to Washington, DC."

The first missile observed by Channel Six in Cheyenne was on a trajectory to intercept the North Korean ICBM. The other two were headed for Pyongyang, the capital of North Korea, and Moscow, Russia, over the North Pole. President McCormick was, so far, honoring his commitment to Saudi Arabia, not to send a bomb their way. He fully expected Russia to counter the missile coming at them, but he hoped North Korea wouldn't have the same success.

Beijing, China, 1:02 p.m. Mountain Time (3:02 a.m. local time)

While much of the world gathered around their televisions and computers to witness the destruction of Washington, DC, the nine member Standing Committee of the Chinese Politburo were gathered in Beijing. President Xi Jinping had called the meeting. In addition to being president of China, he was also the General Secretary of the Communist Party of China—the highest-ranking leader in both the Communist Party and the state. It was unusual to schedule a meeting for the middle of the night, but the terrorist deadline made it necessary.

In a country where disagreement and dissention were not only not tolerated, but were still dealt with quickly and harshly, the Standing Committee was often characterized by a rare bluntness of speech and open disagreement. This never filtered through to the public, of course, but it was the rule within the committee chambers. The current cultural revolution, with its unprecedented reform, had lifted hundreds of millions of Chinese citizens out of poverty, unleashing a massive migration to cities, with better jobs, higher pay, and access to social media. Even so, China still had a long way to go before its people could speak freely, without fear of reprisal or punishment from their government. All political and military bodies in China required complete agreement with the Party position. Every decision was essentially a rubber stamp of a previously determined Party decision.

The nine men of the Standing Committee were the country's most influential leaders. They were, together, the real power behind China's government. Three days after their initial meeting on the subject, they still argued about how they should respond if the U.S. launched a missile at North Korea. Most of the younger members were against a nuclear response. They anticipated that the United States would return a direct attack on China, with superior numbers of weapons. A few of the older members held firm to the age-old position that China's sovereignty was at stake. China needed to show the world that they were now a world power that could not be intimidated or threatened. It was a calculated risk.

One man sat quietly at the table. This was former President Jiang Zemin, who was not a member of the committee. Even though he no longer had an official post in the government, he was the patron of many of the men around the table. As an elder to these men, he wielded influence over their decisions by his mere presence. And everyone at the table knew Jiang Zemin was part of the old guard.

When a military aide knocked, he was admitted to the room.

"The United States just launched a missile at North Korea," the aide bowed and told President Xi Jinping.

"Wait in the corridor," the president told the aide.

The decision of the committee, to retaliate against the United States, took no more than two minutes due to Jiang Zemin's sudden, but not unexpected, statement in favor. The measure passed by a vote of six to three. President Jinping waved a hand at one of the younger members of the Committee, who was seated nearest the door.

"Tell him our decision," the president said gruffly. He had voted in favor of reprisal, because of former President Zemin, even though it was not his first choice. *It would not be wise to go against Zemin,* he thought. He firmly believed the United States would retaliate. All he could do now was go to his hardened bunker, manage the war from there, and hope that the United States ran out of will or weapons before they got to his bunker.

He knew that the aide, as soon as he knew the decision of the committee, would rush to the communications room to notify the Central Military Affairs Commission of China's People's Liberation Army (PLA). It would take less than five minutes for the Commission to give instructions to launch nuclear missiles at the United States.

The Preserve, Aspen Valley, 1:06 p.m. Mountain Time
Inside the Preserve, the group watched as the scene on the

TV changed again. The helicopter pilot could be heard in the background.

"Okay, try again."

The helicopter swung back around so that the camera once again showed the mushroom cloud, farther away and larger than before. Justin faced the camera without blocking the view of the aftermath of the explosion out the window.

"I've got it . . . This is Justin Chase, Channel Eleven, reporting again from Washington, DC."

He was talking faster now, in short, choppy phrases and sentences, and looking over his shoulder out the window every few seconds. He sounded scared.

"The mushroom cloud has changed shape. The upper portion . . . is spreading out to the northeast . . . on the prevailing wind, I assume. The lower portion is dropping back on itself. The destruction on the ground . . . is spreading out in all directions. I never imagined anything like this. The winds from the explosion . . . are knocking down buildings . . . explosively . . . block after block . . . as if they were made of cardboard . . . "

The camera began to shake and the pilot could be heard in the background, speaking frantically.

"Gotta move! Now!"

"Hold on a sec," Justin said nervously, glancing over his shoulder again.

The cameraman had trouble keeping the camera steady with all the shaking.

"Can't. Gotta go *now!*"

The helicopter began to move, but before the pilot could pull away, the shaking became so severe that the camera crashed to the floor.

On the TV screen in the Preserve, they watched as someone's feet tried to find purchase. The camera rattled across the floor toward the nose of the helicopter. Justin fell down, so that his legs were visible on the camera. The pilot cursed in the background as he struggled to control the helicopter.

"I . . . can't . . . control . . . her . . . "

There was more cursing, scuffling, and the banging of bodies shaken around the inside the helicopter. Then the cameraman screamed.

"We're going down!"

The camera twisted so it was facing the outside wall, sliding toward the front of the helicopter. There was more screaming and scuffling for a few seconds, then a loud noise, like an explosion, and the camera died.

1:08 p.m. Mountain Time

The TV program in Amos's office returned to the temporary studio in Chantilly, Virginia. Melanie lurched off screen to the left, her hand over her mouth. Dennis turned to look at her, distress and fear making deep creases around his eyes and on his forehead. He must have received a prompt through the receiver in his ear, since he suddenly turned toward the camera and started talking, filling the air with noise.

"Uh . . . this is Dennis . . . uh, Spaulding at the Channel Eleven temporary studio . . . Melanie has been . . . called away . . . " He looked away to the left—then back at the camera. Melanie could be heard off-screen vomiting. "But she'll be right back . . . I'm sure."

His face twitched. He looked left again, involuntarily, as Melanie continued to dry-heave. He closed his mouth and swallowed, as if trying to keep his own lunch down. Then he nodded impatiently, perhaps receiving another prompt that he was unwilling or unable to obey. He took a shuddering breath and let it out, then seemed to pull himself together for another try.

"We've just witnessed, live, the detonation of a what appears to have been a nuclear explosion in Washington, DC. We've lost contact with Justin Chase and his camera crew in the Channel Eleven Skycam helicopter."

Dennis stopped again and swallowed. His face scrunched up as he swallowed again.

"I'm, uh, sure they're fine. We'll follow up with them . . . later. We're handing off coverage of the explosion in Washington, DC to Brent Close and Holly Stark at our Channel Four affiliate in Boston."

1:09 p.m. Mountain Time

In the office in the Preserve, no one spoke. Amos didn't know what to say, and he was certain the others must feel the same way. Terry turned down the volume without turning off the image. They could see the Boston newsroom, where reporters who hadn't just lost their associates and helicopter to a nuclear explosion were faring a little better—for the moment.

Amos looked around at the others, sure that his own face mirrored what he saw in theirs. The blood had drained from

Mike's face and his jaw was slack. He looked like a cadaver.

"Michael, put your head down. Between your knees."

"Huh?" Mike asked.

Lillie, who was closest to Mike, took him gently by the neck and pushed his head down as low as she could and held it there.

"Everybody okay?" Amos asked. "Matt, you don't look so good."

"I'm okay," Matt said after a moment. "Just a little . . . funny in the stomach . . . and light-headed."

"Let me know if you need any help," Amos said.

Jason looked like he was in a trance, and Amos studied him for a moment. Various emotions flashed across Jason's face in quick succession—surprise, disbelief, shock, disgust, fear, anger, and back to disbelief.

"What do we tell the others?" Terry wondered aloud. "Washington's been obliterated, just like they threatened. And that woman reporter in Wyoming thinks North Korea has launched a missile, too."

"How bad is it going to get?" Mike asked, his voice muffled by his jeans, his head still between his legs.

"I don't know," Amos said. "I think we should all look at ourselves in the mirror before we go back to the family. Let's try to maintain some order and control out there, okay?"

Jason hadn't said a word since Terry turned down the volume. He continued to stare at the TV, his face a mask of disbelief, and Amos decided not to speak to him until he could assess Jason's frame of mind. Then Jason turned to look at him.

"That was unbelievable—impossible."

"You think it was staged?" Amos asked.

"I don't know. I had no idea. I wouldn't have believed it if I hadn't seen it."

"It's hard to believe," Amos said. "We don't want to think that people can be so casual about the lives of others."

"It's just so *much* violence. It's one thing to read about it in history books—like the Crusades, or Hitler, you know—but this is the twenty-first century." He was badly shaken.

"We're more enlightened now, right?"

Amos tried to keep the sarcasm out of his voice, but he didn't entirely succeed. Jason nodded without speaking.

"I don't think human nature has changed much since caveman days, Jason," Amos said. "But the tools we use in our cruelty have certainly gotten worse. Al-Qaeda has been killing people all over the world, even their own, for years now."

"Yeah, but the violence in the streets and at the airports. I mean, I know that kind of rioting can happen, like after the Rodney King beating in California. But this isn't in one place, it's everywhere . . . and that bomb . . . how can they . . . how can anyone believe this is right?"

Jason's face was twisted into a grimace.

Terry watched, listening to the exchange between Amos and Jason. He shook his head, thinking about the explosion.

"It's hard to believe people can have philosophies so different from our own, isn't it? Every time I hear a report of a terrorist bombing, I think about the children being brainwashed into hating so much that they're willing to strap on a belt full of C4 explosive, walk into a crowd, and set it off. They get to go to paradise for doing that, you know. No greater reward for them."

"I've heard the stories," Jason said. "I thought they were mostly exaggerations. Something the media made up to sell news."

"Well, they're not," Terry said sadly. "It's happening all over the world."

Jason didn't know how to respond. It was too much for him to take in. Mouth agape, staring at Terry, he stood up to leave.

"Jason," Amos said.

Jason turned back. He was having difficulty putting his thoughts in a logical order, but he thought he had himself under control.

"I suggest you say as little as possible to the others. They don't need to know anything about this," Amos said, pleadingly.

Jason blinked, trying to make sense of Amos's words and fit them into the jumble of thoughts swirling around in his head.

Amos tried again. "Jason, don't say anything about this to anyone," he said.

"Right," was all Jason could manage. Then he turned and walked out of the room. Moments later he stopped for a moment. *What did Amos say?* It wouldn't come to him.

"Have you ever wondered what it would be like to be in an airplane crash?" Terry asked Amos.

"Now we know," Amos replied.

The president's office in the Prime bunker, Somewhere northwest of Washington, D.C., 3:10 p.m. Eastern Time

"China and Russia just launched missiles at us," SecDef Jim Seymour told President McCormick over the phone. The president was still sitting at his desk. His office was Spartan, but a thin, metallic presidential seal was mounted on the wall behind him.

"I really thought China would stay out of this and let North Korea deal with the consequences of what they did," the president said quietly.

He considered asking Jim for details, but decided against it for two reasons. He'd already pre-approved the plan for what happened next, and he had a meeting scheduled with the entire NSC in half an hour. He'd ask for details then. *Let the military get on with their job,* he thought to himself.

"Follow the plan, Jim," the president said. "You need authorization codes again, don't you?"

"Yes, sir," the general said.

The president bowed his head and once again prayed, asking forgiveness for his part in what was about to happen to the people of the world.

"Ready, sir," Jim said.

24

"That's enough Jason"

The Preserve, Aspen Valley, 4 July, Afternoon

"How bad do you think it will get?" Terry asked.

"You watched the report from the United Nations," Amos said. "I'm sure the missiles the U.S. just launched were headed for Moscow and North Korea. That's what the president said he would do."

"You think China will retaliate against the U.S. for launching a missile at North Korea?"

"That's my guess. So, now, both Russia and China could escalate this into a global thermonuclear war."

"You talked with the president about this, didn't you? What does he think?" Terry asked, the emotion in his voice beginning to rise.

"Yeah. When Greg asked me what I thought about a nuclear weapon in the hands of Al-Qaeda, I told him that if Russian Siloviki are willing to sell nuclear weapons to Al-Qaeda, the terrorists will use them against the United States and our allies. Either we have to stop Al-Qaeda or Al-Qaeda will destroy us.

"What did he say?"

"He's sick about it, obviously. But Jim Seymour, his Secretary of Defense, told him basically the same thing."

"So, you advised the president to retaliate against China and Russia if they launch missiles?"

"Well, I didn't 'advise' him either way. That's not my job. But I told him that unless he can locate the Al-Qaeda strongholds and take them out with conventional weapons, the result will likely be nuclear war."

"I hope the military can stop the missiles."

"If any of those missiles get past the country's defenses, we'll see more of what happened to D.C. The difference will be that now there's no time for people to get out of the way. It'll be mass slaughter. Millions of people could die today. The electric power grid could fail altogether. If the government and military can't stop it here, today, it could go on for days."

He stopped talking for a moment to think about what that meant.

"We'll be fine here," he said. "But I don't hold out much hope for the rest of North America. Or Europe, China, Russia, or North Korea either."

Amos placed both hands behind his head, raised his face toward the ceiling, and closed his eyes, as he thought about the turn of events. Moments later, he lowered his head and looked toward his friend. Terry was staring at him. They looked at each other for several seconds without speaking. Terry's face was ashen and beads of sweat had collected on his forehead and upper lip. Amos wondered if he looked as bad.

"The world may be dying, Terry," Amos finally said. He felt like the life was draining out of him. He lowered his head to catch his breath.

"Had enough for now?" Terry asked quietly. "We should take a break, don't you think?"

"Yeah."

Amos stood wearily, grasping the back of his chair to keep his balance. Terry checked that the recorder was running, then turned off the TV. They walked out together, Terry's hand on Amos's shoulder. Amos was grateful for the support. Mike and Matt, who were sitting silently in the outer office, stood when Amos and Terry arrived.

"Where's Jason?" Amos asked.

"Walked right past us without saying a thing," Mike said. "I asked if he was okay, but I'm not sure he even saw us."

When Amos and the others arrived in the community center, Jason was arguing loudly with Brittany. Amos listened as he walked to his wife.

"What's going on?" he asked Lillie quietly.

"I'm fine cleaning up after myself," Jason complained loudly, "but I'm not going to clean up everyone else's messes. I should be managing people, not washing tables and sweeping floors."

"We agreed to take our turn, Jason," Brittany said, furious. "*You* agreed."

"That's what's going on," Lillie said.

Seeing Amos, Jason redirected his fury.

"I have more management experience than anyone else here," he said to Amos, speaking far more loudly than he needed to. "I should be the one telling others what needs to be done."

We have a war going on, and this is what he's worried about? Amos thought. His stomach churned with anxiety, but he put on his most diplomatic face.

"Jason, nobody's feeling great right now. Maybe this isn't a good time for this discussion."

"There will never be a *good time* for this discussion," Jason bellowed. "You've got us trapped in this hellhole and insist that we kowtow to your demands. I agreed to your rules, but I'm going to at *least* insist that you use my management skills and not ask me to wipe down tables like a . . . a . . . I don't know what."

Amos's inclination was to laugh, but he wasn't in the mood, and it definitely wouldn't help. Instead, he stretched his neck and shoulders, a habit that had started the night Jason had hit him in the head. He kept his expression sober.

"What have you managed, Jason?"

Jason stopped suddenly, like he was expecting an argument and was surprised by Amos's response.

"Well, I had a staff of accountants and auditors," Jason said proudly. "I scheduled their workload, set deadlines, reviewed their results, conducted performance reviews, that sort of thing."

"Well, you know, what our family needs is someone who knows how to encourage teenagers to clean their rooms, bandage scraped knees, negotiate teenager disputes, advise young lovers, that sort of thing."

Jason's demeanor changed a little with each new task mentioned, until he looked ready to explode. Amos looked around at the faces of the others in the room. Most registered surprise, some fear, at the possible outcomes of this confrontation.

"Don't misjudge our situation," Amos said, motioning to the others in the room. "We're a family, and we'll function as a family. Everyone will have jobs and be expected to do them, just like in a family. Maybe you can look over the list of assignments and . . . "

"You're worrying about *teenager* disputes," Jason interrupted, his voice getting hoarse. "When the world outside it tearing itself apart?"

"What do you mean, *tearing itself apart?*" Emily asked, looking at her dad instead of at Jason.

Matt Green, Emily's boyfriend, had come over to stand by her, and now he put his arm around her waist protectively.

"Oh, hasn't your father told you," Jason said sarcastically, taunting Amos. "About the soldiers shooting people in the back . . . ?"

"That's enough Jason," Amos said, barely controlling his anger.

" . . . or the women and children being trampled at airports . . . ?"

"I said, that's *enough* Jason."

" . . . or the bomb that destroyed Washington, D.C. . . . ?"

Amos lunged, punching Jason in the face and knocking him down, then stood over him, breathing heavily, his fists clenched at his sides. Suddenly, Lillie had one of his hands in hers, intertwining her fingers with his.

"Amos, calm down," she whispered.

Emily came up on his other side, taking his arm in her hands.

"It's okay, Dad. It's okay," she said.

Jason looked up at Amos from the floor, working his jaw. He was leaning on his elbows.

"Feel better, Amos?" he demanded, still taunting. "Got that out of your system? Are you afraid to tell the family the *truth?*"

Amos took another deep breath and let it out.

"Jason, you agreed to follow my direction as a condition of coming to the Preserve. I will decide when it's time to tell the family what's happening on the outside and you will respect my decisions. Is that understood?"

"Or what?"

"Don't push me."

Amos couldn't remember being so angry with anyone, ever. Yes, the situation outside was stressful, but Jason pushed his buttons like no one else could.

Jason realized he was at a disadvantage. Amos was standing over him threateningly. He couldn't see a way out of this gracefully. He waited silently.

Finally, Amos looked around the room and Jason followed his gaze. The faces of the family members showed a range of emotions from concern to fear. Jason watched Amos relax, then back up a step.

"Let me help you up," Amos said.

His voice was tight, but he reached out an open hand to Jason, who flinched before realizing that Amos was offering conciliation. He carefully reached out and took Amos's hand, expecting at any time for Amos to play some trick on him.

When he was standing in front of Amos, who was two inches shorter and at least 60 pounds lighter, he realized how angry Amos must have been to hit him hard enough to knock him down.

He caught me off guard, is all, he told himself. *I'll be better prepared next time.*

As Jason looked around, working his jaw with his hand, he saw Nathan staring at him. Nathan's face was blank, but he wondered whether the boy was embarrassed that his dad couldn't defend himself against Amos. There was blood on Jason's hand when he looked at it.

He cut my cheek, he realized. *I swear I'll never be at the mercy of Amos Blund again.*

Lillie pulled on Amos's arm and succeeded in getting him to back up a couple of steps. Amos opened and closed his right hand several times, trying to shake it off. Lillie knew he hadn't struck another person since medical school when he'd done some boxing. She stepped up next to Amos and spoke to the whole group.

"We had an early lunch. There are some grapes and crackers in the dining room. Why don't you all help yourselves."

Lillie saw Sydney take Rylee's arm.

"Let's go eat," Sydney said.

But Rylee didn't respond right away—she was watching Nathan, who was sitting, silent, in a corner, staring at his dad.

25

"Against all the laws of physics"

The Preserve, Aspen Valley, 4 July

As they walked to the lab, Terry and Mike explained to Amos what they'd done to investigate the problem they'd encountered in Logan with the Observer.

"While you were playing car chase games in Logan canyon, Mike and I were checking out the Observer."

Terry paused, clearly looking for a reaction.

"Disappointed that you weren't having as much fun as us, huh?" Amos asked.

He would normally have laughed, but he was still upset from his confrontation with Jason. He absent-mindedly flexed his sore hand and twisted his head back and forth, stretching his sore neck. The stress of the war and the confrontation with Jason had taken its toll on him.

"So, where are we?"

"Remember, you asked me to review the schematics to see if there was something in the controls that could account for the missing medical building?"

"Yes, and . . . ?"

They walked over to the workbench by the Observer.

"We discovered a difference between the design in the schematics and what we actually built in the finished Observer. It didn't look significant. I thought that it shouldn't have made a difference and was inclined to ignore it. But Mike convinced me that we should build a new control board, matching the schematic, and try it, just to confirm."

Terry looked at Mike, nodding for him to continue, and Mike stood up straight, puffing out his chest. It appeared to be a subconscious reaction showing how proud he was of his part in this investigation. Amos smiled. He really wanted to laugh but couldn't make it happen.

"You remember, back in Logan, that we were looking for the new medical center on the University campus and all we saw was an empty hillside?"

Amos nodded and Mike continued.

"Like Terry said, he was going to overlook the error we found in the control board, but I suggested we check it out. Then he was just going to modify the existing board. But I asked if he had the material to build a whole new board."

Amos was watching his son, amused by how animated Mike was becoming.

"I thought that we could swap the boards in and out to see any real-time differences," Mike continued, moving his hands in a back and forth motion. "After that, I helped Terry build the new board and test it. And guess what? There was a difference."

Mike looked at his dad, clearly waiting for his reaction.

"Michael," Amos said with sincerity, "I'm impressed. These

are the boards?"

Mike nodded as he pointed first to one, then to the other.

"This is the original board—the one we used in Logan— and this is the one that matches the schematics. Do you want to see what they do?"

"Yes," Amos said, "but I want to check the ambient conditions in the valley before we turn on the Observer. I want to know if there's any new contamination, since that's probably more important to our situation right now. Is that okay with you guys?"

"Sure," Mike replied.

Amos nodded to Terry, who went to a control panel on the wall to look at several gauges and controls.

"Hmm . . . dust and radioactivity are slightly higher than normal. I don't know if that's significant, but it shouldn't affect a short-duration test," Terry said.

Amos nodded.

"First, the original board," Mike said.

He inserted one board into the Observer, closing the panel. An image about six inches in diameter appeared in the air about six feet away from them. Terry started manipulating the controls and the image started to expand in size.

"*Stop!*" Amos shouted.

Terry stopped, and he and Mike stared at Amos.

"That image isn't projected onto the wall. I thought we were dealing with a projection. But that image is floating in midair."

Amos looked at Terry, who was smiling.

"I wondered how long it would take you to notice," Terry

said.

"Explain!"

Amos walked over to the two-foot diameter image to look at it closer.

"Well," Terry said. "I think it was a coincidence that the image we saw in the lab in Logan appeared to be on the wall. I didn't actually notice this until Mike walked behind it to see what it looked like from the other side."

"Wh . . . ?"

Amos moved around to look at it from the back. He moved back and forth, front to back, several times, to see what differences he could identify.

What he saw was the wooded Aspen Valley, above them. There were trees, grass, and flowers, just as they would see if they were outside. He couldn't see Terry or Mike when he looked from the back, but he noticed that he could see trees over the Preserve, where there shouldn't be any, and the rock face of the cliff above the trees.

"The cliff," he said.

He looked at Terry and Mike, surprised, then looked from front and back several more times.

"Enlarge the image to about four feet in diameter."

He examined it closely again.

"According to the controls, what distance is this image from the cliff?" he asked.

"Thirty feet," Terry said, realizing that Amos was going through the same mental process that he had gone through a couple of days earlier, and was at least as quick at figuring it out.

"That's what it looks like," Amos said. "So, the image should be directly above us, in the clearing over the Preserve. But there isn't a clearing—the trees extend all the way to the cliff."

"Good point," Terry said, smiling.

He'd noticed the same thing when he and Mike had run their tests.

"What do you think?" he asked Amos.

"I think this is going to take some serious investigation," Amos said, rushing to the table. He picked up a pencil and scribbled for a minute on a pad of paper. "We need to analyze why the change to the control board design has this result. Mike, tell me where the change is."

"Dad, can we look at the other board before we get distracted by analysis?"

"Oh, okay Mike. But I want to document what we're seeing here."

"Take pictures?" Mike asked.

"Good idea," Amos agreed excitedly.

He dropped his pencil on the table, hurried to a supply cabinet, pulled out a Nikon digital camera, and took several pictures from each side of the image.

"So, we still haven't resolved the original problem of why we couldn't see the medical building," he said once he had the pictures. "And now we have the same situation in the valley. We're not seeing the valley as we know it to be."

Amos was talking faster, his excitement growing. He ran his fingers through his hair.

"Dad," Mike said with forced patience, "you need to try the other control board."

"Right, Michael. Okay. Anything else I should know about this setup?"

Amos looked at Terry with a question in his expression.

"Why don't we move the image closer to the cliff and see what changes?" Terry suggested.

He was enjoying Amos's boyish excitement.

"Right," Amos said, with enthusiasm. "That's what we were doing when we were interrupted in Logan."

Terry played with the controls. The image remained the same distance from them in the lab, but the objects within the image appeared to move farther away.

As Amos watched, he felt as though he were moving backward through trees and bushes. His brain told him he was moving, even though he knew he was standing still. It was so disorienting that he spread his feet to keep from falling over. When the image stopped moving, he went back to the image and stood behind it. He stuck his head around the edge so he could face Terry, a huge smile on his face.

"This is amazing!"

Terry smiled back, nodding. Amos saw Mike moving his hands in a gesture that said he was getting impatient.

"Okay, Michael, let me get some more photos and then you can play, too."

Mike looked embarrassed, but had a smile on his face. Amos took a few more photos, then realized something.

"Hey, you guys aren't acting surprised by any of this. You already figured out what's happening, didn't you?"

"So far," Terry said, "you've come to the same conclusions we did. Let's switch boards, when you're ready, and see if anything new pops up."

"I'm ready now."

Mike switched the control boards and Terry turned the equipment on again. Amos could see the same forested valley, except that when he went behind the image, there were no trees between him and the rock face of the cliff.

"We're in the clearing this time," Amos said, surprised by the difference. "What's your hypothesis, Terry?"

He could tell from the smug look on Terry's face that he had an idea what was happening.

"It appears that what we see with this *corrected* control board is this valley in this time and place," Terry said, "just as we expected."

"Meaning," Amos said excitedly, "that with the first board—the modified board—what we're seeing is either a different time or a different place?"

"That's my conclusion," Terry said, nodding.

"Wow!" Mike said. "You mean like in the past? That's hard to believe."

"Or the future," Terry said. "But it would have to be quite a ways in the future, because the trees covering the clearing are about the same size as the ones around them."

"That can't be, Terry," Amos said, as he began to piece together what Terry was saying. "We can't possibly be seeing the future. Or the past. That makes no sense."

Amos was baffled. *Terry's conclusion is totally illogical,* he thought. When he saw Terry's wide smile and the twinkle in his eyes, he realized that he was excitedly, and uncharacteristically, waving his arms and raising his voice. He tried to get control of his emotions, but it wasn't easy.

"It seems unbelievable alright," Terry said, still smiling.

"But you *do* believe it, don't you?"

"Amos, I'm not sure what I believe, but I've been thinking about this for two days now, and I can't see any other explanation for what we're seeing here."

"Wow. I mean . . ." Amos trailed off for a moment. "Really? Terry, am I really looking at some other time—other than the present?"

"Dad, come on," Mike said, interrupting. "Could that really be true? You're a scientist. This sounds more like fiction."

"I know it does," Amos said, his voice gone quiet. "The other possibility is that it's a different place, but that can't be the answer because that's definitely our clearing. And what we saw with the other board was our valley without the clearing. Can you imagine the ramifications? It's hard to take in. But Terry, that's the conclusion you came to, right?"

"Yeah."

"But you wanted to see if I arrived at the same hypothesis?"

Terry nodded.

"Well, obviously," Amos began, "this is going to take a bit of time to figure out. We need to be sure. I mean—well, to be honest, I don't know what I mean. I don't know what any of this means."

Amos's voice faded out. He shook his head and looked to the ceiling.

"So, Terry, why didn't you say anything to me?" Mike asked

It was clear that he was disappointed that Terry hadn't discussed the idea with him sooner.

"It didn't come to me until later, after we completed our tests," Terry explained. "I wanted . . . "

Whatever Terry was about to say was interrupted by a loud beeping sound from a panel against the wall.

"What's that?" Mike asked, looking concerned.

Amos rushed over to the wall to deal with it, while Terry began to shut down the Observer.

"Is it air contamination in the valley?" Terry asked.

"Yes, or at least, that's what the alarm is supposed to alert us to," Amos said. "The radiation level reached our low consumption threshold."

He pushed a button. The beeping should have stopped but it didn't. He looked confused.

"The inside monitors went off as well as the outside ones. What's with that?"

Amos pushed another button and the inside alarms shut off. Amos and Terry looked at each other, mouths open, and then at the disappearing image in the room. There was alarm on both their faces.

"I'll get the Geiger counter," Terry said as he ran to one of the cabinets against the wall.

Amos just nodded. When Terry came back, he turned on the Geiger counter—or, more accurately, the Geiger-Muller tube—which, as Amos had explained when he bought two of them, is used to detect and measure levels of alpha, beta, and gamma radiation. He pointed it in the direction of the fading image. It went off, reporting the presence of low-level radiation in the lab.

"What does that mean?" Mike asked.

He looked from his dad to Terry, who were staring at each other, surprise and disbelief etched on their faces.

"It means, Michael," Amos began, but he stopped.

He was still staring at Terry, still trying to understand his own thoughts, and he saw his own surprise mirrored in Terry's eyes.

"I mean, Mike—it *might* mean—that we're not looking at an image. It's—it's a. Hm. I mean, I think it's a portal."

Amos stuttered as he said it, every bit as surprised as Mike and Terry looked. What he had just said, he realized, came out sounding more like a question than a statement. He pushed his hand through his hair as he thought. *What I just said, that's impossible—but no more impossible than looking into the past with that other control board.*

"You mean, like a door?" Mike asked.

Amos turned to look at Mike.

"Or a gate. Yes, I think so. Terry, can that be? This doesn't make any sense. I mean. Terry? A doorway to some other place with this control board, and looking into the past with the other control board? That's insane."

Terry stared at Amos, equally confused. Amos closed his eyes, composed himself, then began again, slowly and deliberately, trying to do a better job with his explanation.

"I think it's some kind of portal. Obviously, that doesn't make much sense. And I can't explain that, just like I can't explain what we saw with the other control board. I can't understand it, but if it is, then this. Um, this portal—I think it allowed enough radiation to leak into the lab to set off alarms."

Amos looked at Terry for any kind of confirmation, or even rejection, of his theory. He realized he still hadn't explained what he meant at all well—because he couldn't.

"I don't know Amos," Terry said slowly, waking from his stupor. "I mean, that makes sense in a way, I guess. But you're talking about something hypothetical. Portals, or doorways, like you're talking about don't actually exist, do they? What you're suggesting goes against all the laws of physics—at least the ones we know."

"So does looking into the past or the future, but that's what we saw before, or so it seems."

"You guys are scaring me a little," Mike said quietly, looking back and forth between his dad and Terry.

"It defies all logic," Amos said quietly, almost reverently.

"This isn't possible, Amos! What the blazes have we invented?" Terry asked.

"Terry," Amos said, "if that's a portal—or door or gate,

whatever you want to call it—the ramifications are endless and, as Michael said, frightening. I don't know. I wish we had more time to test it. But radiation got in. We can't do that again."

"This raises lots of questions," Mike said excitedly. "Like, do both boards create portals? Or, can we figure out some way to incorporate both the old and the new boards into one, to get both effects?"

"You're asking," Amos replied thoughtfully, almost to himself, "if we could travel through a portal into another time or place?"

"Yeah," Mike replied. "And if the portal is directional, which is what it looks like, can we manipulate it to look in any direction?"

"Can we jump from one location, or time, to another?" Amos added.

"Amos," Terry said, interrupting them. "I don't think the level of radiation is bad enough to cause us any permanent harm, but we should probably get out of the lab for the rest of the day to let it disperse."

"Yeah, we need to think about this anyway," Amos said pensively.

Terry rechecked the controls to verify that the equipment was turned off. Then the three men left the lab, locking the door behind them. As they walked down the tunnel toward the community center, Terry turned to Amos.

"Where do you think the radiation came from?"

Amos stared at him, his face blank, shaking his head.

"Too many questions, Terry."

Epilogue

"We're here for you if you need us"

Amos and Lillie were in their bedroom, Amos sprawled out on the bed, his legs crossed, his hands behind his head, propped up on a pillow. Lillie sat on a chair, listening, as Amos tried to explain what they had seen in the lab with the Observer.

"I know it seems impossible, Lillie. It challenges all logic and reason. We were trying to create a new medical technology, not a window on the past, or future, or a gate to some other place or time. It could take us a lifetime just to understand what we have here. I know it all sounds like science fiction. I don't blame you for doubting me."

There was a knock on the door and they heard Emily's voice.

"Can we come in?"

Lillie went to the door to find Emily, Mike, and Rachel standing there, concerned expressions on their faces. Amos sat up, and Lillie joined him on the edge of the bed. Emily and Rachel sat on the only chairs in the room, and Mike stood leaning against the door after he'd closed it. It seemed to Amos that Mike wanted to keep the door from being opened.

"Dad, Mom," Emily started, "We know it's been a long, difficult day for both of you. It's been hard on everyone. We just want to know that you're okay. And we want you to know that we're worried about you."

Amos and Lillie looked at each other for a few moments. Then they looked back at their three wonderful, mature, adult children.

"You want to know if I'm going to begin beating up on people who disagree with me?" Amos asked. "Is that it?"

"Just one person in particular," Mike said with a smirk.

Amos chuckled and shook his head.

"Well, letting him come here was probably the biggest mistake of my life. I don't remember being this stressed out since medical school. At least then I could reduce my stress in the boxing ring. And I only had to worry about myself. But this is so different, with all the people we're responsible for and with what's going on in the world."

"There's so much at stake," Lillie added, taking Amos's hand in hers.

"Well, we want you to know that we're here for you if you need us," Emily said.

"Oh, Emily," Lillie said, a smile tugging at the corners of her mouth, "we know you are, and we love you all."

Lillie and Emily stood at the same time, as if it had been choreographed, and met halfway, hugging tightly for only a moment before Rachel joined them.

Moments later, Lillie looked over at Mike and moved her head from right to left, as if to beckon Mike to the circle. As Mike approached, Rachel and Emily let go, leaving room for him to reach his mom. He reached out and pulled his mom to him, then kissed her on the cheek.

"Luv ya' Mom," he said.

Amos smiled as he watched his family express their love for each other. Finally, he joined them in the center of the room and was crushed as his wife and children swarmed him. After several moments, with all of them standing in the middle of the room, Amos turned to Mike.

"Hey, did you tell your sisters about our discovery?"

"No," Mike replied.

"What discovery?" the girls asked at the same moment, looking between Mike and their dad.

"I know we can trust you to keep a secret, so I'll tell you what we think we've found. Why don't you sit down again?" Amos said, motioning to the chairs the girls had been sitting on. He tried to explain the two control boards and their speculation, that one was possibly a window to another time, and the other potentially a portal—a door or gate—to another place.

"Really? Is that possible? It sounds like science fiction. Can we see it?" Rachel asked, as Emily's mouth hung open in surprise. Mike nodded, a wide smile plastered on his face. The girls promised not to tell, and Amos promised to show them the portal—sometime, but not just now.

After their kids left, Lillie lay down next to Amos, her face inches from his. She draped her arm over his stomach and snuggled into his chest.

"How did we manage to get three such wonderful children?"

Amos just smiled.

Author's Note

This story is a work of fiction. With the exception of some internationally recognizable personalities, all of the characters are fictitious, and any resemblance to real persons is coincidental. Location names, government organizations and functions, and the effects of man-made and natural disasters are as accurate as I could make them.

The idea for this story came to me many years ago, while working as an engineer at a nuclear construction site in Washington State. Being fresh out of school at the time, most of my reading had been textbooks, and I wasn't prepared to write a novel of this size and complexity. When my son, Daniel P. Wilde, asked me to review his first manuscript, *Today We Die*, two years ago, I realized that I wanted to finally tell my story.

I started writing *Omega Crisis*, intending to publish it as a single book, but the story has outgrown these pages. The manuscript for the sequel, *Worlds in Collision*, is already in review, with book three (title yet to be determined) in the works. And there's at least one more story to write after that.

I want to sincerely thank all those who helped to prepare this manuscript for publication. Felicia Osborne reviewed it first and made several constructive suggestions—thank you Felicia. Thanks also to my son, Dan, and to Chris Palmer, Kevin Cook, and Steve Brown, for their priceless suggestions. Thanks to my daughter, Katie Petersen, for her help with the cover design—I had an idea what I wanted, but she brought it all together. Thanks to Saul and Nas at *IndieBookLauncher.com* for their invaluable assistance with editing, finalizing the cover, and preparing the manuscript for publication. Finally, thanks to my dear wife, Marilyn, for her patience with my long hours at the computer, writing this story—I love you.

Read on for a preview of *Worlds in Collision* (Book 2 in the *Gemini Gate* series).

Worlds in Collision

"Have you remembered what was bugging you about the portal?" Terry asked, as he and Amos studied schematics of the Observer and discussed their amazing discovery.

"No, and it's really eating at me. I'm not sleeping well."

"Want to try something?" Terry asked, approaching the Observer.

"What do you have in mind? I thought we agreed to leave it alone until we understood better what was going on."

Terry laughed.

"The way I remember it, *you* decided we should wait. And I don't see how we'll know what's going on if we don't experiment with it."

Amos didn't answer.

"You remember that with Panel B, radiation entered the lab from the valley—our valley," Terry said.

"Yes."

"But with Panel A, no radiation entered the lab. What if we play with Panel A to see what else we can learn?"

"And if the radiation sensors go off again?"

"Well, it'll tell us *something*."

"That isn't the correct way to run an experiment," Amos growled quietly, "but I'll go along if we take careful notes."

Terry nodded toward the notepad on the table as he loaded Panel A into the Observer, turning it on to open a view to the valley.

The vegetation is green with life, Amos thought wistfully as he watched. *Not like the last view we had of our valley, before the sensors malfunctioned.*

Terry kept his hand close to the *off* button and waited.

"No radiation alarm," he said after a couple of minutes. "What are you thinking?

"How beautiful this valley is—it looks so much like our valley before the fire."

"That's what I thought. You have a longing look on your face."

"That obvious, huh? Makes me wish we could go through the portal to enjoy it again."

"Why can't we?" Terry asked with a sly smile.

"You know why not," Amos said. "We don't know enough about what we're looking at—what kind of harm we could cause."

"Or what kind of damage it could do to us?" Terry asked.

Amos frowned.

"I'd love to find out what we've discovered. Is this really our valley? In the past or the future? If it's in the past, is it the near past or distant past? Or is it something altogether different, something we haven't thought of? And what kind of dangers are there?" Amos sighed. "Okay, Terry. What's next?" Amos started making notes on a pad of paper that Mike would later convert to a digital record.

"Well, we've seen the image pass through stationary, inanimate objects, like the building on the university campus. Since we now know that it's a door or gate, shouldn't we be able to get something to come through it into the lab?"

Amos looked up from his notes, staring at Terry.

"You mean, an animal, don't you?"

"Well, so far nothing stationary has entered the lab, so maybe we need to find something that moves on its own power."

"We don't know what kind of animals live in this valley. What if they're dangerous? Or, what if we unknowingly allow some kind of environmental hazard to pass from one side to the other?"

"You mean, like radiation."

"Or a virus or bacteria."

"That's a risk," Terry said without apology. "But we've had the portal open for almost ten minutes now and I don't feel any contamination."

"Now you're making fun of me," Amos said, frustrated. He stared at the portal, fidgeting with his pencil and weighing the pros and cons of risking cross-contamination. Terry waited patiently.

"Okay, let's look for an animal," Amos finally said, his curiosity about their unbelievable discovery overcoming his caution.

Terry smiled at him—he was hooked and it was obvious that his research partner knew it. Terry began moving the image around the valley, passing through trees and bushes that, amazingly, weren't burned like the ones in their version of the valley.

They searched for more than two hours. Each time they saw movement in the bushes—holding their breath until they confirmed that the animal they'd spotted was small or harmless—they moved the portal toward it, but either the animal sensed the portal's presence and moved away, or the image passed right through the animal. In one case it went right through a startled deer, showing them its internal organs, before the animal ran away, apparently unharmed.

"Well, we know we can see internal organs without obvious harm to the host," Terry said. "That's one positive outcome."

"Yeah, but what about more subtle damage, like at the cellular level?" Amos asked pensively. "I just wish we had a way to follow scientific protocols."

Their original goal had been to find a means of diagnosing internal injuries without the use of conventional, intrusive methods. Amos made a note on his pad to see if Mike and Terry could help him figure out a way to record what they observed as the portal passed through an object, dividing his time between that and watching Terry manipulate the image through the valley. Then he remembered the arrangement he'd made earlier with Lillie and looked at his watch.

"Lillie's going to be here any minute with Emily and Matt," he said, sounding exhausted. "Let's give it up for today."

"Just a sec," Terry whispered.

Amos turned to look at Terry, who nodded toward the

portal. Turning back, he saw a small rabbit sitting about two feet from of the portal, looking the other way and chewing on something. Terry held a finger to his lips, then winked at Amos. He picked up a TV control from the table and tossed it through the portal so that it landed just beyond the rabbit.

The rabbit turned toward them and . . .

About the Author

I grew up in Salt Lake City and graduated from the University of Utah with a bachelor's degree in engineering. My wife, Marilyn, and I have five children and fifteen grandchildren. Together we enjoy camping, hiking, travel, and get-togethers with extended family. In my quiet time, I enjoy gardening, genealogy, emergency preparedness, and now, writing. I love to read, and enjoy most genres, particularly murder mysteries and science fiction.

My work as a project manager has given me exposure to multiple industries and specialties, including electric utilities, nuclear power plant construction, water management, global mining, and aerospace, with each of those experiences contributing to my interest in, and the broad perspective needed to write about, the potential effects of global thermonuclear war on the infrastructure and people of the world.

The premise of this story is that, faced with the prospect of nuclear weapons in the hands of madmen, the U.S. government chooses to confront the perpetrators and fight back, rather than sit idly and be abused. Like you, I hope we never see nuclear war. However, what we see in today's headlines led me to speculate on the ability—or inability—of government leaders to control the radical ideologies that threaten to engulf us in world war.

This story about the war to end all wars, the *Omega Crisis*, is meant to entertain. I hope you enjoyed it. Don't miss the second book, *Worlds in Conflict*, available now.

Thank you.